KT-365-379

SAFE HOUSES

DAN FESPERMAN

HEAD
ZEUS

First published in the US in 2018 by Alfred A. Knopf
First published in the UK in 2018 by Head of Zeus Ltd
This paperback edition published in the UK in 2019
by Head of Zeus Ltd

Copyright © Dan Fesperman, 2018

The moral right of Dan Fesperman to be identified as the author of
this work has been asserted in accordance with the
Copyright, Designs and Patents Act of 1988.

All rights reserved. No part of this publication may be
reproduced, stored in a retrieval system, or transmitted in any form
or by any means, electronic, mechanical, photocopying, recording,
or otherwise, without the prior permission of both the copyright
owner and the above publisher of this book.

This is a work of fiction. All characters, organizations, and events
portrayed in this novel are either products of the author's imagination
or are used fictitiously.

9 7 5 3 1 2 4 6 8

A CIP catalogue record for this book is available from the British
Library.

ISBN (PB): 9781788547888
ISBN (E): 9781788547857

Printed and bound in Great Britain
by CPI Group (UK) Ltd, Croydon, CR0 4YY

Head of Zeus Ltd
5–8 Hardwick St
First Floor East
London EC1R 4RG
WWW.HEADOFZEUS.COM

To Liz, as always, and for everything

1

The older man sat down at the kitchen table in the back of the safe house and recited the words for a second time. His monotone made it sound like a lesson, or maybe an incantation—some spell he was trying to cast over his listener:

"To swim the pond you must forsake the bay. You may touch the lake, but you must never submerge, and you must always return to the pond."

The younger man, with his arms crossed, nodded.

"And the zoo?"

"Dry. To all of us, anyway. The pond is also dry, to the zookeeper." A pause, a wheezing intake of breath. "All of their people believe it to be long since drained, and its waters shall forever be invisible. Except of course to those of us with special eyewear. And that's what we're offering, if you're interested."

"Eyewear?"

"So to speak. A new way of seeing. And access, opportunity. More than you've ever dreamed of."

The older man poured some whiskey. He swallowed and set down the glass sharply, like he was knocking for entry.

"You don't understand a word of it, do you?"

"Some of it. Not all."

"We're inviting you in. But before that can happen we have to dry you off."

"From my swim in the bay?"

"Of course."

The younger man frowned and shuffled his feet. But the tilt of his head, the narrowing of his eyes, betrayed heightened interest. He uncrossed his arms and spoke again.

"First you have to tell me more."

"No. First you have to tell me the route you took to get here."

"Just like you said."

"You were alone? No shadows, start to finish?"

"You saw the finish. There was no one at the start, either."

"Positive? Even on the S-Bahn?"

"I took every precaution. The route was clean. I *have* done this before, you know."

A long pause, followed by another gurgle of whiskey, a second knock of the glass.

"Come here, then." The wheeze, yet again. "Sit down."

The younger man took a step forward and then stopped, as if something else had just occurred to him.

"What if it's no sale? This isn't one of those things where if you tell me then you have to kill me, is it?"

The older man laughed, choppy notes from an old accordion.

"Come. Have a drink."

"Was that a yes or no?"

"It wasn't a yes-no question. Sit down and I'll explain. People are dying out there, Lewis. They're drowning with no one in the whole damn bay to save them, and you can change that overnight. As that Polish girl of yours likes to say, time's a-wasting."

"How do you know about her?"

"Rule one, Lewis. Always assume we know more than you think."

Upstairs, in the room with the equipment, Helen Abell took note of the name "Lewis" as she leaned forward on stocking feet, straining to listen through the headset. A cryptonym, no doubt, but something about it was familiar. He wasn't part of Berlin station—or, as the old-timers still called it, the Berlin Operations Base, or BOB—but maybe she had come across his name in a memo, or the cable traffic.

For the next few seconds all she heard was the sound of the younger man's footsteps crossing the kitchen floor—*clop, clop, clop,* as loud as a Clydesdale—and the scrape of a chair as he sat at the table. It made her recall his polished black shoes, clunky, like the ones the East Germans wore.

The men had arrived a few minutes earlier. Helen had peeked out the window the moment she heard the rattle of a key in the lock, and she'd spotted them on the doorstep out front. Unexpected visitors, and neither looked familiar. But the mention of "Lewis" was a thread she could work with.

The wheels of the tape recorder kept turning, twin planets in rotation, absorbing every word. She was afraid to move lest the floor creak, giving her away. Too late to announce her presence. Was she wrong to leave the recorder on? To be listening at all? Probably. *Undoubtedly.* The whole thing was almost certainly way above her clearance. But she'd never heard any conversation like it.

From her brief observation she'd discerned that both men carried themselves with an air of competence and seniority—experienced hands in a special order, one which she aspired to join. It was like eavesdropping on a conversation of the gods. Nonetheless, she was off-limits and it was time to bow out. She should switch off the recorder, remove the headphones, and quietly wait for them to leave. With a sigh, she reached for the off switch.

Then the needles flicked on the dials as the younger man spoke, and her hand stopped in midair. He'd lowered his voice, and Helen, unable to help herself, squinted in concentration to make out the words.

"Do the effies know?"

"Not a thing, or not since Jack kicked the bucket in '72."

"Jack? You mean . . . ?"

"Of course."

"He was a friend?"

"Of a sort. The enemy of my enemy, that whole business. Last of his kind. Here, drink up."

A splash of whiskey, then silence.

Helen was transfixed. *What in the hell were they talking about?* The effies. The zoo. The pond, the bay, and the lake. And now a reference to a former power figure named Jack—probably another cryptonym. Everything about the conversation was baffling, and not just because she didn't know the lingo.

For starters, why speak in code? The whole point of a safe house was to make you feel secure enough to dispense with the mumbo jumbo. You kicked back, put your feet up, traded all the secrets you wanted in the plainest possible language. Safely, and with absolute confidence. That's how she'd rigged these houses, four of them in all across the zones and neighborhoods of West Berlin, available at any given moment for privileged access and secret consultation. Each house was clean, unobtrusive, and practically soundproofed against the curiosity of neighbors, due mostly to her own efforts during the past year.

She was particularly proud of the job she'd done at this location, a crumbling brick townhouse a block south of Alt-Moabit. She had labored zealously to craft the most secure possible environment for the Company's case officers and their agents, or for whoever else among their friends might temporarily need shelter from the cold and lonely hazards of their profession.

Why, then, this strange collection of buzzwords? Unless it wasn't so much a code as a special language—and, yes, there was a difference—an exclusive lexicon for some obscure fraternity of operatives. Perhaps for someone with a higher security clearance this would be no mystery at all.

She also wondered how the men had gotten a key. Helen knew the identities of all six key holders for this house. Someone had given them a key without telling her. That in itself was a serious breach of security.

In addition, the meeting was unscheduled. When people wanted to use one of her facilities—okay, one of the *Agency's* facilities—the rules said they were supposed to provide at least six hours' notice, so she could ensure that no one else would barge in on them, and that conditions would be welcoming and ready. Before she took over, embarrassing run-ins and overlaps had been infrequent but not at all unheard of, a state of affairs that the chief of station had seemed to accept as an occupational hazard. Helen had taken pains to eliminate such snafus. It was all in the details—controlling the leaseholders, managing traffic, making the places easy to use, clean, and functional. She had carefully vetted the current cover tenant for this house, a Pan Am stewardess with Agency connections whose work schedule meant she was home only on Wednesdays and Sundays, and even on those days could clear the premises at a moment's notice.

There were contingencies for unannounced meetings, of course, and also for use by operatives and agents who weren't regular customers. Espionage emergencies were hardly uncommon in Berlin. But the meeting Helen was hearing downstairs had none of the snap or crackle of an urgent rendezvous.

This chat was unrushed, collegial, and despite the age difference she suspected that these men were on roughly equal footing, meaning it probably wasn't a meeting between a case officer and his local agent. Their English was flawless, no trace of a foreign accent. They were either American or very practiced at pretending to be American.

Of course, technically speaking, Helen wasn't supposed to be there, either. That was the rub, and the reason for her deathly silence. Unbeknownst to the Agency, she had begun making surprise weekly inspections of her four properties. It was the most efficient way to uncover shabby upkeep and lax practices. She kept the visits off the books or they wouldn't have worked. Yet another way in which she went the extra mile, a trait she'd become known for since her arrival in Berlin fourteen months earlier.

The job certainly hadn't been her top choice. Not even close. She'd always suspected that the chief of station, a randy old mossback named Ladd Herrington, made the assignment to demean her, to put her in her place.

"You're only twenty-three?" he'd said on that first day, peeping above the frames of reading glasses as he pawed through her file. His eyes wandered quickly from her face to her breasts, where he let them rest long enough to make her uncomfortable.

"You do know you'd be happier as an analyst, don't you? In the long term, anyway. Much better prospects for advancement. For marriage, too, although perhaps that doesn't interest you. Here, on the other hand . . ."

He flapped a hand dismissively, as if they were assessing her chances of discovering a new comet, or of recruiting Leonid Brezhnev as a double agent. Analyst. The default assignment for any Agency female, except the ones exiled to records, or to some other "special branch" of this or that department as long as it was well behind the scenes. Hardly any made it into the field.

Nonetheless, there she'd been, arriving on Herrington's doorstep with only two years of experience for a posting to the city that had defined the Cold War, and he'd responded by slotting her in a position that until then had been largely clerical, staffed by someone two steps below her pay grade. To make it sound less offensive, or perhaps to heighten the joke, he'd come up with a new title: Chief of Administration for Logistics, Property and Personnel Branch, Berlin Station.

Helen had sulked for a week before deciding to make the most of it. She explored and then exploited the job's opportunities, which turned out to be more expansive than anyone had realized. She revetted the tenants, rescouted the locations. Finding all of them lacking, she replaced them several months ahead of the usual rotation. She tightened hiring practices for support staff, upgraded the facilities at minimal cost, and instituted greater accountability among users. Overlaps and screwups disappeared, as did the mice and bedbugs. Complaints from field men dwindled. She made connections, widened her niche, found a lover, and settled in to Berlin's cold, grim majesty with a sardonic viewpoint worthy of a lifer.

And now, here she was, caught in the middle of one of her surprise inspections, silent and still and, for the moment, trapped upstairs on a gray October Monday at mid-afternoon as she wondered what the hell she'd stumbled onto.

She had arrived at the house shortly after 2 p.m., dressed in maid's clothing and carrying a mop and bucket to minimize curiosity from the neighbors, although she already knew enough about their work schedules to be confident that the block would be empty, apart from the usual scattering of *Kinder und Hausfrauen*.

After entering, she proceeded by her customary routine. Locks and latches? Check. General cleanliness? Better than last time, at least. No more mouse droppings beneath the sink, which in this neighborhood was all you could hope for. Refrigerator? Well stocked, nothing gone sour or moldy. Liquor supply? Ample and safe in its usual hideaway, off-limits to the cover tenant.

Last on her checklist was the taping system. She always tested it by walking from front to back downstairs while reciting a favorite poem from Rilke. Sometimes she declaimed in German. Today, in English. She spoke the opening lines while standing in the parlor near the front door.

> *How can I keep my soul in me, so that*
> *it doesn't touch your soul? How can I raise*
> *it high enough, past you, to other things?*

Noting the cleanliness of the carpet and the furniture, she began stepping slowly toward the back of the house. Passing the stairwell into the dining room, she spotted a smudge on the wall to her left; above, a crack in the celling. But she never stopped speaking:

I would like to shelter it, among remote
lost objects, in some dark and silent place
that doesn't resonate when your depths resound.

She entered the kitchen. Rilke had named the poem "Love Song," but for Helen the words never brought to mind any man, past or present. It instead made her reflect on this strange profession of hers, this realm where it was risky indeed to touch the souls of others or, sometimes, even to try and shelter them in some dark and silent place—like this house.

Helen uttered the final lines while peering out the back window into the small garden with its bare plum tree.

Yet everything that touches us, me and you,
takes us together like a violin's bow,
which draws one voice out of two separate strings.
Upon what instrument are we two spanned?
And what musician holds us in his hand?
Oh sweetest song.

With the words still resonating in her head, she climbed the stairs. Her routine was to rewind the tape and play it back, listening carefully to make sure the microphones had picked up every syllable. If no tweaks or repairs were needed, she erased it and was on her way.

Today she'd heard the key in the front door just as she was reaching for the stop button. Heart beating fast, she'd moved to the window. That's when she saw the older man, the key holder.

He looked to be in his late sixties. Salt-and-pepper hair, a bit on the long side, untamed in the breeze. Five o'clock shadow, which somehow suited him. He grimaced as he wiggled the key, which suggested it was a new copy, meaning further cause for worry. How many more copies were out there that she didn't know about?

Then she heard the slide of the dead bolt, the opening of the door. She watched the man on the porch disappear across the threshold. At first she stayed by the window, not daring to move as she listened to the door shutting a floor below. She heard a footstep or two, followed by a few seconds of silence, and then the creak of a floorboard as he settled onto the couch in the parlor. A long sigh, suggestive of a lengthy journey.

She debated whether to announce herself. Why not let him know she was here, so there would be no surprises later? That way she might also find out who he was. She would gently remind him to log his use of the house on the proper form afterward, and then gracefully make her exit.

A knock at the front door preempted her. She again peered out the window. A younger man, early thirties, glancing up and down the street like he knew he wasn't supposed to be there. Hair, dirty blond but neatly barbered. Ruddy face. Like the other man, he wore a tweed jacket and a long wool overcoat unbuttoned in the front, as if they'd both come directly from the moors in some du Maurier novel. Or, no, more like a pair of fellows you'd see in one of those fake Irish pubs you found all over the world, keeping to their own kind while on foreign soil.

She again heard the door open and shut, followed by an exchange of greetings, voices floating up the stairwell as they made small talk in the parlor. Helen instinctively nudged off her shoes. She slid rather than stepped across the floor slowly, to minimize creaks or groans from the boards—until she was close enough to the tape recorder to reach for the headphones. She slipped them on, and for a few seconds held her breath as she listened to their footsteps, trooping toward the kitchen. A slap on the back. A joke about Herrington's sex life that she'd already heard twice, followed by a snort of laughter.

Then and there, she told herself she would use this occasion to further test the taping system, even as she recognized it right away as a dodge, a justification for unauthorized curiosity. Shamed, she was about to slip off the headphones when she heard the older man announce that he needed a drink.

Only if you can find it. The liquor supply was in a lower kitchen cabinet behind a trash can, one of the last places you'd think to look. And you had to manipulate the latch—just so—to click open the door.

His footsteps were direct, nothing the least bit uncertain about the route. Then, the metallic click of the latch, neat as you please, followed by the clatter of bottles as he rummaged among them for his poison of choice.

Well, now.

It was one thing to have an unauthorized key, or for a meeting to be off the books. Quite another to know the secrets of the house. This old fellow sounded right at home. And that was when he had begun speaking of mysterious bodies of water, of hidden lakes and ponds and bays that no one but him could see.

Not long after the younger man sat down, they lowered their voices further, and for the next few minutes there was only a single moment of clarity, when the older fellow, as if intensifying his sales pitch, spoke up and said, "There's never been a better time to jump in, Lewis. We're branching out again. Overflowing our banks."

"Is that so smart? With floods come leaks."

"Not with our clientele, the Vee people and all the rest. Too selfish for any spills. Too intent on winning their next wrangle on the hump."

The hump? The Vee people? And who were all of these clients?

The men then lapsed back into indecipherable muttering. Helen pictured them with their foreheads nearly touching across the table, face-to-face in furtive conversation. It told her that, at the very least, she needed to install new and more sensitive microphones, presuming the bean counters said yes. Budgets were only getting smaller. Congress had its dander up, and Berlin—yes, even Berlin—was starting to feel like a Cold War backwater.

Helen had arrived in the city with expectations conditioned by noir films and spy thrillers, a Berlin where intrigue lurked in every shadow, where every gun had a silencer and every safe house was subject to ambush or takeover. Instead, the ones she ran were paragons of tranquility—safe, just as their name suggested. No one ever showed up armed, and no one ever got hurt.

Even the Wall, with its watchtowers and razor wire, had begun to take on the look of something touristy, a graffiti-covered structure where someday you might stroll the Kill Zone with children in tow and camera in hand, snapping poses for the folks back home. It had been more than two and a half years since anyone had died while trying to cross without permission—poor old Dietmar Schwietzer, age eighteen, RIP. In fact, for all its formidable symbolism, the Wall was the biggest reason her posting had fallen so short of expectations. By cutting off all access to the opposition—the KGB in Karlshorst, the Stasi on Normanenstrasse—its ninety-mile perimeter had long ago robbed their mission of the thrill of the chase. The Agency's work in Berlin was now all defense and no offense. Helen felt like she'd arrived at a wondrous playground only to discover that the most exciting rides had been cordoned off.

Langley's concerns were now focused on Iran, where the CIA-installed Shah had recently fled, ceding power to a scowling, black-turbaned ayatollah who seemed capable of just about anything. Berlin was an afterthought.

The two men downstairs continued muttering, and even as their tone grew heated she could barely understand a word. Did she detect a phrase or two of German? Maybe a snatch of Russian?

Finally, the younger man spoke louder, his voice almost shrill. A chair scraped, meaning he had probably decided to stand. The older man also raised his voice. At last, she again heard every syllable.

"But what if it *does* happen?" the younger man said.

"It won't. I assure you."

"Nothing is foolproof. What's the contingency? And please don't tell me you don't have one."

"Elimination, plain and simple."

"Elimination?"

"Surely I don't have to spell that out for you, do I?"

The answer rendered the younger man momentarily speechless. By then, sweat was prickling on Helen's spine.

Then the second chair scraped, followed by the clip-clop of shoes, the clank of glass as the older man put away the bottle and relatched the liquor cabinet. Water gushed in the sink as someone rinsed the glasses and set them in the drying rack. Mumbled goodbyes, a burst of laughter.

Friends again? Or maybe just allies, partners in crime. Whatever deal had been on the table seemed to have been sealed. Helen heard muffled movements and pictured them shaking hands. The door rattled open. A voice said something indecipherable from out on the front stoop. Then the door shut and the key turned the dead bolt.

Yet again, she wondered: Whose key? And where will it go now?

She slid back over to the window, taking care in case one of them was still downstairs. No. They were both descending the front steps to the sidewalk. She watched through the gap in the curtains as the younger man headed south, toward the Tiergarten. The older one strolled north, toward Alt-Moabit, where unless he turned he'd soon reach the Wall.

Or maybe the Wall was his destination. The closest checkpoint was less than half a mile from here. The mere thought of him crossing into East Berlin with that precious key in his pocket was enough to make her hyperventilate.

Helen exhaled loudly. The beginnings of a headache crept forward from her temples. She recrossed the room and switched off the recorder. Perhaps twenty minutes of conversation were now stored on the tape—all of it contraband, of course. Worse, her own reading of Rilke was on there, too, a preamble that implicated her in this unauthorized taping. Whatever they'd been up to, she had to assume it was according to Hoyle, at least by someone's rules. By every rule *she* played by, she should erase the tape immediately.

She stared at the machine a few seconds longer. Then she hit rewind, letting the reels spin until the tape came loose and slapped against the guide. She switched it off. Now she was supposed to rethread it and hit record, erase this strange conversation forever, as if it never happened.

Instead, she pulled the reel from the spindle and carried it to a side table, where she opened the top drawer and slipped the tape inside. She would erase it later.

Then, another thought, coming at her like a double dare: By using enhancement technology, she might be able to decipher some of the inaudible portions of their exchange. Helen lit a cigarette, inhaled, and considered her options. She shook her head, reached for an ashtray, and stubbed out the reckless idea.

She reopened the drawer, looked again at the tape, and then closed the drawer. To distract herself from any further heretical thoughts she unwrapped a fresh reel and loaded it onto the spindle. A frantic sense of urgency began to build at the base of her stomach. She needed to leave, to get out into the streets, the room now claustrophobic. Hurrying, she slipped on her shoes and ran downstairs. Gathering up her mop and bucket, she headed for the front door. Thinking better of her haste, she set down the mop and bucket by the door and turned toward the kitchen.

She opened the liquor cabinet and inspected the bottle up front, its seal broken. It was an eighteen-year-old Macallan, a single malt Scotch aged in a sherry oak cask. She knew the details because someone in Langley, a middle manager in Facilities whose name she hadn't recognized, had specially requisitioned it only a month ago. It was damned expensive, and at the time she'd thought the order was a bit unorthodox. But she'd written it off as one of those needs that cropped up from time to time in the delicate relationships between case officers and their agents. A Soviet military officer with a rural background had once asked his handler to provide regular copies of *Progressive Farmer* magazine, so he could wallow in the luxuries of state-of-the-art American agriculture whenever he visited the safe house. Being a case officer was a stressful occupation. Being an agent, more so. So whenever someone had a special request, you tried to accommodate them.

Until today no one had opened the Macallan. Whoever the older fellow was, he seemed to have at least one supporter in Langley. She closed the cabinet and paused. Footsteps approached the house on the sidewalk out front, and she held her breath until they passed. What if he returned? The thought sent her rushing back toward the door in such a hurry that she almost forgot the mop and bucket. She didn't begin to calm down until she was out on the porch, snicking the dead bolt into place. Turning, she looked up and down the street from the stoop. North seemed like the best option for now, toward Alt-Moabit where there would be people and voices, shopkeepers and traffic, the company of strangers. Safety in numbers.

Was safety really necessary? She didn't know, and the uncertainty troubled her. For the moment all she knew for sure was that she wanted a drink. Plus some advice, and perhaps a bit of male comfort.

Fortunately, she knew just who to turn to for all of the above.

2

By candlelight you almost didn't notice the modest roll of flab around Clark Baucom's waist. You couldn't very well call it baby fat, not at his age. But at tender moments like this, Helen Abell found such flaws endearing. Nakedness made Clark seem vulnerable, and she thought of his paunch as a mark of experience, the inevitable toll of all those sedentary hours spent at checkpoints and observation posts. Far too much lying in wait in this business of theirs. Not to mention the diet he'd endured in long stretches behind the Iron Curtain. Whether ferrying royalists out of Budapest or relaying vital messages to dissidents in Warsaw, he had often subsisted on potatoes and goulash, pierogies and spaetzle, boiled cabbage and white sausage—a pale, gelatinous cuisine, all of it flavored by cigarette smoke and washed down with Czech beer. Once, right here in Berlin, she'd watched him wolf down the entirety of a fatty old *Eisbein,* a boiled ham hock as big as a severed head.

For all that, he still cut a dashing figure, with lively brown eyes and a face built on classic lines. If he were an actor, she would have guessed that he was still doing his own stunts.

Helen curled up against him and kissed his chest, the hairs tickling her lips. He smiled and reached across her for his pack of cigarettes on the bedside table. Gitanes, an affectation from his schoolboy days in Paris. Some Americans became expats as part of a phase, or for a few years at a time. Clark Baucom had made a career out of it. Since the age of fourteen he hadn't lived in his home country for longer than a year at a time.

"Light one for me while you're at it," she said.

He obliged her, and she inhaled slowly. Strong and unfiltered, but the extra kick of nicotine helped marshal her thoughts. A moment later the words finally fell into place for the conversation she'd been waiting to have all evening.

"Do you know of any spook with a cryptonym of Lewis?"

"One of ours?"

"Presumably."

He furrowed his brow and stared at the ceiling.

"Vienna, maybe? No, I think it's Bulgaria. But only as a fly-in. He comes and goes. Why do you ask?"

"Something I overheard today, out on the job."

In the three hours that had passed before she met Clark Baucom at a café in Charlottenburg, Helen had wrestled with the question of what to do with her knowledge of that afternoon's events. She couldn't very well take the matter to Herrington. *Hey, boss. Just happened to be making an unauthorized visit at Number Three and ran across two fellows I've never heard of, saying all kinds of weird shit. And guess what? They didn't know I was listening, and I taped it!*

Besides, if Herrington already knew about the rendezvous, he'd be angrier at her for nearly disrupting it—or for knowing about it at all—than at any breach of protocol by the participants. For all she knew, the station chief had loaned them his own key, or had authorized the making of a new and secret copy. That would be just his style. Yet another means of knocking her down a peg.

On the other hand, what if something funny was up? Something so far off the books that even Herrington didn't know? Shouldn't someone in authority be notified?

That's why she'd wanted to see Baucom. Yes, for the sex—their affair had been going on since June—but more for the lingering aftermath, when he was always more talkative about tricks of the trade, the lay of the land in Eastern Europe, or his strategies for negotiating the Agency's byzantine interoffice politics. He was part lover, part tutor, and secure enough to not mind that she seemed to value his company as much for the latter as for the former.

They were in the back bedroom of a small house on a grassy suburban tract in Zehlendorf, a safe house in the old American zone of occupation that she'd decommissioned two months earlier. Agency janitors hadn't yet removed the sound equipment, which was terribly outdated, and the lease didn't expire for another two months. By her reasoning—and with Baucom's concurrence, which would count for more if they were ever caught—she had decided that *someone* ought to use it from time to time, if only to convince the neighbors that it wasn't vacant.

Baucom had been a field man since before she was born. He was fifty-five. Robbing the cradle, her mother would've said. People would say what they wanted to say, but the reality was that this relationship had been her idea. It was not built to last, and that was how they liked it. He was charming in an Old Boy sort of way, and he was an attentive and experienced lover. Best of all, he was a raconteur of the first order. If Baucom had one professional weakness, it was his fondness for telling stories between the sheets.

Presumably he wouldn't have been nearly so free with his words if Helen hadn't also worked for the Agency. She nonetheless sensed a certain reckless indiscretion whenever he started talking about his past, and that was fine with her. She savored this vicarious taste of the life she hoped to lead someday, if only people like Herrington could be convinced. After three decades in the field, Baucom's memories were lined up like freighters waiting to be unloaded, and Helen was always eager to coax ashore the payload, with its wonderful color and detail.

"Did I ever tell you about that time with Dixon at that botched dead drop in Prague?" he would typically begin. In this way she came to be a sort of keeper of his flame, or of the flame for that whole core of people who had worked at the heart of things during the Agency's formative years.

"What was it you overheard?" he asked, his voice languid, a little drowsy.

"Well, this Lewis, whoever he was, he and some older hand came into a house while I was making an inspection."

"That must have been embarrassing for you."

"I was upstairs. They didn't know anyone was there."

"And you blithely decided to let them go about their business?"

"Yes."

The bed shook with his quiet laughter. It felt like less of a sin now.

"And now you're wondering if you need to report this to someone?"

"Sort of."

"Don't bother. It will only make a lot of extra paperwork for a lot of people who won't like doing it. Plus, you'll be giving Herrington exactly what he's been looking for."

"I know. It's just . . ."

"Something they said? Is that what's bothering you?"

"Yes. Or no. Not so much what they said, but the way they said it. Almost like they were speaking their own language. Especially the older one. Not a code, exactly, but something like it."

"How do you mean?"

"All kinds of double-talk about lakes, ponds, and bays. Bodies of water. And effies, that was another one. The effies, whose boss used to be named Jack."

Baucom was silent for a while before turning to face her, propping his head on his elbow. For a few unnerving seconds all he did was smoke and stare.

"This older fellow. Did you see him?"

"On the porch, yes. When he was coming and going."

His gaze was steady, attentive. He was fully awake now. It scared her a little.

"Describe him."

She did so. He shook his head, seeming to draw a blank. Then she remembered another detail.

"He sounded wheezy."

"Wheezy?" He narrowed his eyes. "You're sure?"

"Yes. Like he was out of breath, even though they"

were sitting down. And he was drinking. Knocking them back pretty good, too."

"Drinking what? Do you know?"

"An eighteen-year-old Macallan. Brand-new bottle, and he broke the seal. Right out of the special supply, and he knew exactly where to find it."

Baucom lay back on the bed and forcefully exhaled a gray plume. They both stared at the smoke, watching it flatten and curl as it reached the ceiling. She waited for him to speak. Instead, he got out of bed and walked naked to the window, where he louvered open the blinds and carefully looked up and down the street.

"What are you doing?"

"Are you sure they didn't know you were there?"

"Why? What do you see?"

"Answer me."

He said it harshly, a tone he'd never used with her before. She checked his face for any sign of irony, or that he might be joking, but he was serious. It was kind of freaking her out, so she tried thinking back to everything she'd heard that afternoon, rechecking for any possibility they had detected her presence.

"I'm almost positive they thought they were alone."

"Almost?"

"You know what they teach you at the Farm. Never feel a hundred percent about anything."

"Fair enough. But you're reasonably certain?"

"More than reasonably."

"Good. With those people you'd better be."

"*Those* people? You know who they are?"

"I might know who they used to be. But now?" He frowned and shook his head. "Even if I'm right, it's nothing I could ever talk about, so don't ask again. It's not your business. Hell, it's not mine, either." A slight pause, and then: "You didn't, perchance, do something foolish like tape them, did you?"

She looked away. He sighed loudly.

"I was going to erase it."

"But you haven't yet?"

"No."

"I'd do so promptly if I were you. Better still, destroy it. Burn the damn thing if you have to."

"Okay."

"Right away."

"Scout's honor. First thing in the morning."

"No. Now."

"At this hour?"

"*Now*. If you'd like, I'll follow you over there. Cover your tracks and watch the shadows."

"Do you really think that's necessary?"

He thought about it for a second.

"No. I don't. And everything is clear out front. I'd know if it wasn't. But it's nearly eleven, so you should leave before it gets any later. Take a taxi. Have the driver let you out around the corner, but tell him to wait."

"Thanks for the advice, but I *do* know some tradecraft."

"Work quickly. If you're not back by midnight, I'll ring the duty officer."

"Jesus. That's the worst thing you've said all night. Then Herrington would find out for sure."

"Chain of command. Sorry, but that's how it works in these situations."

"And what kind of situation *is* this, exactly?"

"Probably something small and forgettable, as long as you deal with it now, and never mention it to anyone else."

"Okay, then." She tossed back the sheets. "I'll go. Get it over with."

"Good girl."

"Don't call me that." She said it sharply, and he grinned so widely that she wanted to cross the room and slap him. But at least he was no longer looking so deadly earnest, and it helped her relax.

She dressed while he phoned for a cab. A few minutes later it pulled up out front. He walked her downstairs and accompanied her onto the porch.

"Be smart and move fast. Use your skills."

"You act like I'm on a mission."

"You are. Call if you need help. And remember." He tapped his watch. "Midnight, or I phone it in."

"You're never going to tell me what this was all about, are you?"

He looked in both directions, swiveling his head like a bird of prey.

"You're clear. Go."

She climbed into the back of the taxi and gave the driver an address on Alt-Moabit. In Berlin, cabdrivers were accustomed to their fares walking around the corner from where they let them off.

Looking out the back window of the taxi as it pulled away, she saw the glow of Baucom's cigarette on the porch. He stayed there, watching, until the taxi drove out of sight.

3

A bungler's chore. A fool's errand. That's what this was, and it was all due to her lack of self-control. Helen cursed herself as she slid the key into the lock. Mercifully, none of the neighbors seemed to be awake, so at least she wasn't likely to be spotted.

Need to know. That was the bedrock rule she'd violated. Even if something funny *was* going on, it wasn't her business to know it, much less report it. Baucom had seen that right away, just as she should've. He, at least, seemed to have a pretty good idea of what the strange conversation was about, which made her feel somewhat better. If it needed to be reported up the chain of command, then Baucom would do it.

Funny how often curiosity was a liability in this business. When they'd first recruited her they'd assured her it was a strength, one of her greatest. Now? Compartmentalize. Avert your eyes. Mind your own business. Or maybe Herrington used that mantra only on her.

She didn't bother to switch on the lights. Helen knew the house well enough to tour every room blindfolded, and why risk having a passerby see her upstairs before she was able to shut the blinds?

She climbed the stairs, unerringly crossed the room to the side table, and pulled open the drawer. She felt a matchbox, a pen, a pack of cigarettes, and a small notebook as panic began to rise in her chest. But finally, there it was, pushed toward the back by her rummaging. Baucom had advised her to destroy it, and that's what she intended to do—later, at a more suitable location. But there was no way she was going to carry the tape out of the house without first erasing the conversation.

Moving across the room, she fumbled to load the reel on the spindle before remembering that a blank tape was already in place. She groped for the rewind button to free it from the take-up reel, but after hearing the click and then not hearing the slapping of the tape she realized she must have hit either play or record. Some light would be necessary after all, which meant she needed to shut the blinds. She crossed the room to the window and reached for the cord when, like some sort of bizarre replay, she heard the rattle of a key in the front door downstairs. A surprise visitor. Again.

"Shit!" she whispered. "What the *fuck*?"

Calm down. Maybe it was Baucom, having decided she needed backup after all. She let go of the cord to the blinds and looked through the lace curtains. Her heartbeat did a drum roll when she saw a male, medium build, in a long dark overcoat. Definitely not Baucom. Had the older fellow from this afternoon waited for her to return? Had he known all along what she'd done? If so, what next? Fight or flight? Then the man turned his head just enough to show his features by the glow of the street lamp. Dark hair, not graying. Too young to be the older man. Nor was he the one named Lewis. In fact, she knew this fellow.

He was a case officer, cryptonym Robert. Real name: Kevin Gilley, although she wasn't supposed to know that. A fanatic for exotic firearms, a prolific filer of verbose reports. Fancied himself a ladies' man, or so she'd heard. In fact, pretty much all of her knowledge was from in-house gossip. The only thing she knew firsthand was that, as a onetime previous user of her safe houses he'd been supremely tidy, and hadn't left a trace. His operational weakness, according to Agency scuttlebutt, was that his cover as a commercial attaché had apparently fooled none of the opposition, and lately there had been talk of an imminent transfer, either to Latin America or a desk job in Langley. She watched him enter the house and heard the door shut.

A nimbus of light appeared in the doorway to the stairwell as he switched on a lamp downstairs. She heard his footsteps heading toward the kitchen. Another customer for the secret stash of liquor, Helen guessed, although at least Gilley was supposed to know where these things were.

Now she was present for yet another unauthorized meeting, at the facility that was supposedly her most efficiently run. She wondered if this sort of off-the-books activity was again becoming standard practice. Maybe Herrington had circulated a memo among his favored operatives, instructing them to ignore her rules. She knew exactly how he'd word it—a mixture of the practical and the profane, with an overlay of his mannered Anglophilia: *Look, chaps, this officious chick no doubt means well, but if in your judgment these new requirements are cramping your style, then fuck the lot of them. Henceforth, come and go from the facilities as needed, and we'll sweat the paperwork later.*

Yet, she, too, was again here without notice, meaning she should probably get this over with quickly. Swallow her pride, announce her presence, and be on her way, with the illicit tape burning a hole in her purse as she carried all its secrets back across town to Baucom.

There was a knock on the front door. She looked out the window to see Gilley welcoming a young woman. The sound of their voices ghosted up the stairwell. The woman spoke German in an affected Berliner accent, like someone from the provinces trying to pass for local. Probably one of Gilley's agents, meaning it was too late for Helen to announce herself without disrupting their meeting.

Helen sighed, carefully slipped off her shoes, and prepared to wait them out. It wasn't proper procedure, but since when did that matter on this Day of Transgressions? No wonder they wouldn't make her an operative. Screw up like this in the field and someone would be dead. Screw up like this twice within twelve hours and you'd be dead as well.

The young woman downstairs was talking rapidly now. Even from here, she sounded earnest and eager, as if she'd brought Gilley the best possible material, although Helen couldn't make out the words. Helen had warned the cabdriver she was liable to be a while, but who knew how long this meeting might take? The fare would be a fortune. She might even have to ask Baucom for a few D-Marks. She remembered the deadline he'd imposed. Back by midnight, or he'd phone the duty officer. Things could get complicated in a hurry. Maybe this pair would leave in time for her to phone Baucom first. But she probably wouldn't have time to erase the tape before leaving.

The sound of shattering glass broke her train of thought. So much for Gilley's usual neatness. Then a thud, like a chair overturning. What in the hell were they doing? Helen moved toward the doorway, where she heard grunts, as if from a wrestling match.

"Stop it!" Gilley shouted.

"*Nein!*" the woman replied.

"I told you, stop that!" Then, in German: "*Unvorstellbar! Genug!*"

Had she threatened him? If Gilley was in trouble, right here in Helen's most secure safe house, then she needed to act immediately. She slid into the hallway and onto the landing, and then stooped lower to try and see what was happening below.

She eased down a step, and then another. She heard the tearing of fabric, and a pinging of small items—buttons?—bouncing on the wooden floor like sleet against a windowpane.

"Hold still!" Gilley shouted. "Stupid whore!"

Only a whimper from the woman. Gilley had either turned the tables or had been the aggressor from the start. She eased farther down the steps and heard a massive thump.

"That's better," Gilley said, his voice smug. The woman grunted.

Helen, horrified, now saw everything. Gilley had climbed atop her on the couch, which was knocked askew. His bare white back glistened with sweat, and his shoes and trousers were off. He wore only brown socks. The woman lay on her back below him, her face turned to the side and her eyes shut. Black skirt rucked up around her waist. Blouse torn open. The couch shook like a raft on a tossing sea. The woman grimaced and bit her lip.

"*Nein, nein, nein.*"

"Stop it!" Helen shouted.

She clambered down the stairs, nearly slipping as she reached the bottom.

The woman's eyes opened in shock. Gilley looked over his shoulder, but didn't budge from the couch.

"It's you!" he said, almost laughing. "The goddamn station busybody!"

He lurched backward and slung his legs to the floor like a cowboy dismounting a horse. Smiling, he turned to face Helen, his erect penis standing red and glistening with moisture. Helen turned away and, then, figuring that was what he wanted, looked him in the eye.

"I was . . . I was sleeping upstairs," she ad-libbed, even while at another level she was wondering why she was the one having to explain. "What the hell are you doing to her? You're . . . you're . . ." She needed to say the word. He was *raping* her.

"It's not what you think," he said, tossing a hand to the side, flippant in his gestures. "Frieda likes it rough. Enjoys it more when there's a tussle. Isn't that right, Frieda?"

Frieda, if that was indeed her name, was sitting now, with her knees drawn up protectively against her chest. Her feet were still clad in black sneakers. She pulled the front of her blouse together, but the buttons were gone. Then she shook her head and muttered an answer beneath her breath.

"Speak up, my dear."

"*Ja,*" she said. "Yes." She smoothed her skirt and stared at the floor. "It is as he says."

"So you see?"

"I know what I saw. And I know what I heard."

"Then do as you must, of course. But if anyone's out of bounds here, I'd say it was you, interrupting a private meeting between a case officer and his agent. Sleeping, you said? Like hell you were. Nosing around where you shouldn't be, more likely. Way out of your depth. Probably grounds for dismissal, or at the very least, reassignment."

"I'd heard the same about you. Now I think I know why."

He grinned widely. Infuriating. His eyes, the blue-green of a swimming pool, flashed with anger.

"Just the sort of disinformation I'd expect to hear from someone at your level. You really don't know anything, do you?"

Gilley picked up his boxers and slipped them on, and then his pants. He finished dressing as casually as if he were alone in a hotel room. All the while he smiled at Helen, who remained rooted to her spot at the foot of the stairs.

"I know what I saw and I know what I heard," she said again, less assertively this time.

"As do I. Guess whose version will be accepted? Guess which one Frieda will verify. And guess which one of us will be held in violation of policy for their activities tonight?"

He turned toward the woman on the couch.

"Maybe next time, Frieda. When there's a little more privacy, yes?"

She said nothing and continued to stare at the floor. Gilley smiled ruefully and glanced around the room as if checking to see if he had forgotten anything. Then he departed, shutting the door behind him. Helen felt like she had taken a blow to the head. It was as if everything the Agency had ever taught her about tradecraft and secrecy and doing your job the right way had just been spilled onto the floor in a broken mess that could never be reassembled. She drew a deep breath and put a hand to her chest, where her heartbeat was only beginning to slow down. She looked over at Frieda.

My God, practically a girl. Twenty at the oldest, probably younger. One of those pale, undernourished Berliner waifs who wore nothing but black. Hair chopped in a statement against style. Helen guessed she was Gilley's connection to some fringe leftist cell in Kreuzberg, groups notoriously infested with East German operatives. And now here she was tugging at her blouse as she scanned the floor for missing buttons.

Helen opened her mouth to speak, but Frieda beat her to it.

"I was warned," Frieda said in English. "Before."

"By Robert?" It felt like a betrayal to use only his cryptonym, even though she knew it was proper procedure. "He threatened you?"

Frieda shook her head.

"Kathrin, she warned me." She clapped a hand to her mouth. "Her name, I should not have said it. Please . . ."

"Don't worry. I'm cleared for it. What did Kathrin tell you?"

"That I should not go into a house with him, not alone. Dead drops, brush passes. Yes, all of these are fine. In his working ways he is careful. If I am discovered in this work, it will not be from any mistake he has made. But with women, and in places like this?" She shrugged. "She said to stay away unless others are there. Then I come here anyway, alone, and you see it. You see what happens."

"So this was not with your consent?"

"No. It was not." She stood, holding herself, shivering now. Helen stepped closer to console her but Frieda raised up a hand and backed away.

"You were here, then? At the beginning?"

"Well. Yes." Frieda's eyes accused her. "I didn't know he was like this, and I wasn't supposed to be here. I . . . I came downstairs as soon as I knew, and now I want to help you. We can start by reporting this."

Frieda shook her head violently.

"*Nein!* Please, no! He will expose me. I will be as good as gone. I will have to leave, go back to Braunschweig. You cannot tell anyone!"

"We can't let him get away with this."

"*We?*"

She glared at Helen, face streaked with tears. Then she slowly shook her head, as if to say Helen couldn't possibly understand. But Helen did. Report this, and Gilley might burn her to cinders among the groups she worked with. If she was an insert, an infiltrator, then they would not only cast her out, they might also tell the East Germans, the Stasi, whose people would be quite happy to punish her. Brutally, perhaps.

That was how it worked here. Even from the earliest days of the Cold War, the Agency and their Soviet counterparts had operated under a gentleman's agreement when it came to inflicting casualties: Don't touch ours and we won't touch yours. But everyone in the middle—the locals who did their bidding—well, they had better watch their step. And now this one was as vulnerable as a fawn on the Autobahn, all because she had been wronged by her case officer, the man she had entrusted with her life the moment she agreed to work for their side.

"Maybe I can do something through back channels," Helen said. "To try and stop him."

"No. Please." She reached out, but was too far away, so Helen closed the gap and took her hand, squeezing it. Frieda flinched from her grasp and stepped toward the door. They heard the sound of rain.

"Do you think he has gone?" Frieda asked, voice quavering.

"Where do you need to go? I've got a taxi waiting a few blocks from here."

"No."

"It's raining. Let me get you an umbrella. We have some in the closet."

"No. I must leave."

"Tell me your name, at least. Your real name."

"No!" She opened the door and looked out into the rainy night. A downpour, an empty street in darkness.

"Your coat. Here."

Frieda turned, nodding absently as Helen picked up the coat from the chair and handed it over. Frieda slipped it on. Three sizes too large, something from a secondhand shop. So young and helpless, and now she was about to disappear.

"Please, use my taxi. I'll give the fare to the driver."

"No!" But as Frieda reached the threshold she turned and spoke again.

"You will look out for me, yes? Not to report this, but to see that he does not reveal me to the others. You can do this, yes?"

"Yes. Of course." An empty promise, but at the moment it was all Helen could offer.

Frieda looked around the room a final time.

"Safe house," she said disdainfully. She shook her head and walked into the rain and darkness.

Her parting words stabbed Helen as the door shut. For a moment she couldn't move, and by the time she rushed to the window and pulled back the curtains Frieda was gone. Numbly, she began tidying up—straightening cushions, repositioning the couch, sweeping up the shards of broken glass. She checked her watch, remembering Baucom and his deadline. Even if she left for the cab now she'd be cutting it close, assuming the driver was still waiting, so she decided to telephone instead. Tell Baucom to stand down, that she was on her way.

She used the house phone in the kitchen, an unsecure line that belonged to the tenant, and dialed the number for the house in Zehlendorf.

"Yes?"

"It's me. All's well, but there are a few chores I need to attend to, and I didn't want you sounding the alarm."

"Are you okay?"

"Absolutely."

"You don't sound very convincing."

"Long story, but not on this phone."

"Of course."

"I'll be back within the hour. Don't wait up."

"As you wish."

After hanging up she wondered what she would tell him later. Handle this rashly and Gilley would get away with everything. She wondered how many other times he'd done something like this. She shook her head, trying to clear her mind. Was she forgetting anything?

The tape.

She ran upstairs, her stomach hollow, and switched on the light in the room with the equipment. The reels were turning. Which button had she hit earlier? The red record button was pushed down.

That meant every spoken word, and every noise from the struggle between Frieda and Gilley, were now on tape. So were Frieda's words afterward. Feeling her heart lift, Helen hit the stop button and exhaled in relief. She rewound the tape, removed it from the spindle, and put it into her bag alongside the other one. Two reels, with two stories. Her own little archive of the forbidden, collected in a single day.

Enough trouble to last her a lifetime, she supposed. The only thing she knew for sure was that none of her training or experience offered the slightest bit of guidance as to what she should do next.

4

Helen awoke at the house in Zehlendorf to the smell of brewing coffee. Baucom stood by the window in his boxers, raising the blinds onto a gray Berlin morning. She felt as wrung out as if she'd endured hours of nightmares, and then she remembered why. A gust of rain pelted the windowpane, and she wondered if Frieda was still out in the elements, too scared to take shelter in any of her familiar places.

Baucom climbed into bed and handed her a steaming mug. Frothed milk on top, the way she liked it.

"Thank you."

"The way you were last night, I figured you needed it."

"What do you mean?"

"You were in quite a state when you got back."

"How would you know? You were fast asleep."

"Later. Tossing and turning. Shouting in your dreams."

"What did I say?"

"Incoherent. But your face?" He shook his head. "You looked scared. Hunted. I shook you once, to wake you, but that only made it worse. I was afraid to try again."

"Clark Baucom, master spy, afraid to wake a sleeping harpy."

"I take it that everything didn't go as planned?"

"What makes you say that?" She wasn't ready to tell him what she'd witnessed, not yet.

"Well, for starters, your handbag seemed a little full this morning."

"Those tapes are none of your business!"

"I seem to recall you making them my business. Or one of them, anyway. But if you don't want me to interfere, fine."

"All right, then. If you're going to poke around in my things, the least you can do is help. What can you tell me about Kevin Gilley?"

"*He* was there?"

"Who says this is about last night?"

"Then why do you ask?"

"Just curious."

He smiled, not fooled a bit, but answered, anyway.

"One thing I know is that for security reasons you're supposed to call him Robert."

"Isn't he supposed to be out of favor? I heard he was up for a transfer."

"That's the cover story, anyway. It must be working if you've heard it."

"What's the real story?"

Baucom shook his head, frowning.

"He plays in another part of the sandbox from me. Sorcery and black bags. Deals with things I wouldn't *want* to know, and would shut my ears if someone started to tell me."

"Supposed to be quite the Casanova, isn't he?"

"That would cover half our field men, present company excluded."

"Does this rep extend to his treatment of female agents?"

Baucom frowned and shook his head.

"What are you saying, exactly, that you caught him with his pants down?"

"Something like that."

"Last person I saw drop trou in a safe house was a prim little Bohemian who used to bring me telexes from the Czech Foreign Ministry. He'd smuggle them out of the office by taping them to his ass in the washroom. Always made me turn around when he took his pants down. He'd offer a proper little 'Excuse me,' and then all I'd hear was the rattle of his belt buckle, a quick zip, and a bunch of ripping sounds while he tore the tape off with little grunts and shrieks."

"I believe we were talking about Kevin Gilley."

"I believe we were. And I told you all I know about the man, and even that was too much."

He went silent, and for a while she thought the subject was closed. Then he moved closer, slid his thigh against hers, and slipped his arm beneath her head like a pillow. She sat up, took a swallow of coffee, and set the mug on the bedside table before easing back down. His body felt like a bulwark, a firewall. His next words emerged in a whisper, directly into her ear.

"Every now and then I do wonder who Robert's really working for."

She was careful not to move.

"You think it's them?"

"Oh, no. Robert would never work for them. But there are times I suspect he's mostly working for himself."

"How so?"

She felt him shrug, and waited for more. He said nothing, and a few moments later he asked where she'd like to go for breakfast. Perhaps that new *Bäckerei* around the corner on Teltower Damm? The one that dusted everything with confectioner's sugar and made the strongest coffee for blocks? She said that sounded fine, and then she tried one more time, sidling up to the subject carefully, as if it might reach out at any moment and grab her by the arm.

"You think Robert is just selfish, then? Looking out for number one?"

"Why do you ask?"

His new favorite question, which irritated her, and made her wonder if Gilley's predatory nature was common knowledge, even a subject of Agency banter among the select, and therefore not a topic for discussion among those at lower clearances, like her.

"Well, let's say, just as a hypothetical, that Gilley *was* at the house last night. As a customer, but not exactly playing by the rules."

"Like us, you mean? Intimate acts in an Agency facility?"

She blushed, and was grateful he was staring at the ceiling.

"I wouldn't call his behavior intimate by anyone's definition. Besides, this house is decommissioned, and I'm authorized to be here. To keep the place looking occupied, show my face to the neighbors until we've had time to remove the equipment, close up shop."

"True enough."

"So, then."

"What?"

"The hypothetical. What do you make of it?"

"I don't engage in hypotheticals. Not for people like Kevin Gilley."

He again let the topic drift away, off into the smoke from the Gitane he'd just lit.

"So, then," he said at last. "Breakfast?"

"I think I'll sleep a while longer."

"Wise decision."

He climbed out of bed and began to dress.

"The only problem," she said, "is that I'm not sure I *can* sleep."

"Well, it all depends on your approach."

"What do you mean?"

"How you approach sleep. How you prepare yourself to enter it."

"You act like it's a place, a destination."

"Don't you think of it that way?"

"Usually I'm so tired that I just fall right in."

"I enter it willfully, with gratitude. It's the only way I was able to sleep at all sometimes during the war, or later, during some of those scrapes I got myself into. I'd think of sleep as a warm shelter on a cold night. I'd be lying there in a tent, maybe, or in one of those huts full of soldiers, everybody snoring, their breath clouding the air, and I'd picture sleep as this realm where you must prepare yourself in order to be admitted, like a sanctuary."

"A sanctuary. I like that."

"It's kind of like the feeling I get when I arrive at a safe house in hostile territory, that moment when you lock the door behind you and realize you're going to be fine. You stop and listen to the quiet, to the familiar little noises a place always makes. The hum of the refrigerator, maybe, or a car outside crossing a loose manhole cover. The drip of a downspout. Things you've noticed before, so that when you hear them again it's a reassurance and all the tension drains right out of you. The way the dirty oil comes pouring out of a car when you unscrew the oil pan."

"An oil pan. How poetic."

Helen was about to smile when she was reminded of poor Frieda, who had also put her trust in a safe house, despite being warned about Gilley. And if a safe house wasn't really safe, then maybe sleep wasn't, either. But it was an appealing notion.

"A destination," she said. "That's good."

Helen curled up in the bed. Baucom tugged the covers into place and lightly stroked her hair.

"I don't know what happened last night, and I won't press for details," he said. "Whatever it was, I'd say you've earned some peace. Sleep as late as you want. I'll cover for you with Herrington."

"Thank you," she said lazily, already easing through the gates toward a necessary oblivion. She sensed her troubles and anxieties remaining behind, refused entry. Even the haunting image of Frieda, pale and wet and frightened, floated off into the shadows like an untethered soul.

And from that day onward, no matter how tired or shaken or upset, Helen held fast to the idea of sleep as a secure destination, a welcoming refuge, up to and even including the night thirty-five years later when she was murdered in her bed.

5

On the night Willard Shoat killed his parents, he walked barefoot to the edge of town with a can of red spray paint, out to the sign that said, "Entering POSTON, pop. 924." He shook the clicking can, raised on his tiptoes, and opened fire. First he slashed out the number. Then he painted a new total to account for the subtraction of Mom and Dad: 921.

Willard never was much for math.

But it took the police a while to figure that out, and for two days running they dug holes all over the family farm in search of a third body. They ran backhoes and unleashed sniffer dogs, going after anything that hinted at rot or decay. Being a farm, there was plenty of both. The manure heaps alone kept them busy for an entire afternoon, and they tore up the better part of an acre before concluding, as almost everyone else in town already had, that Willard had simply gotten his sums wrong.

Henry Mattick, new to Poston and living in a small frame house less than a block from the scene, took a contrary view. Dumb as the boy was—an unkind word, perhaps, for a twenty-four-year-old whose mind never made it past kindergarten—Henry believed Willard was simply counting himself out of the game as well. For what better way to negate yourself than to do away with the two people who brought you into the world?

Henry got wrapped up in the story almost from the moment he first heard the sirens.

It wasn't as if he had much else to do, marooned in a rural village on the Maryland Eastern Shore. He was between jobs and romantically unattached, quartered in a spartan rancher owned by a distant relative who'd offered temporary refuge at a bargain rate. Or so Henry told the neighbors on the few occasions they induced him to talk. They knew he was from Baltimore by the stickers on his car, but when they asked about that he only nodded.

His only companion was a brindled, underfed mutt left behind by the previous tenant, a dog so accustomed to neglect that he would disappear for days at a time, showing up only to eat, accept a scratch or two on the head, and poop in the grass by the porch before again wandering off. Henry, deciding not to take it personally, gave the dog a name—Scooter—and accommodated his unpredictable schedule by keeping his bowl filled at all hours.

Watchful by nature, Henry kept an eye on the house down the street as the police came and went. He followed the saturation media coverage almost minute by minute, and when the cable networks began to lose interest he switched to the Internet.

By the lurid and violent standards of the age, the case struck Henry as fairly run-of-the-mill. And with only two fatalities it probably would have attracted little media attention if not for Willard's strange sojourn to the sign at the edge of town. Otherwise, the basics were simple. The murder weapon was a hunting rifle, a .30-06 bolt action Ruger American that Willard's dad had bought him for his fourteenth birthday. Up to then he'd used it only for shooting at deer. He shot both his parents in the face—Dad first, Mom second. Investigators settled on that order of events partly by reading the spatter of blood and gore, but also because his mother's body was found sitting upright in bed, meaning she had probably awakened after the first shot.

Neither the boy nor his parents had been drinking in the hours beforehand. Toxicology tests weren't yet complete, but none of the three had a history of drug use, and Willard had been reasonably lucid, all things considered, at the time of his arrest. Both deaths were almost certainly instantaneous. Estimated time: Between 4 and 4:30 a.m.

Based on the blood trail, Willard had dropped the gun on the bedroom floor and proceeded immediately out of the house, pausing only to pick up a spray can of tractor paint, which he'd apparently set by the front door before the shooting.

As for motive, the family's oft-interviewed friends and neighbors offered no plausible theories, despite the best efforts of the reporters who saturated the town. (Henry himself turned away six of them, and for three days they went door-to-door with the fervor of Jehovah's Witnesses.)

The townspeople's accounts were almost identical in tone and content. In the weeks leading up to the event, Willard had exhibited no apparent anger, no violent tendencies, no signs of mental illness. He was just "slow," everyone said. Slow and sweet and impressionable, with a special fondness for fried chicken, cotton candy, fireworks, and marching bands. And although he went hunting with his father every deer season, no one could remember the last time he'd bagged one—or, indeed, if he'd ever even hit one.

A few people raised a history of bullying as a possible instigator, although everyone said the problem had mostly disappeared years ago, when his contemporaries went off to jobs or to college. And by then Willard had grown large enough to make picking a fight with him seem like a bad idea.

There was no suggestion of parental abuse. His father, Tarrant, sixty-three, was known as a hard worker and devoted parent, and was well thought of in the community. His mother, Helen, fifty-nine, although a bit chilly and aloof, had always been fiercely protective of his interests. No one had ever heard her raise her voice to him. In fact, people said, as if suddenly awakening to the realization, for years no one seemed to have heard her say much of anything to anybody. In a way, she had become as much of a closed book as her son. Those who thought about it the longest dated her withdrawal to the year the Shoats' daughter, Anna, went off to college—six or seven years ago, they guessed, before inevitably realizing on second thought that it had been more like a dozen, a calculation that left everyone shaking their heads at the fleeting nature of time. Anna, who now lived in Baltimore, wasn't quoted anywhere. Apparently she'd gone into seclusion, and wasn't expected in town until the day of the funeral.

Deprived of any obvious answers, some of the more pious citizens of Poston finally concluded that the Shoats' failure to find a church home must have contributed to their downfall. A boy of unshakable faith, they said, never would have done such a thing. That body of opinion, quoted most prominently on Fox, provided Henry with a welcome moment of comic relief. Typical, he mused, and yet another reason he wouldn't be sticking around Poston any longer than he had to.

Yet, he, too, believed there had to be more to the story, if only because his most recent employments had taught him that, even for the simple-minded, motive is often buried deep within a welter of complexity. And as he searched for answers from his amateur's perch, the one aspect of the murders that he kept returning to was the same one that had captured the public's imagination: Willard's half-mile walk to the edge of town. Henry was so haunted by the image of the boy's lonely, purposeful stroll that he decided late one night—or, rather, very early one morning—to retrace Willard's steps, if only to share in the sensory cues that the young man must have worn like a second garment as he strolled out to correct the town's population total, as single-minded as a census taker.

Henry began at the head of the Shoats' driveway, where the front flap of their empty mailbox hung open like the tongue of an exhausted dog. The neighboring houses were dark. No one stirred. It was that hour before dawn when shooting stars still tumble dimly across the sky, farm ponds smoke with morning mist, and the acrid smell of skunk floats across fields of corn and soybeans. Crickets and tree frogs offered the night's final chorus. Soon the songbirds would begin to stir. Henry was barefoot, just as Willard had been. The pavement was still warm from the previous day, but its roughness soon forced him onto the grassy shoulder, cool with dew.

He inhaled the scent of the dying night—pine resin and moist earth, that slight essence of skunk—and as he proceeded he pictured Willard just ahead, rumpled and blood-spattered, and gripping a can of paint. He imagined the boy passing these silent houses, the hems of his denim overalls rasping in the wet grass.

Henry rounded the curve of Willow Street and turned onto Highway 53, the narrow slab faintly aglow in the last wash of moonlight. Off in the distance, the red lights of a radio tower flashed like a homing beacon.

The boy's weight, girth, and sedentary lifestyle must have made his breathing labored by this point, Henry thought, as he passed the Basnight place on his left, a brick rancher with a triple garage and a satellite dish sprouting on the lawn like a giant mushroom. On the pavement just ahead was a blackened splotch of road kill—a flattened squirrel, crusty enough to flip with a spatula.

Next Henry overtook the playground, where it seemed every kid in town had laughed at Willard as the oaf who couldn't read, couldn't add, couldn't do much of anything but shake his head and say "I dunno" whenever anyone asked him a question. Finally, breaking free of the houses, he reached the welcome brigade of signs from the Ruritans, the Civitans, the First Baptist

Church, the Farm Bureau, and the VFD, their rusting posts twined with trumpet vine.

Then, just beyond, the Poston sign, where Willard had stopped to complete the task at hand.

Why?

Henry considered the question yet again, but had no answer. The walk, for all its heightened awareness, had tuned him to a blank signal, a hiss of dead air.

Willard had then walked home, straight back the way he'd come. Two hours later the paperboy had found him, curled up and snoring on the concrete deck of the Shoats' front porch. Seeing that the door was ajar, and noticing enough blood to make him uneasy, the paperboy had promptly swerved his bicycle around to pedal straight to the office of the town cop, who arrived with gun drawn to find Willard still asleep and the house already abuzz with flies.

It took only two days for a Maryland state highway crew to replace the sign, which must have set some sort of record for bureaucratic efficiency. But in a macabre twist the boys from the DOT went with Willard's revised total of 921. They toted away the old sign for evidence, and within hours of its departure the story began making the rounds that Willard had actually painted the number in blood.

Henry returned to his house feeling more foolish than enlightened. He climbed into bed as the birds began to chirp, and the last thing he heard as he fell

asleep was the slap of the newspaper on the porch—
same paperboy, same bicycle. When he finally awoke
to retrieve the copy, the funeral procession was passing
down Highway 53 with its sad assortment of vehicles:
two hearses, a courtesy limo, three cars of friends and
family, five TV vans.

A story on the front page told him over a late breakfast
that the service was closed to the public. Accompanying
it was the first photo he'd seen of Willard's sister, Anna.
Her face surprised him. Compared to the rest of the
family, she looked cosmopolitan and aware, seemingly
the product of a wider world. The set of her jaw lent
her a certain fierceness, yet there was also a touch of the
demure. Henry's most recent boss would have described
it as the kind of face juries loved—guileless and open,
the very picture of honesty and sincerity.

She was thirty, the second-in-command of some do-
gooder outfit that lobbied on behalf of children and the
poor, which made Henry wonder what her relationship
with her brother had been like. Had she taken the job
out of sympathy with his plight, or out of guilt for
leaving him behind?

A gloomy choice.

After a dinner of takeout fried chicken—Willard's
favorite, it belatedly occurred to him—Henry swore
off any further coverage. He shut down his laptop and
flipped on the television to watch a baseball game. It
would soon be time to leave Poston, anyway.

In the fourth inning he opened a bottle of rye whiskey he had vowed to ration until October. By the ninth he had downed more than half. He switched off the game just as a pop-up settled into the shortstop's glove for the final out. Then he shut his eyes and dreamed of Willard on his nocturnal walk, alone yet not alone, stepping resolutely while some presence loomed just behind him in the roadside shadows, watchful and knowing.

6

Next thing Henry knew, someone was hammering at the screen door, every blow striking at his temples. He rose groggily. Rubbing a hand through his hair, he wondered if he'd imagined the noise. The bottle of rye was still open on the floor, and its fumes almost made him wretch. He was screwing the cap back on when the knocking resumed.

"Coming!"

Shouting made his forehead throb. No sign of the dog, and the bowl was still full. The clock on the cable box said it was 10:24 a.m.

Henry opened the door to be greeted by the face of Anna Shoat, as if she'd stepped straight off the pages of his newspaper. The photo's harsh caption flashed instantly to mind: *Anna Shoat, who has refused to comment.*

"Are you Henry Mattick?"

"Yes."

"I'm Anna Shoat. I'm the—"

"I know who you are."

"Of course." She nodded, resigned to her notoriety. He looked up and down the street, to see who else might be out there to witness her arrival on his doorstep.

"Don't worry," she said. "They're all gone."

"Who?"

"The reporters, the cameras. First day I've been left in peace since it happened. May I come in?"

"Sure."

He stepped back to allow entry, feeling callous and impolite. As she stepped inside he hazily realized that she, too, had been a part of his overnight dreams, although his only clear memory was that she had moved just as she was moving now—with a brisk, nimble assurance.

Turning to follow her, he saw with fresh eyes the forlorn nature of his lodgings. The only seating was a sagging gray couch and a green corduroy easy chair. There was a scuffed coffee table, a wall-mounted television with wires dangling from the back. He'd hammered together a set of bookshelves out of unfinished pine, large enough to hold a three-month supply of reading. The ceiling had cobwebs in every corner, same as when he'd moved in, and the dingy off-white of the bare walls was a perfect match for the thin beige carpet, which was so new that it still smelled like chemicals. Make a place bleak enough and no one will want to visit. That had seemed like a pretty good plan until now. He could have used some help from Scooter, if only to demonstrate that, yes, he did have a warm and fuzzy side.

"It's just temporary," he said of the house, but her eyes showed only exhaustion as she settled into the green chair. Henry took the couch.

"Can I get you something? Coffee, maybe?"

She shook her head.

"I hear you're some kind of investigator?" she said.

"Was. And not really."

Now where had she learned that? Probably from Stu Wilgus, a nosy retired lawyer from Baltimore. Henry had let himself be drawn into conversation with the man a few weeks ago in the checkout line of the general store—yes, they still called it that in Poston. Henry had sensed even then that he was revealing too much.

"Was. Okay. But supposedly you're looking for work?"

"I'm between jobs, but that's by choice."

"Oh."

She nodded and put her hands on her knees, like she was on the verge of leaving. Then she sighed and sagged into the chair.

"I ask because I'm looking for somebody who . . ." She paused, searching for the words. "Somebody who can help me understand this. You know, at first they wouldn't even let me see him. Can you believe that?"

"Willard, you mean? Your brother?"

She looked up abruptly, eyes shining with gratitude.

"Thank you for calling him that. My brother. The whole damn week no one else has done that. Not even the pastor. 'What shall we say at the service about Willard?' The police, too. 'What are your wishes for a lawyer for Willard?' Never once 'your brother.' Like we're no longer related. I'm not even convinced he did it." She thrust out a hand, as if to halt that train of thought. "Check that. Of course he did it. That's indisputable. But not of his own mind. He couldn't have. That's why I'm here. I need someone to help me figure out why, and I'll pay for your services."

"I think what you need is a doctor. A psychiatrist, maybe, to examine him."

"If I thought that was the answer, I'd do it in a heartbeat. But I don't think he's reachable that way. I'm not sure he ever has been. And after this? A closed book. Right now I'm only interested in what I *can* do, and my best hope is to figure out what he was up to in the days before it happened. Learn where he was, who he saw. Retrace his steps to find the trigger, the thing that set him off."

"The cops were no help?"

"What do you think? And, really, why *should* they care? Their only job is to figure out who did it, and Willard definitely did it."

"What about a PI?"

"A friend gave me a name in Baltimore. I called but he said he'd be wasting my money. When he told me his rates, I agreed. The travel expenses alone would wipe me out. So, to be blunt, that's another reason I'm here. I'm thinking you might be cheap, or at least affordable. You won't have to travel, for starters. I can pay seventy-five a day, plus mileage, for up to a month. I know it's peanuts, but if you're not making anything right now, well . . ."

"Money's not the issue."

She nodded, like it was the answer she'd expected. Then she exhaled loudly, seeming a little less burdened after unloading her sales pitch. It occurred to him that she hadn't had anyone to talk to since arriving in Poston. Mom and Dad were gone, her friends were in the city. She hadn't seen the neighbors in ages, and that left only cops, newshounds, the pastor for a church she hadn't attended in years, the creepy funeral director, maybe an estate lawyer. By default, Henry Mattick had become her sounding board.

Henry felt almost honored. It helped that his throbbing hangover was beginning to fade. But, for reasons of his own, he knew he wasn't the right choice, and he wanted to find a gentle way to tell her as much.

"I'm really not a professional."

"Still, it was the U.S. Attorney's office in Baltimore, right? Isn't that where you were working before?"

"Stu Wilgus must have told you that."

"He was at the funeral. One of the few who had the guts to come."

Or the curiosity, Henry thought but didn't say.

"Well, like I told Wilgus, I wasn't even full-time. A contract job, then I was out on my ass."

"Before that you worked for some congressional committee, right?"

"Right." He wasn't happy she knew all this, and he must have let it show.

"Sorry. I looked you up online."

"Must have looked pretty hard. Look, the gig with DOJ, mostly what I did was watch a lot of investigators do their work, but I've never been trained as one myself." Not exactly true, so he hedged. "Or not really. It's like the old ad, 'Hi, I'm not a doctor but I played one on TV.'"

"Fine, then we'll make it fifty a day."

"Well, let's not get carried away." This finally coaxed a fleeting smile out of her. "Seriously, I'd help if I could, but I doubt there's a single thing I could find out that you couldn't find out on your own. Chances are your brother just snapped. I'm not saying that to discourage you, I'm saying it because I wouldn't even know where to begin."

"With his hunting, that's one place."

"What do you mean?"

She leaned forward, renewing her pitch.

"Last time I talked to Dad, maybe a month ago, he said Willard had started hunting on his own. It made Dad a little nervous, but he figured maybe it was good for him, a sign of independence. I asked where he went, how he got there. Dad didn't have the slightest, which to me was kind of alarming. He never once came back with anything, but there were always a few rounds missing. And the other thing was, Dad never heard any shots. So he wasn't hunting our land."

"Maybe he was just walking a long way."

"Dad figured he was meeting somebody with a car."

"Did he ask?"

"Yes. Willard said no, but he wouldn't look Dad in the eye, and that wasn't like him."

"Who were his friends?"

"None. He's never had any. That's one reason Dad didn't push it. If he finally had a friend, why spoil it?"

"Unless he was walking the whole way."

"Willard didn't like long walks. Besides, our property's only forty acres, and the woods run out at Hallam Road. He would've crossed into someone else's land inside fifteen, twenty minutes."

Henry locked on to that image: Willard emerging from a stand of pines onto a gravel lane, his breathing labored, boots caked with mud and wet leaves. The thought took him back to the edge of town, where he again saw Willard with his spray can, raised on his tiptoes to log the new total. He looked up to see Anna staring at him, awaiting a response.

"Let's say he did go off with somebody else," Henry said. "Even then, unless somebody saw them, or knows who it was, it's just another dead end."

"So we ask around until we find somebody who saw them. Then we're one step closer to finding out who put the idea in his head, or confused him enough to do what he did."

"Why does this friendship, if that's what it was, have to be something sinister? From what you've said, it sounds like exactly what he needed."

"Then maybe his friend dumped him, and that's what set him off. Or Dad found out, or Mom, and they put an end to it, so he got angry and killed them. Either way, it's a step toward an explanation, and that's all I'm looking for."

"Have you asked him?"

She nodded and again looked at the floor.

"They let me see him late yesterday, after the funeral, but he barely said a word. I walked in and he perked right up, actually smiled and said, 'You came back!' Then he asked where Mom and Dad were, and what was I supposed to say to that?"

"What *did* you say?"

"I told him they were dead. I guess I should have been nicer about it, gentler. But, Jesus Christ, he'd fucking killed them. He just kind of crumpled, his whole face. Then he turned around and wouldn't look at me, wouldn't say another word."

"You think he'd forgotten? Or blanked it all out?"

"Maybe. I'm seeing him again tomorrow. I'll take you with me, if you want." She paused, sinking back into her thoughts. "He looked terrible. He hadn't bathed or shaved or combed his hair. He asked if I could bring him a toy."

"A toy?" It put a lump in his throat.

"One morning he kills our parents. Then he's asking for his model of the Millennium Falcon."

Henry let that sink in for a few seconds before speaking again.

"The numbers he painted, that whole thing with the sign. Did you ask about that?"

"Oh, that part's easy." She flicked her hand dismissively. "Willard counts everything. Keeps tallies and writes them down everywhere. On paper, on pieces of wood, whatever's handy. Lists and running totals for all kinds of stuff. How many tubes of toothpaste he's used, how many bars of soap. How many cardinals on the bird feeder. The number of times he saw Elmo on *Sesame Street*."

"But the number itself, well . . ."

"Because he subtracted three?" She shook her head and almost smiled. "That's one where the assholes who always made fun of him were probably right. He just got it wrong. He's not used to adding or subtracting. He's too busy notching up the latest totals. Half the time you can't even figure out what he's counting. He can't always spell the words, so sometimes he uses little symbols that only he understands. A compulsion, that's what the shrink said."

"He's got a shrink?"

"Wrong word. He went to a doctor for a while, more like a counselor or therapist, somebody who worked with the developmentally disabled, and it was years ago. It was as much for us as it was for him, to help us understand the way he was, and how to keep him happy. Mom thought it did him some good."

"What did you think?"

"It did explain all the lists. She said it was normal, and gave him focus, a sense of purpose."

"Have you been to see her?"

"He stopped going when he was around seventeen."

"Too bad."

"Yeah, I've thought that a few times, too. But even with her, it wasn't like he ever really opened up. Like I said, a closed book." For a second or two her eyes had a faraway look. Then she refocused on Henry. "So what do you think?"

He shook his head.

"This isn't my area of expertise."

"All I'm asking for is a week of your time. One week, when all you're doing now is sitting here in front of your TV, doing shots of rye."

Well, at least she was observant.

"Look," she continued. "It's either you, or I take potluck from the Yellow Pages over here on the Eastern Shore. Dial G for gumshoe, and hire some rube who tails cheating farmers for a living. Yes, I'm grasping at straws. But right now you're my only hope."

She laughed bitterly and shook her head.

"I sound ridiculous, don't I? 'Help me, Obi-Wan Kenobi, you're my only hope.' That's his favorite movie, as you might have guessed from the toy request. Although I'll be damned if I repeat that in public unless I want CNN using it in their latest stupid theory: *Murder boy had Darth Vader fixation.*"

She sighed.

"Maybe I'm losing my mind. My apologies for bothering you."

"No, it's okay. And I can see why you'd want answers. I understand that."

"So you'll do it then?" The light returned to her eyes, and for a moment the jury in him wavered, edging toward a yes vote. Then the naysayers spoke up: *You're falling for the face. This isn't why you're here.*

"Let me sleep on it."

She should sleep on it, too, he thought. Maybe by

tomorrow she would feel better simply for having talked things over, and that might be enough.

"Okay," she said. Then, glancing down at the rye. "But maybe you could sleep on it with a clearer head than last night."

"It's not a habit." He was a little unnerved by how badly he wanted her to believe him.

"I wouldn't sweat it. The neighbors have plenty of theories about you, but none of them seems to think you're a drunk."

He escorted her to the door, and then pulled back the curtain to watch her depart. She was walking up Willow, back toward the murder scene. A morbid part of him wanted a peek inside the house. But he had no intention of taking her up on the offer, even though he, too, would like to know what made Willard Shoat snap.

Instead, he would give Anna a contact or two from his past—people with similar skills who might even agree to her bargain rate. He would offer to let them stay here, gratis, to help cut costs. As for Henry, the best thing now would be to pack up and get moving. But first he had to make a phone call. There was no landline, so he picked up his cell phone and punched in a number with a Washington area code. The first ring had barely started before someone picked up—Mitch, who must have recognized the incoming number.

"Mattick. Been wondering when you'd call."

"I figured it was your turn."

"What, worried we'll stop paying you?"

"The opposite. Nothing really left to do here, the way I see it."

"That's for sure. Who'd have guessed it, huh?"

"If you really want to know, the whole thing's given me the heebie-jeebies. Talk about being in the wrong place at the wrong time."

"Understandable. We're at a loss, too. Just when you think you've got an easy, uneventful assignment, huh?"

"Tell me about it. One thing you should probably know. Her daughter was just over here."

"Anna?" He said it almost like he knew her.

"Yeah."

"What for?"

"She wants to hire me."

"Hire you?"

"To look into things. She thinks someone must have put the idea in her brother's head. Controlled him somehow."

Mitch paused, digesting the news.

"How'd she hear about you?"

"How wouldn't she, the way this place is."

"What do you think of her theory?"

"Same as the cops, probably. She's grasping at straws, looking for anything to make her feel better."

"Maybe so. But it's perfect, don't you think?"

"Perfect how?"

"For keeping you on the payroll, now that you've actually got an excuse to snoop around in a way you never could have before."

"Mitch, she's dead."

"But the reason we hired you isn't."

"And that reason is?"

"We've been over this, Mattick. I've already told you all you need to know."

"Nothing, you mean."

"Just do the job. The one we're paying you for, and the one she'll be paying you for."

"I don't even know what you could still want at this point. Not that I was giving you much to begin with."

"Isn't it obvious? If this actually gets you into the house, then take a look at everything she left behind. Phone bills, finances, letters, appointment books—anything, recent or ancient. Don't worry about relevance, we'll know what's important. Make copies when you can, and forward them."

"I don't know, Mitch."

"You didn't turn her down, did you?"

"No, but . . ."

"Good. Make her happy. Accept her offer."

"And if there's a conflict? Between what she wants and what you want?"

"There won't be. After the way this whole thing just got turned on its head, we'll be happy to let her take this wherever she wants. Anything we get out of it now is gravy. Trust me, Mattick. It'll be hand in glove. Hand in glove."

Sure, he thought, as they ended the call. Henry had heard those kinds of assurances before. He looked out the front window, but the street was empty. By now Anna Shoat was probably back inside the house where she'd grown up, surrounded by silence, spooked and lonely. How long did violence linger in the atmospherics of a place where something terrible had happened? He supposed he would find out soon enough.

It troubled him, the idea of intruding. Even on the off chance Henry was able to help, he wanted nothing to do with deceiving someone so vulnerable. With any luck, she'd do them both a favor and give up. He'd phone Mitch again, tell him sorry but no deal, and then pack his bags.

Henry walked to the bedroom and pulled his suitcase from beneath the bed. He cleared out his T-shirts and boxers from the chest of drawers and piled them inside. Then he sat on the bed and reconsidered. When you said no to people like Mitch, they just shrugged and found somebody else. And that was a problem. Henry didn't want just anybody doing this, now that Anna was part of it—sad and abandoned Anna, with a face a jury would love. She deserved better.

He put his clothes back in the drawers and slid the suitcase beneath the bed. Returning to the living room, he grabbed the bottle of rye and set it on the highest shelf in the kitchen. He turned on the television, watched blankly for a few seconds as a guy with a loud voice demonstrated the many uses of a folding ladder. Then he switched it off, placed his hands on his knees, and stood. There was work to be done. If he was going to do this, then he had better do it right.

7

Anna was back on his doorstep at 7:30 a.m. Henry had already showered, shaved, and brewed a pot of coffee. Even Scooter was back, having scratched at the screen door for entry an hour earlier. He was now curled on the cool linoleum of the kitchen floor, watching Henry and Anna enter from the hallway. On the stove, two eggs popped in a slick of bacon grease in a cast-iron skillet.

"Want some?" Henry asked, pointing with a spatula.

She shook her head, all business until she spotted the dog.

"Ah. So there he is."

"You've met Scooter?"

"The neighbors mentioned him. They see your willingness to take him in as a vote in your favor."

"Didn't know there was a referendum."

"The court of public opinion. Poston's has always been pretty busy."

"I've noticed."

She poured herself a mug of coffee. Henry slid his eggs onto a plate where two strips of bacon were already waiting. Scooter's ears went up but otherwise he didn't budge.

"Sounds like you've done some more asking around."

"I have. It was fruitful."

His stomach did a tiny somersault. He wondered if she was about to fire him before he even said yes.

"You spent a year in Europe."

"That's no big secret, although I doubt you found it on Google."

"Talked to a friend of yours."

"A friend?"

"Is it that unusual?"

"Well, no." Although he had to admit that no obvious names leaped to mind. His most recent job had imposed a certain degree of isolation, as had this one. "But it's fair to say I'm not the world's most social creature."

"He said that, too. 'Bit of a loner' were the exact words."

"Wouldn't mind knowing your source."

"I'm fine with loners as long as they're competent, and he spoke well of your skills. I like the whole Europe thing, too. Anyone who can go over there without a plan or a job and manage to stay an entire year must be resourceful."

"Fifteen months, actually. And it wasn't that hard."

But he *had* been resourceful then. Happy, too, for the most part. He'd been in law school at the time, only a semester shy of a degree. Pointless, he'd concluded, before dropping out to hop a budget flight to London. He knocked around the U.K. on a bicycle for a few weeks, striking up conversations in rural pubs and bunking with farm families for weeks at a time as the seasonal chores demanded. He crossed the Channel and gradually made his way across the continent before reaching Germany, where he lived hand to mouth for eleven months in Berlin. By the end he had acquired a loose network of friends—Germans and expats—but was so broke that he had to bum a loan for a return ticket to the States.

Henry loved it there. Not the cold, or the clouds, or the short summer, but everything else, all of which seemed especially tailored to his preferences. Berliners walked places. They had clean and wonderful parks, and weren't always in their cars. Even old ladies bicycled to the grocery store. No one seemed to mind having an American in their midst, and once they accepted you they'd do almost anything to help. The locals read books and newspapers, bought their bread from bakers. Spending an hour in idle contemplation in a bar or café was a virtue, not laziness, and restaurants weren't so goddamned noisy. Nobody had guns, religion was passé. His kind of living, at least until he ran out of money.

The moment he got back to the United States he recognized what he had somehow never noticed before about the country he grew up in: People ate too much, bought too much, and then climbed into huge cars and trucks to go out and buy more. Bigger was always better, or at least more admired. Everyone was too distracted to read anything beyond the texts on their phones or the crawler on cable news. Voters opted for whoever promised to crack down on the people or groups they most despised. Greed and guns were rampant. At a time and place like this, it felt dangerous to be loyal to anyone or anything. And so it was that Henry fell into the perfect job for nursing his lonely contempt, a staff opening on Capitol Hill.

"Your bud says it was you who got that senator in trouble a few years back," Anna said. "The one with the floozy on the payroll."

"Opposition research. The people I was working for wanted him off a certain subcommittee. He made it easy for me. I was lucky."

"People who are good at what they do almost always say they're lucky."

"And vice versa. In Washington, anyway."

"Anything more I should know about your time there?"

"Nothing that's relevant."

Or nothing he cared to mention, because plenty was relevant. The job on the Hill had taught Henry most of what he knew about discreetly investigating someone's past, following a paper trail, and doing surveillance while hiding in plain sight. The fellow who hired him had done the tutoring, a rumpled old gnome named Rodney Bales. Staffers referred to Bales in hushed, deferential tones as Sir Rodney, at least partly due to the remnants of an upper-crust British accent in his rumbling baritone.

Henry's official employer was a senator from the Midwest, although Henry didn't actually meet the senator until his third week on the job. His real boss was Bales.

Trying to figure out Sir Rodney's past was like working on one of those cryptic crosswords filled with puns and confusing wordplay. Some people said he'd been with MI6. Others swore it was CIA. Now and then Bales casually dropped a clue to past assignments and whereabouts, like the time he joked about a talking parrot that had made him laugh in a wartime bar in Beirut. Henry was with him on K Street when he bumped into an old foreign correspondent who blithely mentioned, through gales of laughter, "that drunken old Serb who nearly took your head off in Pristina." Then there was the time Henry came upon Bales in his office, poring over a Czech magazine.

Oh, yes, his office. Rather than quartering himself with the rest of the senator's staff in the Russell Building, Sir Rodney's home base was in the Capitol itself, a windowless chamber at the back of the senator's hideaway. That's where Bales first interviewed Henry before hiring him on the spot.

"You know what I like best about your résumé?" Bales had said. "Your senior thesis on Metternich, focusing on his minions instead of the man himself."

"How did you even find that?"

"And your year abroad. You made your own way, you improvised."

"Barely."

"See? I like that, too. Almost every other chap who comes through that door is overselling himself before he even sits down."

"If you really want to know, I've never been all that impressed with people in this line of work. Senators, I mean. Or even congressional staff."

That was when Henry first heard Sir Rodney's laugh, wet and caustic, like something bubbling in a cauldron. Bales then told Henry that before doing a single day of work he would have to endure a month-long training course known around the office as the School of Night.

"How late are the hours?"

"No, no. It's a euphemism. From Shakespeare. A reference to a bunch of schemers and deep thinkers who were up to no good. Or so they say. Have you heard of the Farm, the CIA's little training camp?"

"Sure."

"Well, this is the *Cliff's Notes* version, minus all the

physical stuff. We also throw in an hour or two on data mining, and so on. Not just to show you how to do it, but to give you an inkling of what you'll be up against. No such thing as a secret in this town anymore. Not for anyone who knows what the fuck he's doing."

Henry might still be working there if the senator hadn't been unseated in the 2012 election. Bales, unsurprisingly, remained employed by switching over to committee staff, where he managed to at least keep Henry aboard part-time until the summer of 2013, when the gig at DOJ came open. Henry got the nod solely on the strength of Sir Rodney's recommendation.

And, now, here he was tucking into his eggs and bacon under the gaze of his prospective next employer.

"Sure I can't make you some?" he asked.

Anna shook her head.

"I can't help but notice that you haven't yet said no to my offer."

"I also haven't said yes."

"And what will it take for you to say yes?"

"A little more information on my employer."

"Fair enough." Her cell phone began ringing in her purse. "Shit."

Anna frowned at the incoming number but answered. "Yes?"

Then a pause, followed by a look of embarrassment. She grimaced and touched a hand to her forehead.

"I'm so sorry. I meant to do that on the way out of

town and it completely slipped my mind. Her pills are on the kitchen counter. The food's in the pantry. Oh, and her name is Princess, not that she ever answers to it."

Another pause, Anna nodding with a hint of impatience.

"I'm not sure. Cheryl will be back on Saturday, though, so you can just hand her over then. I'll text her your number and address . . . Okay, good . . . And thank you again."

She sighed and put the phone back in her purse.

"Princess?"

"A cat. Not mine. I was babysitting for a friend who's out of town, so I had to pass her along to someone else. One more change of venue and she'll start feeling like one of my clients."

"Clients?"

"Children. Runaways, foster kids, juvies. I did have my own cat once, but gave it away after three months."

"Allergies?"

"No. I just didn't like having it around. My mother's daughter, I guess. We never even had a dog growing up."

"What's a farm without a dog?"

"That's what my father always said. All he ever wanted was a retriever for hunting, but Mom always put her foot down. I think Willard and me were already more critters than she could handle."

As if on cue, Scooter stood and sauntered toward the back door. Henry walked over to let him out.

"Think I offended him?" Then she turned somber. "Maybe with a dog this never would've happened. Another set of eyes on Willard. Or maybe a dog would have distracted him, or been his friend."

Henry decided it was a good time to change the subject.

"Those children you work with, who's minding the store while you're gone?"

"My coworkers. They'll manage. So will the children." Then she looked at the floor, as if ashamed for saying it so dismissively. "What more do you need to know about me? I'm thirty, I live in a third-floor walk-up in Mount Vernon with no roommates and, as you heard, no pets. My job is important but not all-consuming. I like baseball, hate football, never vote Republican, avoid Facebook like the plague, and eat out at least five times a week, which is probably why I can't afford a better apartment or a real PI. Any other questions?"

"None that can't wait."

"I'm beginning to see how you go about your work. Watching, listening, waiting for slipups. Maybe you even arranged for Nancy to make that call."

"What if I really had?"

"I'd be impressed. But not in a good way."

"Useful to know."

"You sound like a man who's made up his mind."

"I have. But I won't take your money for any longer than two weeks."

"Fair enough. Will you be needing an advance?"

He shook his head.

"What changed your mind?"

So, then. Already having to lie. Henry took another bite of his eggs to avoid looking her in the eye, and then answered with his mouth full.

"Curiosity, I guess."

"That job of yours in Baltimore, with the U.S. Attorney. How'd you end up on their radar?"

Still interviewing him. Maybe she was having second thoughts.

"A friend on the Hill. Told me they were looking for something a little unorthodox, and said it matched my skill set."

"Skill set?"

"Mostly the ability to keep my eyes open and my mouth shut while looking for anomalies and paper trails. Plus the law school background. They liked that, too."

"What did DOJ want you to do?"

"Do you really need to know?"

"Now that you're my employee, do you really need to ask?"

"They detailed me as support staff on a special investigation, an antidrug task force, working with city cops. It was an infiltration, plain and simple. Justice was convinced one of their people was tipping the bad guys, and they wanted to find out who."

"Sounds dangerous."

"Not if you're careful. I'm a chickenshit at heart, so I was careful."

"Did it work?"

"They got their man, and I got a bonus. Which is why I don't need an advance."

The last part was another lie, but the first part was true. In fact, he'd built such an airtight case, and did it so quietly and efficiently, that DOJ was able to handle the whole thing without going to court, which greatly pleased his bosses because it allowed them to keep everything out of the public eye. It worked for Henry, too, because his role never had to be revealed in depositions, charging documents, or in open court. And in the departmental shake-up that followed, so many people were fired or transferred that no one could have said for sure who the snitch was. The U.S. Attorney showed his gratitude by offering a full-time job. Henry, having seen the lay of the land, turned it down.

"That looks good," Anna said. "I've changed my mind about that egg."

She stepped around him to the stove to turn on the gas and cracked an egg into the skillet with a single pop against the rim.

"One other request, if you're really going to do this," she said.

"Okay."

"Keep me as busy as you can, don't let me feel sorry for myself, and don't act like I'm made of glass."

"Understood."

"When do we start?"

"How 'bout now?"

"Good. I scheduled a nine-thirty visit with Willard. I told them I might be bringing my own investigator, and they said fine."

"That gives us more than an hour to spare. Would you mind if . . ."

"If what?"

"Well, this won't be pleasant, but I need to look at the scene. The house."

She held the spatula in midair, the egg bubbling beneath it.

"Okay." Barely audible. "Sure. That makes sense."

She ate only half the egg and slid the rest into the garbage. He grabbed a notebook and they set out on foot down Willow.

8

They must have been an odd sight to the neighbors. Henry, who knew every name behind every address, saw the Larrimores eyeing them from the breakfast nook, peeping out between the crape myrtles. The town mailman, Sarris, out on his early rounds, nodded gravely as he motored slowly past them in his van. By noon everyone in town would know that he and Anna were up to something, or at least had become a duo of sorts—the prodigal daughter of the murdered family teamed with the hermited newcomer. He didn't like feeling this exposed and scrutinized, but for better or worse he would be out in the open from here on out.

The Shoat house was a one-story rancher. Red brick with white trim. Door near the middle, two windows to the left, three to the right. Gray shingle roof in need of repair, eaves still dripping from a thunderstorm the night before. Two dogwoods on the lawn, one of them blighted, plus a pin oak that had probably been planted around the time Anna was born.

Anna tore off the crime scene tape from the wrought iron railing of the front steps and wadded it into a black-and-yellow ball that she threw to the ground before getting out her keys. Henry picked it up as she unlocked the door.

"All that land out back, it's your family's?" he asked, although he already knew the answer.

"Forty acres. Corn, soybeans, a barn, and a patch of woods. Plus two big-ass chicken houses, way at the back 'cause Mom hated the smell."

"Who's looking after the chickens?"

"The feeding and watering are automated, so that's taken care of unless something breaks or the power goes out. You don't really own the birds. Washam Poultry is coming out around midday to pick 'em up, says they're as big as they're gonna grow. So that will be the last of it except for cleaning out the shit, which of course we *do* own. Or I own. God knows who I'll hire to do it, or to harvest the corn and beans in the fall. Can you grab the mail?"

Henry reached inside the mailbox. An electric bill, two ad circulars, and a catalog for L.L. Bean. Nothing that would interest Mitch, although he supposed other items would keep rolling in. Like fingernails and hair, your mail kept growing after you died.

They stopped just inside the door, as if both of them needed a moment to acclimate. The air was damp and stale with a sharp overlay of disinfectant. A sunken living room was to the right, its walls almost as bare as in his house. There was a gallery of family photos atop an upright piano in one corner. A younger version of Willard smiled back at him from a frame on the left. At the far end of the living room, two steps led up to a small dining room with a glass-fronted cupboard showing off the good china.

The entryway opened just ahead onto a hallway, and that's where they headed. To the left were the bedrooms. They turned right into a family room with a brick fireplace and a big screen TV, and crossed the carpeted floor to an eat-in kitchen. Anna, as if sleepwalking, went all the way to the stove, which smelled faintly of bacon grease, before doubling back toward the family room. Henry dropped the wadded ball of tape into a trash bin beneath the sink and followed silently. A shaft of sunlight peeped through an opening in the curtains, filled with dust motes, probably the same ones that had been tumbling through the air on the night of the murders.

They went down the hallway toward the bedrooms, Anna's shoes echoing on the hardwood floor. There were three doorways. The two on the left were open, the one on the right was closed. Anna stopped, as if unwilling to take him farther.

"Have you been staying here?" he asked, belatedly realizing how harsh the question sounded.

"Only the night before the funeral. I got in too late for a motel, and I'd been too zapped to make any plans. Either way I was going to have to confront it. All or nothing, that's me." Her voice was a monotone. "The next day I checked into a B&B, the one Mrs. Hollis runs across town. This is the first time I've been back since then."

Henry nodded, trying to imagine what that one night must have been like for her.

"I slept pretty soundly, believe it or not. Exhaustion, probably."

Henry stopped by the door to Willard's room.

"Okay if I have a look?"

"That's why we're here."

The bed was made, the floor swept, and almost everything was in its place. The only anomalies were scraps of paper here and there, marked with lines and slashes—the numerical tallies that Anna had told him about. Three were on the bedside table. One was labeled, BOOKS, another MILK, and the third had a drawing of something dotted and circular.

Here and there were plastic model airplanes and cars that Willard had built, or tried to build. Most were half finished. A few that he'd completed were hanging by fishing line from the ceiling, including the Millennium

Falcon. Anna gave it a tap, which made it swing back and forth.

"I don't suppose they'd let me take this to him in jail."

"Probably not."

He had his own little flat-screen TV, mounted above a DVR player. A Luke Skywalker poster hung above them. More scraps of marked paper were on his dresser. On one, the tally reached at least a hundred.

"That's the one for how many times he's watched *Star Wars*," Anna said.

Henry picked up a scrap labeled SOCKS, with the total at sixteen. Two others had drawings that Henry couldn't decipher.

"I see what you mean about the obsession with counting."

"Mom used to try to pick up after him. But he'd get so upset that she gave up."

"You don't think that maybe . . . ?"

"That he'd kill her over that? No. If you'd ever seen them together, you'd know. She was his Lord and Protector, and he was devoted to her."

"What about your dad?"

"Oh, they were fine, too, but it wasn't the same. They'd hunt, go on walks, do chores, but never really said much. But Mom? It was sweet. I used to envy him sometimes. Stupid, huh?"

She turned away from him, like she might be on the verge of tears. Henry pretended not to notice and opened the closet door. Camouflage hunting overalls hung next to flannel shirts, a few button-downs, three pairs of khakis. There was a sport coat for dress-up occasions, along with a single clip-on necktie, which struck Henry as deeply poignant.

Even in the closet, Willard's tallies were in evidence—pencil scribbles on the door frame and the back of the door. Someone, probably his mom, had tried to scrub them off but had given up. From the words and symbols it was apparent that Willard had kept count of his lifetime supply of belts, shirts, pants, and shoes.

A small footlocker sat at the end of the bed.

"What does he keep in there?" Henry asked.

"Be my guest."

Henry unbuckled the hasp and pulled open the lid. Anna gasped in surprise. It was practically stuffed with papers—page after page torn from yellow legal pads and spiral notebooks, some of it neat and folded, the rest crumpled or wadded. All of it was marked with Willard's lines and slashes—probably more than a hundred tallies. Most of the paper looked relatively new, and none of the ink was faded.

"Good God," Anna said, a little horrified.

"This wasn't normal?"

"Not to this degree."

Henry pulled out a few of the folded sheets. They

were labeled with strange symbols, indecipherable. He uncrumpled a few more and the story was the same. No one but Willard could have told them what he had tallied, or why.

Anna sighed and put her hands to her face.

"I guess it was getting worse. Maybe if I'd come home more often . . ." She lowered her head.

"It wasn't your fault."

"No. But I was avoiding the place. That's what I think now. I used to visit every few weeks. Lately, nothing. I was telling myself it was because I was so wrapped up in my job, and with my friends. I'd joined a book club, a health spa, a dinner group, anything to keep me busy on weekends. It was almost like I could feel what was happening here and knew I wanted nothing to do with it."

"Or maybe you were just building a life, like everybody does."

Henry shut the trunk, stood, and gently steered her back into the hall. Nodding toward the closed door across the hall, he said, "I'm sorry, but do you mind if . . . ?"

"Go ahead. I'll pass, if you don't mind. Been there, done that."

He opened the door, the smell hitting him right away, like a public restroom that has been mopped down with industrial cleaners. He felt like he'd released an unwanted spirit into the rest of the house.

There was no crime scene tape. The sheets and mattress were gone, with only the box spring remaining. Here and there on the headboard were dried brown spatters of bloodstains. The curtains were shut—he wondered if gawkers had tried to peep in from the back lawn—which made it so gloomy that Henry had to resist the urge to throw them open and pull up the sash, let in some fresh air.

The door to one of the closets was open—Anna's mother's, judging by the dresses hanging in a neat row, a sparser selection than he would have guessed for a woman of her age. Stacked on a top shelf was a sheaf of papers and a couple of cardboard boxes. Exactly the sort of thing Mitch wanted him to paw through. Maybe later. On the bedside table, next to the telephone, a checkbook was splayed open with unpaid bills underneath. An uncapped pen lay to the side.

"Hate to say it," he called out over his shoulder, "but you're going to need to go through some of this stuff."

"I know."

He turned, surprised to see her in the doorway.

"I haven't had the willpower for it yet. There's so much of it. Those boxes in the closet, four more in the mudroom. Old letters, old photos, all kinds of stuff. Plus the laptop."

"Your dad's?"

"Mom's. Out in the barn, of all places. She had a

little office built after I went off to college, a place all to herself with a coffeepot, a space heater, and everything."

He nodded, already curious about the office. All in good time.

The phone rang, making them jump as it jangled on the bedside table like an alarm, along with the echo from the one in the kitchen.

"You should answer it," he said. "Probably junk, but you never know."

"I need to get the line disconnected. Another item for the damn to-do list."

The bedroom phone was closer, but Anna walked down the hallway to the one in the kitchen. Henry followed at what he hoped was a discreet distance and stopped in the doorway to listen.

"Hello?" A pause while someone spoke, then she put down the receiver.

"Robocall."

Henry saw the light flashing on the message machine and gestured toward it.

"Probably more of the same, but you never know."

She frowned and pressed the button.

There were three messages. The first was from Stu Wilgus, whose voice Henry recognized right away. He offered his condolences, then asked whether her parents would have wanted flowers or a memorial donation. Henry guessed that what he'd really wanted was gossip from the scene of the crime. The second message was dead air. The third one got their attention.

"Hi, this is Douglas Hatcher. I'm a claims administrator for the Employee Benefits Security Administration, and I'm calling for Mr. Tarrant Shoat, or for the next of kin of the late Helen Abell Shoat, or any surviving heirs or assigns, with regard to the final settlement of her severance agreement. So if whoever gets this message could please call me back at my office in Silver Spring, I'd greatly appreciate it."

He left a phone number.

"That's odd," Anna said. "Do you think it's a scam?"

"No idea. Who did your mother used to work for?"

"Nobody. Except years ago, when she was a paralegal for some real estate lawyer in Easton. It's how she met Dad. She drew up the settlement papers when he bought this property."

"Well, his title sounded official enough."

"Unless he was really calling from some phone bank in India."

"Only one way to find out."

She grabbed a pencil and pad from a basket on the kitchen counter and played the message back, this time writing down the number. Then she called it while motioning Henry closer, angling the receiver so he could listen in. Douglas Hatcher picked up on the second ring.

"Yes, hi. I'm Anna Shoat, returning your call. My

mother was Helen Abell Shoat, and you left a message for my father, but he's also deceased."

"Oh. Sorry for your loss."

"And who do you work for again?"

"The Employee Benefits Security Administration, U.S. Department of Labor. And you're Helen Shoat's daughter?"

"I am. Your message said this was about some kind of severance agreement?"

They heard him moving a pile of papers, and he spoke the next words as if reading from a script.

"Yes. Under the terms of your mother's federal severance package, I have a check to administer to the relevant beneficiary, which seems to be you."

"Her *federal* severance package? From what?"

"Her term of federal employment."

"Are you sure you have the right Helen Shoat?"

"Perhaps you could give me the last four digits of her Social Security number, then we'll know for sure."

"Just a second." She grabbed her handbag from another counter, reached inside for some folded documents, and rifled through them. "Here we go."

She read the numbers aloud.

"Yes, that's correct. Full name, Helen Abell Shoat?"

"Correct. And she was employed by the government?"

"For two years only, and it was quite a while ago, from 1977 to 1979. Not long enough to vest for a pension, but apparently there was a severance agreement, and the terms of its fulfillment call for a check to be issued to her closest surviving relative on the event of her death."

"What department was this?"

"Labor, the Employee Benefits Security Administration."

"No, I mean my mother. Who did she work for?"

"Oh." More rustling of papers. "This doesn't say. But it indicates that her final place of employment was abroad. The United States consular office in Berlin."

"Berlin as in Germany?"

"Yes. So she was probably working for the Department of State."

"Probably?"

"Like I said, none of the paperwork says for sure. Is that important?"

"Kind of. It would be nice to know."

"Well, somewhere in the file is a contact name, probably for whoever sent over the documentation."

"Do you think you could find it for me?"

A sigh.

"Give me a second."

The receiver thudded on a desk. They heard some banging around, a file drawer opening and shutting, more shuffling of paper. Telephones were ringing in the background. Then, a muffled sound, followed by:

"Got a name and number for you. Ready?"

"Please."

"Wallace Barringer." He spelled the last name and

rattled off a phone number with a 703 area code, followed by a four-digit extension. "He's probably in Human Resources. A benefits administrator, if I had to guess."

"Thanks."

"Oh, and your check. I'm going to mail you a few forms, which you'll need to fill out in order to prove your relationship to the deceased. We'll also need documentation that you're the closest surviving next of kin, plus a copy of your mother's death certificate, some proof of your own citizenship, that sort of thing. Once we've received everything, you should have the check within four to six weeks."

"Goodness. And all because Mom worked two years for the government?"

"As I said, it was a severance agreement. They aren't customary, but they're not unheard of."

"Can you tell me the amount?"

"Sure. Let's see. There was an initial payment in 1979 of seventy-five thousand dollars, which, as stipulated by the terms of the agreement, was deposited into an interest-bearing account, compounding annually at a rate of four percent, leaving a current value of $295,956.67."

Anna's mouth dropped open in surprise. She looked quickly at Henry, who felt like they'd just moved closer to the heart of something—not the information Anna wanted, but the kind that Mitch was after.

"Wow. Okay, then. Why don't you send the paperwork to this address, since I'll be checking by here pretty regularly."

"Would that be the one on Willow Street in Poston, Maryland?"

"Yes."

"Very well. This will go out today. I'll send it by Express Mail, so you might even receive it tomorrow."

"Great. Thanks."

She hung up.

"I'm rich," she said. "By my standards, anyway. Is it wrong to be excited about that?"

"Not at all. And your mom worked in Berlin?"

"So it seems. Isn't that amazing?"

"She never mentioned it?"

"Not once! I never even knew she worked for the government, much less overseas. The only job she ever talked about was the one in Easton, which she hated. I wonder if Dad even knew. I guess he would've had to have known, right?"

Henry shrugged. The ground rules of marriage were a mystery to him.

"I wonder why she was there? She would've been, well, let me think . . . about twenty-three or -four. Six, seven years younger than me. Almost the same age as Willard."

"You know," Henry said, "with that kind of money you could afford a pretty good PI, a professional."

She shook her head.

"Too late. You're the man now, the way I see it. And the meter's already running, seventy-five bucks and counting, so let's keep moving."

"You should call that number he gave you."

She punched it into the phone, again angling the receiver so he could listen. Henry leaned closer, heard two rings and then the click of the receiver and a woman's voice:

"CIA, Human Resources."

They looked at each other, eyes wide, mouths open. Anna answered in a rush.

"Sorry. Wrong number."

She practically slammed down the receiver, and then clapped one hand to her heart and the other to her mouth.

"Oh my God. The CIA?" She took a step backward, as if to regain her balance. "No *wonder* she never talked about it. Do you think my mom was a freaking spy?"

But Henry was already thinking of Mitch, and of whoever in Washington had put him here and was paying his salary, renting the house, reading his dull and news-less reports—some nameless bureaucrat who was still seeking information on this poor woman who was no longer living. Give us all of it, Mitch had said—recent or ancient. And now, having tugged on the first available thread, it had unraveled from a surprising connection deep in Helen Shoat's past. Surprising to him, anyway, and to Anna. No wonder they'd hired him. He found himself reassessing his own ignorance in this affair, an ignorance which suddenly felt like a foolish liability.

"What's wrong?" Anna said.

"Nothing. It's just strange, that's all. We should leave now if we're going to make your nine-thirty appointment."

"Okay. But don't you think it's weird? Maybe even a little funny?"

Henry forced a smile on her behalf.

"Absolutely. Let's come back later. Maybe we'll find more answers in all those papers of hers."

"Oh, definitely. After that little bombshell, we're going through all of Mom's stuff with a fine-tooth comb."

"So you truly had no idea? She never said a word, not even about Europe?"

"My mother wasn't the type to drop hints. She either told you something or she didn't. And when it came to any kind of information about herself, she mostly didn't."

"Do you think your dad knew?"

Anna shrugged.

"Dad never talked about the past, his own or anyone else's. He was too busy worrying about the weather, or the price of corn, or the latest marching orders from Washam Poultry. When you're a farmer, that's how you have to be."

They walked out to her car in the driveway to set out for the county jail. Turning from Willow onto Highway 53, Henry, for all his misgivings, was now glad she'd hired him. He, too, wanted to know what was going on.

As they drove out of town he reflexively glanced over his shoulder, back toward the scattered homes and storefronts of Poston, where every blank window now looked like a lens, following their progress.

9

Ladd Herrington pushed his reading glasses down to the end of his nose and peered at Helen above the frames. He leaned back in his swivel chair, arms crossed, a pose of distance and disdain.

It was nearly noon, but Helen was still waiting for the caffeine to kick in from her belated first cup of coffee. The station chief had summoned her to his office the moment she got to work.

"Robert was in here earlier about you," Herrington began.

"Gilley, you mean? Kevin Gilley?"

Herrington snatched off his glasses and leaned forward, palms flat on the blotter, a lumpy old toad poised to spring across the desk.

"You'll refer to him as Robert, if you please. You're not even cleared for that information!"

Helen shrugged, already regretting that by sleeping late she'd let Gilley get the jump on her, although she was shocked he'd chosen to mention it at all. But if that's how he wanted to play it, fine. She had the ammo to outlast him. The tape, for starters, her very own nuclear option if push came to shove. But, like all nuclear options, it offered the possibility of mutually assured destruction, so she would first appeal to reason. The challenge would be controlling her temper.

"He said you behaved most inappropriately last night," Herrington continued. "Violated your own rules, introduced yourself to an agent without authorization, and interrupted a sensitive meeting between a case officer and a contact."

"Sensitive meeting? Is that how he described trying to fuck one of his agents? And I mean that literally. The figurative sense applies only to what he's trying to do to me."

This momentarily put the brakes on Herrington's offensive. He frowned, backed off a bit, and shoved his specs to the side of the desk. The chair creaked beneath him.

"What are you saying, exactly, Miss Abell?"

"What is *he* saying, exactly, since he's the one who chose to make an issue of it? Was I at the safe house unannounced? Yes. So was he. Although I was there in the course of my management duties, on a night when there was no scheduled usage by any case officer. When he and his contact arrived they were unaware of my presence upstairs, a situation I was prepared to suffer in silence, and with all due respect for their operational privacy—until it became clear from all the noise downstairs that he was forcing himself on a young female agent. At that point it became clear to me that their rendezvous had everything to do with Robert's sexual gratification and nothing to do with Agency sources and methods."

Herrington opened his mouth to speak, but Helen kept going.

"So, yes, at that point I went downstairs and introduced myself to an agent without authorization, just as he said, but only to put a stop to his misbehavior. Robert and I had a few words, and then he left. He smirked and he snarled, but he left, and he did so *without* his agent, who by then was in tears. And afterward it was up to me to calm the poor girl down. If anything, I limited the damage he might have caused."

Herrington exhaled loudly, seemingly as out of breath as Helen. He looked off to the side while fumbling distractedly with a small bronze bust of Lenin that he used as a paperweight. A shiny spot atop Lenin's bald dome suggested that he rubbed it fairly often, just as he was doing now, either for luck or inspiration. He noticed her watching, set it aside, and glanced toward the shuttered window. She wondered if this wasn't the first time he'd heard something like this about Kevin

Gilley. How had Baucom described the man? Someone in it for himself, yet also a practitioner of the Agency's darker arts. Sexual predation would hardly seem to be out of the question under that setup.

"Yes, well . . . Robert did imply you might allege something of the sort. Predictable, I suppose, given your own tendencies."

"My *tendencies*?"

"Oh, come on. You can't be completely oblivious to what people say."

About her and Baucom, he must have meant. Had to be.

"Last time I checked, sir, all of my intimate relations involved consenting adults, and none with subordinates or direct supervisors. Would you prefer that I sleep with some foreign national who's never been vetted? Although I'm told that's quite popular in our office."

Herrington's mouth fell open. For a moment he was too shocked to reply. Rumor had it that his latest paramour was a typist at the French consulate.

"Sir, he was raping her, and if you somehow find such behavior excusable in a man of his position, then at least consider the matter pragmatically. Can you imagine the unholy mess if he had been allowed to complete the act, and she had then gone to the authorities? Alleging, no less, that it had happened in one of our very own facilities?"

By the time she finished, Herrington had collected himself for a counterattack.

"Was Robert's behavior unprofessional? Yes, I suppose so. Assuming you're telling the whole truth, of course. But your use of the word 'rape'? Come on, Helen, you know better. Or would if you actually had experience in the field. Relationships between case officers and agents are complex and multilayered. If we start telling our field men exactly how to conduct their business then we might as well shut them down."

"I know what I saw, sir. I know what I heard. It wasn't consensual."

"It didn't *sound* consensual, maybe because you're not familiar with the context of the relationship. You may think you know what you observed, but you don't, so I urge you to take this no further."

"Then exactly what *did* I observe, sir?"

"You're not cleared for that, Miss Abell. And don't think I'm not aware of how you must have learned Robert's real identity."

"I learned it, sir, not from any pillow talk, but because this entire station leaks like a sieve."

Herrington reddened.

"As for your own choice of sexual liaisons, Miss Abell, since you *did* ask for my preference on the matter, what I would prefer is that you were married and stable, with a home life that didn't so obviously interfere with your official duties."

Helen's first impulse was to quit on the spot. Tell him bluntly what she thought of his opinions and leave, never to return. But that was probably what he wanted. It would certainly be the easiest way to make this mess go away.

Her second impulse was to say she'd feel more comfortable working for the Soviets than for someone as clueless and overmatched as Ladd Herrington. But he was just stupid enough to take it seriously, and so were the paranoid snoops in counterintelligence who would zero in on the statement the moment it appeared in her file.

"Very well, sir. In that case, provided I'm able to meet your expectations for my domestic arrangements, just how would you prefer I approach the state of matrimony? Faithfully, or like you?" She stood before he could answer. "And not to worry, sir. I'm quite done with this matter. For now."

She let the final words hang in the air as she bustled out the door, as angry as she'd been since her arrival in Berlin. She knew it wouldn't help to slam the door, but she slammed it all the same.

Everyone in the office heard, and everyone saw her leave.

10

"What you need," Clark Baucom said, "is a dose of forgetting. Here, drink up."

Helen shook her head. Strong drink sounded like the perfect prescription. But the last thing she wanted right now was to follow someone else's orders.

Baucom poured brandy into her glass, anyway, and she didn't push it away. She'd get to it when she felt like it.

They were in a narrow, gloomy bar a few blocks from Savignyplatz, a run-down place in a spiffed-up neighborhood, meaning that it was almost never crowded, and the regulars were generally too drunk to listen to a word you said. Tradecraft in drinking, if there was such a thing. Baucom had taken her there the moment he heard the news, and he'd selected a small round table in the back.

The proprietor, Lehmann, had appeared at Baucom's shoulder almost immediately, nodding and leaning closer while Baucom muttered an order under his breath as if conjuring up a spell. Lehmann nodded gravely and disappeared into the cellar, emerging moments later in a draft of cool, damp air with a dusty bottle that he toweled off at the bar. He brought it to the table with a corkscrew and two snifters, and did the honors as smartly as if they were in a Paris bistro with a Michelin star. The two men exchanged knowing glances. They had a past, then. Yet another chapter from Baucom's big book of lore. Maybe Berlin was quieter now, but at moments like this you could still feel its history, its importance at the fulcrum of East and West. Come what may, spies still counted for something here.

Helen, eyeing the glass, gave in and took a sip. Heavenly, although she didn't dare ask how much it cost, especially after she downed the first glass as quickly as a half liter of cheap Pils.

Baucom topped it up.

"Erasure," he said. "First your mind. Then the tapes. That's your ticket back to safety. No more thoughts of that mystery fellow Lewis. No more thoughts of Robert."

"Kevin Gilley. I'll say his name if I please."

For the first time that evening Baucom looked mildly put out. His eyebrows angled in disapproval as he leaned across the table.

"My dear Helen, I know we've chosen a nice dark corner, and I can certainly vouch for Lehmann. But we're not alone here, in case you haven't noticed, and in Berlin the walls have ears. Remember?"

"Sorry. But did you really just mention my safety? Do you think that's actually in doubt?"

"The safety of your career."

"Ah, my *career*. That vast edifice of pride and achievement." She took another swallow. "At the moment, 'unsafe' would probably be a charitable description, don't you think? And funny you should mention Lewis at all. I hadn't even thought of that name since last night, although I suppose in its way the contents of that tape are a lot more intriguing than—"

"See?" He smiled, but not nicely. "Already backsliding. More." He nodded toward her glass, which she raised to her lips. Such a wonderful elixir, probably older than her, and as mellowed as Baucom, a complex vintage in his own right. In drinking it, however, she was again reminded of Lewis—or whatever his name really was—and his older companion, the wheezing gray eminence with his fancy Scotch. A touch of the urbane in his manner of speaking, despite all that nonsense about various bodies of water.

What did it all mean? What was "the bay," and why did Lewis need to be cleansed of its polluting waters? Who was Jack, their powerful pal who had died in '72?

And why on earth had the older fellow, there at the end, spoken so cavalierly of "elimination, plain and simple," one of the few remarks that had needed no translation at all?

She set down the glass and licked her lips. When she looked up, Baucom was watching her carefully.

"You know exactly what they were talking about, don't you?" she said. "All that gobbledygook about water. That's why the tapes scare you. Not because of Gilley—oh, all right then, *Robert*—but because of Lewis."

Baucom shook his head, his expression passing from irritation to worry.

"I should have known better than to bring you here in your current state of mind."

"My current state of mind is a pleasant sort of buzz giving way to inebriation. By your own design, Clark. Oh. Excuse me. *Charles*. I keep forgetting we're supposed to be speaking operationally, for some damn reason you haven't told me yet. And I hope you weren't referring to the female state of mind? The scold who must be silenced? The woman scorned?"

"Your words."

"But you're not denying them, which makes you sound more like Herrington every time you ask me to forget."

"Now that's a low blow. All I'm counseling is discretion."

"Discretion I'll grant you. Discretion is half of what we're paid for, so I'll zip it for now. But erasure is out of the question, in either sense of the word. You might as well ask me to stop being so curious, and that's the other half of what we're paid for. Or are you too old to be curious anymore?"

It stung him, she sensed it right away, and she tried to atone by taking his hand. He let her, a start, but in searching his eyes she saw more disapproval than pain, and after his next swallow he set down the glass as sharply as the older man had in the safe house, the knock making a few heads turn in the quiet bar. He shook his head and chuckled under his breath.

"You belong in the field," he said. "You're tougher than anyone we've got out there, yet here you sit, a desk jockey pushing a pencil and handing out keys to Agency real estate like the night porter in some pay-by-the-hour hotel."

"Thanks for making me feel so vital to the cause."

"It's a compliment, my dear. They don't know what they have in you. Tell me, because this is something I've always wondered, when did you first know you wanted to get into this racket?"

"You tell me. You know all about my formative years. Bible-thumper dad, obedient housewife mom."

"The joys of East Bumfuck, North Carolina."

"*Wixville,* North Carolina. East Bumfuck was the next town over." And the worst day of every week had been Sunday, she couldn't help but remember. Sitting through her father's droning sermons, followed by long dinners at parishioners' homes where the man of the house always took ten minutes to say grace to impress her dad, and then all you got for your patience was overcooked roast and a rice pudding.

"It was in a dry county, I'll bet."

"Good guess. You had to drive thirty miles for a fifth of whiskey, and hope that nobody from church spotted your car outside the ABC store. Coming from a place like that, who *wouldn't* want to go overseas to snoop for Uncle Sam?"

"But there has to have been a moment, a turning point. You're a woman of epiphanies, Helen. That's as plain on your face as those beautiful eyes."

She wanted to deny it, but he was right, although it had taken her years to realize it. In retrospect, her urge to be a spy, a snoop, a keeper of secrets, went back to one summer night around a card table in her mother's kitchen, a sultry evening of distant thunder and the sound of crickets.

Helen had just turned twelve. Her father was out for the evening, ministering to the ailing and bereaved of his flock, and their home was quiet. It was 1967, a July when you were almost afraid to turn on the television for fear of being alerted to yet another upheaval in some northerly city like Newark or Detroit, or more casualties in Vietnam, although Helen's memory of that night's fare was that at 8 p.m. she switched on *The Man from U.N.C.L.E.*, the signal coming and going on their little black-and-white depending on how deftly she could adjust the bent coat hanger that passed for a UHF antenna. In those days she was fixated on the costars, two dapper spies, especially the blond Russian heartthrob named Illya, reigning obsession of all the teenybopper magazines.

Almost as soon as she settled in to watch there was a knock at the door—Uncle Lester and Aunt Grace, from her mother's side, stopping by with a deck of cards and a box of poker chips. Helen's mother, usually a slave to house rules against alcohol and gambling, got out the card table from the coat closet without a moment's hesitation, although she did pause when Lester suggested adding Helen for a four-handed game.

Sensing an opportunity to breach a new opening on the discipline frontier, Helen leaped from the couch to demand inclusion.

"Pleeease, Mommy?"

"Oh, all right, then. But the minute your father turns into the driveway you run back to your room like this never happened, you hear me?"

"Yes, ma'am."

And that set the tone for the evening—the thrill of forbidden pleasure, a state of high alert. To make it even better, her mother staked her to a small pile of chips, offering the possibility she might win a few nickels and dimes.

Uncle Lester spelled out the rules, explaining the difference between a straight and a flush, and teaching her how to ante up and make bets. "We'll keep the rest simple," he said. "Five-card draw until the little missus is ready for something more complicated."

To keep track of which hands were the strongest, Helen got down the P–Q volume of the encyclopedia her Mom had bought month-by-month at the A&P, and opened it to the write-up for "Poker." She set it on the floor by her feet for easy consultation.

But the few times she lucked into good hands, everyone else folded before she could win many chips, and she couldn't understand why. The moment of revelation came a few hands later, when, after folding, she stepped around the table to peek at Uncle Lester's hand.

He slapped down his cards before she could steal a glance.

"Don't you come looking at my hand!"

"But I folded."

"That's beside the point."

"No it isn't. I can't possibly win."

Uncle Lester shook his head as if she just didn't get it, which left it to Aunt Grace to explain.

"It doesn't matter if you're out, honey. If you see his hand, you'll be able to read his play. You'll know whether he's bluffing, or holding, or whatever."

"So."

"So?" Her uncle again. "Well that's the whole point of poker, ain't it? Reading other people? How do you think we've all been knowing what you've got? Every time you look down at that book on the floor we figure you must have something pretty good."

A few hands later, after again folding early, Helen went to the refrigerator for a Cheerwine. She returned to the table by an elliptical route that let her see her Uncle Lester's cards just as he was fanning them out after the draw. Jack high. Weak. She then noted his every gesture—the flick of his eyes, the movement of his hands, the flash of his tongue to wet his upper lip—as he bluffed his way to a huge pot.

Three hands later she took back nearly all those chips after noting the same movements just before he doubled the stakes. When he finally called and she revealed her winning hand as a measly pair of nines, he dolefully shook his head.

"You see?" he complained, as if he'd known all along what she'd been up to. "Betty, this girl of yours is a fast learner, but she's also a sneak!"

Her mother winked at her from across the table, and it was still one of Helen's fondest memories.

From that moment onward, Helen had an insatiable appetite for ferreting out secrets. Not gossip, exactly, but all sorts of hidden stuff no one else seemed to know—about her friends, her parents, her teachers, people at church. Watch carefully, learn the signs, and before long you can discover the key to just about anyone. Her biggest coup came at summer's end, when she finally learned why her mom was always so drowsy after lunch, right up until it was time to fix dinner.

In good weather, her mother's midday routine almost never varied. She would make lunch for Helen and then haul a load of wet laundry to the clothesline out back. The chore always took an inordinate amount of time, and it always rendered her droopy and slow, fit for little more than an afternoon of soap operas while she dozed on the couch, leaving Helen to her own devices. Was hanging out the wash really that strenuous? Or did she simply need to catch up on sleep after staying up too late the night before? Helen aimed to find out.

So, the next day, after her mom put lunch on the table—peanut butter and banana on white bread, with potato chips and a bowl of Campbell's Cream of Tomato—Helen took a few quick bites while waiting for her mom to head outside with the laundry. The moment she did, Helen tossed the rest of her sandwich and rinsed her plate and bowl before exiting through the front door. She crept around to the side of the house and took up a concealed position behind a big holly bush at one corner.

So far, nothing looked out of the ordinary. Her mother was hanging shirts and trousers, the bigger items that would wrinkle the most if left wet for too long. Once they were in place her mother glanced side to side, checking in the direction of both neighbors. She also glanced back toward the house, and Helen held her breath. But her mom didn't see her, and none of the neighbors was out and about. Her mother then set out for the woods behind the yard, where she parted the underbrush and stepped into the trees.

Helen wanted to follow, but knew she'd be spotted the moment she broke cover. Peering through the holly she watched her mother proceed maybe ten feet deeper before stooping lower and rummaging for something below. She then turned and sat down—on a tree stump, perhaps?

Shadows and underbrush made it hard to see what she was up to, but she was barely moving. There was a glint of sunlight, as if from a mirror, but little else. Helen marked her mother's position in relation to a big oak, the one in which her father had long ago built a tree house, now in disrepair. Her mom sat there for a good fifteen minutes while Helen swatted at gnats. Finally her mother stood, turned, and stooped again for a few seconds longer, reaching down into the weeds before fording the underbrush back to the clothesline. She pinned up the remaining socks, T-shirts, and underwear, picked up the laundry basket, and walked back into the house. From previous experience, Helen knew what came next. Her mother would turn on the television and make a beeline to the couch, lost to the world for the next several hours.

Helen waited a few minutes and got to work. She set out across the lawn, running in case her mother happened to look out the window. Reaching the woods she paused to check for poison ivy, and then stepped through a thicket of goldenrod, trumpet vine, and scrubby pine toward the big oak. Cicadas whirred like a giant windup toy. From the oak she took ten paces to her left and came upon a rusted milk crate, like the kind they used to leave on the porch for deliveries before everyone started buying at the supermarket. She opened the top flap and looked inside. Nothing but spare clothespins, although the idea her mother would buy this many extras was so preposterous that Helen reached inside and discovered they were piled atop a false bottom.

Below lay a bottle of Nikolai Vodka, with a red-and-white label, alongside an empty jam jar that her mother must have used as a drinking glass. Helen unscrewed the cap and sniffed the spirituous but otherwise odorless vapors. That probably explained her mother's choice. Nothing to mark her breath. And if anyone had happened upon her while she was drinking, the liquid in the jam jar would have looked as clear as water.

So here it was, then, her mother's secret for daily survival, cached like treasure—a bottle she must have procured on one of those sixty-mile round-trips to the next county. Or maybe she'd arranged for a trusted go-between, a cutout as they called it in the spy game. A dark secret, especially for a preacher's wife, and Helen found it to be sad and desperate, but also reckless and exciting. She felt that way about her own behavior as well. Snooping around like this was a bit sad, but very exciting, and she knew this would not be the last time she was willing to take furtive action when something needed figuring out.

Helen tipped the bottle for a test sip. It burned so much that she coughed, and she wiped her lips on her T-shirt. She capped the bottle and put it back into the milk crate along with the jam jar. Then she circled back to the front of the house, eased inside, and sneaked down the hall to her room.

She told Baucom only the first part of that story— about the night of the poker game—as they sat in Lehmann's little hideaway. The other part she'd never told to anyone, and probably never would. Baucom laughed when she described how she called her Uncle Lester's bluff.

"From that night on," she said, "he would never play

poker with me again. Which also taught me something. Use your best information sparingly, and pick your shots well."

"And what does that lesson tell you about how you should play your hand with Herrington?"

She considered the question while swallowing another measure of the wonderful brandy. Beats the hell out of Nikolai Vodka, she thought with a smile. She searched for an answer—not the real one, but the one she figured Baucom wanted to hear.

"I suppose it tells me I should try to get a better read on things before making my next move. Get a little more information, to give me a clearer idea of what to do next."

"Splendid. A self-taught prodigy. That poker game was probably more valuable than any single thing you ever learned at the Farm."

"I'm not so sure about that. But, speaking of playing it smart." She pushed away her glass, even though there was still a swallow or two left. "The last thing I should do tonight is have too much to drink."

He shrugged, unconvinced.

"Even when it's this good?"

"Yes, even when it's this good." She picked up the glass, eyeing the amber liquid a bit wistfully. "My mother certainly never had anything of this quality."

"Your mother was a drinker, the parson's wife?"

She shrugged, noncommittal. She then laughed to herself, remembering a review for Nikolai Vodka she'd spotted years later by some whiskey snob in a magazine: *Easy on the wallet, but few flavors other than alcohol and a light burn.*

"But you'll erase the tapes, yes?"

Helen eyed him carefully. For the first time she wondered where his real loyalties lay in this matter, and the possibilities were disconcerting. Crafty old veterans were wonderful for their stories and lore, but they also had the skill to nudge you in directions more advantageous to the Agency than to yourself. And, let's face it, Baucom was Agency to the core. No one could have lasted this long without being a Company man.

"I should go," she said, a little sharply. He rose with her, reaching for her hand, but she moved away. "And I should sleep in my own bed tonight. Alone, if you don't mind."

This time she did detect hurt, unless he was just playing for sympathy. Her slightly muddled state of mind made it too dangerous to stick around long enough to find out. She closed the gap between them and touched his sleeve.

"Maybe tomorrow? And here . . ." She opened her purse. "Let me split this."

Baucom laughed.

"Not at your pay grade. Lehmann and me will work it out."

Across the room, she saw Lehmann glance their way as he swiped at the bar with a towel, nodding as if he knew what they were discussing. She instantly envisioned cooperation between the two men, both informally and operationally. A mail drop behind that loose brick by the bar, perhaps, or beneath those framed George Grosz lithographs from the 1920s. Their relationship probably dated back a long time. What the hell, then. Let Baucom pay the whole damn bill. Lehmann probably would cut him some slack for old times' sake.

That left her feeling better as she walked toward Kantstrasse to catch the U-Bahn home. It was a blustery evening. The north wind whirled her hair like some stylist trying something new at the *Friseur*. She let it slap against her face, enjoying the briskness with its bite of coal smoke, its tang of brine from the far Baltic. She wondered if Baucom was watching from the stoop of the bar, but she was too proud to turn around. Look straight ahead, she told herself, before nearly tripping on a loose cobble. One fewer drink might have been wiser.

She vowed to ride this out. She would remain strong and resolute because she had truth on her side, and wasn't that supposed to set you free? Just as the Good Book said, that verse from John that they'd inscribed on the floor of the main lobby at Langley. Her father had once quoted it in a sermon, never imagining that it would be the motto of his daughter's future employer.

The brandy was jumbling her thoughts. Mom's secret stash, Dad's windy sermons, Baucom's fond tales of the old days, and, still flickering here and there, fresh images from what she'd witnessed at the safe house. She felt a twinge of apprehension. Even with the tape, would facts alone be enough to protect her? She would need cunning as well, and connections. Not just Clark, but others.

But she was too addled to devise a strategy now, so why not give in to the cool wildness of the evening? From a barroom doorway to her left, three students tumbled onto the sidewalk and set out arm in arm, laughing and then singing in English a punk lyric that Helen had seen spray-painted on the Wall only days earlier: "I wanna be sedated!"

Say what you will about the Wall's effects on her profession, for young West Berliners it had evolved into a protective moat, holding back not only the austere tyranny of the East but also the brisk get-to-work mentality of the West. Young people came here now to frolic on an island of hedonism where rent was cheap, tuition was free, and everyone was exempt from the draft. So go ahead and watch us through your binoculars and rifle scopes, we'll turn out the lights at dawn.

The students burst into laughter yet again as they

rounded a corner and moved out of sight. Helen smiled. Everything would be fine. With the Agency preoccupied by Iran, they might even act sanely when confronted by a personnel problem in Berlin. Surely the powers-that-be couldn't afford to tolerate rape. Her burdens seemed to lift. She laughed aloud and broke into a skip for a few steps before resuming her brisk walk.

In all her introspection she never once noticed the fellow in the black leather jacket with silver studs up the sleeves, who was watching her carefully from a block to her rear. He, too, let his hair flutter in the breeze, only his was oily and untamed, a Jolly Roger of dark mischief as he moved along the shadows. His young face was ruddy, as if he were accustomed to the outdoors. Dropping farther back, he eyed her through the kind of scope that you might mount on a rifle.

When Helen caught the southbound U-7 at Wilmersdorfer Strasse he boarded the third car just as the doors were closing, and he easily followed when she transferred to the U-3 at Fehrbelliner Platz. Exiting behind her at Dahlem-Dorf, he remained in her wake for five blocks more, all the way to her street. By then, Helen had lowered her head in weariness, not even a pretense of alertness as she approached her building and unlocked the main door. He saw her enter, pocketed his scope, and took out a small notebook.

11

Helen sensed her new status as a pariah from the moment she entered Berlin station. Averted glances in the hallway. Murmured hellos from clerical staff who refused to look up from their typewriters. Over by the coffeemaker, two men known as notorious flirts scattered so quickly at her approach that you would have thought the fire alarm had sounded.

It might have been bearable if there hadn't also been practical consequences, which she discovered on a trip to the records room. She was looking for recent cable traffic with any references to "Robert," "Frieda," or "Kathrin," the friend who had supposedly warned Frieda about Gilley. She filled out a request for each subject and dropped it onto the desk of the chief records officer, Eileen Walters.

Walters was blessedly easy to work with—a good egg, as Baucom liked to say. Being married and stable, she was also Herrington's kind of employee, but Helen liked her because she never played favorites. She worked just as assiduously on behalf of the lower-ranking officers as she did for the most senior operatives, a quality that had engendered a fierce loyalty throughout the station. Only two weeks earlier, Helen, not much of a cook, had slaved for hours over a baked pasta dish for a Sunday potluck at Walters's home in Zehlendorf.

This morning, however, Walters glanced cursorily at Helen's requests before saying, "You're not cleared for this."

"Of course I'm cleared. I'm not asking for the most sensitive material, just the regular stuff, the same sort of things I send out myself."

Walters looked up with a glint of sympathy in her eyes.

"I'm afraid you're not, effective this morning." She glanced around as if to check for eavesdroppers, slid open a desk drawer, and retrieved a single sheet of paper.

"Here, but give it right back. I shouldn't even be showing it to you."

It was a Herrington memo addressed to "ALL," a group which apparently no longer included Helen Abell:

FYI, until further notice, all clearances for Helen Abell shall be strictly limited to those items and matters that pertain directly to her daily

*administration of the physical facilities under her
immediate jurisdiction.*

In other words, he was cutting off any avenue by
which she might build or buttress a case against Kevin
Gilley. No cables, no reports, no offhand conversations,
no access to agents. Nothing.

Walters already had her hand out. Helen briefly
considered making a copy, but her access number for
the copier would have been deactivated by now as part
of her punishment. And why make an enemy of Walters,
who at least had showed her the memo? She handed it
over. Walters sagged in apparent relief, which in its own
small way was the most disconcerting thing Helen had
seen all morning.

"So," Helen said tersely. "That's that, I guess."

"I know why he did it," Walters whispered. "Everyone
does, and believe me, a lot of us sympathize. Be aware
that you're not alone."

In Helen's turbulent state of mind, the words struck
her as potentially sinister.

"What do you mean, 'not alone'?" She, too, was
whispering now. "Am I under surveillance, is that what
you're saying?"

"God, no! Or I don't think so. I just meant, don't be
surprised if you start hearing from others. Privately, of
course. The word is out, and not only in Berlin."

"About Gilley, you mean?"

Walters again averted her eyes.

"Sorry," Helen said. "Robert, I mean. Or I suppose I shouldn't have said that, either."

"As I said, the word is out. Give it time."

"Out with who? Who do you think can help me?"

"Please. I can't say anything more."

Helen heard the door opening, and the sound of footsteps. Walters lowered her voice further, and Helen had to lean closer to hear.

"I probably shouldn't be talking to you at all because, well . . ."

"Well, what?"

"Herrington phoned me a few minutes before you came in. He ordered me to confiscate your key."

"To the records room?"

"I'm afraid so." She held out her hand.

"What if I never came in?"

Walters nodded toward the other side of the room, where a case officer, MacIntyre, had opened a drawer. In other words, there was now a witness to Helen's presence.

With a rising fury, Helen removed the key from her key ring and tossed it onto the desk, making a ringing noise that caused MacIntyre to stop what he was doing. The room was deathly silent.

"Oh," he said, noticing Helen.

She felt the color rising in her cheeks as she turned to go, and by the time she got back to her desk she was on the verge of vomiting up her breakfast. Her cheeks burned as if she'd been slapped, but she was determined not to display anger or pain. It's what everyone would be watching for. She gently shut the door to her office and sagged into her chair, her head in her hands as she squeezed her eyes shut.

She reopened them to the sight of another fresh memo from Herrington sitting atop her desk, which must have been delivered while she was in records. It wasn't the one he'd sent to everyone else.

Miss Abell,

Langley has brought it to my attention that you are more than a week behind in filing the regular safe house usage reports. Please bring your work in this area up to date no later than the close of business today.—LH

Below was a handwritten PS, in which he offered the real news:

Until this disciplinary matter is settled, you will be working under a reduced security clearance. While you will still be expected to stay abreast of your duties, I should clarify that until your clearance is restored you shall not be present, either as a facilitator or as an operator of recording equipment, for any clandestine meetings at our facilities. I have appointed temporary stewards from our clerical pool to assist in such duties until further notice.

For the moment, paperwork was her only duty. She was reminded of Baucom's characterization of her from the night before as a desk jockey, a pencil pusher—wartime terms that his generation had coined, and in her case they were painfully apt. With her clearance gone, she officially ranked even lower than a typist on the scale of Agency trust. She took out a sheaf of blank usage reports and scrolled one into her typewriter. She was so flustered that she had to use Wite-Out six times in the first five minutes.

All day she waited for the cavalry to arrive, based on Walters's vague assertion that others might soon rally to her cause. Not a single person knocked at her door. Her phone was silent. On her three trips into the hallways—one to the break room, two to the ladies' room—no one approached or called her name. She was so intent on looking straight ahead that she didn't know if anyone even dared to look at her. She did train her ears for the sound of Baucom's avuncular voice, but came up empty. Perhaps he'd been warned off as well, and was holed up in that restricted-access conference room in the back, where the Old Boys liked to gather.

Around 4 p.m. she completed the usage reports. She sipped at the cold remains of her midday coffee and reviewed her remaining options for investigating Gilley's misbehavior. Slim pickings. Copies of earlier usage reports were filed right here in her office, so she at least had access to them. Maybe there were records of previous meetings involving Robert, Frieda, or Kathrin.

She checked back through a year's supply, but found only a report for one previous visit by Robert, to a safe house in Steglitz that had since been decommissioned, and there was no mention of whom he'd met. If Robert was a more frequent customer, then he'd never reported his other visits. She did, however, find a record for previous visits by Frieda and Kathrin, one apiece. Each had met with Linden, a case officer whose actual name was Rick Ford.

That was something, she supposed. Ford would still know how to get in touch with them, although by now he, too, would have received Herrington's memo. Helen was damaged goods.

But Baucom could ask Ford on her behalf. This was war, and she should act accordingly. As far as Helen was concerned, Herrington had already fired his heaviest weapons—short of suspending her outright—and she would eventually have to use hers, meaning the tape. The nuclear option. But first she had to come up with the best possible means of deployment, because she would probably only have one chance to use it.

It was nearly 6 p.m. She was exhausted and disheartened. She locked her office and headed for the exit. The route took her by records where, to her surprise, the door was ajar, a rare lapse in security by Walters. With a stab of wishful thinking, she wondered if Walters might have left it open just for her. Maybe this was the sort of help Walters had been hinting at earlier?

Helen pushed through the door. Walters looked up from her desk and frowned right away. So much for that theory. Helen was about to slink away in shame when a man's voice called out from across the room.

"*Guten abend,* Frau Abell!"

It was Erickson, a field man whose German was notoriously bad, and whose Russian was worse. "*Was ist los?*"

"I should be asking you that," she answered, seizing on his greeting as an excuse to linger. "Must be something important if you didn't even bother to shut the door behind you."

Walters was glaring now.

Erickson smiled. Had he not seen Herrington's memo? Or maybe he didn't give a damn. Rumor had it that he'd been relegated to the most undesirable assignments until he improved his German.

"Oh, nothing all that earth-shattering," he said. "Major cleanup over in the produce aisle, and I'm the designated mop."

Walters cleared her throat. Erickson didn't notice, and Helen didn't dare look her way.

"A cleanup?"

"Some agent of ours—a *minor* one, thank God, but ours all the same—seems to have gone smash on the floor."

"Blown?"

"Dead."

"Good God!"

"Oh, it's not an operational casualty. Still, there are procedures to be followed because this one's going to make the papers."

Walters again cleared her throat. Helen again ignored it.

"How terrible."

"Yes. A lot of drinking involved. These young ones do put it away, although I'd always credited you gals with being more under control in that department."

"Gals? The agent was a young woman?" Helen strained to keep her voice under control.

"Anneliese Kurz," he said, looking at the file. "Nineteen years of age. Ever come across her at one of your houses?"

"Well, not by that name."

"Oh, of course." He smiled, silly him. "I guess you only know them by their cryptonyms."

She held her breath. By now even Walters wasn't stirring.

"Here we go, then. Frieda, it says here. Lovers' quarrel, or that's the working theory of the Polizei.

Some young anarchist on a rampage, also drunk—over in jolly old Kreuzberg."

Helen wished he would shut up, but he kept on chattering. She tried to smile as he continued but could barely mask her agony and astonishment.

"So, off I go. Mop in hand and official ID at the ready." He rolled his eyes. "By the way, you wouldn't happen to fancy a drink, would you? Later, of course, when I'm free and clear of all this? Helen? *Helen?*"

"What? Oh. Sorry, but no. I'm, uh, busy."

"Ah. So I've heard. The lucky old dog."

The innuendo bounced right off her, and she barely noticed as Erickson departed. Walters stood from her desk and bustled forward.

"Leave!" she hissed, her face a thundercloud. "You can't be in here, Helen. Leave now."

12

Willard Shoat, quiet and barely responsive on Anna's first jailhouse visit, was talkative this time, even with Henry hovering nearby. It took only seconds for him to reduce his sister to tears.

They met in the visiting room of the county lockup, face-to-face through a reinforced glass partition while seated on round stools bolted to the floor. Armed guards were posted on both sides. The room could hold five visitors at a time, but, due to Willard's infamy and mental limitations, the jailer was letting Anna visit outside normal hours.

They spoke to each other over an in-house telephone. The deputy who escorted Anna into the room insisted that Willard had showered the night before, but he looked dirty and disheveled. The orange uniform was clownishly baggy, and as Willard crossed the room to

take his seat he kept shoving the sleeves up his arms.
When he saw Anna, his face bloomed with a shy smile
as he picked up the phone.

"Hi, Anna."

"Hi, Willard." To Henry, her voice sounded fragile,
and the next exchange broke her.

"You're still here, so that part's happening."

"What part, Willard?"

"Have they got up yet? Mom and Dad? Have they
got up?"

Anna bit her lip and lowered her head. When she
looked up, her eyes were glistening.

"Got up?"

"From bed. Ain't they got up *yet*?"

"No, Willard." Her voice cracked. "They ain't got
up."

She pressed her free hand against the glass, maybe
hoping he'd do the same. But either he hadn't seen that
movie or didn't understand. Instead he looked down at
his lap, seemingly befuddled.

"Why ain't they?"

"They're in the ground now, Willard. They're at
peace, but they're in the ground."

She pulled her fingers away from the glass to wipe
her eyes. Willard rocked back and forth on the stool.
It was plain on his face that these weren't the answers
he'd expected.

"I'm sorry, Willard. Give me a few seconds, okay?"

"Okay," he said meekly.

Henry felt awkward being there, but couldn't look away. He was surprised by the familial resemblance, which hadn't been evident in newspaper photos. It was mostly their eyes, oval pools of brown, although Anna's were more animated. There was a similar sculpting to their face, although Willard's cheeks were flabbier.

The guard perked up when Anna reached inside her purse, then lost interest as she withdrew a handkerchief to blow her nose. She folded it and dabbed her eyes before picking up the phone again.

"Okay, then. Let's talk about you, Willard. Tell me how you're doing."

He shrugged.

"I eat a lot. But there's no chicken. No cotton candy. There's no movies here. I sleep. They let me sleep a whole lot." Then his face lit up, and he sat up straighter. "Can I go home with you?"

"No, Willard. You have to stay."

"When can I go?"

"I don't know, Willard, but it might be a long time."

"Real long?"

"Maybe."

"Can you count it, count the number? How many days?"

"No one knows yet. It depends on . . ." She paused,

again biting her lower lip. Henry stepped forward to offer his handkerchief, which again brought the guard to attention, but she waved it away.

"Depends on what?"

"On what the court decides about what happened to Mom and Dad. Can you talk about that? Do you know why it happened?"

He shrugged, as if she'd just asked why the jail wasn't serving chicken, yet another question beyond his ability to answer. Anna's fingers squirmed on the receiver, and her voice sharpened.

"Tell me why it happened, Willard. Why you did that to Mom and Dad. With your rifle, I mean. Why'd you shoot them, can you tell me?"

They stared at each other, faces rigid. Henry wondered if there was a history behind these sibling confrontations. Even between such different minds there must have been jealousies, rivalries, some fights along the way.

Willard's face folded in on itself and he gasped for air with a sound like a sob.

"Those numbers!" he said, louder than he'd yet spoken. The guard on his side frowned and stood a little straighter.

"What numbers, Willard?"

"The numbers! Why hasn't it happened?"

"Why hasn't what happened, Willard? What numbers?"

Henry, unable to contain himself, stepped toward the glass and spoke toward the mouthpiece. "The numbers on the sign? The sign for Poston? Is that what you mean?"

Willard looked up in surprise, recoiling at the sound of a new voice.

"Sorry," Henry whispered.

"Do you mean the sign?" Anna asked, drawing her brother's attention back to her.

Willard nodded slowly.

"What do the numbers mean? What was supposed to happen?"

Willard grimaced and shook his head. He looked lost in thought. Anna repeated the question, but he remained silent. She lowered the receiver to her side.

"This was a bad idea, the whole thing—hiring you, coming here, all of it. I'll never know why. *He'll* never even know, so how the hell will anyone else?"

"It's okay."

"No. None of this is okay. I'm wasting your time, and God knows what I'm doing to my brother. When we came in he seemed fine. Now look at him."

Willard was slumped on the stool. He stared at the floor, his face red with frustration.

Henry rested a hand on Anna's shoulder.

"Don't give up. Too early for that."

Willard's voice crackled from the receiver.

"He said . . . He said that the numbers, that they would finish it."

The words affected them like the crack of a whip. Anna picked up the receiver and asked slowly, carefully, "*Who* said that, Willard? Who said the numbers would finish it?"

Willard looked from Anna to Henry, and then back at his sister. His eyes widened and, for the first time, he looked mistrustful, maybe a little scared.

"No!" He backed away, nearly stumbling as he stood from the stool.

"It's okay, Willard. You're all right. You're okay."

She placed her free hand back against the glass. Willard's grimace softened and he slowly settled back onto the stool.

"Are you better now? Do you feel okay?"

He nodded.

"It's just one small question, Willard, that's all. And it's okay to answer it. Who said the numbers would finish it? Was it someone like Joey? Is that the kind of person you're talking about?"

Willard shook his head. His gaze returned to the floor.

"Not Joey," he said sullenly.

"I know that," she said. "I know Joey wouldn't do that. But was it someone *like* Joey? You know, someone I wouldn't be able to see?"

He continued to stare at the floor.

"Who was it, Willard. Who told you that?"

When Willard looked up, his eyes seemed to be pleading for mercy, or a little understanding.

"I can't. I promised, Anna. I *can't*."

"You promised him?"

Willard nodded.

"Promised him what, Willard?"

"No. I *can't*. I can't, Anna, or it won't *never happen*!"

He dropped the receiver, which bounced against the partition as he again slid off the stool. He raised a hand as if to wave goodbye and then thought better of it. Then he turned and walked away, toward the back of the room where the guard stood. Anna knocked on the glass and shouted.

"Willard. *Willard!*"

He kept going, not even turning to say goodbye.

13

Anna was silent all the way to the parking lot. They slid onto their seats and Henry started the car. The only noise was the rush of cold air, the thrum of the tires. As they were turning onto Highway 53, Henry could wait no longer.

"Who's Joey?"

"Imaginary friend. When Willard was twelve or thirteen. Lasted a whole summer."

"Maybe this time it's somebody real."

"Or maybe that's what I'd like it to be. It's pretty much why I hired you, isn't it? Find someone else to blame—anyone but my brother? Well, here's an alternate theory: Maybe that's what Willard is doing, too. He used Joey the same way."

"Like some kind of bad boy alter ego?"

She nodded.

"Joey was Willard's excuse for doing pretty much

anything he knew he wasn't supposed to do, so maybe that's what he's doing now."

"Then why did he look scared?"

"You thought he looked scared?"

"Yes. When you were asking him for a name, anyway."

"I thought he looked horrified. At himself. You saw how he reacted when I told him Mom and Dad weren't getting up. I think maybe it's just hitting him what he's done."

"Well, you know him better than I do. Still, his eyes . . ."

"What?"

"I've seen that look before, and I don't think it's horror, or self-loathing. He's scared of something. Or somebody."

They drove another mile toward Poston, green fields of ripening corn and soybeans flying past them in full sunlight. Anna drummed her fingers on the dashboard.

"Maybe you're right. I was so upset I didn't know what to think." She laughed harshly. "And now I get to go meet Washam Poultry, aiding and abetting in the corporate slaughter of sixty thousand birds. You don't have a smoke on you, do you?"

"Sorry. Gave it up."

She switched on the radio, one of those classic rock stations, and it of course just happened to be playing "Psycho Killer" by the Talking Heads, which made her laugh again, harder this time. Henry reached over to switch it off but she stayed his hand.

"No, no. Leave it on."

You're talking a lot, but you're not saying anything. When I have nothing to say, my lips are sealed.

Then she switched it off, shook her head, and wiped her eyes.

"Isn't that just perfect? Like my whole fucking day, my whole fucking *life*. Sorry, I shouldn't be unloading on you."

"At seventy-five a day I'd say you've earned the right."

"Oh, yes. I almost forgot. My big 'investigation'!" She made quote marks in the air. Then she took a deep breath. "Oh, Willard, you poor, dumb bastard. *What were you thinking?*"

She pounded the dashboard and sobbed loudly, but only once. Henry looked away as she blew her nose. The car had slowed to forty-five, and a big semi rig blew around them in the passing lane with a shriek of its air horn and a blast of grit.

Anna reached over and pressed the horn.

"You, too, asshole!"

Henry waited a few beats and then, in what he hoped was a calming tone, said, "I'm guessing Willard must have had it pretty rough. Growing up, I mean."

"Oh, God yes." She settled back into her seat. "Most of it started when he turned five or six, school age. I was around twelve, right when you're starting to worry about where you fit in, right when having a brother like Willard was the worst possible thing to have on your teen résumé. So for a while I just tuned it out."

"Understandable. Hormones and all that."

"Then one Saturday when I was sleeping in I heard him crying and screaming. I looked out the window and they were chasing him right through our yard. His own damn yard. I flew out the back door in my PJs, mad as hell, the wrath of God. And from then on I had his back. Of course by the time *he* hit twelve I was off to college, way up north. And I'll admit it was a relief to leave it behind. Later I felt like I'd deserted him at his greatest hour of need, but I guess I needed a life."

"We all do at that age."

"Then, after my freshman year, that was the summer of Joey. Willard probably just needed someone else to take the heat, or to do his acting up."

They were cruising along at sixty now. The only features on the flat horizon were a distant line of trees and a couple of chicken houses. Anna switched off the air and rolled down her window. The stench of chicken manure came in on the breeze like something you could touch.

"Jesus, what a stink," she said. "They use it for fertilizer. That and about a thousand chemicals. Pesticide and everything else. Maybe that's what finally got to him." She paused. "So you think this person might actually be real?"

"Like I said, to me he looked scared. Imaginary friends aren't usually scary. At the very least we might as well ask around, like you said earlier. See if anybody ever saw him with somebody else—hanging out, maybe, or hunting in the woods."

"Sounds so dark and sinister now, doesn't it? The idea of Willard out there on his own with a rifle?"

"Or not on his own."

She nodded, looking straight ahead.

"You're right, we should check."

They were nearing town when she practically grabbed the wheel.

"Turn into that store up there!"

He braked hard and swerved into the parking lot of a convenience store in a slide of gravel. She unlatched the door.

"If we're really going to do this, then I need cigarettes. Backsliders Anonymous. Want anything?"

"Beer. A six of anything that isn't light."

"The rye's not enough to keep you going?"

He smiled but didn't answer.

"We're quite the pair, aren't we?"

They hopped out of the car, and bustled off to buy their supplies.

14

Anna had gone quiet again by the time they reached the Shoat house. The Washam Poultry catch crew was due in half an hour, so Henry gave her some space to catch her breath. He walked down a gravel lane toward the crops, and was standing in a field of soybeans when the trucks rolled in.

A white pickup hauling a forklift led four tractor-trailers down the long dirt road to the two chicken houses. Each house was five hundred feet long, a shed of corrugated metal with big fans and a feed silo mounted at one end. The beds of the tractor-trailers were piled with empty cages that were shedding feathers like a torn pillow.

Henry watched from a distance as Anna greeted the foreman with a handshake. He wore a black Washam ball cap and a red flannel shirt, and handed her a clipboard with papers to sign. Nine men spilled from the cabs of the tractor-trailers, calling out to each other in Spanish.

They were scruffy and bedraggled. They stood to one side, preparing as if for battle. Several pulled on heavy work gloves. Others covered their arms with torn panty hose, presumably for protection against beaks and talons, and donned respirators and dust masks. Some wore goggles.

A funny place, the Eastern Shore. Less than a two-hour drive from Capitol Hill, and a frequent stopover for beachgoers on the way to Ocean City and Rehoboth. But it looked, felt, and operated more like a state in the American South. In recent decades it had turned over its scut work to thousands of new arrivals from Latin America, whose presence was now evident in bilingual signs and a boomlet of Mexican restaurants—all of this happening in small towns that had previously been about as ethnic as a jar of mayonnaise.

Yet, in the more prosperous and picturesque waterfront villages, there was a layer of urban gentry that had silted down over the years from the better neighborhoods of Baltimore and Washington. Old money and privilege, embodied by people like Stu Wilgus, or new money and excess, which showed itself in gargantuan new houses. You didn't have to dig beneath the surface very far to find a sediment from the power corridors of Capitol Hill, K Street, perhaps even

Langley—the sort of people Rodney Bales might once have investigated. Yet another reason for Henry to stay on his toes.

The forklift hauled a stack of cages into the end of one of the chicken houses, and the workers followed. A sudden uproar of clucks and shouts announced that their labors had begun. A cloud of dust rolled out the open door. Henry had read that the trick to this job was to grab as many as four chickens at a time with each hand, snatching them up by their feet. Even from where he stood, he could smell an ammonia stench from the drifts of wood chips and manure that covered the floors of the houses, ankle-deep.

After a few minutes the forklift emerged, the cages now filled with a flutter of dingy white birds. Henry had expected Anna to flee at the earliest opportunity, sparing herself the sight of the carnage. Instead, she was riveted to her spot, arms folded. And he was watching her. It felt somehow appropriate to once again be twice removed from the real action, just as he'd been on his previous assignment, watching the cops and the feds as they had, in turn, watched the drug bosses and the dealers on the corners—an extra layer of detachment that had insulated him from the consequences of his actions.

After an hour or so the crew emerged from the first house and moved into the second one. Two of the tractor-trailers had already rumbled off toward the processing plant where, within an hour, all those chickens would be headless and hanging by their feet.

Henry saw a catcher tending to a bloody scratch on his arm. The wind was picking up, and the next gust brought a powerful whiff of ozone and rain from the west. Henry looked behind him to see dark clouds rolling closer. A gust thrashed the soybeans against his trouser legs, tickling his ankles through his socks. He glanced downward to see green leaves dusted with insecticide and fertilizer, the work of Anna's father from only a week ago.

Anna and the foreman headed for the shelter of a nearby shed, and Henry decided he'd better join them. The first fat raindrop slapped his forehead as he crossed the final row of beans, and he reached the shed just as the skies opened.

"There you are." Anna sounded relieved. The foreman with the Washam Poultry cap nodded.

"This is Ben Halloran," she said. "The . . . I'm sorry, Ben, what did you say you were called?"

"The live-haul manager. I come out to the catches a few times a week, to make sure the crews are up to snuff. Are you family?"

"A friend. Henry Mattick."

They shook hands. Anna looked ready for the day to be over.

"I'm real sorry we won't be coming here no more, ma'am. It was always a pleasure working with, well . . . I'm assuming it was your mom and dad?"

"Yes. It was."

"I was, uh . . . real sorry about your news."

"News," she said. "Yes, I guess that's pretty much what it was. It was news all right."

The poor fellow shifted his weight from one foot to another and tried to redeem himself.

"They was good folks. Always treated our people right. Willard, too, even." Now he was in even deeper, but it was too late to stop. "I'm kinda surprised old Merle didn't latch on with today's crew, given his attachment to the boy."

In the awkwardness that followed it took a few seconds for the words to sink in. Anna looked at Henry, who raised his eyebrows.

"His attachment to Willard?" she said.

"Yes, ma'am. Rest his soul." He actually took off his cap, as if Willard, too, had passed away.

"How do you mean, his attachment?"

"Well, ma'am, they always got to talking afterward, when we'd break for lunch. Your mom would put on a spread for the crew. Coca-cola and an ice bucket, sandwich fixin's and some chips."

"Oh, I'm sorry. If I'd known I would have—"

"Oh, no. I didn't mean that."

"But you said they'd talk, this guy Merle and my brother?"

"That's right. Merle always requested special to be on any crew coming to your place, so I expect they must have been pretty good pals."

Henry was all ears.

"Merle who?" she asked. "What's his last name?"

"Oh, hell, ma'am—pardon my language—but I don't know the full names of half the fellows on these crews." He put his cap back on. "Especially with, well, you know." He grinned and made a yacking motion with his hand. "All that Habla Español. Except when they've got a complaint about their check, of course. Then all of a sudden their English is pretty damn good."

"At the rates you pay, who can blame 'em? You do keep records, though, right?"

"On the regulars, sure. They get paychecks, W-2s, the whole nine yards. But Merle, he's a hustleman."

"Hustleman?"

"Part-timer. Cash basis only. No receipts, no records, nothing. We pick up a few every day, for when we're running short. And with the full-timers jumping from company to company, well, we're just about always running short."

"So this Merle, he just kind of shows up at the job site?"

"Oh, no, ma'am. He's part of a labor pool, over at Henson Point. That's where we always go first when we're looking for hustlemen. He wasn't there this morning, though, which, like I said, kinda surprised me, because he was always looking to be on any crew coming here. And you folks were due. He would've known."

"He would've? How?"

"Oh, the grow schedule, mostly. He kept track."

"Did he, now? Well, I'd like to find him if I could."

"Find him?" Halloran, seeming to finally register her intensity, looked a little uncomfortable.

"To thank him, for being such a friend to my brother. In light of what happened and all."

"Sure, ma'am. But I, uh . . . I don't really think they'd like the idea of me helping you track down one of our hustlemen. Not that I'd personally object."

"I understand, Ben. So where's this labor pool, then? You said Henson Point?"

"Yes, ma'am. One of those informal things. They start showing up in the Walmart lot around six. Every morning but Sundays, looking for any kind of work they can pick up."

"Undocumented?" Henry said.

"Well, mostly, although you didn't hear that from me. They get some drunks, too, the usual down-and-outers. Cash basis, like I said, which is the way those types like it."

"Merle doesn't sound like a Hispanic name."

"Oh, he ain't, ma'am. He's as white as you and me."

"Then which is he, a drunk or a down-and-outer?"

"I don't rightly know, and that's the truth of it. Always works hard, though, when he bothers to show. That's usually how it goes with the drinkers and the druggies. Reliable until they're not. Although, well . . ."

"Well, what?"

"He's always been kind of a fish out of water with that crowd. Dresses like 'em, I'll say that. But clear-eyed, never bloodshot. It's why our crew chiefs like having him. They know they'll get a good, sober day's work. 'Scuse me, ma'am. Looks like they're about finished."

He stepped into the rain and headed off toward the trucks. Henry looked at Anna.

"What do you think?" he asked. "Could he be the new Joey?"

"Better. Joey made flesh."

A few hours ago she'd looked beaten. Now she looked invigorated, determined.

They had work to do. It was a slim thread, but it was a lead.

15

Helen drank alone until three in the morning—her very own dark night of the soul, catered by two bottles of cheap Gewürztraminer. She contemplated the various ways in which her actions had doomed the poor, benighted Frieda, and speculated on what she might have done to save the girl. Her sorriest conclusion was that Frieda would have been better off if Helen had remained upstairs, listening in impotent agony while Kevin Gilley raped her. A horrible prospect, but Frieda—or Anneliese, as Helen now thought of her—would still be alive.

Damaged, yes, but alive.

Toward the end of the first bottle, Helen settled on an even better alternate outcome.

"Should've killed him," she muttered to herself. She remembered the fear in the girl's face as she had fled into the rain bearing little more than Helen's parting vows of aid and secrecy. Empty promises.

Helen supposed there was a chance that the murder was some sort of terrible coincidence. Raped in one venue, killed in another, but for different reasons. The world was always a dangerous place for drifting young women like Anneliese. Helen clung to that thread as she drank her way through the second bottle.

Then Baucom's words about Gilley's field of endeavor flashed to mind—sorcery and black bags—and her torment resumed. Of course it was connected. She swallowed more wine.

For dinner she ate half a box of crackers and a heel of stale bread slathered with the final scrapings from a jar of Nutella. In the course of the evening she got two phone calls. Probably Baucom, so she didn't answer. After the second one Helen unplugged the phone.

A little after four she vomited up everything, spattering her jeans, her blouse, and the floor beside her bed, where she'd nodded off an hour earlier. If she'd been lying on her back she might have choked to death, and what a great loss that would have been to the Cause of the West, she reflected from her seat on the floor, the room spinning.

Helen stumbled into the shower fully clothed to wash off the mess, and then stood dripping on the bathroom tiles as she stripped off her soaked garments. She put on a soft heavy robe, climbed into bed and fell into a dizzy stupor. No sanctuary to be found this time, despite Baucom's kindly advice. No realm of sleep yet existed that would have admitted her for protection in this frame of mind.

But when she awoke there was a plan stirring inside her throbbing head. If she couldn't pursue or investigate Gilley from inside Berlin station—and that seemed clear, given all the restrictions Herrington had imposed—then she would do it from the outside. From here on out she would set her own limits, take risks. The one thing she wouldn't risk was letting Gilley go unpunished or unnamed.

It was already past 9 a.m., so the first thing she did was phone Herrington.

"I'm not feeling well. Some sort of bug."

"Then by all means take a day." He sounded relieved.

"I might need more than one, but I'll be available in any emergency, and I won't fall behind in my paperwork."

"Take as long as you need. Whatever it takes for the old, reliable Helen Abell to return to form."

"Thank you, sir." *You fuckwad bastard.*

"Thank *you*, Helen." Smug as ever, even in trying to sound gracious.

Obviously he believed he'd won. *Problem solved! Another administrative coup for the chief of station!*

She threw on the first clean clothes she found—black jeans, a blue cotton T-shirt, a brown Irish fisherman's sweater. Then, reconsidering in light of her planned destination, she dug out a more professional getup. A navy business suit with a white cotton blouse. Something that looked not only very American but vaguely spooklike, because that's what she was shooting for. She swallowed three Tylenols, drank two glasses of water, and grabbed her ID and shoulder bag. The last thing she did before leaving was to check inside the bag for the two reels of audiotape. From now on she would keep them with her at all times. She was glad she wouldn't be going into the office, where it would feel like she was carrying a load of smuggled plutonium.

Helen headed straight to the nearest café, where she ordered a *Milchkaffee* and a chocolate croissant. She grabbed a copy of *Tagesspiegel* from a stack by the door and then steeled herself by gulping half the cup before opening the paper. She found the item boxed among the local news briefs on an inside page, and her first reaction was to wretch, barely able to hold down those first swallows. This drew an indignant stare from one of those older *Hausfrau* types who were always correcting your behavior. Helen glared back until the woman looked away. She took a bite of the croissant and another swallow, letting the coffee scald all the way to her stomach. Then she read the story.

The murder of Anneliese Kurz merited only four paragraphs, and the details were scant. Strangulation and a severe beating. A suspected lovers' quarrel, just as Erickson had said. No suspect was in custody, or was named, but an eyewitness had apparently spotted a young man running from the scene, and then saw the body through an open door. So, then. Not Gilley, but that was hardly a surprise.

The most valuable item was the name of the policeman handling the investigation: Otto Schnapp, a detective with the Kriminalpolizei, or KriPo. He was based in the cop shop for the *Abschnitt,* or precinct, for Kreuzberg. She borrowed a phone book from behind the counter and looked up the address on Friesenstrasse. Schnapp was probably the fellow Erickson had dealt with, and his task would have been simple enough: Hush it up or, at the very least, keep the Agency's name out of any further discussion. Erickson also would've requested access to Frieda's personal effects, and by now a team would have searched and sanitized her apartment.

The precinct house was a complex of imposing nineteenth-century red-brick buildings, five stories high. With their turrets and arched windows they were grandiose, like something built in the age of the Kaisers. Her walk from the U-Bahn took her past Templehof, the horseshoe-shaped air terminal that had been the main landing strip of the Berlin Airlift, which kept the western half of the city fed and watered during the Soviet blockade of 1948. Now it was a minor hub for commuter flights, but Helen could never pass it without recalling the postwar photos of spindly German boys standing atop piles of rubble as they watched the incoming American cargo planes—back when the East-West struggle really was a matter of life and death.

She found Detective Otto Schnapp on the third floor, in an office with glass partitions. His door was open, so she entered without knocking. He was standing with his back to her, dressed in a police-issue ribbed green sweater as he rummaged through an open file drawer.

"Herr Detektiv Schnapp?"

He turned calmly, a rangy man in a blond buzz cut, and assessed her with steady blue eyes.

"*Ja?*"

She handed him her official ID and addressed him in German.

"I am Helen Abell, here on behalf of my employer with regard to the homicide of Anneliese Kurz."

He raised his eyebrows as he inspected the ID. Then he handed it back.

"Again?" he said in English. "Your Mr. Statler was here yesterday on this matter. I told him all that I know. And I am assuming that by now his representatives have already visited the scene, as well as Miss Kurz's place of residence."

Statler. Erickson's cryptonym.

"Yes, and thank you for your cooperation. But further questions have come up, so I'm here to double-check. And, please, do speak German."

Schnapp settled in behind his desk and gestured toward a chair. He steepled his fingers, and looked her in the eye long enough to make her uncomfortable.

"It is best if I speak English in these sorts of . . . situations. I do not wish to be told later that something was lost in translation. Although your German is certainly superior to Mr. Statler's."

Hardly surprising. Schnapp was impressive, not least because she already sensed he wasn't buying her story.

"Pardon me a moment," he said.

He picked up the phone, dialed a number from memory, and, following a brief pause and the squeak of an answering voice, said in English, "Miss Helen Abell, please."

She started to object, then thought better of it. He nodded and spoke again.

"Very well. I shall try later. No, there is no message."

Neatly done. He'd managed to check the validity of her name, but without blowing the whistle on her to Berlin station, and she wondered why.

"Tell me," he asked, steepling his fingers again, "what is so important to you—or, rather, to your employers—about this case?"

"As I said, I'm only here to double-check."

"Even with so little information at hand? What details of the case, in particular, did you wish to 'double-check,' as you say?"

He leaned forward and opened a small notebook. He was calling her bluff, asking for specifics.

"The eyewitness, for one. I'd like to review his statement, and his contact information."

"So, I see that you have read this morning's newspaper."

"We'd hoped there would be no coverage. Now, about that statement . . ."

Schnapp smiled.

"Why don't you ask Mr. Statler for his copy?"

"As I said, I'm here to verify. We do that sometimes."

He eyed her a moment longer. Then he shook his head slowly, opened a desk drawer, and retrieved a glossy photo clipped to some paperwork. He tossed it toward Helen.

It was a crime scene photo of Anneliese Kurz. Helen reflexively looked away, but the image was already embossed on her memory. A white, thin neck, twisted at a horrible angle. Glassy lifeless eyes. That pale skin, and the same blouse that Gilley had torn open, buttons missing. Helen swallowed slowly and glanced again. The girl's mouth was agape. Her temple was bruised.

"May I get you something to drink?" Schnapp sounded solicitous. He seemed taken aback by her reaction. "Mineral water, perhaps?"

"No, thank you."

She steeled herself and unclipped the photo to read the report, although she could barely focus on the words.

"I'll need a copy of this," she said, her voice sounding to her like it was coming from another room.

"Your colleague has already misplaced his?"

"Just being thorough."

"Of course. You may keep that one. I have others. The photo remains here."

She slid it toward him without comment and again tried to focus on the words. She cleared her throat and spoke again.

"Any luck in identifying or locating a suspect?"

"None. The eyewitness account, as you will see, was not so detailed." He recited from the report by memory: "Male, early twenties, medium build, long blond hair, blue jeans, white T-shirt—"

She held out a hand to halt him.

"You know, my German really is quite good. As long as you're quoting the witness verbatim, you might as well give me his exact words."

"Those *were* his exact words, Miss Abell. The eyewitness was American."

"American?"

"Yes, as you will see in the report. Kurt Delacroix, age nineteen. Some sort of hippie, it would seem, or perhaps simply a fellow traveler of all those *Autonomen* anarchist trash who live in that building."

"I see. And the report contains his contact information?"

"Such as it is. Some flophouse calling itself a youth

hostel. Bedbugs, syringes in the stairwell, that sort of place. A room on the fifth floor with six beds. But as I spoke with him I saw that he only had one bag. A duffle, I believe you call them, so at this moment he may be anywhere."

"You think he's left Berlin?"

"I do not know. I asked him to remain in the city in case we arrested a suspect. For a lineup, you see. The victim supposedly had a boyfriend, whose description matches that of the suspect, but no one seems to know where he has gone. Delacroix promised he would stay, but when I went to question him a second time he had vacated the building. His current whereabouts are not known to me."

"Does the report give his physical description?"

"It is not our customary procedure to log descriptions of eyewitnesses, Miss Abell, not when we have already spoken with them face-to-face. Nor was your Mr. Statler much interested in such information, so there is nothing to 'verify,' as you put it. But would you like to know for yourself?"

They were looking intently at each other. Helen sensed that Schnapp didn't really care if she was here in an official capacity or not. For whatever reason, he seemed to be enjoying their back-and-forth. Curiosity, maybe.

"Yes, please. Describe him."

"Fairly tall, perhaps a hundred eighty-eight centi-meters." Schnapp paused. "Ah, yes, you are not metric. Allow me." He reached into a desk drawer for a pocket calculator and punched in a few numbers. "About six feet, two inches. Broad-shouldered, but trim. Brown eyes, a reddish complexion, clean-shaven. Long black hair, greasy and uncombed. When I saw him he was wearing black leather pants and a black leather jacket, with silver things up his sleeves—do you call them buttons?"

"Studs, I think."

"Yes. Silver studs. A white T-shirt. Black boots, of the sort that the anarchists wear for kicking in the teeth of fallen policemen. He speaks as they speak, with contempt in every word. I gathered that he enjoys their company, perhaps, but does not share their taste for fighting simply for its own sake. So, then, an *Autonomen* in appearance only, but not by personal manifesto."

"What sort of progress have you made in the case?"

"None. Nor do I anticipate making much more in the days to come, unless our crime scene technicians come up with some sort of wonderful discovery, or unless Mr. Delacroix suddenly reappears with more information. There was no blood at the scene. Whoever killed her was quick and efficient, and was unusually tidy about cleaning up after himself."

"Well trained, then."

"Or lucky. It happens."

"How do you know he was quick?"

"The room showed no signs of a major struggle, and the doctor who examined her said there was no skin beneath her fingernails. Only the dirt of the streets."

A plain enough statement, but it nearly moved Helen to tears.

"But if this was some sort of lovers' quarrel, shouldn't someone have a name?"

"Miss Kurz's friends, such as they are, did not know a name for any such lover. That theory, which the newspaper and your colleague Mr. Statler seemed to accept, was solely because of Mr. Delacroix's account. He said he heard the suspect shouting just before he ran into the hallway from the apartment. 'You bitch, sleeping with everyone.' Spoken in German, he said."

"What else do you have?"

"Nothing."

Schnapp shrugged, almost blasé, and it pissed her off.

"So you're just going to let this one fall through the cracks?"

"The cracks, Miss Abell? You speak as if we have these sorts of murders flowing like a liquid, like there is some sort of spree of crime here in Berlin. I am not your TV Kojak with a lollipop in his jaw and too many bodies to keep track of, yes?"

"Who said anything about Kojak?" Although she had watched it—the New York detective with a head like a bowling ball. She had even seen episodes here— dubbed, of course. *Who loves ya, baby?* wasn't half as catchy in German.

"My point, Miss Abell, is that this is not New York. Nor is it even Chicago or L.A. At most we will have fifty murders in the city this year. That is fewer than one each week, and of course not all of them occur in this district. So I can assure you that my attention to this matter will be . . ." He paused, searching for the right word.

"Undivided?"

"Yes. Undivided. But for the moment the simple truth is that there are not enough leads to keep me busy."

"What about next of kin?"

"For the girl?"

"Yes. Maybe they would know something."

He sighed and flipped through his notebook.

"I have not yet been able to find anything to tell me of a previous address, or of any family. She has been registered as a resident of Berlin for only a year and nine months. But she had no job, and she was not a student."

"She said something to me about Braunschweig."

He raised his eyebrows.

"You knew her?"

"I met her only once, and for only a few minutes."

"Yes?" He waited for more.

"She was in a hurry to leave."

"Yet she had time to tell you she was from Braunschweig? Where was this meeting? On what day, and at what hour?"

"I'm afraid I'm not at liberty to say."

"I see. Yet, I am the one to blame for not working hard enough."

For a moment she was tempted to tell him everything. About the rape, the confrontation with Gilley at the safe house, the girl's plea for silence and her disappearance into a rainy night. Schnapp nodded, as if to encourage her. But Helen's resolve failed, and she remained silent, the good employee, unwilling to go any further in her defiance of the Agency.

"What will you do next, then?" she asked, the question sounding feeble.

"There is nothing that I can do, or not at this time of day. These sorts of people tend to live mostly in the later hours, and mostly in places where a policeman is not typically welcome."

"The club scene?"

He nodded.

"Punks, I believe they are calling themselves now, with all of that loud and pointless music. Plus all of the anarchists, or *Autonomen,* as they call themselves. Hoodlums, that's what you'd call them in America.

They believe in nothing but destruction. They all dress as she did, and also in the way of our American witness, Mr. Delacroix."

He stood, signaling the end to their meeting.

"If you decide that you have more to tell me, Miss Abell, then I hope you will call."

He handed her a business card. She nodded as she took it, and then lowered her head.

"Yes," she said meekly. "I will."

"Should I inform your office of the satisfactory nature of your visit?"

"That won't be necessary."

"I guessed as much."

He smiled, and she felt his eyes on her all the way to the stairwell.

16

Helen waited until midnight to go looking for Delacroix. She picked up one of the free weeklies to scout their listings of night spots for the local punk scene. The two likeliest places seemed to be Dschungel and SO36, which didn't close until the last patrons stumbled out the door at daybreak.

She pondered what to wear. At twenty-four she was young enough to fit in, but clothes were another matter. She didn't own a shred of black leather, nor any makeup that could possibly make her look as pale or ghostly as the countless anarcho-punks she'd seen on the subway and S-Bahn.

One fashion quirk she'd noticed was a preference for safety pins as earrings, so she spent the next ten minutes looking for one, only to conclude that she wouldn't be fooling a soul. Achieving the right look would require a makeover worthy of Hollywood, not to mention an attitude she didn't possess. So instead she threw on her black jeans, blue cotton T-shirt, and brown fisherman's sweater—the very getup she'd rejected that morning. At worst she'd be seen as an uncool older sister, a naïf, or maybe a tourist. At best she'd be invisible. Most of the people where she was going, she assumed, would be too drunk or stoned to care.

She realized her mistake not long after arriving at Dschungel, where, to her surprise, there was a strict door policy and a long line of people hoping to get in. She suspected the exclusivity had something to do with its location, only a few blocks off the prosperous shopping district along the Ku'damm. A stout, bearded troll seemed to be in charge of selecting those worthy of entry. He sat on a folding chair by the door, keeping the line moving by muttering either a bored and dour, *"Nein,"* which happened in most cases, or by leaping to his feet for a hug and a slap on the back, followed by the shouting of a name. "Jorg! *Komm rein!*" "Ulrike! *Willkommen!*"

He needed less than a second to pass judgment on Helen, who, despite mustering the most sullen possible pout, merited yet another *"Nein."* She lingered a while longer to size up the people waiting behind her. None matched the description for Delacroix.

SO36 was grungier and more freewheeling, a perfect match for its environs on Oranienstrasse in Kreuzberg, a few blocks south of the Wall. Helen paid a cover charge and entered a miasma of smoke and noise. The place was packed. A band named Katapult was banging out a song called "Angst." Half the people were bouncing up and down. The rest were either free-form dancing or, like Helen, eyeing the scene. The only offstage lighting was a strobing spotlight directed at a glitter ball dangling from the ceiling, like the ones in disco clubs. It cast out whirling beads of light, which gave the room a frenetic feel.

To Helen's dismay, roughly half the young men had long, stringy hair and were wearing black leather. Trying to find Delacroix here based on Schnapp's description would be like searching a beehive for a male with a striped belly.

She decided it would be better to proceed by ear, which became possible as soon as the band moved offstage for a break. Jostling through the crowd, she listened closely for anyone speaking English, male or female, or even German with an American accent. The moment she heard either, she zoomed in to ask, without preamble, "Have you seen Delacroix?"

Her first attempt was greeted by a puzzled look from a short young woman with a Midwestern accent and purple bangs. Her second, to a fellow who would have looked like a surfer boy if not for his shredded leather jacket, produced a quick shake of the head and a terse "No, man. Fuck off." The third, directed at another woman, also produced a "Fuck off." She was about to try for a fourth time when she felt a tap on her shoulder just as someone shouted, "Miss Abell!"

She turned to see Otto Schnapp, who, despite being clad in jeans and a gray sweatshirt, fit in far better than Helen. Maybe it was the buzz cut, or those unwavering eyes.

"You will not find him here," Schnapp said.

"Find who?"

"Delacroix. I have looked myself. He is not here."

"Why are *you* looking for him?"

Schnapp glanced to either side and nodded toward the door. She followed him into an alley, where it was suddenly and blessedly quiet. Her ears rang, and she smelled of smoke, sweat, and weed, but out here the air was cool and crisp.

"Your Mr. Statler telephoned me today, not long after you departed."

"Oh."

That was that, she supposed. She might as well turn in her resignation first thing in the morning.

"You are not working this case in an official capacity, that much is clear."

"Did Statler tell you that?"

"He did not need to. His interest was in another matter, that of Mr. Delacroix. In fact, from all that he said and did, I surmised that he is far more interested in Mr. Delacroix than in either Miss Kurz or the so-called suspect."

"So-called?"

"Mr. Statler suggested strongly that I refrain from any further contact with Mr. Delacroix. Only twice before in my nine years as a detective has your employer asked me to have no further contact with someone, and in each case do you know why they made this request?"

Helen shook her head.

"It was because those people were employees."

"I see."

"I am sure that you do. Except this time your Mr. Statler made no such admission to me, even when I asked."

"I wish you would stop calling him *my* Mr. Statler."

"As you wish. But his behavior is why I decided to look for Mr. Delacroix again. Just in case. It is also why, in speaking with . . . with Mr. Statler, I neglected to tell him of your visit to my office."

She sagged in relief. No resignation necessary. Not yet, anyway.

"Thank you."

"Do not thank me, Miss Abell. I suspect that what I should really be doing is discouraging you from further involvement. You saw what became of Miss Kurz."

"That's a reason to keep going. Besides, you're not exactly taking your own advice. I doubt that policemen who spy on spies get very far in this town."

"I am a lifelong Berliner, Miss Abell. For us, some behaviors are second nature."

"I bow to your local expertise, and apologize for my hubris."

"Then you are a rare American." He offered a half smile and eyed her a bit longer, as if weighing whether to say more. "I do have a few items more of information concerning Mr. Delacroix, items that I had planned to put into a supplemental report until Mr. Statler asked me not to. But you are an Agency employee, so I suppose it is only proper that you know them, yes?"

"Yes."

"He is a student. Tufts University, in the state of Massachusetts. His parents are Jill and Walter Delacroix. They live in Bethesda, Maryland."

She took a pen and a notepad from her bag and wrote it down.

"Anything else?"

"Nothing. Which is why I would like to find him. I think he would be a person of interest to me. Not on the Kurz matter, perhaps, since that is now closed to me. But for future reference."

"I understand."

"Good. Then my secret will be as safe with you as yours is with me?"

"Absolutely, Detective Schnapp."

She scribbled the phone number for her apartment and gave it to him.

"Will you let me know if you find him?"

"I think we both know that is unlikely. I suspect by

now that Mr. Delacroix, as your Kojak would say, is in the wind, yes?"

"Yes."

They locked eyes for a moment. Finally he nodded.

"Take care with yourself, Miss Abell."

He headed off into the night.

Thirty minutes later, Helen was pressing the buzzer for Baucom's apartment. It took more than a minute for him to answer on the squawk box.

"It's me. I'm coming up." She tried to sound as forceful as possible, but there was still a long pause before he buzzed her in.

Baucom lived in Charlottenberg, one of the few neighborhoods of West Berlin that had retained most of its Old World charm after the *Trümmerfrauen* cleared the rubble of 1945, brick by brick. He lived on the third floor of a grand old building with a marbled foyer and high ceilings, in a spacious apartment with old rugs and a huge porcelain furnace in the middle of a living room with bookcases on every wall. The windows across the front stretched almost from floor to ceiling.

Helen knew she was imposing on him. He didn't like surprise visitors, and he wouldn't like her plans to stay for the night. She had been there once before, for drinks only, and even that brief stopover had made him uneasy. He had darted to and fro the entire time, retrieving napkins, emptying ice trays, setting out coasters. His dictum was that of many an older spy: Always sleep elsewhere when you take a lover. Your lair is your own.

Yet, here she was, ignoring all that in search of counsel and solace, her footsteps echoing like rim shots as she mounted the cavernous stairwell. At least she hadn't come by taxi, which would have infuriated him—a colleague giving out his address, and then stopping right out front as a convenience to anyone who might be following her.

Baucom answered the door in a bathrobe, cigarette in hand, like Robert Mitchum in cranky PI mode.

"Rough night?"

"The worst." He took her in his arms, ashes crumbling onto her shoulder.

"Light me one of those."

"You'll need more than a smoke, I'm afraid. By sundown you were quite the topic of conversation around a few select people at the office. Word was that you'd strayed off the reservation. Under cover of a sick day, no less."

"About Frieda, you mean? The agent who was killed?"

"That was the story."

"Shit!"

Schnapp must have lied to her. How else would they have found out?

"Fortunately, the damage appears to be limited.

Herrington is not among those in the know. As of now, anyway. But you should have come to me first. About the girl, I mean, and Robert."

"I thought I already had?"

"Only in the vaguest of terms."

"Because you told me to drop it. A helluva lot of help that was. Besides, whatever happened to your 'need to know' philosophy? Shouldn't you just have let me find out all this for myself?"

"If that's how you want to play it, then why are you here at two in the morning? I've got a 7 a.m. flight to Vienna, by the way, so there's that, too."

"Fine. I'll go."

He sighed and took her by the arm.

"Grab a seat on the couch. I've got just the tonic."

She considered plopping onto the easy chair instead, then decided that would be churlish, so she curled up at one end of his creased leather sofa and pulled a blanket across her knees. His suitcase was already packed and standing by the door, with a fold-up umbrella hanging from the handle. She felt bad about keeping him up, but Baucom was her last remaining ally in Berlin, especially if Schnapp had turned on her. Had she misread the cop? Or were her own employers tailing her now?

She stood and went over to a window, where she pulled back the heavy curtain just enough to glance at the sidewalk below. Bare trees that couldn't have hidden anyone. No one was lurking in a doorway, or by the shuttered storefront of a camera shop across the street. Nothing but the shadows of the lampposts, the flutter of fallen leaves along the curb.

"Come away from there."

Helen joined him on the couch. He had returned with two snifters and a dusty bottle of something that, on first sip, revealed itself to be almost as fine and restorative as the brandy Lehmann had brought up from his cellar.

"Thank you."

"You needed it."

She took another swallow and waited a few seconds before speaking again.

"So I suppose I'm 'for the chop,' as our British friends would say."

"I'm not so sure."

"No?"

"You've got more defenders than you realize." The same thing Walters had said, making her wonder who they were talking about. He sniffed at her shoulder and wrinkled his nose. "Good lord, where have you been?"

"To another world and back. A very loud world, and I've returned empty-handed."

"Well, my dear. All I can say is that first thing tomorrow you'd better make a full and penitent confession to that gasbag Herrington, in the clearest possible language."

"Even though I still have a card to play?"

"You're hopelessly overmatched."

"You wouldn't say that if you knew what was on that tape. I know Gilley is well connected, but—"

"Helen!"

He took away her glass and set it on an end table. Then he leaned closer, held her hand, and lowered his voice.

"Listen to me. And listen well, because this will be my final word on the subject of Kevin Gilley." Baucom's tone had turned imperious, a roll of thunder from deep within. No more euphemisms or "my dears" to soften the blow. This was someone preparing to deliver the gospel from on high, a man in a pulpit—just like her goddamn father.

"Okay," she said, not daring to move lest she set off some random noise that would remind her of the creak of a pew, the cough of a parishioner. Baucom nodded solemnly and squeezed her hand, and for a moment or two he seemed to rumble, as if the words were still forming.

"It is not his connections, per se, that make him untouchable. Don't you see that by now? It is the nature of his work, the things he does and arranges for the Agency."

"Sorcery, you said before."

"You're damn right it is! Vanishings and disappearing acts. People who are there one minute, gone the next—with all of it appearing to be oh-so-random or accidental. Seeming acts of fate that are weeks or even months in the making, courtesy of our careful illusionist, Mr. Gilley. And, believe me, he never leaves a single footprint, no trace at all."

"So you're saying that he—"

"Just listen! What I'm saying is that these . . . *activities* of his, and his connections to *them,* and not Gilley himself, are what make any sort of remedy off-limits as far as you're concerned. So it's pointless and maybe even dangerous to try. Do you understand me?"

"But, if—"

"Helen! Do you understand me?"

"Yes."

He released her hand but held her gaze. She still had questions, but knew they would only yield further admonishment in that terrible tone, so she remained silent.

Vanishings and disappearing acts. Meaning killings and assassinations, of the sort that never found their way into the news. Except on those occasions when he had to act hastily, even sloppily. No weeks or months of careful planning had been possible where Anneliese was concerned. Helen thought again of the photo, the girl's mouth agape, her face contorted by the violent twist of her neck, all of it arranged by the man whom she would never be able to touch or harm.

Baucom handed back the glass. He drank with her

for a few quiet moments, letting things subside. Then he put up his feet on an ottoman, threw an arm behind her across the back of the couch, and told her one of his oldest stories. It was from back during the war, when the State Department had sent him to Moscow, an odyssey involving planes, trains, a bicycle, and an oxcart.

She'd heard it before, but he knew that. It was a comfort to see and hear him spinning a yarn, his eyes alit with the wonders of his memory and the amber of the brandy.

"And then, of course, while I was knocking around a year or so later, in banged-up old Budapest after the war, that was when I first got into this racket."

He'd never mentioned that part before, and she wondered if there was a reason he was doing so now.

"With the OSS?" she asked.

"I've never claimed to have worked for them."

"Well, no. But who else was there to work for back then? Army G-2?"

"Have you ever heard me mention them before?"

"Okay. Army CIC, then, the Counterintelligence Corps."

He smiled and shook his head, like they were playing 20 Questions and she was missing by a mile.

"Well, there wasn't anyone else." A pregnant pause. "Was there?"

He looked away and reached for his Gitanes. Then,

after a decent interval that left her stewing over his insolence, he spoke again, his words issuing with uncharacteristic somberness from an oracular cloud of smoke.

"Tell me, my dear. That conversation you heard back at the safe house. The first one, I mean, with all that fraternal mumbo jumbo about various bodies of water. You ever make heads or tails of that?"

"No."

"Well, then. There you go. The answer to your question."

And that was the way Baucom chose to tell her, in his own maddeningly elliptical fashion, that whatever Lewis and the wheezing man had been talking about was somehow connected to his own past, presumably involving a network of spooks she'd never heard of.

"Okaaay," she said slowly, after a contemplative sip of brandy. She took another of his cigarettes and deliberated over what to say. "I *think* I know what you're saying, but why are you telling me now?"

"To help you sort out your priorities. I still don't know what you saw or heard later that day, when the talented Mr. Gilley came calling. What I do know is that the conversation you heard earlier offers—if you're careful, if you're smart—a greater chance at leverage. But even there you must wield your knowledge judiciously. *That's* your road to redemption, my dear, especially if you're disciplined enough to hold your fire on the other front. Then, after a decent interval of time, maybe someday you'll be in a secure enough position to revisit it."

"A decent interval? A young woman is dead. There is no decent interval."

Baucom shook his head.

"I've said all I'm going to say on that subject. I have moved on, and you had better do the same. For you there is only one road forward, and I just drew you the map."

She stewed for a few seconds longer. It rankled, but maybe by following his suggestion she could at least regain her footing.

"Assuming I take this advice, will you help me?"

"Overtly? Out of the question. But there are certain things I can do—and, more to the point, that others can do—as long as you stay the course."

"Such as? And who are the others?"

He frowned and shook his head, and his meaning was clear: Not her business. Need to know. Plus all the other usual operational rules that made perfect sense professionally, but were no less maddening for it.

"I'll have to sleep on it," she said. "Preferably here, and preferably on the couch."

"Take the bed. At this hour I won't be going back to sleep, anyway, and I'm leaving for Tegel at five."

He kissed her on the forehead, which was a shade too fatherly for Helen. She pulled him into an embrace and kissed him on the lips.

"Thank you," she said. "I think."

He smiled ruefully and gestured toward his bedroom. She headed down the hallway, and he did not follow.

17

Helen awakened early in an empty apartment. There was a handwritten note from Baucom on the bedside table. He'd lived overseas for so long that he formed his letters and numbers just as a German would, which made her smile.

> *Helen,*
>   *Please forgive the nature of my departure. Rest assured that it was necessary in all respects.*
>
> *—CB*

His way of apologizing for leaving without saying goodbye, she supposed, although she hadn't wanted him to wake her at such an ungodly hour. She stretched, luxuriating beneath the duvet. Out in the drawing room she could hear the big porcelain furnace steaming like a teakettle, and she crossed the floor barefoot to the bathroom, where she took a long shower before remembering belatedly that she'd be wearing the same smelly clothes from the night before.

Baucom had left his coffeemaker loaded with fresh grounds and a full reservoir of water. She pushed the button and sawed a thick slice from a brown loaf in his bread box. He'd left a carton of yogurt on the counter next to a banana, and she made short work of both.

She wondered whether she should again call in sick. Would that be risking getting fired over the phone? Baucom seemed to think Herrington didn't know what she was up to, and with any luck—and a little help— maybe he'd never find out. But Schnapp must have spilled the beans to somebody. She cursed the detective beneath her breath.

But, without any worthwhile leads on Delacroix, maybe she should follow Baucom's advice and lay low on Gilley for a while. She could instead start poking around on the question of Lewis and the strangely coded conversation. Maybe the two men she'd overheard had strayed out of bounds, and Baucom thought they needed reining in? She could start by looking further into the requisition of the fancy brand of Scotch. Who had requested it, and why? She also wondered who her so-called allies within the Agency must be. These were questions she would only be able to answer by returning to Berlin station.

After deciding on a quick detour to her apartment for a change of clothes, Helen gathered up her things to leave. It was nearly 8 a.m.

Reflexively, she felt in her shoulder bag for the two tapes, which she'd last checked on while riding the subway to Baucom's apartment, but she couldn't find them. She dropped the bag onto the couch and pawed through it a second time. No luck. Growing frantic, she dumped the bag's contents onto the coffee table in a great clatter, and quickly surveyed the wreckage.

The tapes were gone, both of them.

She looked wildly around the room in case Baucom might have gotten them out and then left them sitting in plain view, on a table or chair. Nothing.

Her fury rising, she searched the apartment room by room, checking every closet, every shelf, every drawer, beginning in the kitchen and finishing in the bedroom. Fruitless, as she knew it would be.

"Fuck! What the hell, Clark?"

She then spied Baucom's note on the bedside table and finally saw it for what it had been all along—a confession. Forgive me, for I have sinned against you on behalf of the Agency. He'd stolen the tapes, and by now they were probably in Herrington's hands. He had then disappeared into the ether, leaving only yogurt and a banana in compensation.

"You duplicitous *asshole!*" she shouted, realizing as she said it that, as a spy, she had just paid him a handsome compliment, which prompted her to kick the end of the bed. This caused a pile of books on the bedside table to totter and then tumble to the floor.

"Clean it up yourself, you jerk. Unbelievable!"

She threw her things back into her bag and left in a rage, not even bothering to lock the apartment. Downstairs, she intentionally left the main door ajar, only to have it latch anyway as she rushed down the steps to the street.

"Fuck!" she said, drawing a disapproving glare from a passing shopper. "Fuck all of them!"

She stopped on the sidewalk, momentarily at a loss as to where she should go and what she should do. Home was a bleak prospect, even with clean clothes awaiting. A trip to the office in her agitated state would probably lead to another confrontation with Herrington, which she couldn't afford right now.

Then she thought of Otto Schnapp, conceivably the one person she could scream at without consequence. What more could he do, turn her in twice? She walked around the corner to the nearest phone booth, took out his business card, and dialed the number.

"Schnapp," he answered.

She lit into him in English, and without even saying her name.

"The first thing I want to know, Herr Kojak, is why you lied to me."

"Miss Abell?"

"Yes, it's Miss Abell. And I need an answer."

"Lied to you about what?" He sounded wounded. He was either a good liar or an innocent party.

"You didn't phone my office?"

"Yes, but only the one time, when you were present at my desk. Has something happened to you?"

"And they haven't phoned you again? Or paid another visit?"

"No. Even if they had, why would I want to damage the one person with your organization who might actually help me later? Although I will confess I never really expected to hear from you again. Nothing personal, of course. It is the nature of your job."

"Well, you're hearing from me now, and as long as that's the case I might as well make it worth your while."

She then told him most of the story of what had happened in the safe house between Gilley and Anneliese Kurz, although she only identified Gilley as "one of our senior case officers," and she didn't tell him the address of the house.

"And you believe Mr. Delacroix is working for this senior case officer?"

"Yes."

"You realize I will still not be able to, how do you say it, lift a finger on this matter?"

"Yes. But I figured you were entitled to know."

"I thank you for that."

"And I was thinking that, well, you might at least be able to help me find him. Delacroix, I mean."

"Even if I did so, I would not be able to take him into custody, not unless he did something of further provocation."

"I wouldn't ask you to. All I want is a location, an address. For myself."

"Is that wise for you?"

"Probably not."

There was a long pause. She imagined him frowning, or rubbing a hand through his buzz cut as he thought it over.

"I will do what I can, Miss Abell."

"Thank you."

She felt better now, even though by this time Delacroix had probably left Berlin. At least she'd tried. She'd been a bad employee but a good citizen of the world, which for now would have to be enough. Alone, that's what she was—personally and professionally. Unarmed, too, now that the tapes were gone. The only tangible result of her efforts of the past few days was that Anneliese Kurz was dead. Dead and unmourned, by anyone but Helen and a powerless Berlin policeman.

Where to now, then? A café? A bar, to drink it off? Too easy, too predictable. So was the idea of taking another sick day. She would go to the office. Swing by her apartment first, for more professional-looking clothes that didn't smell like a *Bierstube,* and then she'd waltz into work to sit at her desk, fill out her forms. If allowed she would find some way to seek out more information about the first conversation at the safe house, the one between the wheezing man and the contact named Lewis. Baucom may have betrayed her, but he wouldn't have offered his advice if he hadn't meant it. He had revealed too much of himself in doing so for it to have been an empty gesture.

It was time to tread boldly. If anyone stared, she would stare right back. When Baucom returned to Berlin, she would cut him off at the knees. And if Herrington cut her loose, then so be it. At this point, with a young woman's blood on her hands, she deserved nothing less.

18

They set out for Henson Point at seven the next morning.
On the console between their car seats were foam cups
of coffee and a bag of doughnuts.

Steam rose from a dewy field of soybeans to their left.
Seagulls circled above a county landfill to the right. As
they crossed the Choptank River, the expansion joints
of the bridge thumped beneath the wheels. Across the
water, low-slung white boats patrolled the shallows.
Watermen in ball caps and overalls hauled up crab pots
and trotlines, already well into their workday.

"What happens if we find him?" Anna asked. "Merle,
I mean."

"I'm guessing we won't. Or maybe hoping is the
better word."

"Why?"

"Well, if he did have something to do with this, don't you figure he's gone by now?"

"Unless he's more disturbed than my brother."

"In which case we'll have to tread carefully, try not to stir him up."

"But you think he's gone?"

"If he had a part in it, yeah. But we should keep an open mind on that."

"For seventy-five a day aren't you're supposed to have tunnel vision?"

"Plus expenses. Which reminds me, hand me another doughnut."

"Keep the receipt or you won't get reimbursed. Glazed or powdered?"

"Glazed. Always. Sharpens the mind."

Pulling into the Walmart lot they spotted a group of about twenty men gathered at the far end, where it bordered the lot for a Home Depot that was already doing a brisk trade. Henry stopped and let the engine idle as they watched from a distance.

"See any likely suspects?" he asked.

Most were dark-haired and wore jeans or canvas pants, with work gloves stuffed in their back pockets. Ball caps and paint stains. Stubbly faces. Some held coffee cups, or carried water bottles. Most of them looked Mexican or Central American, plus a few African Americans. Slouching off to one side were a couple of pale outliers, more like Merle's type, although both were too young and too short to fit the Washam foreman's description of a fiftyish guy over six feet tall, and neither fellow had a salt-and-pepper beard. Clear brown eyes, the foreman had also said. Never bloodshot.

"No Merle," Anna said. "That's a good sign, right? I mean, if we think he was involved."

Henry nodded, threw the car into drive, and eased toward the laborers.

The men looked up in interest as the car approached, and crowded closer as it braked to a halt. With the windows down you could hear a low rumble of Spanish, and smell the soap from their morning showers. One fellow, moving with an air of brisk authority, forded the crowd to the window on the driver's side as the others made room. He was tanned and fit, late thirties, and spoke with barely a trace of an accent.

"How many?" he asked.

"We're looking for someone," Henry said.

"Just one? What's the job?"

"It's not a job. We're looking for Merle. He's supposed to be a regular here."

The man turned aside to say something in Spanish to the others. Their postures sagged and they began to drift away.

"Go," he said, waving them forward like a patrolman directing traffic.

"He's an Anglo in his early fifties. Six feet, a beard. You know him?"

"Go! These men need work!" He whistled loudly, and the men cleared a path.

Henry rolled forward.

"Who made him boss?" Anna said.

"I suppose somebody has to, or it would be total chaos. I'm guessing he decides who gets what, then takes a cut for himself."

They pulled into a spot thirty yards away and watched a white panel van approach the workers, who again converged like paparazzi at a Hollywood premiere. The same guy leaned into the window, and emerged holding up three fingers.

"Carlos!" he shouted. "Paquito! José!," pointing as he went. His selections walked toward the back of the van. A door flew open and they climbed inside. The van drove away.

"One-stop shopping," Anna said. "That van was just over at the Home Depot. Bought his supplies then popped over here for a crew."

"And all of it tax-free. Wonder what the boss man would do if we got out and tried to talk to some of them? How's your Spanish?"

"I'm good at food. That's about it."

"Same here." He popped open his door. "I'll try the two Anglos. Take the wheel, and keep the engine running."

Both of the men standing off to the side wore white T-shirts and jeans, and both were smoking. As Henry approached, the heavier one tossed his cigarette to the pavement and pointedly crushed it with a steel-toed boot before turning his back on Henry. The second one wasn't exactly welcoming, but at least he looked Henry in the eye.

"Looking for a guy name Merle. I'm told he's a regular."

"Sorry, man. Can't help you." He kicked at the ground and turned away.

"But you know him, right? Older guy with a beard?"

The first guy, the bigger one, wheeled and spat at Henry's feet.

"Fuck off, man. We need work."

The boss man approached, wagging his finger.

"No, no. I told you. Go!"

"And I told you, we're just looking for somebody."

"Only if you've got jobs. Then we can talk."

"I've got a twenty, how's that for starters?" He held out the greenback, and it took the guy only a second to snatch it.

"You said Merle? Anglo with a beard?"

"That's him."

"Mostly does chicken catching. Hates construction. But he hasn't been here in at least a week, so there you go."

"Know where he lives?"

"No idea. These other guys won't know, either."

"How 'bout if I ask them?"

"They don't speak your language."

"What about these two?" He nodded toward the white guys.

"They know better."

"Than to cross you? How much do you get out of all this?"

He grabbed Henry's forearm and led him back toward the car.

"Out of here! Now!"

By then a white pickup had pulled up to the crowd of laborers. The boss man released Henry's arm and trotted toward the truck. Henry took out his notebook, scribbled his name, address, and cell number and tore out the page. He trotted back over to the white guys, approaching the less hostile one as he folded the scrap of paper and held it forward.

"Fifty bucks to anybody who can help us find Merle, and this is where you can reach me."

He held out the paper. The shorter guy took it and then hesitated, like he was about to toss it aside. Then he stuffed it into the pocket of his jeans.

"Tell the others," Henry said. "You can always take a cut, just like the boss man."

There was a shout from behind.

"You still here, asshole?" The boss man, already trotting back toward him. "Get the fuck out of here!"

"I'm on my way," Henry said. Anna pulled the car alongside him with the passenger door already ajar.

Henry climbed in as a rock flew toward them from out
of the crowd. It sailed across the hood before striking
the asphalt.

"The proverbial shot across our bow," Anna said as
she accelerated away. "He's worse than Simon Legree.
What did you give to the down-and-outer?"

"My name and number. If anything comes of it, we're
in for fifty."

"Fair enough, as long as El Jefe doesn't get a cut."

Back at the Shoats' house the postman had just arrived.
Atop the pile of junk and bills was an Express Mail
envelope for Anna from the Employee Benefits Security
Administration. There was a form to fill out, plus a list
of the documentation she'd need to get the check.

"Want to help me round up some of this stuff?" she
asked. "It's as good a reason as any to start poking
around in all my mom's old junk."

Just what Mitch would've wanted to hear.

"What have you already gone through?"

"Bills, mostly, like this crap. And farm stuff. A
neighbor told me the beans needed spraying in another
week. Now, if I just knew what to spray them with."

"What will you do with this place?"

"Sell it. If Willard was around I might at least keep
the house, find him a caretaker. But I guess the state will
be handling his accommodations from here on out."

Then she turned away and opened the refrigerator, as if to hide behind the door. He listened to her rummaging through bottles and plastic containers. She heaved a sigh of exasperation and emerged holding a head of limp, rotting lettuce.

"Everything in there is turning five shades of green." She kept her face averted as she turned toward the garbage bin beneath the sink. "The fridge, yet another chore. But that can wait. Mom's things should be a lot more interesting."

"You said she had an office?"

"Out in the barn. Her hideaway. The key's right here."

Anna rummaged through a wicker basket by the phone, and pulled out a plastic garage door opener attached to a silver key. He followed her out back into the mid-morning sun, the breeze smelling of manure and insecticide. The barn was a few hundred yards farther on.

"Did *she* call it a hideaway?"

"No. I came home at the end of my first semester and there it was. She liked to come out here whenever things got too hectic, or noisy. Once, during a big snowfall when I was home for Christmas, she spent the better part of a day out here. Her way of dealing with cabin fever, I guess. I think sometimes she just came out here to read and smoke."

"She was a smoker?"

"That's the funny part. She'd supposedly quit years ago, when she was pregnant with me. But whenever she'd come in from the barn I'd smell it on her clothes, and I'm sure Dad did, too. She'd be chewing gum so it wasn't on her breath. Just like a high school kid."

"Your dad never said anything?"

"That wasn't his style. He figured that when she wanted to talk about something she'd let him know." Anna paused as they reached the barn. "She could be that way about a lot of things. Keeping them to herself. Going off on her own."

"Maybe the CIA gave her a taste for secrecy."

"Or maybe a taste for secrecy is why she joined."

Anna clicked the opener. The door lurched open and rose with a clatter, like a big aluminum curtain.

19

To Henry's eye, the barn was more of an oversized garage, housing machinery instead of animals. The floor was a slab of concrete. There was no loft. A mammoth John Deere tractor was parked in the middle, surrounded by all sorts of attachments and equipment. The hideaway, as Anna called it, was in a rear corner with its own door, which Anna opened with the silver key.

It was small, about nine by nine feet, but felt instantly comfy. The walls were painted a soothing green, and there was a custom-made desk along the back with drawers, cabinets, and shelves all built from the same blond wood. A MacBook sat on the desk, folded shut. In the corner was an easy chair with a reading lamp mounted just above it. There was no window, but the lighting was warm and homey. The overall effect was like something you'd see in an IKEA catalog. The only items that seemed out of place were a small space heater and an air-conditioning unit that had been built into the outer wall where a window might have gone.

His eyes were drawn to the highest shelf, where an old bottle half filled with an amber liquid was perched by an empty wineglass.

"Mom's little tipple?" Anna said.

"I doubt it was a regular habit or she wouldn't have put it somewhere she'd need a chair to bring it down."

"The voice of experience?"

He climbed onto the office chair for a closer look. The bottle was dusty, the writing in French.

"Brandy," he said. "A label I've never heard of, probably because it's well out of my price range. But it's definitely got some years on it."

"Only one glass. That's kind of sad."

"I can see why she might want a solitary nip now and then."

"Says the man who drinks alone."

He was about to climb down when he noticed something else pushed toward the back of the shelf, which made it invisible from below—a big, touristy snow globe with a gilded Eiffel Tower inside, mounted on hulking plaster base with "Paris" painted in blue letters.

"Boy is that ever ugly."

"What's ugly?"

"I'll show you." Henry raised up on his tiptoes and stretched out his arm. It was covered in dust.

"God, it weighs a ton. Take a gander."

Anna burst out laughing.

"Wow, that's hideous."

"And broken. Looks like somebody knocked a chunk off the bottom."

"Why would she even keep it?"

"Did your parents go to Paris on their honeymoon?"

Anna snorted. "Are you kidding me? No way. Ocean City, a week at the beach. It was probably all they could afford. Dad's never even been out of the country. Maybe Mom went while she was in Berlin."

He set it back on the shelf, climbed down, and wiped the dust on his pants.

"Did your Dad build all this furniture?"

Anna shook her head.

"She wouldn't let him near the place. She hired some cabinetmaker out of Easton. I always thought it looked like something you'd see in Europe."

"Definitely. Like Germany." The word hung in the air for a moment.

"I guess you'd know. Never been there myself. I still can't imagine Mom being there. In the middle of the Cold War, no less."

"Well, that's why we're here. To find the real Helen Shoat. Should we fire up the Mac, or save the hard stuff for later?"

"Why would the Mac be hard?"

"Password protected, don't you think?"

Anna smiled.

"Mom told me once that she used the same password on pretty much everything. Her phone, her ATM, her library card. She said she could never keep them all straight otherwise. Osprey. Her favorite bird. She was kind of an idiot about those things."

Henry was skeptical but typed it in.

"Damn. You're right. Not exactly a super spy." He wondered if Anna was as disappointed by that as he was. Mitch probably would be, too. Although, for all Henry knew, Mitch was looking for something completely different.

Icons came up across the bottom of the screen for a web browser, a mail account, search engines, photos, a word processor, and a few other items. He clicked open the browser and got more icons—for Google, Netflix, AccuWeather, and a local bank. He checked her browsing history and it came up blank. The search history on Google gave the same result. The photo archive was empty, and her mail basket only had a half dozen unopened items that had come in since the night she was killed. All of them were junk.

"I'm beginning to see why she didn't worry about her password. Either she rarely used this, which I'm doubting, or she was good at covering her tracks." He made a few more clicks. "Look at this. No search histories, no way to follow her footprints. And I'm guessing her emails purged as soon as she read them."

"What about document files?"

Henry clicked some more.

Nothing.

Anna took a crack at it, and they pecked around a while longer, but it was like scrounging for food in an empty kitchen.

"You said she was an idiot about these things? Looks to me more like she got advice from a professional." In fact, based on everything Rodney Bales had once taught him, he knew she had. With a sigh of exasperation, he shut it down.

Next to the desk was a two-drawer filing cabinet. Locked.

"Now we're getting somewhere."

Anna searched for a key inside the top desk drawer, but found only pencils, pushpins, and paper clips.

"We could force it with a crowbar," Henry offered.

"We could. But they're handmade, and I'd hate to damage them. Give me a few minutes in the house. I've got a decent idea where she might have kept it."

Henry waited until he could no longer hear Anna's departing footsteps. Then he reached into a hip pocket and pulled out a slender black case about double the size of a matchbook. Inside was a set of tiny stainless steel tools, like needles with various shapes at the ends. Rodney Bales had given it to Henry as a "graduation gift" from his School of Night, along with a gag gift of disposable surgical gloves, for rummaging through people's garbage.

He quickly selected a tool and slipped it into the keyhole. Within seconds he'd maneuvered open the lock, although he also noticed that the mechanism was already loose, and when he looked closer he saw faint scratches around the keyhole. He pocketed his tool case, reached into the desk drawer for a paper clip, and waited in silence for Anna's return.

"No luck," she said, coming back through the door. "But I did find this, on the top shelf of her closet."

It was a hatbox. Inside was a blond wig, in a layered cut that looked fairly retro.

"What do you think? The master of disguise?"

"You never saw her wearing it?"

"God, no! Anyone around here would've laughed her out of town, my father included."

Then she spotted the file drawer, standing ajar.

"You found the key?"

"Picked the lock," he said, holding aloft the paper clip. No sense letting her know how he'd really done it, or she might start asking some unwelcome questions. "But the lock was already loose. If I had to guess, I'd say it's fifty-fifty somebody beat us to it."

"And then relocked it?"

"To cover their tracks. Wouldn't be that hard for someone who knew what he was doing."

"Especially if he had the right tools," she said, eyeing him closely. "You know, like a paper clip."

Henry shrugged and offered what he hoped was a convincing smile. He then stood aside as she checked inside the drawers. Both were full, front to back, although it quickly became apparent that the contents were mostly routine paperwork—tax returns, car loans, repair invoices, bills for hospital visits (the births of Anna and Willard, Anna's tonsillectomy). The fattest folder held warranties and user manuals for seemingly every household appliance the family had ever owned. There were insurance policies, banking statements, and reports for a small investment account. Most of the bottom drawer was devoted to records from Washam Poultry, along with invoices from agricultural suppliers, seed companies, and other farm business. There were school report cards, copies of standardized test scores, and catalogs from at least a dozen colleges that Anna must have considered applying to at one time or another.

"I can't believe she kept all this," Anna said.

At the back of the top drawer they found a Last Will and Testament for Anna's parents, which silenced them for a moment. Anna flipped past a few pages of boilerplate until reaching the beneficiaries.

"Looks pretty basic. Says that if they were both to die that everything goes to me, et cetera, et cetera . . . As does the guardianship of Willard. Then there are a few pages of 'selected personal effects' for special distribution."

"Like what?"

"Well, let's see." She flipped another page.

"Wow. I had no idea they were such detail freaks. Listen to this: 'To the Rev. Martin Wister, if surviving, the small bronze figurine of a feeding heron.' Probably because he'd complimented the pot roast when they had him over for Sunday dinner, and then maybe said something about liking the heron. Here's something about a few old books for Willard's first teacher in kindergarten, who he adored. It goes on for another two pages. Endless junk and glory from stuff around the house. The lawyer who drew it up is also the executor, so I guess I need to make an appointment."

She closed the folder with a sigh.

"Maybe this is as good as it's going to get," Henry said.

"Maybe." She dug back into the lower drawer. "Ah. Here we go, way in the back. This one's marked 'Personal.'"

She placed the folder on the desk. Out spilled birth certificates, Social Security cards, vaccination records, and expired driver's licenses.

"What's this?" Henry said, picking up a laminated ID. "Your mom got a researcher card at the National Archives."

"The photo's pretty recent."

"These things are good for a year, and this one expires next June, so she must have gotten it a few months ago. What do you think, genealogical research?"

"If it was, it's nothing she's ever mentioned. You think maybe she was looking up her own records? CIA stuff?"

"Doubtful. Agency files stay classified at least fifty years, and the stuff they do release is available online."

"How do you happen to know that?"

"My job on the Hill." Sir Rodney, yet again. "When you're paid to dig into other people's secrets, you end up burrowing into all kinds of archival hidey holes."

He held aloft the ID card.

"What do you think? Something worth following up?"

"Maybe." She rummaged some more. "Look, pictures!"

Anna pulled out a small pile of photos.

"Didn't she keep a family album?"

"Tons. There's a whole shelf of them in the house. Maybe these are special."

A few were mug shots of Anna's mom, like the ones you'd use for passports and visas. There were different sets that appeared to have been taken at different times in her life. Others seemed to have sentimental value—family shots at Christmas, one of both kids with their Easter baskets. There was a shot of Willard and Anna from when Anna must have been about ten. They were barefoot, standing by a picnic table on a summer lawn. She stood behind her brother in a protective pose, hands on his shoulders and her face a bit fierce. Willard grinned goofily. A pink wisp of cotton candy was stuck to the left side of his mouth.

Anna grew quiet and picked up the next one, a shot from a few years later of her family out on the Bay, seated on the windward side of a sailboat. She was eyeing Willard as if he might be about to fall overboard. Seated just behind her was a handsome middle-aged man with sinewy muscles and a farmer's tan.

"Your dad?"

"Yes."

Anna had her mother's eyes, but her father's cheekbones and oval face. His hair color, too. In the photos that had run on TV he'd looked a little haggard, and most of his hair was gone. In this one, with a full head of reddish brown locks tossed by the breeze, he looked downright dashing.

"What was he like?"

"Strong and silent type. Self-made man."

"This wasn't his family's farm?"

"Oh, no. He saved his money, bought small, and kept adding. He even made the chicken houses work. So many people get into that and get in over their heads, because Washam pays you depending on how your birds stack up against everybody else's. But his flocks always rated near the top. He started with almost nothing. His dad was an electrician who kind of bounced from one job to the next. I think his wiring burned down somebody's house."

"Ouch."

"Dad used to tell a pretty funny story about it. He didn't say much, but whenever he told a story he hit all the right notes."

"Brevity is the soul of wit."

"He never wasted a word. He was sneaky smart, and solid. I think that's what must've caught Mom's eye when they met. He was older, by four years. Maybe it's what she needed at the time."

"A CIA gal who ended up in the middle of nowhere, clerking for a real estate lawyer. What was her family like?"

"Holy rollers, from rural North Carolina. Her father was a preacher, Assembly of God. Supposedly he wanted to baptize me, but Mom refused. Dad said that later she changed her mind, but by then he was in the hospital after a massive coronary and he never recovered. I think Dad told me that so I wouldn't make the same mistake, waiting too late to tell them something important."

She looked away. Henry waited for a moment before speaking again.

"Do you remember your mom's parents?"

"Not the preacher. I vaguely remember my maw-maw, but she was kind of a nervous wreck. Not at all the doting type. She kept her distance, especially from Willard. She died a few years after my grandfather, and by then I think she was drinking pretty heavily."

There were a few more photos of Anna and her brother, and she sorted through them quietly. Toward the bottom of the pile was a fading color shot from an old Instamatic, curling at the edges, of a man in his fifties, handsome in a way not unlike Anna's father. He was seated in a café, smiling rakishly but with a hand thrust forward, as if he didn't want his picture taken.

"Who's he?" Henry asked.

"No idea."

Henry looked closer. On the rear wall of the café you could just make out the word HERREN on a sign with an arrow.

"From Germany, I'm guessing. That sign is pointing to the men's room. Interesting."

"A lot of character in that face."

He flipped it over, but there was no writing.

"Look at this one," she said, pulling out the last photo in the pile.

"Is that you on the left?"

"When I was a little girl."

The young Anna stood on the Mall in Washington next to her mom and another woman maybe twenty years older, in a business suit, with the dome of the U.S. Capitol in the background.

"Is that one of your grandmothers?"

"No. No idea *who* it is. I vaguely remember that trip, mostly as a lot of standing in long lines and too much walking. Although now I'm thinking that maybe this woman took us to lunch."

"So they were friends?"

"Maybe. Those smiles don't exactly give you the warm and fuzzies, though, do they?"

"Anything on the back?"

She flipped it. Blank.

The final item in the file was a six-by-nine cream-colored envelope, closed with a metal clasp. Inside were three passports, two blue and one black.

"Whose are these?" Henry said.

"I didn't know Mom and Dad had one, much less Willard, although I guess Mom would have had to have had one, if, well . . ."

"For working in Berlin. Right."

He opened the first blue one, which looked brand-new. It belonged to Anna's mother, and was still valid. She had obtained it only three years earlier.

"Did they take trips overseas?"

"Never, as far as I know. Dad had no desire whatsoever. And Willard would have been such a handful."

They flipped through the back section for visas and entry stamps, but the pages were blank.

"Looks like it's never been used."

"How sad. I wonder why she even got it."

Anna picked up the next one, which was black and said "Diplomatic Passport" on the cover. There was a hole punched in it, meaning it was expired. Helen Marie Abell had obtained it in 1977, the year she joined the CIA. The photo was a revelation, a young woman full of energy and life, a hint of mischief. Henry was thinking how much she looked like Anna, especially in the eyes, when Anna said, "Look at her. She was beautiful."

"She's got your eyes for sure."

"You think?"

"Don't you?"

Anna shrugged. "I never used to like it when people said I took after Mom. Too afraid I'd end up like her, I guess, giving up on herself the way she did."

"You think she gave up?"

"Well, look at the life she'd made. Farm wife with soybeans and chicken houses. Three meals a day to cook, a grown son to take care of. She'd kind of painted herself into a corner."

"And this little room out here was her corner."

The passport's back pages had entry stamps for Germany, plus a few more indicating she had passed through East Germany, probably on her way to and from Berlin. The only other entry stamps were for the United Kingdom.

"Guess she didn't go to Paris, then," Anna said. "Not

exactly the globe-trotting mystery woman if she spent the whole two years in Germany."

"Don't sell it short. Plenty of intrigue to go around in Berlin in those days."

"Secretarial job, that's my guess."

"I doubt they give severance packages to secretaries."

"Unless some boss tried to knock her up."

"In those days that's probably how the boss got promoted."

Anna smiled.

"Hand me the last one."

It, too, was dark blue, but the writing on the cover was a shock.

"*Canadian?*" Anna said. "What the hell?"

They opened it. The younger version of Anna's mom again stared back at them—the same photo as the one from her diplomatic passport, but with one important difference.

"She's blond! Do you think it's the wig?"

Henry took the wig back out of the box.

"Can't be. This one's almost new. But look at the name in the passport."

The Canadian passport had been issued in the name of Elizabeth Waring Hart.

"Holy shit. An alias?"

"I think they're also called cryptonyms."

"So she was undercover?"

"Let's see if she used it."

He flipped through the pages and found entry stamps for France and Germany.

"So here's the Paris connection," she said. "Look at the dates. October of seventy-nine."

"Wasn't that about the time of her severance?"

Anna checked the materials the government had sent her.

"This doesn't add up. The date of her severance is before all of those entry stamps."

"Maybe they kept her on unofficially a while longer. For a last hurrah."

"For something sneaky, you mean?"

"Isn't everything they do sneaky?"

He flipped through the passport again. A scrap of yellowed newsprint fluttered out like a moth. Anna caught it in midair. It was a news story, only four paragraphs. Handwritten across the top was *Tagesspiegel*, with a date from October 1979.

"This is also dated before her severance," Anna said. "Can you translate it?"

She handed it to Henry, who read it quickly but carefully.

"It's about a murder. A young woman, beaten and strangled. A suspected lovers' quarrel in an apartment in Kreuzberg, meaning it was probably a dump. She was only nineteen."

"American?"

"German. Anneliese Kurz."

Anna gasped, a sudden intake of breath that caused Henry to look up.

"You've heard of her?"

"No. But her name, it's . . ."

"It's what?"

"The same as mine. Anneliese. Look, it's even spelled the same, with an 'e' in the middle. It's my first name. I've always hated it."

"Did you ever ask where it came from?"

"She just said it was a name she'd always liked. I hated all my names, but that one especially."

"*All* your names?"

"Anneliese Audra Claire Shoat. Two middle names, for God's sake. Try fitting *that* on your driver's license. I wanted to go by Claire, but she wouldn't let me. She said Anneliese was noble and honorable."

"Noble and honorable enough for your mom to quit her job?"

"And then go traveling around Europe under a false identity, doing God knows what?"

Anna was quiet, thinking it over. Then her eyes widened.

"What? What is it?"

"I just remembered something. A moment with Mom, from the summer before I went off to college. August, it would've been. In 2002."

She stared into space, eyes blazing.

"We were shopping, buying a bunch of clothes for

me at Hecht's. We'd driven all the way across the Bay Bridge so I could go to a mall. I'd just come out of the dressing room in some god-awful thing she made me try on, and she must have seen something over my shoulder that made her stop, because she dropped her shopping bag and just stared. So I turned to look, too, and there was some man in a suit on the other side of the store, standing there with his arms crossed and staring at us. Then he nodded, like he was about to come over to say hello.

"I asked her who it was, but I don't think she even heard me, 'cause then she said, real quiet, 'You see that man over there, honey?'

"I said, 'Yes,' also real quiet, because by then I could tell it was something serious. And when I turned back around to look again he was smirking, and she said, 'I want you to remember his face. If you ever see him again—at school, at home, or *anywhere*—then I want you to let me know right away. Do you understand?'"

"Did you ask who he was?"

Anna nodded.

"Her answer was really vague. 'Somebody Mommy used to know.' That's all she'd say. I remember the words exactly because for a second or two she sounded like she was talking to a ten-year-old. Then she said, 'He's the reason you have your name.'"

"Meaning 'Anneliese'?"

"That's what I assumed, because it was the name

I'd always bugged her about the most. I was in second grade before she let me shorten it to Anna."

"And this guy, what did he do next?"

"Nothing. Next time I turned around he was gone. I never saw him again, and Mom never mentioned it again."

"That's quite a story. Would you remember him if you saw him again?"

"I don't know. It's been, what, twelve years? He was older than Mom, so he might even be dead by now."

"It wasn't this guy, was it?" Henry slid out the photo of the man in the German café.

"No. Or I don't think so. Although maybe I'm saying that 'cause the guy in the picture looks friendly. This other guy had a pretty nasty smile."

"Let's hang on to this," he said, setting aside the clipping with the passports and a few of the photos. They poked around for another half hour, but found nothing of interest. Anna was more subdued, and they said little as she collected the items she needed for the severance check.

"You said the lock was already loose?" she asked, just before closing the file drawer.

"Yeah."

"Makes me wonder what might be missing."

"Maybe nothing."

"We can hope."

As she prepared to lock up, Henry gave the room a final once-over. Then he looked up at the ceiling, and his gaze stayed there.

"What is it?" Anna asked.

"That."

He pointed to an air duct, one foot square, with a louvered metal vent. "If you've got a space heater, and an air-conditioning unit in the wall, what's that for?"

"Fresh air from outside?"

"Maybe. But wouldn't that be mounted on an outer wall?"

Henry pulled over the office chair.

"Hold this steady for me," he said, stepping onto it. He reached into his pocket for his tool kit, thought better of it, and instead retrieved a dime, which he used to unscrew the bolts on the vent cover. He dropped the screws into his shirt pocket and handed the cover to Anna.

"What's up there?"

"Nothing I can see."

He reached inside and felt around. The recess in the ceiling was of the same dimensions as the opening except on one side, where it extended at least a foot farther onto a small shelf above the ceiling. He groped back, reaching as far as he could until he felt the edge of a small envelope.

"Got something."

He grabbed it and slid it free. Then he stepped down

from the chair. The envelope was tiny, only two by three and a half inches, with a clasp closure. On the outside, in cursive lettering in black ink, was the word *Sisterhood*.

"A hideaway within a hideaway," Anna said.

"What do you think?" He handed it to Anna.

"Definitely Mom's handwriting. But 'Sisterhood'? Not her style."

Anna undid the clasp and turned the envelope endwise. Out dropped a small key. There was nothing else. Anna tried it on the file drawers, but it didn't fit.

"It's numbered," she said, taking a closer look. "Like for a post office box."

"Or a safe deposit box."

"Also not her style. And wouldn't there be some kind of bill for it?"

They rechecked the banking records, just in case, but it was all pretty standard, and there were no mysterious service charges.

"It could be for some other bank, so she could hide it from your dad."

"Or in Switzerland," Anna said, which made her giggle. "I'm thinking the post office is more likely."

"What's the Sisterhood, then?"

"Nothing from around here, as far as I know."

"But you've been gone awhile. This could've been something recent. Whatever it is, she went to a lot of trouble to hide it."

Anna turned the key over in her hand.

"We might as well try the post office first. See if the slipper fits."

"After you, Cinderella."

They locked the office and set out for the middle of town.

20

That night, after a fruitless visit to the nearest post office and further scrounging among photo albums and boxes of old junk, Henry was back at his house and had just opened a bottle of beer when his cell phone rang.

It was Mitch.

"Thought you would have checked in by now, Mattick."

"Not much to tell you yet."

"You never know. Run it down for me."

He summarized the visit to Willard and the trip to the labor pool without fielding a single question, but Mitch perked up when Henry got to the part about the items in the barn.

"And she called it a hideaway?"

"It's an office. Farm and financial records, mostly. And there was nothing on her laptop, far as I could tell."

"But she kept the place locked?"

"Well, it's out in the barn, so that makes sense."

"Anything interesting?"

He went over their findings. He figured Mitch would get excited when he mentioned the old news clipping about the dead girl in Berlin, dated so close to the time of Helen Shoat's departure from the CIA, plus the Canadian passport issued in another name. But Mitch just grunted and said "Yeah" a few times, so he kept going.

The news of the researcher's card for the National Archives seemed to intrigue him.

"And that was recent?"

"A couple months ago."

"What was she looking for?"

"No idea. Family history maybe?"

"Find out."

"I'll put it on the list. Anna didn't seem all that interested."

"Who's at the wheel here, you or her?"

"If I steer too sharply, Mitch, she'll get suspicious."

"I get that. But steer it all the same. Find a way."

Mitch also wanted to know more about the photos.

"Who was in them?"

"Family, mostly. Holiday shots and vacations. There was one of an older guy in Germany who looked like he was in a café, probably from her CIA days."

"Got a name?"

"No idea. But he'd be ancient by now, if he's even alive."

"Who else?"

"A shot from a day trip to Washington, Anna and her mom with some friend of hers."

"Friend of Anna's?"

"Of her mom's."

"Describe her."

He did so, quite generically, further piquing Mitch's interest.

"What year would that have been?"

Henry did the math. Anna said she'd been five or six at the time.

"Maybe '89 or '90."

"Send me a copy. Take one with your phone, and shoot it to me on an email."

"Sure. First time I get a chance."

"Just make sure you do. Anything else?"

Henry was about to offer the day's pièce de résistance, their discovery up in the ceiling vent in the envelope marked "Sisterhood." But something about Mitch's attitude had rubbed him the wrong way, and made him uncomfortable. Just this once, Henry figured he'd hold something back, at least for a while. The School of Night had not offered a single lesson on how to avoid or obstruct your handler, much less on how to balance divided loyalties, so he was winging it now.

He wished Anna's mom were here so he could pose the question to her. They could swap a few Berlin stories while they were at it. From the scantiest of findings, he'd begun to feel a kinship with the woman.

"You still there, Mattick?"

"Yeah, just trying to remember if there was anything more that was worthwhile. But that was pretty much it."

"Pretty much? I told you, Henry. I want it all."

"And you'll have it, as soon as I've got it."

"Okay, then. And send that photo ASAP."

"Sure."

He hung up. Then he stared at his phone, feeling more conflicted than ever.

Mitch carried no label, no address, no office number, and no line of authority. Above him lay only the darkness of the unknown, and the further Henry proceeded on Anna's behalf, the more troubled he became by the known.

He turned off his phone. From now on, Henry would be the one who decided when they talked.

21

Helen checked her watch. One full hour at her desk, and not a single visitor. More to the point, Herrington hadn't yet summoned her to his office. Still employed, then, at least for the moment. Even more miraculous was that someone had left her key to the records room right there on her desk, plain as day.

She hadn't yet gotten up the nerve to use it, lest Eileen Walters chase her away. Although, judging by the key's precise placement—squared perfectly to all four sides of her desk—Helen was guessing that the always orderly Walters was the one who'd returned it. It was as if, with the disappearance of the tapes, the entire drama of Helen's apostasy had disappeared as well. From the moment of her arrival her coworkers had offered smiling nods and measured words of welcome, as if to show her the way toward salvation.

Only Baucom could have engineered it. Even an early flight wouldn't have prevented him from passing the word to Herrington that she was no longer a danger. And Baucom would know, since he was the one who had rendered her harmless. With that thought her anger rose anew. She was tempted to pick up where she'd left off, by requesting all files and cables relating to Kevin Gilley.

But where would that get her? Without a job, she would no longer be able to act on Anneliese's behalf. Even so, Helen wasn't yet comfortable with this new status quo. So, she remained at her desk, drearily attending to paperwork.

By noon, she had come up with a way forward. Alas, it was the same course Baucom had recommended. A failure of the imagination, perhaps, and certainly a failure of daring, but it was better than nothing.

Shortly after lunch she filled out a few blank request forms to give to Eileen Walters. One asked for all recent cable traffic involving the cryptonym "Lewis." The other sought further information on the source of the requisition of the Macallan Scotch whisky for the Alt-Moabit safe house.

She walked to the records room and unlocked the door. Walters looked up from her desk, and smiled when Helen handed her the forms. Across the room, a low-level researcher named Duane stopped what he was doing to peer at Helen from across an open file drawer.

"These are both for Langley," Helen said. "Do they look okay to you?"

Walters took a glance.

"Everything looks to be in order," she said, in apparent relief. "I'll send it right on through."

Across the room, a file drawer latched shut. Duane had already lost interest in her. Helen was boring again, a repaired and functioning piece of the daily machinery. It was almost disappointing, and for a moment she was tempted to do something outrageous. But, no. Live to fight another day.

"Thank you," she said.

"And welcome back," Walters replied. "I was so pleased to hear it."

Helen turned to go, then wheeled back around.

"What exactly *did* you hear? I've been wondering all morning, because no one actually told me anything."

Duane again went silent on his side of the room. Walters peered over Helen's shoulder and said, a bit sharply, "Will that be all for now, Duane?"

"Oh. Yes, of course."

He cleared his throat, gathered up a sheaf of folders, and departed. Walters waited for the door to shut behind him.

"No one said much of anything, actually. All I got was a very brief call from Herrington first thing this morning telling me your clearance had been restored, effective immediately. When I asked for written confirmation, he said that would not be forthcoming. I gathered he wasn't all that happy about it. I decided to return the key on my own initiative."

Well, that was something, Helen supposed. No wonder Herrington hadn't shown his face.

"Thank you for telling me."

"As I said, you're not alone in this."

Helen wondered again about the deeper meaning of that remark. Who were her supporters, and how widely were they placed? Maybe Baucom was responsible for that as well. He might even have done her a favor by removing her single greatest temptation for rash action, although she would never forgive him for the way he'd gone about it.

The rest of the workday passed without incident. She saw Herrington only in passing, in the hallway. Expecting him to look away, she trained her eyes on him. Instead, he met her gaze and nodded.

"Miss Abell," he said frostily.

"Hello, sir." She refrained from smiling so he wouldn't think she was gloating, and then felt like a suck-up for having done so.

It confirmed her belief that Detective Otto Schnapp really *had* stayed mum about her, because surely Herrington wouldn't have been so forgiving if he knew she'd been poking around on a police matter. But if that were so, how had Baucom known what she'd been up to? Whatever the case, for now she seemed to be in the clear.

She made one more trip to the records room, only to run into Erickson—Mr. Statler, as Schnapp knew him. He, too, said nothing about Anneliese Kurz or the police. His only inquiry was to again invite her out for a drink. She didn't need long to consider the offer. Sleeping with Erickson, or spending time with him at all, would be more of a punishment than what Baucom had done.

"No, thanks. I'm busy this evening."

"Doing what?"

"Oh, you know. Subversion and malfeasance, the usual."

He laughed a bit nervously and left without a further word.

Sitting in her apartment that night she found herself feeling chastened and proper. She microwaved a box of frozen lasagna, sipped abstemiously from a single glass of wine, and watched a dubbed episode of an American cop show—Kojak, as luck would have it. She changed into PJs, slippers, and a bulky terry-cloth robe before brewing a mug of ginger-lemon tea, which she took to bed along with a self-help book about mother-daughter relationships that a college friend had recommended.

Within half an hour she drowsily concluded that the

book had no relevance at all to her own life. She then thought about her mother for a while, remembering her seated furtively in the woods, nursing her jam jar of cheap vodka, her means of coping with a shuttered life in a small town in the Bible Belt.

"At least I'll never end up like that," she announced to the empty bedroom, just before switching off the light. There were worse things than being on Herrington's shit list, she supposed, just before thinking yet again of Anneliese—her ghastly white face, her horribly twisted neck.

Helen switched the light back on and looked for something to read. It was hours before she could sleep.

22

Arriving at her desk early the following Monday, Helen almost immediately found herself reimmersed in the realm of forbidden pursuits. All it took was a terse interoffice phone call from Eileen Walters.

"I have something for you. See me."

She hung up before Helen could reply.

Helen arrived at her desk a few minutes later. Walters looked around as if to reassure herself they were alone. Then she leaned forward and lowered her voice.

"Was anyone else coming down the hallway?"

"No."

"Good. We need to wrap this up as quickly as possible. If anyone else comes in, we'll stop what we're doing and then finish when they've gone. Understood?"

"Yes."

Walters reached into her desk and pulled out a sealed envelope.

"This arrived this morning by diplomatic pouch, over at the consular office. It was addressed to me but the sealed parcel inside was intended for you."

"By diplomatic pouch?"

"To avoid the usual cable traffic, encrypted or otherwise. A courier brought it by. Herrington knows nothing about it."

Helen flushed with anticipation.

"I told you there were others. Well, this is one of them. I'm a go-between, nothing more."

"Who is it from?"

"She's in records, in Langley, someone I've never met but have often been in touch with. All I can say for sure is that she appears to know a little bit about everything, so I've always gathered that she's fairly senior. Beyond that I can't tell you anything, so please don't ask. And you're not to reply through me. That's also been made clear."

"All right." Helen's palms were tingling as she took the envelope. "Thank you."

"You should probably go now, before someone else sees us talking."

"Of course."

Helen moved breathlessly away from the desk and went out the door. The hallway was still clear. She carried the sealed envelope back to her office, shut the door behind her, and then set it on her desk, as if it might open of its own accord. Taking a few seconds to collect herself, she decided to lock her door. Then she took a letter opener from her desk, tore through the tape, and slid out a single folded sheet of CIA stationery with three typewritten paragraphs.

The sender was someone named Audra Vollmer. Helen had never heard of her. Her letterhead said she was chief of records for the analytical group of the Information Operations Center. An archivist, located at the heart of all Agency records. Like Walters, but to the tenth power. For anyone needing the kind of information Helen had been seeking, Audra Vollmer was a connection of the highest possible value.

Vollmer's inclusion of her name and title was a bit surprising, as was her use of official Agency stationery. For someone who seemed so intent on keeping this communication a secret, she seemed just as determined for Helen to know not only exactly who she was, but also what sort of authority she wielded.

The message was concise and, as Helen soon realized, intriguing:

Your concerns with regard to Robert are not isolated. Information that I believe to be pertinent is available. Toward that end, an asset will soon be in contact.

On housekeeping matters, my perusal of your safe house usage reports and associated records indicates that your secure facility on Sachsenwaldstrasse is overdue for maintenance. In keeping with suggested protocol I have scheduled a resupply of cleaning materials for delivery at approx 19:00.

I will forward instructions for further communication. Do not reply until you have received them. Please destroy this message and envelope upon receipt.—AV

No wonder Vollmer had contacted her this way. She had apparently decided to enlist in Helen's secret war on Kevin Gilley, cryptonym Robert. Somehow—perhaps through Walters—word had reached her of what had happened in Berlin. This told Helen that Gilley had his enemies, Baucom's warning notwithstanding, and that they were interested in joining forces.

It was promising. Check that. It was fantastic.

Helen slowly reread the message. Obviously, a third person was about to become involved—the "asset" to whom Vollmer referred—and apparently that would happen at seven o'clock this evening via some sort of delivery at the safe house on Sachsenwaldstrasse. The message, with its vague reference to "cleaning materials," made her wonder exactly who or what would be arriving at the house. She wondered what Vollmer's prior experience was.

The Sachsenwaldstrasse safe house was on a leafy street in Steglitz, and was the smallest of the four locations Helen administered. It was a third-floor flat in a bland stucco apartment building, near a children's playground that the Agency sometimes used—albeit rarely—for dead drops and brush passes, two ways of handing off messages between agents and case officers.

On the pecking order for hypersensitive meetings it probably ranked last among the four locations. But, due to its tenant's full travel schedule and the neighborhood's high level of pedestrian traffic, it was often the handiest for crash meetings and other emergencies. In that sense, Vollmer had made the perfect choice. She had done her homework. She must have studied the fine print of Helen's reports and lease agreements, copies of which were all on file in Langley.

Helen's first action was to follow Vollmer's final command by shredding the message. Her second was to give notice in writing that she would be making a maintenance visit to the Sachsenwaldstrasse safe house between the hours of six and nine that evening. If Herrington happened to see it, he'd be pleased to see that she had returned to her tame role of Agency domesticity.

She kept to herself as much as possible the rest of the day. Shortly before six, which was well after sunset in Berlin in late October, she departed for Steglitz, first by bus, then by taxi, and then by U-Bahn, a roundabout journey that took forty minutes but left her satisfied that no one had followed her from Berlin station.

She let herself into the safe house and took up a watchful position at the front window, louvering the blinds open at an angle that would allow her to see anyone approaching the building downstairs without being seen from the street. The nearby playground was dark and quiet. Last-minute shoppers headed home with full tote bags. Bicycles came and went.

At two minutes before seven, a mailman in a Deutsche Post uniform approached with a push cart. He reached into his mail bag and carried a stack of envelopes up the steps and into the building. It was certainly a bit late for a real postman to be on duty.

Helen unlocked the door to the stairwell and held it ajar to listen to the sound of the mailman on the floor below as he opened the bank of mailboxes in the entryway. A moment or two later it clanged shut, and she heard him leave. She took the tenant's mailbox key and descended the stairs. Awaiting her was a phone bill, an advertising flyer, and a white envelope that appeared to be a personal letter. All were addressed to the tenant, Gerthe Schneider. But the envelope for the personal letter was neither stamped nor metered, and the name *Vollmer* was scribbled above the return address. Helen took it upstairs. She opened it in the kitchen.

Folded inside was a single sheet of paper with a two-line message. It was typewritten, but not in the same font as the message that had arrived by diplomatic pouch.

The first line read: *Call at 20:00. Use phone box and coins.*

The second line was a phone number with the country code for France. The message was unsigned. Looking closely at the paper and envelope, it was obvious that all the materials had been acquired locally. Whoever Audra Vollmer was, she seemed to have a lot of resources in the field at her disposal. Helen memorized the number, burned the message over the toilet, and then flushed away the ashes.

Helen knew from her own scouting of this location that there was a phone booth only two blocks away. But with extra time on her hands she decided to go farther afield, partly for security and partly to walk off her nervous energy. She stopped in a bar down the street to change some bills for D-Mark coins. She considered buying a shot of whiskey to brace herself, and then thought better of it. Instead she bought a copy of *Tagesspiegel*.

Twenty minutes and many roundabout blocks later, she chose a phone booth on a relatively busy stretch of Bismarckstrasse. There was a fallback location just around the corner in case someone jumped into this one at the appointed hour. Helen checked her watch. Six more minutes. She sat on a nearby bench and opened the newspaper, checking the time obsessively until a minute before eight, when she stepped into the booth.

The overhead light flickered on as she shut the door. She dropped in a handful of coins and punched in the number. A woman answered on the third ring.

"Hello? Is this Berlin?" American accent, someone about her age.

"Yes. Hello." She had given a lot of thought about what to say—not her name, certainly—but she had never come up with an opening line she was comfortable with, so she settled for something fairly bland. "I'm, uh, calling about Robert?"

"Splendid. I have instructions for you." So cool and competent, this one. And a surprisingly friendly tone, which helped put Helen at ease.

"Go ahead. I'm ready."

"First, if I may step out of operational character for a moment, I'd like to say what a relief it is to finally have an ally on this. Thanks for sticking your neck out."

Under other circumstances the woman's approach might have made her suspicious. But Helen detected the same notes of relief and release that she was experiencing, so her answer came naturally.

"Thank you as well. You're right. It's good to have an ally."

"Now, if we could only share a drink afterwards."

They laughed. The tension eased.

"I suppose you're working for the same firm as me."

"Yes. As is the old gal in the home office who got in touch with both of us."

"I've never met her. Have you?"

"No. Not sure I'd want to. Very formidable, even in print. Okay, down to business. A little post office has been set up for you, at some kiddie playground you're supposedly already familiar with?"

"Yes. But that seems sort of chancy. I think some of our people are already using that."

"This spot for us is along the back wall, beneath a corner brick by the drinking fountain. Same place?"

"No. The usual operational location is over by the swing set."

"There you go. Same PO, different box. Here's the protocol. Everything is to be typewritten. We'll use our respective three-letter airport codes for identities, which means TXL for you, for Berlin Tegel. I'm CDG for Paris Charles de Gaulle. And it will be IAD, for Washington Dulles, for our mother ship. Got it?"

"Got it. It occurs to me that here I am trusting you when I don't even know your name."

"Same here."

Not that it would be all that hard figuring out either of their IDs, Helen thought. Neither Berlin nor Paris station was exactly overflowing with females, and she supposed her new ally was as aware of that as she was.

"But we both know hers," Helen said, "or at least I'm assuming you do, right?"

"Yes. I was a little surprised she offered that. Speaks to her position of power, I suppose."

"Or maybe that's wishful thinking on our part. It would be nice to know that someone with real clout was on our side."

"Definitely wishful thinking. Run aground on this and we'll be swimming for the lifeboats. The key is to not run aground. Rely on what you've learned in the field, and I'll do the same."

Helen didn't have the heart to tell her that she had no experience in the field. And if Audra Vollmer had also never been a field operative, then they'd be relying on two pencil pushers. Meaning she had better let her new friend in Paris set the tone.

"Where do we start?"

"IAD briefed me on what you saw. I had a similar sighting. I didn't file anything official, but I did include a version in my weekly report. Nothing came of it, of course. How she heard about it is beyond my clearance."

"Beyond mine, too. I still haven't gotten around to putting anything on paper, and doubt I'd even be allowed to at this point."

"That bad?"

"Oh, yes."

"Nasty piece of work, isn't he?"

"Yes. And the repercussions . . ." Helen's words trailed off. She faltered for a moment. "The girl in question, well . . . I'll fill you in soon enough."

"I'll be waiting."

"These dead drops, presumably you're using one as well?"

"She assigned me a location. Nothing from our usual assortment, as far as I could tell. I changed it to a location more to my liking."

"Who's servicing them?"

"That's also her department. Madame X, as I've come to think of her. A very together lady. Or she'd better be. An hour ago I was starting to panic, wondering if we were both fools for trusting her. Then it occurred to me that maybe she's the fool, for trusting us. All right, then. More to come. Send something tonight, if you can. Madame X promises pickup will be speedy and delivery prompt. She also wanted you to know that she's at the hub of a lot of useful information, so if you have any requests then send them immediately. But to her only, and only through our channels."

"Perfect."

"I thought so, too. Then I started wondering, what happens if that channel goes silent?"

"The one to the home office, you mean?"

"Yes. She'll have more at stake if things begin to fall apart. Which is why I think we need a contingency. One other channel, just between us, if you're game."

Helen liked the idea. And then she didn't. This woman was friendly, but maybe it was part of a ruse, an effort to make her expose herself more than she should.

"Do you mind if I think about that?"

"I'm sorry. I've spooked you."

Something in her readiness to retreat restored Helen's trust. And she had a point. Pinning all their hopes and logistics on a single network, run by a single friend in Langley, left few alternatives if that channel was cut.

"No, you're right. What would you suggest?"

"Nothing fancy. Just remember this number. If you're ever in a jam, and the usual channel isn't an option, ring me at the same time as today. Twenty hours. I'll make this phone box a regular stop at that hour until you tell me to stand down. How does that sound?"

"Perfect."

"Great. Are we done, then?"

"Yes."

"Until the next time, then. Goodbye."

Helen hung up, and almost immediately felt lonely and isolated. The only sound was the buzz of the overhead light. She popped the door ajar to shut it off, and to allow for a moment of privacy in the dark before she ventured back into the streets. She smiled, feeling triumphant, a small victory to build on. Then she scanned her surroundings. For a brief panicky moment she half expected watchers to emerge from a listening van, or from the hedgerow across the street.

But when she stepped from the phone booth, no one approached. No one stopped to stare, or to snap her photo. She walked briskly back toward the safe house, and upon arrival she got right down to business, typing out a message to IAD, putting it into an envelope, and then locking the house behind her. Walking to the playground, she carefully checked her flanks and then posted the message to the dead drop, where the brick came loose easily and then fit snugly back into place.

She took a roundabout route home to shake any surveillance, and by the time she reached her apartment she had concluded that with the help of her new allies she might actually be able to do this. Step by step, and ever so carefully, she could succeed. They all could.

23

The dividends were immediate. By the following night, a fresh message was waiting for Helen behind the brick in the playground. She pried it loose after dark, when the only possible witness was an old drunk, a neighborhood regular she'd noticed on enough previous visits to have him vetted, just in case.

She didn't open it until reaching her apartment. It was typed on half a sheet of paper, double-folded, and was a reply to her request the night before to Audra Vollmer for more information about Kathrin, the cryptonym for the agent who'd warned Anneliese Kurz about Gilley.

Magda Elisabeth Henkel (Kathrin), DOB July 8, 1959. Activated: May 12, 1978. Reports on leftist student groups. Case officer: Rick Ford (Linden)

Rick Ford was fairly low on the pecking order of operatives at Berlin station, meaning Kathrin was probably a low-priority agent. If so, then why would she have ever worked with Gilley, the so-called high priest of the Agency's darkest arts? From the way Baucom described him, Gilley was a professional of such exacting standards that he presumably had access to the most experienced and competent personnel the Agency could offer. Yet, from what Helen had seen he had recently employed two of their most inexperienced agents.

Pasted below Kathrin's name was a thumbnail photostat mug shot—narrow face, large eyes, dark spiky hair—next to a telephone number and an address in Kreuzberg. Helen decided to again use a phone booth. This time she chose one four blocks from her apartment.

A young woman answered in a somewhat shy tone, but in the German fashion, by stating her last name.

"Henkel."

"I am a friend of Mr. Linden. He suggested that we meet."

"We should not speak of this here."

"I understand, but this is somewhat urgent. We need to . . . to adjust your protocols."

"My what?"

"Your protocols."

It was bullshit, of course, but during her time in Berlin Helen had learned that if there was one sure way to appeal to a German's sense of duty, even one who ran with a crowd as supposedly countercultural as Kathrin's, it was by citing some sort of bureaucratic necessity.

The young woman sighed.

"All right, then. Where, and at what hour?"

Helen had previously decided that it would be best to meet at the scene of the original crime. She had already put in the proper forms to reserve a block of time, just in case.

"Alt-Moabit, you know this location?"

"Yes."

"Seven tomorrow night, then."

"Okay."

Helen placed her fingertips against the chilly windowpane of the darkened room as she peered into the night. Outside, snowflakes fell from the late-October sky, drifting like ash through the beam of a street lamp.

She spotted Kathrin approaching from around the corner, the young woman's gestures giving her away—looking over her shoulder, quickening her pace, a bad actor trying too hard. The opposite of how an agent should deport herself on the way to a rendezvous. No wonder she'd been farmed out to Rick Ford, and even he probably thought of her as a throwaway. Helen moved away from the window and headed downstairs.

The day had passed with agonizing slowness. Word had filtered through the office that Baucom was back in town, but he hadn't yet been in touch. She supposed he was feeling awkward about his thievery. Just as well. If Helen were to meet him now, he'd probably sense within minutes that she was up to something.

He might also ask about her progress in investigating Lewis and the wheezing man, and she had none to report. Her query for information on recent cable traffic involving "Lewis" had been returned with a terse, unsigned note informing her that such information was beyond her clearance. There was no longer any record of the requisition of the Macallan Scotch, so that was another dead end.

She had arrived at the safe house an hour ahead of schedule to narrow her margin of error. She spent most of the extra time nervously tidying up. She also searched every room, half convinced she would discover someone in stocking feet preparing to turn the tables on her, the tape recorder already running.

When she checked the liquor cabinet, she would have sworn that the Macallan was an inch or two lower than before, although her own records said there had been no official activity in the house since her last visit.

Helen considered pouring some of the Scotch for herself before opting for the vodka, which made her think of her mother. In the fridge she found a carton of orange juice, which she poured atop the vodka. Her glass was empty, rinsed and drying on the draining board by the time Helen went upstairs to watch for Kathrin. She was standing by the front door for the first tentative knock.

"You're Kathrin," she said, recognizing her from the photo—a frightened and ghostly face. A girl, really, cut from the same mold as Anneliese, in clothes that she might have picked up from a charity table at a homeless shelter.

"Yes."

"I'm Betty." Helen had settled on her mother's name for her cryptonym, since Herrington had never felt the need to assign her one. Having never run an agent before, she wasn't sure how to begin, although at least her German was good.

"Anything to drink?"

"No, please."

Kathrin lit a cigarette and sat on the couch, the very one where Gilley had assaulted Anneliese a few nights ago. The thought was enough to keep Helen from sitting down. Instead she began pacing slowly back and forth. Kathrin spoke first.

"You said something about my protocols?"

"Yes." Helen stopped and looked her in the eye. "That was for cover. What I really want to do is talk to you about Robert."

Kathrin emphatically shook her head.

"I cannot speak with you about that."

"Kathrin, it's all right."

"I cannot speak with you!"

Helen sat next to her on the couch. Kathrin looked away until Helen touched her forearm.

"The first thing you should know is that I am not a friend of Robert's. The second is that your case officer, Mr. Linden, does not know of this meeting, nor should you ever tell him. But I am operating under the highest authority on behalf of Mr. Linden's firm, and I will do what I can to keep you safe."

A couple of whoppers, but she needed to know Kathrin's story. Kathrin looked away from her, drew a deep breath, and spoke toward the far wall.

"If I speak with you of Robert, then you must supply me with an escape and evasion kit."

"With a *what*?"

"A kit for leaving this place, with a new identity. Linden told me he had one for himself. For use in an emergency, he said. A passport from another country, and with another name. He said you have people who make these things for you. Cobblers, he called them."

Good lord. Linden had been showing off, puffing up his importance to this low-level agent, probably just to impress her, and in the process he'd revealed matters he should've kept to himself. It made her wonder what else he might have said.

"Even if we could do that for you, Kathrin, it would take days, maybe weeks."

"Then I cannot speak. I will not."

"There are other ways of keeping you safe."

Were there? Not really. Not when you were up against someone with the purported skills of a Kevin Gilley. The only safe way forward was to keep this meeting a secret, so Helen would do her damnedest to ensure that.

"I'm not asking just for me, Kathrin. This is for Anneliese. Frieda, I mean. You'll be doing this for her."

"Why for Frieda?" Kathrin's brow furrowed. "Has something happened to Frieda?"

"Have you truly not heard?" The girl shook her head. "It was in the newspaper, just the other day."

Kathrin's eyes widened at the mention of the newspaper. Helen gently took her hand.

"I'm so sorry to tell you this, but she was killed."

Kathrin pushed her away. She looked down at the floor, gasping as if she'd just broken the surface from a deep dive into the ocean.

"Was it him?" she said, looking up suddenly. "Was it Robert?"

"The witness described someone else." True, but misleading, and she hated herself for the deception.

"But does this not mean that Robert's people . . . ? Well, you know what I am asking."

"I do. And that is why you must speak with me. So that this will not happen again. When I last saw Frieda, she said that you had warned her. About Robert, I mean."

Kathrin lowered her head and nodded slowly.

"She said you had told her not to be alone with him. Had he tried something with you? Sexually, I mean."

Kathrin nodded again, still with her head lowered. Then she spoke, barely audible.

"In a friend's apartment, where he had arranged to meet me. He had business to do, a job to discuss, and that is what we did. Then, when that part was done . . ." She hesitated.

"It's all right. I am quite aware of what he's like."

"He began trying to remove my clothes. I stood. I tried to push him away. But, well, he is very strong. He said he would report me, would tell the others."

"The others?"

"His employer. *Our* employer. And the student groups, the ones I was reporting on. He would tell them all and then, well . . ." She shrugged. "So what could I do?"

"I understand."

"And then . . ." Kathrin looked away.

"And then what, Kathrin? What did he do?"

"Do I really need to say it? Do I really need to describe it, moment by moment? It happened for five minutes, maybe longer, and even then he kept laying on top of me, sweating on me, breathing into my face. And smiling, always smiling, like he thought that would make everything okay for me."

Then she seemed to deflate, folding in on herself at

the end of the couch. Kathrin pulled up her knees and clasped them with her arms. Helen placed a hand on her back but Kathrin pushed it away.

"Why were you meeting him, Kathrin? Had Linden arranged it?"

"No, no. Robert called on the telephone. He said he had an operation to run, one that Linden should never be told about, the same as you said tonight. I was to help arrange it."

"What did he want you to do?"

"A small thing. I was to obtain two keys. One to a garage, and one to a car inside of it. I was to steal them from a man's coat pocket, a man who I would meet in a bar. I only had to keep them long enough to make wax impressions. The garage key would be red, he told me. The car key would be for a BMW."

"Did Robert arrange the meeting at the bar?"

"No. The target was a regular at this bar on Tuesdays. We were to go there because Robert said that we were both 'his type,' and that if we approached him, he would want to talk with us."

"We?"

"Frieda and I."

"You were working together?"

"Yes. But only this one time. I had not met her before. I did not know her. You said her real name was Anneliese?"

"Yes. Anneliese Kurz."

She nodded, but her expression did not change.

"So the two of you went to the bar, then, on a Tuesday night?"

"Yes."

"Together, or did you meet her there?"

"Together. Someone picked us up in a van, on two different corners."

"Robert?"

"No. Someone else."

"Who?"

"He did not say his name. He only said that he was working with Robert."

"Why two of you?"

"To distract this man. Whichever one of us was closest to his coat would reach in for the keys and then make the impression, for copying, while the other one kept his attention."

"Had you ever done anything like this before?"

She shrugged and lowered her head.

"It's all right, Kathrin, you can tell me."

"When I was younger."

"Shoplifting?"

"Yes."

"And you were caught, too, I'm guessing, which is how Robert would've known."

"Yes, I was caught once. In my hometown in Sachsen-Anhalt, when I was seventeen. It is why I ran away to Berlin."

Another waif on the run from family and boredom, alone and especially vulnerable, like Anneliese.

"Did the plan work? Did one of you get this man's keys?"

"Frieda took them. It was easy. She didn't even have to sneak it. We just waited until he went to the men's room, and he left his coat on the bar stool. We pressed both keys into the wax and were done. She put the key ring back into his coat pocket well before he returned."

"Do you know why Robert wanted them?"

She shook her head.

"How did you know who the target would be?"

"Robert had showed me a photo."

"Did he tell you the man's name?"

"No, but the man told us himself. It was Werner. Werner something, maybe with a 'G.' Gernhardt or Gernholz, I cannot remember. But he was wealthy, or dressed that way. And, well, he drove a BMW. Or at least that was one of his keys. He liked to brag about his work."

"What did he do?"

"Something political, for the SPD."

"The Social Democrats?"

"Yes, a policy job, he said. He tried to make us believe he was very important, but Frieda and I had never seen him on television."

"Did you leave with him?"

"No. That was not the plan. We were only to imprint

the keys, and then deliver the wax kit to the van."

"And that was the night when you warned Frieda about Robert?"

"Yes, as we were leaving the bar. She had told me she would be meeting him soon."

"What for?"

"She did not know. But she said it would be at a safe house. This one."

"The man who was working for Robert, the one in the van, what did he look like?"

"He was younger, more like one of us."

"Like you and Frieda, you mean?"

"Yes. Longer hair, a leather jacket, like someone you'd meet in the clubs."

"A German?"

"No. American. Or his accent was American."

Helen felt a cold spot at the base of her stomach.

"Long hair, you said, and a leather jacket?"

"Yes."

"Black leather? With silver studs up the sleeves?"

"How do you know this?"

"And his hair. Black? Stringy?"

"Yes. You know this man?"

"Possibly."

Delacroix again. It seemed obvious. No wonder Erickson had asked Detective Schnapp to back off.

"Have you seen him since then?"

"No."

"But you would recognize him if you did?"

"Yes."

"If you do see him, Kathrin, you must contact me right away. Not later, but right away, do you understand?"

"Yes."

"But do not approach him, do not try to follow him."

Kathrin grew very still.

"Did this man kill Frieda?"

"I don't know. He might have."

She put a hand to her mouth.

"Kathrin, listen to me. I'm going to help you leave here safely, all right?"

She nodded slowly.

"There is a back way out of this house. Did Linden ever show you how to use it?"

Kathrin shook her head.

"I'll show you now. Come with me, let's get you going, and I'll watch to make sure you're away safely and securely, all right?"

They stood, Kathrin a bit unsteadily. Helen took her gently by the shoulders and steered her through the kitchen to the back door, where she pulled back the curtains. It was no longer snowing. The clouds had thinned and were racing across the sky, lit by a half-moon. The spindly limbs of the plum tree waved in a cold breeze.

"At the back of the garden there is a steel gate into an alley. It's locked, so you'll need to punch in a key code, okay?"

"Okay." Her body was rigid, but she was paying close attention.

Helen told her the numbers and had Kathrin repeat them back.

"Very good. Would you like something to drink first?"

"No. I only wish to leave."

Kathrin had never bothered to take off her shabby overcoat, but it was hanging open in the front. Helen helped her button it up, feeling like a mom on the first day of school, sending her child out into the unknown. She clasped the girl by the shoulders and looked into her face.

"When you reach the alley, turn right."

Kathrin nodded.

"That will take you to Alt-Moabit, where there should be plenty of people. Turn left when you get there. Don't linger, don't look over your shoulder. Act as if you know exactly where you're going and as if you don't have a care in the world. And be in touch if you have to be. You have my number, yes?"

"Yes." Barely audible. She was trembling now.

"It's going to be all right, Kathrin. And thank you. Because of your help, I think we can stop Robert. Okay, it's time to get going."

Helen shut off the light in the kitchen and opened the back door. Kathrin stepped carefully down into the garden. Helen watched through a gap in the curtains as the girl crossed the narrow lawn in the stilted motions of someone traversing a cemetery at midnight. Not a promising start, but what could you do? When she reached the keypad it took her two tries to open the gate. She stepped into the alley, headed right, and disappeared into the shadows.

Helen relocked the door and swallowed hard. She poured another vodka, and this time didn't bother to add orange juice. Half an hour later, having steadied her nerves and reassured herself that she was doing the right thing, she headed home. Checking behind her on the way to the U-Bahn station, she noticed nothing out of the ordinary. No black leather jackets with studs up the sleeves. No young men with long, stringy hair.

Yet, the moment she entered her apartment, the buzzer sounded from the door downstairs, meaning that someone had either been waiting nearby or had followed her home. Too close for comfort. She reluctantly pressed the button for the speaker.

"Who is it?"

"Otto Schnapp."

She sighed in relief and buzzed him in. His footsteps echoed up the stairwell in a rhythm that was steady and precise, almost military. Or did she think that only because he was a German cop with a buzz cut?

He entered frowning, and stopped only a few feet inside the door.

"Can I get you something? Coffee maybe?"

"*Nein.* No, thank you. I have information for you, then I must go."

Helen nodded, a bit breathless. Finally, some help.

"Kurt Delacroix. I have found him."

She reached instinctively for her handbag to pull out a notebook and a pen.

"Yes?"

"I have no address for you."

"But—"

"I know only his present whereabouts." Schnapp pointed at her window, with its view of the street below. "He is down there, a block away. Or was when I last saw him. He was following you, directly from the U-Bahn station at Dahlem-Dorf."

Helen's pen fell from her hands and clattered on the bare wood floor.

"You're sure it was him?"

Schnapp nodded.

"He is dressed differently tonight. A green army coat with a torn collar. His hair is gathered in a horse tail—"

"Ponytail?"

"Yes, ponytail, and it is pushed beneath a woolen cap. But it is him. It is Delacroix. Of this I am quite sure."

"Did he see you?"

Schnapp shook his head.

"He did not bother to check behind him. I think this is because he was so intent upon watching you."

"I see."

She glanced down at the pen on the floor. She had no idea what to say next.

"I am sorry. But I thought that you should know."

"Yes, of course. Thank you. Do you mind if I sit down?"

Her cautious optimism from half an hour earlier was gone. In all her worrying on Kathrin's behalf, she had neglected to worry about herself. A mistake. A grave and serious mistake.

24

Henry and Anna drove away from the third post office they'd visited that morning. Like Cinderella's slipper, the Sisterhood key was proving to be a tough fit.

"I'm beginning to think it's not for a post office box," Anna said.

"Well, we know it's not a box at a bank. We'd have found something by now in her records. Or maybe the key's obsolete, for something she either lost track of or didn't renew."

"If you hid a secret key in the ceiling, would you lose track of what it fits?"

"Okay. Then maybe I'm just tired."

"Or having a doughnut crash."

"You know, before we met I was eating yogurt and fruit for breakfast."

"On the morning I hired you, weren't you frying eggs and bacon?"

"I didn't say it was yogurt *every* day"

Anna's cell phone chirped in her handbag. She glanced at the number.

"Sorry, I need to take this."

Henry reached over to turn down the radio for her, with the welcome side effect that he could hear every word. It was apparent right away that the call was about her job, and for the next few minutes Anna spoke about various children. Tywon would need more meds soon. Holly had to be kept away from her uncle at all costs. Darren was a handful, yes, but with coaxing and the right treatment could be a dreamboat, too. She spoke with an undertone of affection.

The last minute or so of the conversation returned to the topic of logistics for Princess, the itinerant cat. Then she signed off, reached for the radio and turned the music back up.

"Another Princess update?"

"You know, it just occurred to me why I've never wanted a child of my own. What if, after the first three months, I decided to give him back? Too many parents like that already, don't you think?"

"I doubt you'd be that way. Like mother, like daughter, you said that the other day, and she never gave up on you or Willard."

"True. And it couldn't have been easy for her. Maybe that's what really worries me—having another Willard because of something in my genes."

Henry was trying to come up with a tactful answer to that when her phone chirped again.

"Shit," she said, eyeing the number. "I need to take this one, too."

This time she turned in her seat to face the passenger window. Henry reached again to turn down the car radio, but she shook her head. Obviously she wanted some privacy, so he acted as if he wasn't the least bit interested even as he tried to listen in. She sounded annoyed, and her body language came across as one big frown. Briefly she raised her voice, and for a few seconds he heard every word.

"You know, we've been over this before. And if you can't see why this is a bad time to go over it again, well . . ." A pause, while Anna nodded rapidly. "I know, but you're just going to have to be patient . . . Okay, then . . . Right. Bye." Followed by a muttered "Jesus!" as she dropped the phone back into her bag.

"Sorry you had to hear that," she said.

He let that hang in the air for a moment before following up.

"Some guy?"

"Does that have any bearing on our work?"

"No."

"Then it's really none of your business."

"Sorry."

"No need to apologize. It's your job to ask questions. Just don't expect me to answer all of them." An awkward pause, ten seconds that felt more like sixty. "But yes, I am involved with someone. I guess you might say he and his needs are on probation. Until I'm done with all of this. Or until I've got my head back on straight, whichever comes first. What about you?"

"Me?"

"Involved or not?"

"Not."

She nodded as if it was exactly the answer she'd expected.

"The kind of work I was doing didn't leave much room for forming attachments."

"Or maybe that's how you were already inclined, and the job was the perfect excuse for staying unattached."

It was close enough to the truth to make him uncomfortable.

"How about pulling into that store up ahead for a cigarette break," she said. "I keep telling myself I'm buying my last pack, then the minute I run out I want another one."

Henry flipped on the blinker, happy for the opportunity to change the subject.

He followed her into the convenience store, which was chock-full of the usual junk and glory. Anna went straight to the checkout counter, where a fairly jolly-looking fellow with a potbelly and a plaid flannel shirt eyed her closely as she scanned the tobacco offerings along the back wall. Henry rummaged among the cheese curls and potato chips.

"Pack of Newports," Anna said.

She was scowling, still in a bad mood after the phone call, and the attentive clerk noticed.

"Smile!" he said, all cheerful and chirpy.

Anna leveled him with a glare.

"That'll be seven seventy-five," he said meekly.

Poor, clueless fellow, Henry thought, having instantly known the remark would piss her off. His previous job had forced him to spend more time than he would've liked on social media, searching for behavioral clues among the staffers who were the subjects of his investigation. Most of it was crap—snapshots of meals, or of children and pets. The only worthy takeaway had come from studying the postings of various women and their like-minded friends, a witty commentary with a subterranean lava flow of anger directed against the male of the species. Not him, or anyone else in particular, but the general cluelessness and violence of his gender.

At first he was bewildered, a little stung. Had they always felt this way? He then began to view it from a more analytical and, finally, more sympathetic frame of mind, and he was soon thinking wryly of himself as a fly on the wall in the Facebook equivalent of a Maoist reeducation center. Even from that jaded perspective he couldn't help but be influenced.

Henry thought of all that as he watched Anna snatch up the cigarettes and head out the door. In lieu of advice—*Hey, buddy, they hate it when you tell them to smile*—he bought a cup of scorched coffee and left a one-dollar tip. He said little for the rest of the drive.

Back at the Shoat house, where Anna was hoping to plow through the last two boxes in her mother's closet, the message machine was blinking. When Anna pressed the button, the voice of Stu Wilgus filled the kitchen.

"Anna? Sorry to bother you, but I figured you'd want to hear this. Ran into Cilla Miley this morning over at the grocery store, a friend of your mom's from way back, and she tells me she saw Willard a few days before . . . before all the unpleasantness, walking across the far end of one of their fields with his rifle next to some other fellow who, as far as she could tell, wasn't even armed and definitely wasn't your dad. Bearded fellow, she said. So, maybe they were hunting and maybe they weren't, but she was kind of surprised to see him way over on their side of the county, since they live probably ten, fifteen minutes from your place. So, anyhow, you might want to touch base with her. That's Cilla and Stan Miley, right off of Showalter Road. Hope all is well with you, and take care of yourself."

The message ended. Anna paused the machine and looked at Henry.

"Bearded," she said. "Like our pal Merle."

"You know this Cilla Miley?"

"From years ago. Did some charity work with Mom, and we'd have dinner over there sometimes, but it's been ages. Shit."

"What?"

She was looking at her cell phone.

"I also missed a call on my cell. It's from the county cops. They left a voicemail."

She put it on speaker so he could listen. It was a Captain Saunders, who'd called only a half hour earlier, probably while they'd been in the convenience store:

"Just thought you'd want to know, ma'am, that the forensic report is in, plus the last of the postmortem results from the state medical examiner. You'd wanted to know when they were available and you might want to come in for a look before we release them to the media."

"You got that right," Anna said, as the message ended. "Let's go."

The police, to their credit, were solicitous and gentle, and didn't seem to mind she'd brought along her own amateur detective. Captain Saunders, an older guy with a brush cut and an outdoorsman's tan, led them to an interview room where the reports were already stacked on a table next to a water bottle.

"I can make copies, if you'd like."

"Thank you," Anna said.

"Can I get you any coffee?"

"No, thanks."

He paused at the doorway of the interview room.

"I knew your dad, back in the day. Not long after high school. Good man. It was a terrible thing."

"Yes it was. About these reports, have you looked at them?"

"Yes, ma'am. About an hour ago."

"Anything stand out?"

"Well, that footprint, the one in the mudroom at the back of the house—you'll see it in there—that's the only item that was a little curious, but I wouldn't lose sleep over it. Probably one of the first responders."

"Show me."

He grimaced a bit, like he wished he hadn't said anything. But he dutifully picked up the report and flipped to the third page.

"Down toward the bottom," he said, pointing. "There's a photograph of it, too. Although I wouldn't recommend you look at all those pictures. They're kind of, well . . ."

"I understand. This says the print is from a Vibram sole?"

"A partial, from the heel. Yes, ma'am."

"So, like a hiking boot?"

"Or some kind of work boot. Those would be your possibilities."

"Is that normally what the EMTs wear?"

Captain Saunders shrugged.

"At that hour of the day I'm guessing they throw on whatever's handy. The call came in around six a.m., I believe. I'll get those copies for you. That's the one for the press room that you're looking at, by the way. Fair warning, we'll probably release it around seven this evening. Might want to keep the phone off the hook tonight."

"Thanks."

"And could we also see the photos?" Henry asked. "Or at least the one of the boot print."

"They're digitized. I'll pull it up for you on my desktop." He looked down at the floor, shuffling his feet. "Just the one, if you like. To minimize your, uh, your exposure."

"Yes," Anna said quickly. "Thank you."

"Just let me know when you're ready, and I'll escort you back to my desk."

He left like he couldn't get out of there fast enough.

As Henry expected, the crime scene report made for gruesome reading. There were explanations of patterns of splattered blood on the bed, the ceiling, and the wall. There was a vivid description of Willard's face when he was found on the porch that mentioned numerous red speckles and traces of something darker and more gruesome. Anna stared at the wording for about ten seconds before abruptly setting the page aside.

On the next page, someone had mapped out Willard's movements after the shootings, based on his bloody footprints, and also on the dew, dirt, and blood that ended up on his trousers and bare feet. Anna shook her head and set it aside, but Henry picked up the page.

Accompanying the text was a drawing of Willard's entire journey, all the way out to the highway sign and back. It put Henry out there again on the dewy shoulder in the stillness before dawn, and he again wondered what idea or motivation must have sent Willard on his single-minded errand.

Of further interest to Henry was the investigator's conclusion that Willard hadn't simply curled up on the porch when he returned home. The trail of footprints showed that he had instead walked back to his parents' bedroom, as if to check on his mother and father. He'd stopped by the bed and then turned around, bypassing his own room to go out to the front porch, where he left the door open and fell asleep.

When they were done, Anna flipped the pages back to the mention of the partial boot print. The print was made with her mother's blood, meaning that whoever made it had either been in the bedroom or had stepped on one of Willard's tracks.

"If it was a first responder, why weren't there more of them?" Anna said. "It's almost like somebody was being real careful not to leave a trace and then made one false step right before he left the house."

"It was pointed toward the door?"

She nodded.

"And it was the only one," she said. "From the heel. Like somebody was walking on clean tiptoes and lost his balance."

"I can see where a first responder might do that, trying to not contaminate the scene."

"Okay. But if he was that careful, wouldn't he have put on those plastic overshoes they use?"

"I don't know. I'm not familiar with their procedures in this county. Maybe you should ask a real detective."

"Maybe I will."

For the first time she sounded a bit disappointed in him, and he was surprised by how much it bothered him.

"Let me do the asking," he said. "Earn my keep."

"Fine. Let's go see the photo. Then we can read the medical examiner's report."

They tracked down Captain Saunders, who cleared his throat and turned to his keyboard.

"Maybe you should stand over there until I find the right one."

Anna nodded stoically.

He clicked around for a few seconds, his mouth in a tight line. The brightness of the screen flashed in his eyes as he scrolled from image to image.

"Here we go. I'll get out of your way. Click on print if you want a copy. When you're done, just X-out in the upper right corner."

He retreated to the coffeemaker as Anna settled into his chair. Henry watched from over her shoulder.

The photo took up most of the screen. It was a heel print, just as advertised, with the waffle pattern you'd expect from a Vibram sole. By the time the photo had been snapped the blood had already turned brown. Anna clicked for a copy, and they heard the printer hum to life across the room.

She hit a keystroke by mistake, and before Henry could stop her she'd advanced to the next photo, a garish shot of her parents sprawled in the bed, shot to pieces like in a gangland movie, blood spattered across the sheets and headboard. Her father's head was practically exploded, and her mother's eyes were bulging half out of their sockets. Anna froze, mouth open, a strangled gasp trapped in her throat. Henry leaned in, took the mouse in his hand, and clicked. The image disappeared. Left in its place was a scattering of icons across Captain Saunders's wallpaper, a photo of him proudly holding aloft a two-foot rockfish in the back of a fishing boat.

Anna exhaled loudly. Henry touched her right shoulder.

"I'll get the printout."

She drank some water to calm down, and then announced that she was ready to read the medical examiner's report.

"We could wait. Since they're making copies, I mean."

"No. Let's get it over with."

She skimmed it, while Henry read over her shoulder. It wasn't as if there had been any doubt about the cause of death, but at least there were no photos. She didn't slow down until reaching the results of the tests for toxins, narcotics, and pharmaceuticals.

"What the hell? This says Willard was taking an antidepressant."

"Which one?"

"Zolexa."

"Is that new?"

"New to me. I'm surprised Mom never mentioned it. I didn't know he had any issues like that. Or not lately."

"He did earlier?"

"In puberty. The whole hormonal mess everybody goes through, except worse for him, for obvious reasons. That doctor I mentioned, she prescribed something for a while, but I don't think they were happy with it. Later he stopped altogether."

"But you said they'd stopped seeing that doctor."

"They did. Ages ago. I finally remembered her name the other day. Sandra Patel, over in Easton."

"Maybe they went back. That's a half-hour drive. We could be there by three."

"Anything to get all this stuff off my mind."

They collected their copies, thanked Captain Saunders, and left.

25

Dr. Sandra Patel had one of those bright, cheery offices that looked like it had been decorated by Fisher-Price, with bold primary colors and big windows for plenty of sunlight. There was a play area in the corner with a Lego table where a boy, five or six, was building something. Henry watched in fascination as the boy spent several minutes putting blocks together and then gleefully ripping them apart, as if torn by competing urges to create and destroy.

They'd stopped at the Shoat house on the way over, to look for pill bottles with Willard's name on them and any other sign of recent prescriptions. Nothing. They looked up Zolexa online and found the usual bold claims of success in treating depression, but also some alarming side effects. Sometimes it worked, sometimes it didn't, sometimes it was a disaster.

The young receptionist reacted to their mention of

Willard's name with a gasp, quickly suppressed. She then called Dr. Patel on the in-house line for a hushed consultation that ended with her asking Anna and Henry to have a seat. Henry half expected her to call the cops. She kept a careful watch on them, as if they might try to kidnap the boy at the Lego table.

The boy's mom, at least, remained oblivious, so absorbed in a *Highlights* magazine that she didn't even notice when they were summoned to the doctor ahead of her son. The receptionist led them down a hallway with the solemn air of a funeral director.

Dr. Patel rose from behind her desk to greet them. She was a thin woman in her late fifties, slightly stooped, with brooding brown eyes that projected calm and concern. Her black hair was pulled back tightly in a bun.

"Thanks for seeing us without an appointment," Anna said. "This is Henry Mattick, a friend who's helping me look into things. About Willard, I mean."

"I was so upset when I heard about him. And your poor parents, of course. I have followed the case closely. I even thought about getting in touch, but decided that you needed your privacy. But it was so unlike him, or unlike the Willard I used to know. He was never a violent boy. Never."

"You sound like you haven't seen him in a while."

"Oh, not for years. But we kept his file. Until last month, of course, when his new doctor took over.

Although even then I never spoke directly to your mother or father, much less Willard himself."

"His new doctor?"

"Have you not seen him? Has he not participated in, well, any of the diagnosis after the fact?"

"I wasn't aware there *was* a new doctor. And if he's been in touch with the police, they haven't mentioned it."

"Oh, dear. I'm so sorry to hear this." She looked a little flustered.

"Do you have his name?"

"Dr. Wallace Ridgely, in Cambridge. I'll get his information for you. I wish I would have known, I could have saved you the trip."

She picked up the phone.

"Yes, Andrea. Could you please bring me the paperwork on the transfer of Willard Shoat's records? Thank you."

The receptionist must have pulled the materials earlier, because she entered seconds later with a slim manila folder for Dr. Patel, who opened it on her desk.

"Here is Dr. Ridgely's letterhead, with his address and phone number. And here is the fax I received from your parents, requesting that I send the records to Dr. Ridgely."

Anna eyed the fax carefully.

"Are those their signatures?" Henry asked in a low voice.

"Looks like it."

"Would you like me to phone Dr. Ridgely for you? I'd be happy to make an introduction. I am so sorry you weren't aware of this."

"Thank you."

Dr. Patel punched in the number.

"Yes, please. This is Dr. Sandra Patel from Easton, calling on behalf of Anna Shoat, the sister of one of Dr. Ridgely's patients, Willard Shoat. Would it be possible to speak with him?"

She frowned as she listened. Then she slowly spelled out Willard's first and last name and waited a few seconds longer.

"Excuse me? None? There must be some mistake. May I please speak directly with Dr. Ridgely? Dr. Sandra Patel in Easton . . . Yes, I'll wait."

She frowned again and held the receiver aside.

"This is very odd. She says they have no record of your brother as a patient. But I transferred his file as requested, so they must have *something*, even if there was never an actual consultation."

"And you said this was about a month ago?"

"As you can see for yourself." She nodded toward the consent form, dated in early July. "I suppose they could have switched doctors again, but I doubt your parents would have acted so rashly."

She perked up as a voice came back on the line.

"Yes, Dr. Ridgely. Thank you for taking my call." She pushed a button to put the conversation on speaker.

"I'm calling on the matter of Willard Shoat."

Ridgely's voice crackled loudly into the room.

"Shoat? You mean the fellow who murdered his parents, that whole bizarre thing over in Poston?"

~~Yes. But~~ ...~~and~~ shook her head in embarrassment.

to inquire about his recent medical ~~his~~ ...~~d's~~ sister, who wishes

"Didn't Donna tell you we have no record of him? He's never been a patient of ours. Believe me, I'd have remembered."

"But surely you received his file? Your office contacted me in July, and had them delivered by courier."

"I assure you, Dr. Patel, we don't have even a scrap of paper with his name on it. Nor have I ever requested any."

"But I have your own letter, here in front of me. Dated in July."

"With my signature?"

"Yes, and under your letterhead."

"Could you fax me a copy of that?"

"Absolutely."

Henry and Anna exchanged glances.

"And you said the file was delivered to my office?"

"By courier, yes. Your own, as I recall, because the charges were prepaid."

"FedEx?"

"UPS, I think. Yes, because here is the copy of the invoice." She held it up from the file folder. "And I remember it fairly clearly, because this happens quite seldom in my practice."

"Our courier account is with FedEx, so I'm not sure who would have made that request, but I can say with absolute confidence that it was no one from this office."

"You're positive?"

"Entirely. But send me that letter, because I'd like to get to the bottom of this."

"As would I, Dr. Ridgely. I'll send it straightaway."

"Thank you. Good luck tracking this down."

Dr. Patel looked ashen as she hung up the phone.

"You said you remember it clearly, this courier's visit?" Henry asked.

"Fairly well, yes. As I said, it's an infrequent occurrence. And even though it had been years since I had seen Willard, he made quite an impression on me. I often wondered what sort of young man he had become."

"And this was in July?"

"Yes. Here is the receipt."

"This delivery man," he said, "was he white, black, Hispanic?"

She squinted in concentration.

"An older white guy. He was wearing the standard uniform." She raised a finger in the air. "And a beard, he had a beard."

"What color was the beard?"

"I don't remember. Dark, that's all."

er?" Anna asked.

...ed.

...een, but I can't say for sure."

...rother's, what was in it?"

...rything. The entire record of his treatment. He was my patient for six years, until he was seventeen."

"Would it have included records of any prescriptions?"

"Of course."

"Including Zolexa?"

The doctor frowned.

"I had almost forgotten that period, because it was so brief. But, yes, he did take Zolexa for a while. We discontinued it fairly quickly after there was, well, an episode."

"An episode?"

"Fairly dramatic, I'm afraid. The effect on him. He was somewhat depressed at the time. So we gave it a try. Zolexa evened out his disposition, but it also made him very compliant, very suggestive. Too much so for his own good, as it happened. Some boys at his school, they were very quick to take advantage. They had him doing all sorts of things that he would not have done otherwise. Jumping from the top of a jungle gym, for one, and Willard was no daredevil."

"That's for sure."

"The worst of it was that he shoved a poor girl right off her bicycle, simply on their say-so. She had to be taken in for an X-ray of her arm, but fortunately there

was no fracture. I don't remember all the particu~~
but everything would have been in the file."

"The file that's now missing," Henry said, which cast
a pall over the room until Anna broke the silence.

"Would the effects of Zolexa still be the same for him
as an adult?"

"There is no way of knowing for sure, of course.
His hormonal balance would obviously be altered.
But given his previous reaction, I certainly would
never recommend prescribing it for him at any time,
especially when there are so many alternatives. Why?
Do you think he may have taken some?"

"It showed up in his bloodstream in the tests by the
medical examiner, from the night he killed Mom and
Dad."

Dr. Patel's mouth made a small, horrified "O." She
raised her hands to her face and sighed.

"I'm very distressed to hear this. *All* of this. Someone
did him a great disservice."

"Yes," Anna said. "That's what we think as well."

She turned toward Henry with a look of grim resolve,
and nodded toward the door.

26

They piled into Henry's car with renewed determination, but still no clues on Merle's whereabouts.

"Should we tell the police?" Anna asked.

"Tell them what? That some day laborer whose name might be Merle drugged your brother and made him do it? They'd laugh us out the door. Politely, of course, since they seem to like you."

"You know, until a few minutes ago I was almost ready to throw in the towel. I mean, so what if some friend of my Mom's saw them hunting off in the woods? Even if that was Merle, the moment he heard his hunting buddy had just blown away his parents—and with his trusty deer rifle, no less—if that's me, then I'm heading for the hills. But this shit with the medical file and the Zolexa?"

"He'd have had to forge a lot of signatures, fake all those letterheads, the UPS stuff, everything."

"You said the lock might have been forced on my mom's files. Maybe that's where he started."

"If all this is true, then we're dealing with a professional."

"Which can only mean it's got something to do with Mom. Or with what she used to be—the spy with the fake passport."

"Plus a nice severance package to keep her quiet."

"You're right. The cops would have us committed. *I'm* almost ready to have us committed. Should we check with UPS?"

"For what? We don't even have a name. The uniform would be easy enough to fake, and you can pick up shipping waybills at all their storefronts."

Henry slapped the steering wheel.

"Shit!" he said. "UPS!"

"What?"

"Your mom's key. UPS has a mailbox service. What's their closest location?"

She checked on her phone. Five minutes later they pulled into the lot of a UPS Store only two miles away. There was a row of mailboxes along the left wall, and they marched straight to the one with a number corresponding to the one on the key.

It didn't fit.

"What's the next closest?" Henry asked.

"Stevensville, just off Route 50, right after the Kent Narrows Bridge."

"We could make it by six-thirty if the traffic isn't bad. What time do they close?"

"Seven."

"Call them. Use your mom's name, tell them you're checking to see if your account is up to date."

"Sounds like fraud."

"It's not the U.S. Postal Service, so we're not breaking federal law."

Anna called the number, introduced herself as Helen Shoat, and asked the scripted question while Henry watched.

"Okay," she said, frowning. "Thank you."

She sighed and disconnected.

"Strike two," she said. "This is hopeless. We're never going to figure out where this key goes."

"Unless . . . Hand me your phone."

He waited a few beats for the sake of decorum, and then punched in the same number.

"Hi, my name is Henry Mattick, and I'm the executor for the estate of the late Elizabeth Waring Hart. I'm calling because my records show that she had a mailbox account with your store. Is that correct?" Then, a few seconds later. "Thank you, but that won't be necessary, I have the key with me. Very good. See you soon."

He smiled.

"Jackpot. Paid up through November in the name from her Canadian passport. For whatever reason, your mom must have decided she needed a cryptonym again."

27

Berlin, 1979

Helen reached behind the loosened brick and felt the edge of an envelope, the first new message in days.

She had redoubled her counter-surveillance tactics since the night Schnapp saw Delacroix following her home. Every trip, no matter how small, was now a labyrinth of evasion. It was wearing her out, but it was the only way she felt secure. Even at home, she felt vulnerable. She no longer opened her window shades.

For the same reason, stopping at the mail drop every evening was making her uneasy. She needed to set up another location, and soon. Nor was she at all keen on the idea that someone outside their immediate circle— the Sisterhood, as she had already begun thinking of their trio—was acting as courier, venturing to and fro with these explosive little parcels.

Following her meeting with Kathrin, Helen had fretted for the better part of a day about how she might best protect the girl. She didn't yet have an answer, apart from benign neglect. Trying to keep tabs on Kathrin might only draw unwanted attention to both of them, especially now that she knew Delacroix was on her tail.

In the meantime, she had learned more about the Social Democrat whose keys Kathrin and Anneliese had copied for Kevin Gilley. His name was Werner Gerntholz—Kathrin's memory had only been off by a single "t." As with most reasonably prominent German political figures, East and West, Berlin station had a file on him. Eileen Walters had promptly let Helen view it. But the file was fairly thin, and most of the contents were newspaper clippings.

Gerntholz ranked high in his party as a behind-the-scenes operative, not as a public face. He belonged to the party's most leftist wing, and had written policy papers sharply critical of U.S. ambitions to deploy modernized nuclear weapons in Europe. In doing so he had drawn the ire of the State Department, which had triggered a brief round of scrutiny from the Agency. At least one senior analyst in Langley had questioned his loyalty, citing Gerntholz's earlier ties to a government official later unmasked as a Stasi double agent.

Not long after viewing the file, Helen spotted Gerntholz's name in a story in *Der Spiegel* quoting him on economic policy, so he was apparently alive and well. Nor was there any hint of recent scandal. Perhaps the reports of Gilley's dark powers were exaggerated.

She had also tried to find out more about Kurt Delacroix, with little success. Erickson, besides meddling with Schnapp's investigation, had also commandeered Delacroix's Berlin file, and even Walters was powerless to reclaim it, although she did relay a request to Audra Vollmer to search for any records at Langley. But Langley had no personnel records for Delacroix, nor any information citing him as an intelligence source. If he was working for Gilley, then he was either off the books or, likelier still, Gilley's paperwork was handled with a higher security clearance than even Vollmer commanded.

Either reason would explain why Delacroix apparently felt no need for a cryptonym. The more Helen thought about it, the more she decided Gilley was smart to use him that way. No need for fake ID documents, which, if discovered, could attract unwanted attention from local authorities. By navigating deeper channels than anyone else, Gilley was apparently allowed to operate by his own rules.

Not that Helen wasn't doing the same thing, a realization that made her short of breath as she strolled away from the mailbox, turning left out of the playground with the envelope poking from the top of her purse. She wanted to find a secluded place where she could read the message, and she was so preoccupied that at first she didn't notice the man coming up quickly from behind on her right. He pulled even just as she reached the dark midpoint between two street lamps, and she gasped in surprise as he grabbed her forearm.

"Sloppy, Helen. Sloppy!"

It was Baucom, looking very cloak-and-dagger in an outdated fedora and belted trench coat, a cliché from central casting, although there was nothing at all humorous or mannered about his behavior as he forcibly steered her forward. She tried to wrench free, but his grip was unyielding.

"Let go of me!"

"Fine," he said, releasing her arm. "But you're playing the fool."

It sank in that he must have watched her collect the envelope, which made her slow down even as her adrenaline surged.

"How were you able to follow me?"

"Follow you? Who the hell would need to follow you when you come here every night? As I said, sloppy. Although as far as I've been able to tell, I'm the only other person who knows about this place. Except for whoever's servicing the mailbox, of course."

She didn't dare tell him how relieved that made her feel. If Delacroix had been in the vicinity, then surely an old pro like Baucom would have spotted him, right?

"Do new friendships always make you so reckless, my dear?"

"How much do you know?"

"Enough."

"You didn't leave me any choice, did you? Thief. Did you destroy both reels, or just give them to Herrington?"

"Herrington has nothing to do with this. And he knows nothing of the tapes."

"Does he know you're here?"

Baucom again grabbed her forearm and pulled her to a halt. She bristled, and pried his hand off her arm, but did not resume walking. They faced each other like quarreling lovers. Maybe that's what they still were.

"Look at you," she said, trying to sound disdainful. "That ridiculous hat."

Rather than answer he reached skyward and snapped his fingers. A taxi materialized from seemingly nowhere and rolled to the curb. Baucom opened the rear door.

Helen hesitated. If he'd burned her once, he might burn her again.

"Where are you taking me?"

"Where else? To Lehmann's, if only because his truth serum tastes better than mine, although by now someone might even be keeping an eye on my place. So there's that to consider as well."

"Why would someone be watching your place?"

"My reckless taste in women? Get in, for Chrissakes, the meter's running."

He slid in behind her and gave the address for Lehmann's little dive off Savignyplatz, which at least showed he wasn't lying about their destination. She needed a calming drink, and she might as well drink it at Lehmann's, their own little safe house.

They were silent throughout the drive. Helen stared out the window, and when they got to the bar she pointedly took a different chair from the one he pulled out for her. She saw Lehmann noticing, and flashed him a smile as if to soften the rebuke. Reading their body language perfectly, the saloon keeper flipped an immaculate dish towel over his shoulder and headed for the cellar. The brandy was at the same level as where they'd left off before.

Baucom didn't speak until after his first swallow.

"Are you going to let me read it?"

"Of course not."

He nodded, as if it were the answer he'd expected.

"Good. That's a start. Change the goddamn mailbox. That would also be a start."

She swirled the brandy in her glass, angry with his belittling tone even though she agreed completely.

"So, then, is that all for tonight? A free lesson in the obvious, plus a toot of Lehmann's finest?"

Baucom leaned forward, his voice practically a whisper.

"Edward Stone. Cryptonym 'Beetle.' Spelled like the bug, not the group."

She waited for more. All he did was stare.

"Am I supposed to guess the rest?"

"You said that he wheezed, and that he went straight for the good stuff, the Macallan."

"How did you—?"

He raised a hand.

"That's all I will say. Plus a word of advice. Use this information as judiciously as you would consume this wonderful elixir, because it is every bit as rare and valuable. And equally intoxicating. Do not share it with just anyone."

"But you *do* want me to use it, or why tell me?"

He said nothing.

"And you're not telling me out of any sense of love or loyalty, are you? You're just hoping to use me. Promoted to shadow operative for Clark Baucom, sly old hand of Budapest."

"Yes, I want to use you. As do your newest friends, so spare me the indignation. In this little business of ours, almost everyone finds ways to use his friends and connections, or haven't you noticed? Cliques and factions and competing agendas, all of it beneath the big wonderful tent of the Company. Everyone with his own sideshow at one time or another, and if that counts as using your friends, then I plead guilty as charged. But I'm not betraying you, and haven't, even though I know that's what you believe."

"What else am I supposed to think after you stole the tapes?"

"That depends on what I do with them."

"And that would be?"

"Not your business at this point, nor do you want it to be. 'Need to know' isn't just a means of thwarting curiosity. It keeps you safe. Or safer. Especially when you seem to be doing everything you can to ensure that safety is a foreign concept. Which is why I have one more item for you."

Baucom reached into his jacket and withdrew an envelope, which he slid across the table. There was no writing on the outside. Helen briefly considered sliding it right back. Then she picked it up.

"May I look now? Here?"

He shrugged but didn't object, so she pulled back the flap. Peeping inside she saw a Canadian passport, plus a Eurail pass that would be good for a month from its first date of usage. It had been purchased only yesterday.

"Who's this for?"

"Who do you think?"

Nudging the rail ticket farther out, she saw a name printed along the side.

"Elizabeth Waring Hart," she read aloud. "Am I supposed to know her?"

"Fairly well, I'd say. Although lately she hasn't been herself, so maybe it's an open question."

She thumbed open the passport and saw her own photo—as a blonde, no less.

"Clark, what the hell?"

"It's not official, but it's top-of-the-line. The cobbler is an old friend who owed me a favor. Hope you like the photo. He did that as well. You'll need a wig, of course, or a dye job, if you ever plan to use it. But you'd probably want one, anyway, as part of the whole package."

"An escape and evasion kit?"

"How about if you don't say that aloud? And it's not enough. You should also have a pair of sunglasses, a ready supply of currency. D-Marks, but also something for wherever you might want to go first. Francs, pesetas, whatever place you settle on."

"What, no rubles?"

"This isn't comedy, my dear. I'm deadly serious."

"I know. No need to act like I'm some G-7 from the steno pool."

"My worry is that you won't bother to act on your knowledge until it's too late." He leaned closer. "So what I'm saying is *do this now*!"

"Now you're scaring me. You've developed a knack for that, you know."

"Good. You should be scared." He swallowed some brandy, looking for the first time that he needed it as much as she did.

"What do you know about all this that you're not telling me?"

"Not a fair question."

"It is among friends."

"Not a fair argument."

"Oh, for Chrissakes, Clark! What's unfair if we're talking about someone who operates beyond all the usual rules?"

"Why do you think all my worries are only about Robert?"

"Gilley. And here's another name for you. Delacroix, who works for Gilley. Heard of him, too?"

Baucom looked stumped for the first time that night, and for once she wasn't happy about it. She'd been hoping he'd say that this Delacroix fellow was a minor matter, easily controlled.

"Can't say that I have," Baucom muttered. "But you're still missing the point."

"Well, Gilley *is* the scary one."

"What, exactly, about the wording of 'Elimination, plain and simple' doesn't sound scary to you?"

They were the words that the wheezing man—the one she now knew to be Edward Stone, cryptonym Beetle—had uttered at the close of his meeting at the safe house.

"So you listened to the tapes."

"Of course I listened."

"And?"

"These questions." He shook his head in exasperation. "I told you. Enough."

"So that's all the explanation you're going to offer? A name and a warning, plus an escape kit?"

"As I said. Cliques and factions, each with its own sideshow."

"This Beetle fellow, I take it you're not fond of him."

He shrugged and picked up his glass.

"Fuck you and your selective silence, Clark. I don't know what's worse, the stupid riddles or the whole 'need to know' firewall you put up every time I have an important question."

"As I said, it's for your protection. For everyone's. And it's my own way of saying that I have now done all I'm capable of doing on your behalf."

"And Herrington doesn't know? About any of this?"

"Not yet. And if he doesn't, then the Central Europe desk in Langley doesn't. So whoever your others friends are, they at least seem to be capable of more discretion than you've demonstrated to date."

"I thought you knew all about them?"

"I have my theories. But I also have my limitations and blind spots."

"Cliques and factions and all that."

"Yes."

She shook her head. Then she knocked back a bracing shot, hoping that it would help clear things up. Instead, she experienced the first stirrings of a luxuriant slide into a mellow stupor, which, if unchecked, might lead straight to bed, a thought that took deeper root when Baucom took her hand and again leaned closer. But instead of offering a caress, or saying something suggestive, he squeezed her hand and said, "Carry yourself wisely, my dear. Whatever it is you're doing, wrap it up soon. Because you won't go unnoticed by the wrong people forever. And if and when you are caught, it won't be my doing. Know that."

"All right."

"One further caution."

"Yes?"

"In all these messages back and forth between you and God knows who else, you had best not bandy about any of those coded words that made you so curious when you overheard them at the safe house. Lakes and ponds. The bay. All that body of water stuff."

"Why?"

"Just do as I say."

"Let me see if I have this straight. You'd like me to do a little nosing around on your behalf about this Edward Stone. But without mentioning his name, or anything that he said. That should be easy as pie."

"Since when is our work ever easy? It's why I brought you the other little gift, in case the going gets so tough that you need to get away for a while. But that's all I can do for you. Finis."

He abruptly released her hand and stood from the table. He reached for his wallet and put a wad of bills onto the table. Then he nodded, as if to say goodbye.

"Your brandy," she said, hoping to lure him back. Half a glass remained.

"Take it. You'll need it more." Baucom turned and, with a knowing glance at Lehmann, strolled off toward the door, departing like a film star toward his golden years, or a once great athlete toward retirement. It was an exit of such grace and quiet drama that Helen almost immediately felt wistful. She even wondered if it might be the last time she'd see him.

A few minutes later, having finished her own drink but leaving his untouched, she stood. Lehmann walked over with the towel across his arm.

"May I call you a taxi?"

"Thank you, Lehmann." She paused, then took the plunge. "Tell me, how long have you two known each other?"

"Oh, quite a while. From the worst and earliest days. The winter of '46."

"And how long have you worked together?"

"Worked?" A puzzled expression, very convincing. He was quite good. "We are friends, *Fräulein*. Old friends, yes, but that is all."

"Of course," she said. "Cliques and factions and all that."

He frowned uncertainly, which left her feeling that she had at least given him something to think about, one small puzzle as a counterpoint to the three or four whirling in her own head.

28

Since her arrival in Berlin, Helen had almost never been homesick. Wixville was barren ground for nostalgia. As a preacher's daughter she had been hounded at every turn by classmates who maligned her for her brains, and for her penchant for solitude. The surrounding countryside had only added to her misery. It was flat and unforgiving, a tangle of scrub oak and poison ivy. The forests were mostly tree farms, endless pines lined up like bowling pins. The few stands of natural woodland were almost invariably infested by briars that tore at your jeans and bloodied your arms. Even a ride into town offered scant relief—a dreary promenade of strip malls, billboards, car lots, trailer parks, and discount stores with parking lots bigger than football fields. Crossing their blacktops on a hot summer day was like tiptoeing through a lava flow.

She did miss America from time to time, if only for that feeling of limitless joy she used to get whenever she eased free of the flatland clutter, driving into green hills with a friend at her side and good tunes on the cassette deck, lured toward adventure by the promise of the open road. So many Germans that she'd met since coming to Berlin were enchanted by the American West, less for its cowboy mythology than for the spacious vistas they'd seen in the Technicolor of films and dreams. She'd always found that a bit amusing.

But now, surrounded on the S-Bahn by silent, unsmiling commuters—most of them dressed in black and smelling of the damp and the cold—Helen felt overwhelmed by a deepening sense of Eurogloom. She was out of place and out of sorts, a naive American in over her head among secretive, violent people. Out the window, lengthening shadows announced the approach of winter, and the usual three layers of clouds were closing in from the west. This was the time of year when the sulfurous smell of coal smoke began to haunt every street in Berlin.

Take me back to the States for just one deep breath, she thought, back to a land where history was only a matter of a few hundred years, and its more fractious moments could be patched over by unstinting optimism and the heroics of Lincoln and MLK, by baseball every summer and by football in the fall. A place where, rightly or wrongly, even the most complex problems were routinely summed up by bumper stickers. She was not at all religious, this preacher's daughter, yet she offered up a silent prayer all the same: Deliver me from these pale and earnest strangers, among whom my worst enemies may be lurking. Or, if that's not feasible, God, then simply leave me in peace and safety until I've had more time to think.

If Baucom's intent had been to buck her up, or put her on high alert, then he had failed. She instead felt only burdened—by the weight of her struggles, by this city's grim history. What was the Cold War to her, really, other than the means to a job? A job going poorly, by any measurement. She again scanned the faces on the crowded S-Bahn car, everyone swaying and bouncing as the train rounded a curve. In doing so she locked on to a teenage girl reading a book. Raven hair, skin as white as talcum. A younger version of Frieda. Helen pictured the girl's dead face laid out against the cobbles of an alley, collecting raindrops in its creases and divots. Anneliese, she reminded herself. Not Frieda. Stay in this business a few years and you didn't even recall people by their real names. There was Frieda, Robert, Beetle. Masks, each and every one. And now she had her own mask snug in her purse, the Canadian passport issued to Elizabeth Waring Hart. She wondered how Baucom had chosen the name. From an old girlfriend, perhaps?

For her health and well-being, he'd said, even as he'd gently urged her to pursue matters that might get her fired, or worse.

If this was what it meant to learn the deeper secrets of the trade, then why had she yearned for so long to be admitted to the club? Even now she was still only a gate-crasher, an unauthorized entry caught in a place she'd rather not be.

The train car rattled onward, everyone silent beneath the noise of the tracks until finally, mercifully, it screeched to a halt at Helen's stop. She stood, jelly-legged, as the sliding doors thundered open.

Then, in spite of every dragging counterweight, she hauled herself off to begin completing the necessary chores. It was time to buy a wig—blond, to match her hair in the passport photo. Time to gather cash in several currencies. Time to select a new and safer mail drop and then notify the Sisterhood of the change. Time to fire off a discreet inquiry with regard to Edward Stone, aka Beetle. Only when all of that was done would Helen allow herself the luxuries of food and further medication. Only then, she vowed, would she deem it permissible to drift away to that distant refuge of sleep. Gate-crasher or not, she was a professional now, and had better start acting like one.

29

In the morning, calmer, Helen considered blowing off
Baucom's request entirely. Why should she stick her
neck out to find out more about this "Beetle" fellow?
But by the time she was halfway through her first cup
of coffee, she'd reconsidered.

Baucom was not a man who did things offhandedly.
If he could have pursued the matter himself, he would
have done so. If he had deemed it unworthy of pursuit,
he never would have mentioned it to her. And while, to
her, the more pressing interest was still Kevin Gilley—a
rapist and probably a murderer—she was undeniably
curious about the strange conversation she'd overhead
between Edward Stone, aka Beetle, and the younger
man, Lewis.

Was it part of some conspiracy? Toward what end?
And for which masters? To help the Soviets? To help
themselves? And who, she wondered, stood to be

eliminated as part of their plans? At the very least, she ought to do some poking around at the fringes.

She settled on the records room as the best starting point, if only because she had Eileen Walters on her side. Cryptonyms. There must be a file somewhere containing all the cryptonyms in current use by operatives and sources for Berlin station.

Not long after she reached the office, Helen popped into the records room and loitered toward the back of the filing cabinets while Walters conversed with a field man named Haller about a new restaurant that had just opened in Steglitz. By the time Haller left, she had settled on an approach.

"What is it, Helen?" Walters said, looking up from her desk. "Is there something I can find for you?"

"Oh, probably not. I'm just a little confused at the moment."

"Over what, may I ask?"

"A stray cryptonym that popped up in one of my usage requests. 'Beetle,' like the bug."

The words sounded forced the moment they left her mouth, and she was about to blush when Walters, not seeming to notice her discomfort, cheerfully said, "Oh, you must mean Eddie Stone."

"Possibly."

"Has to be."

"He works here?"

"Goodness, no. Vienna. And not for years. Not

surprised you haven't heard of him. He was well before your time. Whenever he came to Germany it was usually to Bonn."

"So you know him?"

"Knew. I was posted to Vienna then. Still remember the send-off they gave him when he retired in '73."

"He's retired?"

"Yes. And quite the bash it was. I was the only decently dressed female in the room, apart from the chief of station's secretary. Like something out of *Cabaret*. All very louche." She laughed and covered her mouth. "I'm afraid I only lasted half an hour, but of course by then most of them were three sheets to the wind. Boys and their libidos, you know."

"All too well. Where did he go after hanging it up?"

"Now, that's a very good question. I seem to recall he found a soft landing with some multinational. That was around the time that hiring international security consultants was all the rage in the corporate world, what with the Red Guards kidnapping business executives and that sort of thing."

"Ah. So he went back to the States?"

"No, I think he stayed over here. London, maybe? With Philips, the electronics firm. Or, no, I think it might have been Uniroyal, the tire maker. Why, is one of his old contacts looking for him?"

"Something like that."

"Langley would know his current whereabouts. Would you like me to put a trace on him for you? I could send out a request on your behalf and probably have an answer by tomorrow."

"Yes. Thank you. Thank you very much, Eileen."

Well, that was easy. Helen practically floated back to her office.

For the rest of the morning she worked quietly at her desk, and by early afternoon she'd caught up on her administrative chores. That evening, she activated the new mail drop she'd selected the night before by sending off a test message to her two allies, CDG in Paris and IAD in Washington.

That night she slept soundly. Maybe this wasn't going to be impossible, after all.

30

Helen arrived at Berlin station early the next morning in hopes of finding a reply to her query on the whereabouts of Edward Stone. Instead, she encountered Herrington prowling the hallway outside her office. It was an uncharacteristically early hour for him, and he already looked haggard, as if he hadn't slept. His tie was loosened and his face was unshaven.

"In my office," he said.

Helen put down her purse and began taking off her coat. Before she could finish, Herrington moved up in her face and put a hand on her arm.

"Now," he said. "As in, right this moment."

So much for everything going smoothly. Had someone spilled the beans on her work over Gilley? Had her new mail drop been discovered?

There was an unmistakable air of crisis outside Herrington's office. A younger man, unfamiliar to her, stood in a pose of readiness, with arms folded and rolled-up sleeves. He looked up as she approached but wouldn't meet her gaze. Neither he nor Herrington spoke to each other as the station chief passed by on his way to his desk.

Herrington shut the door behind her as she entered. He gestured to a chair, where she seated herself as meekly as possible. This time he did not bother to rub Lenin's head for luck, nor did he even glance at her chest. He locked his fingers in a prayerful pose atop his blotter, looked her straight in the eye, and delivered the blow.

"We're letting you go."

"*What?*"

"You heard me."

"As of when?"

"As of now. That gentleman you saw outside will be escorting you from the premises."

"I have to at least clean out my desk."

"You'll take nothing from this office."

"Not even my purse?"

"He'll collect that for you. Along with your official ID."

"But—"

"There will be no discussion. You will contact no one, here or at Langley or anywhere else. Failure to heed this order will result in prosecution, and we'll spare no expense in pursuing charges. Do you understand?"

"What charges? What have I done?"

"As if you needed to ask."

"But—"

"I told you. There's nothing to discuss." Then he raised his voice to shout to the man outside. "Allen?"

The door opened immediately. The fellow with rolled-up sleeves stepped inside.

"She's all yours." Herrington stood. "Allen here will escort you home to gather your belongings. You're allowed a single suitcase. Anything that doesn't fit will be shipped to you later, and be advised that whatever you do take will be thoroughly searched upon arrival."

"Arrival where?"

"Allen will drive you to Templehof for a military flight back to the States. Any further word on the plane, Allen?"

"Gassed up and waiting on the tarmac, sir."

"Good." He turned back to Helen. "You'll be landing in about nine hours. Someone from Langley will be waiting, and they'll sort it out from there."

She opened her mouth to speak, but the only thought that came to mind was that it was over—everything, and on every front. Not just her investigations but her career, her life, her hopes, her great European adventure—all of it was ashes, emptiness. She wanted to vomit.

Allen gripped her arm, a bit roughly at first, and then with a gentle nudge as he seemed to realize how stunned she was.

"Miss?"

She turned to face him. He was about her age, probably an ex-jock, but his eyes showed intelligence, maybe even compassion.

"We have a plane to catch. Come with me."

He made it sound like he was taking her on a date, and her first impulse was to laugh. Then she noticed Herrington's look of triumph— the smug set of his mouth, the gleam in his eyes, and she wanted to lash out. But an outburst was probably what he was hoping for, something to share later with the others over celebratory drinks. So she turned away from him, shook off Allen's grip on her arm, and walked out of the office with as much fortitude as she could muster.

A car from the consular section was waiting outside at the curb. A Marine guard in full dress uniform was at the wheel, which made it look like she was a government big shot, a visiting celebrity here to toss a bouquet of roses at the base of the Wall. She swallowed hard, still feeling nauseated as she slid onto the seat with Allen close in her wake. In the confined space of the car she could smell his cologne, a brand she detested, so she pressed the button on the armrest to open her window. It would only lower by a few inches, just enough to allow the raw dampness of a Berlin morning, which usually made her bones ache, to pour in.

"I'd prefer if you didn't do that." Allen said.

"I'd prefer if you hadn't doused yourself in a quart of English Leather. I can't exactly climb out the opening. It stays."

Neither of them spoke for the rest of the ride, and she left the window open even after she had to hold herself rigid to keep from shivering.

31

What did you pack for a journey of exile, a deportation from your life? More to the point, what sort of clothes and belongings did you throw into a bag when you knew that some snoop in gloved hands was going to toss all of it onto a table for close inspection almost the moment you landed?

Helen stood with hands on hips as she stared at her suitcase, opened on the bed like an empty clamshell, a beige Samsonite, her mother's going-away gift from the day she'd left for college. Up to now it had represented freedom. From here on out it would remind her of disgrace. She sighed, and then she got angry at herself.

"Buck up, Abell!" she said.

"What was that? Are you talking to someone?"

The voice of Allen, who was waiting in the living room. They'd trudged up the stairs in silence. He'd still seemed to be smarting from her crack about his cologne. Now his face appeared in the bedroom doorway, head swiveling from side to side as if searching for infiltrators, a communist conspiracy.

"I was just talking to myself while I pack."

He left without a word. She heard him switch on the television, an outburst of loud voices and canned laughter. Yet another American rerun, expertly dubbed by the Germans. *Hogan's Heroes,* of all things. Fat and jolly Sergeant Schultz, proclaiming in a doltish Schwabian accent that he knew nothing. What a comfort it must be for Berliners to view Wehrmacht officers and Gestapo men as ineffectual boobs. Courtesy of the Americans, no less.

Helen walked over to her window and pulled open the blinds. Gray upon gray, with trailing wisps of coal smoke thrown in for good measure. But she would miss it. She would miss these rooftops with their pigeons and their chimneys and their Old World gloom.

Glancing to the right, she noticed something outside her bathroom window that had never seemed significant until now. An idea took root. Somewhat foolish, but an idea all the same. Heart beating a little faster, she walked to her closet, got out an overnight bag, and began filling it with underwear and clothes. And, then, from the very back of a dresser drawer, from where she'd stowed it the other night, she took out the escape and evasion kit that Baucom had given her. Fortunately she had already stocked it with currency, just as he'd advised—D-Marks and French francs, enough for at least a week.

From another drawer she withdrew the blond wig and the sunglasses and dropped them on the bed. She turned and walked to the door, poking her head out just enough to see Allen laughing at something Colonel Klink had just said.

"If that flight's going to be nine hours then I'll need a shower before we go." She kept her voice neutral, calm. "How much time do we have?"

He shot a cuff and checked his watch.

"Is half an hour enough? We're the only passengers, so it's not exactly a rush job. But we don't want to keep them cooling their heels all morning."

"Understood. Half an hour it is."

Helen shut the bedroom door, stuffed the wig and some clothes into the overnight bag and then carried it into the bathroom, where she locked the door behind her. She looked at herself in the mirror and drew a deep breath, gathering herself for the next move. It was probably a blessing that Baucom had taken the tapes. For the moment they were in a safer refuge than she could provide, as long as he hadn't destroyed them.

She turned on the tap in the bathtub and pulled the lever for the shower. The water screamed out in its usual roar as she pulled the plastic curtain shut. She took the wig out of the bag and put it on, checking the fit in the mirror. Then she turned toward the window and wrenched it open. Without a moment's hesitation she climbed with her overnight bag out onto the platform of the fire escape, into the cold and damp of the Berlin morning. By pressing hard against the glass, she was able to nearly shut the window behind her.

She was three stories up. Straight below her was an alley. Too obvious. She looked up. The stairs climbed for another two floors, to where a steel ladder led to the roof. Better. Helen secured the overnight bag by pulling the strap over her head so that it angled across her chest like a bandolier. Then she climbed—first the steps, and then the ladder—while the coal-smoke breeze whipped at her wig, someone else's hair blowing into her eyes and mouth until she clambered onto the roof and was able to push it out of her face.

She looked out across the city. To the east, the giant spire and silver ball of the Funkturm loomed over Alexanderplatz like a golf ball on a tee, waiting for Brezhnev to smack it into the Baltic Sea. No sense heading in that direction.

She crossed the rooftop, hesitated at the edge, and then backed up a few steps before making a running leap across the four-foot gap to the next apartment building. Her heart fluttered as she landed, but the second crossing was easier and the third was almost fun. No worse than jumping all those briar bushes in the woods around Wixville. As an unexpected bonus, the last building in the block offered an easy leap to the one around the corner. Another series of crossings led to the end of a side street.

All this took only a few minutes, and by the time she'd descended another ladder and another set of fire stairs to the ground she was all the way around the corner from where she'd started. Allen probably wouldn't get suspicious for at least another five minutes, or even ten as long as Sergeant Schultz kept him laughing.

Helen briskly covered three blocks until she reached Clayallee, a four-lane boulevard busy with traffic. She crossed as the light was changing, and was lucky enough to flag down a taxi almost the moment she reached the other side. Other than the driver, the only person who saw her climb in was a younger fellow running up the side street in her wake. His long hair was tied back in a ponytail, which bobbed as he ran. He wore a surplus army jacket. Helen spotted him as he reached Clayallee.

"Where to?" the driver asked her.

Where to, indeed? And what could she do about Delacroix?

"Bahnhof Zoo," she said, directing him to the nearest train station.

Delacroix crossed the four lanes against the light, waving his arms for any approaching taxi as he darted between oncoming cars. Horns honked, but a cab heeded his signal and pulled to the curb.

"Shit!" she said.

"Is something wrong?" the driver asked.

"I need to make a call. Pull over at the first phone box."

"There's one in a few blocks."

"Perfect."

Helen took out Otto Schnapp's business card and prepared to dash out the door the moment the taxi pulled over. She ducked into the phone booth, dropped in a coin, and dialed as fast as she could. By the time she noticed the second taxi pausing a block behind hers, Schnapp had answered and she'd said what she had to say. Would it work? That would be up to Schnapp.

"Let's go," she said, climbing back in.

Only when she looked out the back window, and saw the second cab resume its pursuit, did she begin to doubt herself. What in the hell did she think she was doing? And who would protect her now? With no easy answers, Helen leaned forward and again spoke to the driver.

"On second thought . . ."

"Yes?" he said, turning his head.

She was on the verge of asking him to turn around and head back to her apartment. Even apart from the matter of Delacroix, this was foolish, insane. It was one thing to be banished in disgrace. Quite another to go on the run, and convince them that every worst fear they'd ever had about her was absolutely correct. They'd panic, go berserk. They might even conclude she'd gone over to the other side.

Then she thought of Herrington scrambling to react, frantically trying to explain her disappearance to his superiors. A fuck-up of epic proportions. A career changer. She also imagined the dirgelike ride with Allen to Templehof that awaited, followed by the long flight home, and her humiliating arrival. No. She wasn't ready for any of that, nor would she submit to the likes of Herrington. Not after the way he'd treated her.

"Yes?" the driver said again.

"Same as before. Bahnhof Zoo, quick as you can."

Twenty minutes later the taxi arrived at Zoo Station. By then the second taxi was a full block behind, stopped at a light. Helen bustled up the stairs into the terminal, scanned the departures board, and settled on a train leaving for Hamburg in eleven minutes.

She strolled toward the stairway that led to the platform, knowing without looking that Delacroix would soon be following. Too much time remained to simply wait upstairs, so she ducked into a bookstore where she pulled a sweater and a scarf out of her overnight bag and slipped them on, covering her hair. She bought a pair of reading glasses and put them on.

There were still eight minutes until departure, but she would be able to board in only a minute or two.

Emerging warily from the bookstore, she spotted Delacroix outside a crowded café across the terminal, where he was eyeing the tables for any sign of her. Trying not to panic, she headed for the stairs at a deliberate pace while averting her face toward the timetable at the far end of the terminal.

She reached the stairs and began to climb. Maybe she'd lost him.

Just as she was reaching the platform she heard a clatter of footsteps coming up from behind. The train was to her left—already boarding, thank God, so she quickened her pace, ducked into the nearest doorway, and briskly made her way down the aisle of the first car before settling into a window seat of the second car.

Looking out onto the platform she spotted Delacroix twenty yards down, hands on his hips as he scanned the windows. It was hopeless. Inevitably he would come aboard, and once the train left the station there would be no escape. She grabbed her bag and was about to make another run for it when she spotted the buzz cut and green policeman's sweater of Otto Schnapp. The detective had just come up the stairs and was sprinting toward Delacroix, who had nearly reached the door of the train.

Delacroix was about to step aboard when Schnapp

grabbed his shoulder from behind. He wheeled reflexively, assuming a threatening posture that looked like something out of a martial arts manual, but he lowered his arms and relaxed into a slouch when he recognized Schnapp. He nodded, seemingly dazed, as Schnapp began to speak. Then he handed over his passport.

Delacroix pointed to his watch and then toward the train. Schnapp slowly shook his head. He pocketed the passport and motioned toward the stairs. Delacroix pivoted suddenly, as if to make a dash for the train, only to have Schnapp grab an arm and wrench him to the platform, flat on his back.

The doors of the train slid shut. The cars lurched toward Hamburg just as Schnapp was helping Delacroix to his feet.

Helen turned away from the window, elated. She took off the reading glasses, sank into her seat, and allowed herself a gleeful smile. After a minute or so, the smile disappeared, and so did her euphoria. She had taken the leap. Now came the fall, which promised to be considerable. The trick would be in managing the landing.

Helen drew a deep breath and wondered what the hell she was supposed to do next.

32

The UPS Store was tucked between a tire shop and a sushi joint in a small shopping center on Route 50. Henry and Anna headed straight for the mailboxes, in an alcove to the left. There were about three hundred, most of them small, although box 218 was in a quadrant of eight larger ones with five-by-ten-inch doors.

"Do the honors," he said.

Anna unlocked and opened the door while Henry stooped to share the view. Inside was a pile of several dozen envelopes.

"Good God," she said. "Could all of this have come in the past week?"

"I'm guessing she stored them here."

"You're right. Look at the one on top."

It was a plain white envelope with no return address, postmarked from McLean, Va., in late August of 2002.

Twelve years old. Below it in the pile, more white envelopes were interspersed with powder-blue airmail envelopes.

A UPS clerk appeared from around the corner, and they looked up like a couple of thieves caught in the act.

"Are you the guy who called? The executor for Ms. Hart?"

Henry stood a little straighter.

"Uh, yeah. And this is Ms. Hart's daughter, Anna."

"Hi there. Sorry for your loss. She was one of our regulars."

"Thank you," Anna said. "She always spoke highly of the service."

"I don't suppose you'll be renewing. Would you like a refund for the extra three months?"

Henry answered, "Why don't we just let it run its course, in case any more mail comes in?"

"Sure." He turned toward Anna. "You look kinda familiar. Have you been here before?"

"No. First time."

He probably recognized her from the newspapers, Henry figured. Or from TV footage at the funeral. All the more reason to get out of here quickly, although judging from the clerk's reaction Henry doubted he'd made the connection to the murders. The fake name must have thrown him off, so Henry decided to prod for more information.

"Some of this stuff looks like it's been here for years," he said. "Did she ever take anything with her?"

"Just that big envelope the last time she came in. I think it might've been the oldest thing in there."

"The big envelope?" Anna said.

"One of those nine-by-thirteen jobs, with padding. She put it in the day she first rented the box. Always made it a little crowded for the letters, but it wasn't my place to complain as long as everything fit. Then she took it with her a couple weeks ago, right before, well . . . it must've been right before she passed away."

"Oh."

"You sound like you knew her pretty well," Henry said.

"Just enough to say hello, maybe talk about the weather. But she was one of my first customers—I manage the place—and she was always real nice. A stylish lady, your mom."

"Stylish?" Anna's tone was incredulous.

"For her age, I mean. Must have been quite the blond bombshell at one time. No disrespect, of course."

"Blond?"

"Sure."

The wig. Had to be.

"You're right, Mom had style. Guess I never realized how much until recently."

They scooted out the door before he could ask another question. Anna headed for the car, all business.

"Want me to read them aloud?" she asked. "Or we could pull over, stop at a Starbucks along the way."

"With this stuff? Out in public?"

"Right. Okay."

"Let's take them to my house. But tell me about the postmarks."

Anna picked carefully through the pile, as if handling the rarest of artifacts.

"You saw the one on top. McLean, Virginia, August of 2002. But no name or return address on the outside."

"That's near Langley, CIA headquarters. Is it definitely the oldest one?"

"Yes." She thumbed through to the end of the pile. "Oh, my God." Her tone went from giddy to somber. "The most recent one is from only a week ago. She never even opened it."

"Where's it from?"

"There's no return address, but it was postmarked in York, Pennsylvania. Cream-colored envelope, nice stationery. And it's handwritten." She rearranged the pile and started going back through it more slowly. "Same handwriting as on the airmail envelopes from earlier, which also go back to 2002. Whoa!" Suddenly, the bounce was back in her voice. "And all of those were postmarked in Paris. A woman's writing, if I had to guess."

"So they're not all from the same person?"

"Two different people, it looks like. About half of

them are typed, or maybe from a printer. Those are the ones from McLean . . . Check that. The last typed one was postmarked from some town in North Carolina. Currituck?"

"Near the coast. The first one from Paris, in 2002, what month was that one?"

"Late August, just like the first one from McLean."

"Which was right around the time you and your mom saw that creepy guy at the mall, when you were heading off to college."

"You think that's what started this?"

"Just thinking out loud."

"Interesting timing."

"In looking around the house have you come across much old mail?"

"Just a box of Christmas cards. I think the only reason she kept those was to know who to write next year."

"What about that big envelope the UPS guy was talking about? He said it was nine by thirteen. Seen anything like that?"

"No. And you saw for yourself, it wasn't in her office, either."

"Maybe she hid it somewhere else."

"Or sent it away."

"Or took out what was inside, and tossed the envelope."

"Right before she died."

That thought kept them quiet for a while. By then the smell of the letters filled the car, an essence of old paper, faded ink, the mustiness of an archive.

Scooter was waiting on the front porch when they pulled into Henry's driveway, as if he knew something was up and didn't want to miss it. Henry dumped a fresh supply of food into his bowl, and Scooter got straight to work while Anna spread out the letters on the coffee table in the living room, arranging them in chronological order.

The day was getting toward sunset, so Henry threw open the curtains to let in the last of the sunlight. The view through the picture window seemed to catch Anna by surprise, and he immediately saw why. The first thing you noticed was her parents' house, right down Willow.

"I never realized what a front row seat you had for all the goings-on."

"Yeah, that's for sure." He looked away from her, feeling like it was too risky to say anything more.

They were about to get started when they heard a low growl coming from the front door, where Scooter stood looking out through the screen. The fur on his back was bristled, and he was baring his teeth.

"Is he like that all the time?"

"He's never like that. Laziest watchdog on the planet, unless there's a squirrel within range. What is it, fella?"

Scooter growled again, and then H
A scruffy-looking fellow in jeans an
was coming up the sidewalk to the door.

"You know him?" Anna asked.

"Never laid eyes on him."

They reached the door just as the fellow w
to knock. Henry started to open it, only to have
lunge for the gap with a snarl. The fellow reacte
a boxer ducking a punch, taking a step back
and crouching slightly as his eyes widened. Then
uncoiled as he realized the dog wasn't getting loos
anytime soon.

"Lookin' for Henry Mattick."

"That's me." He kept the screen door closed. "Who
are you?"

The man grinned, spit a brown stream of tobacco
juice off the side of the porch and then wiped his mouth
with his sleeve.

"Ron at the labor pool says you was looking for
Merle. Says you're paying fifty to anybody who can
help." He reached into his pants pocket for a folded
scrap of paper. "Gave me your address. I ain't got
no phone, but I just finished a catching job over the
Morrison place and figured I'd come on over."

"The Morrisons live across town," Anna said in a
lowered voice. "This guy must not have a car."

"No, ma'am. Not since the repo man took it. Trans
Am, too, and only four months behind on my payments,

fuckers." He wiped his mouth again. "So I'm here
my fifty."

"What do you know about Merle?" Henry asked.

"Ain't seen him goin' on a week now."

"I already knew that."

"You gonna invite me in, so we can talk proper and
all?"

Henry, mindful of all the letters on the coffee table,
shook his head.

"Not sure my dog would handle that too well. How
'bout we just conduct our business right here on the
porch?"

"Suit yourself."

He grinned, eyes shining. Henry guessed he'd either
been drinking or was high, probably not a bad idea if
you caught chickens all day. Anna grabbed Scooter's
collar while Henry stepped onto the porch. The dog was
no longer growling but his fur was still tufted along his
spine. Henry folded his arms and stood a few feet away
from the visitor. They faced each other from opposite
sides of the slab porch.

"You never told me your name."

"You wanna hear what I got to say, or you wanna ask
questions?"

"Depends on how bad you want the fifty."

"He was livin' in a motor court, Merle was. Out on
Route 50."

"How do you know that?"

"Why's it matter?"

"For fifty, it matters."

"'Cause I stayed there myself. Not in his room, I ain't no fag. But same place, and he was there. Saw him coming out his door one morning."

"Which motor court?"

"Where's that fifty?"

"In my wallet. If you want it, keep talking."

He grinned again, and then nodded.

"Place called the Breezeway, just this side of the Nanticoke Bridge. She's back up in the trees a little."

"How long ago was this?"

He shrugged.

"Three weeks, maybe. You gonna pay up or not? 'Cause I can always come back and get it some other way, you know." He nodded toward Anna, who was watching through the screen.

Henry, the color rising in his cheeks, took a step forward and put a finger on the man's chest, nudging him toward the side of the porch until his back was pressed against the prickly leaves of an overgrown holly. Up close he smelled like sweat and chicken manure, and his teeth were the same color as the tobacco juice.

"Keep talking like that, my man, and you'll never get a dime."

"Just funnin' with you, 'cause I reckon you're good for it, right?"

"You make sure that's all it is."

Henry stepped back and took out his wallet. By the time he'd pulled out a pair of twenties and two fives the fellow was practically salivating.

"Never did say your name."

"Nope. Never did." Another grin as he eyed the bills.

"If this turns out to be bullshit, the first thing I'll do is tell that crew chief over at the labor pool about our little transaction, and I'm sure he'll want a cut."

"That spic with the mouth? I can deal with him." He spit again, putting down another brown streak across the crabgrass. Henry handed him the bills. The fellow counted them twice, as if the math was a little complicated. Then he stuffed them in his pockets and mimed tipping a cap to Anna.

"Pleasure, ma'am. Nice doing business with the both of you."

They watched him walk away until he turned the corner toward the highway. Only then did Henry let Scooter out. The dog sniffed at one of the brown streaks and sauntered off in the opposite direction.

"What do you think?" Henry asked. "Tackle the letters, or chase down this tip?"

"After that creepy little visit? Let's check out the tip. Those letters aren't going anywhere, but Merle probably is."

Henry carefully stacked the letters in order, and then stashed them in a kitchen drawer behind a loaf of bread. They locked up and headed for the highway.

33

The Breezeway Motor Court looked like it had been down on its luck for a while. It was a long, low-slung block of fifteen rooms. Red-brick, peeling white trim. Brown doors and smudged picture windows with the curtains drawn. A No-Tell Motel if there ever was one.

There was a gravel parking lot and, just as the tipster had said, the place was set back from the highway in a grove of pines that only added to its gloom. It was dusk when they arrived, and the orange neon "Vacancy" sign was buzzing on the wall of the office, next to a jalousie window that was obscured by a tangle of trumpet vine. Out front, a hand-lettered plywood sign announced a weekly rate of $90.

"Quite a bargain," Henry said.

"Bedbugs at no extra charge."

The screen door of the office was unlocked, so they walked on in. The desk clerk looked up from an issue of *Motor Trend*. A breeze from a ceiling fan curled back the tops of the pages. The clerk was in his early twenties, with a porn star mustache but otherwise clean-shaven, and more neatly dressed than the place deserved. He stood and greeted them with a cheerful smile.

"One room or two?"

"Actually, we're looking for somebody," Henry said. "Guy named Merle. White guy in his fifties, had a beard, was staying here maybe a week ago?"

"Oh, sure. Merle Watkins. Rolled in more than a month ago and paid in advance. Around here, that makes an impression."

Henry looked at Anna, who nodded. A last name, and a last known whereabouts. Finally, the trail felt a few degrees warmer.

"Any chance he's still around?"

"Nope. Took off about a week ago with three days left on his tab. Don't see that every day, either. He owe you money or something?"

"Or something. We just want to talk to him. You wouldn't have his check-in card handy, would you? I'm Henry, by the way. And this is Anna."

The clerk set aside his magazine and stood a little straighter.

"Derrick, pleased to meet you. And if it were up to me I'd be happy to show you, but, well . . ."

"Rules?"

"My boss is kind of a stickler for privacy stuff. Said it's what most of our customers are paying for."

"Never knew privacy was that cheap. What's he paying you an hour?"

"'Scuse me?"

"Your manager. I guess what I'm really asking is, if you could pick up an extra twenty just for letting somebody take a quick look at a check-in card, he wouldn't begrudge you that, now, would he?"

Derrick smiled uncomfortably and gazed up at the ceiling fan, as if thinking it over.

"Tell you what. For twenty bucks, what I *can* do is give you the key to Merle's old room. Number eight. Nobody's been in there since he checked out. That way you could have a look-see and come on back. But— and here's the good part—*first* I'd need to go out there myself to make sure that, you know, nobody's illegally occupying the space. And while I'm doing that, well, you two could make sure nobody goes poking around in that card file over there. 'Cause that would be wrong."

"The gray box?"

"Yep."

"We'll watch it like a hawk."

Derrick grabbed a key from a slot and let the screen door slam shut behind him. Henry slid over the box from the end of the counter, opened it, and began thumbing the cards. There were blessedly few at a dive like this, and he quickly found what he was looking for.

"Here we go." Anna leaned closer for a better look. He could feel her breath on his ear. "Merle Watkins, checked in on June 27th. Run this address on your phone."

"Go ahead."

"Forty-four North Main Street. Latham, New York. Damn."

"What?"

"I was hoping for a tag number, but there's no car listed."

"And the address is a fake. There's no forty-four North Main, not in Latham. There's one in Cohoes, New York. Or in Harriman, New York. But not in Latham." She clicked around a while longer while Henry waited. "There's no Merle Watkins listed in Latham, either. On any street."

"Fake name. To go with his fake address."

"Anything else?"

"Not unless he paid with plastic. If he did, for another twenty maybe Derrick will let us keep an eye on the receipts."

But, as Derrick informed them a few minutes later, Merle had paid in cash.

"Did he have a car?" Henry asked.

"Oh, yeah. Sure did."

"You get a tag number?"

"Nope. But it had Virginia plates, I remember that, mostly because he had such a sweet ride. Camaro SS, a 2010. That's the year they finally brought it back."

"Brought what back?"

"The Camaro. Best thing Chevy ever built. He had a V-8 with four hundred horses. Sweet, like I said."

"Remember the color?"

"You bet. Silver. A real nice look. Oh, and here's the key if you want to take a look."

He tossed it to Henry, attached to a plastic green oval with the room number in white.

"Make it quick, though. The owner likes to drop by some nights around this time. To make sure I'm not throwing any parties, I guess, and, well . . ."

"We'll be out of here before you know it."

By now it was almost dark, especially in the deep shadows of the pines. Number 8 was about halfway down. There were only three cars in the lot besides Henry's, so it wasn't surprising no one had needed Merle's room since he'd checked out. Henry unlocked the door and switched on a light. The place smelled of pine resin, disinfectant, and cigarettes.

"So this was his home for more than a month," Henry said.

"Lovely. The orange curtains are a nice touch."

"He did have cable, though."

"And he spent his days grabbing five chickens at a time, forging doctor's signatures, impersonating a UPS man, and going hunting with my brother. For what?"

"Either he's a real pro or this whole idea is crazy as hell."

"Just about everything I've learned in the past few days is crazy as hell."

She stooped down to check the wastebasket.

"Nothing in the trash."

"I doubt we'll find anything. This guy doesn't strike me as the careless type."

Anna went into the bathroom and switched on a fluorescent light, which flickered and hummed while Henry checked beneath the bed. There were a few empty peanut shells, a crushed cigarette butt, but nothing of interest. He pulled a chair across the room to place it beneath a heating duct high on the far wall, climbing up for a closer look just as Anna emerged from the bathroom.

"Find anything?" he asked.

"Dead cockroach. What are you doing up there?"

"Checking the ducts. The paint is scratched on these screws, and they feel a little loose."

"Are you saying Merle and my mom have the same taste in hiding places?"

"Got a dime?"

"You sure you don't want your magic paper clip instead?"

"Very funny."

"Here."

She handed him a dime.

"Move that floor lamp closer, so I can see." She

switched on the light just as he was removing the last screw.

"Anything?"

He raised on his tiptoes and peered inside.

"Empty, but there's a path through the dust, like something has been dragged through the duct."

"Maybe that's where he kept his cash."

"Or anything else he didn't want people to know about."

Henry put the grate back on, tightened the screws, and hopped down. He noticed Anna looking around with a restless, unreadable expression.

"What are you thinking?"

"I'm imagining my mom, holed up in some room like this in Europe, doing whatever it was that she did in those days. Hiding from the Russians, maybe. Or meeting some contact."

"She would have been in much better digs than this."

"Oh, yeah? Like what?" She touched his arm.

"A cozy little pension in Paris, maybe. With a sloped ceiling and a charming view."

"Keep going." She squeezed his arm.

"Or maybe a chalet at the base of the Alps, with a fireplace."

"And a hot tub in the back?"

"Now you're making it almost sexy."

"Meeting people in secret places is pretty sexy all by itself, don't you think?"

"I suppose it is."

He concentrated on her eyes, and her touch. For a moment they hung in that delicate balance between affection and passion, with Henry aware of the beating of his heart. He drew her closer and they kissed.

Within seconds her hands were under his shirt, and his were pulling up her blouse. She backed him against the mattress and they tumbled onto the bedspread. She grabbed for his zipper. He undid a button, and then another. Groaning bedsprings and gasping breaths.

There was a loud knock at the door, followed by a shout from Derrick.

"Y'all 'bout done in there?"

They stopped, a freeze frame, chests heaving. Henry looked into her eyes, and she broke into a flushed grin.

"It's the KGB!" he whispered. She giggled but held on tight.

"Hello in there?" Derrick again, this time with a note of panic.

"Just about done!" Anna shouted back, and they collapsed in laughter, molded to each other, Henry alive with the heat of her body. But the spell was broken, and with a creak of the springs Anna rolled off the bed and hopped to her feet.

"Damn," she whispered, buttoning her blouse while Henry zipped his jeans. "Guess we should've hung out the 'Do Not Disturb' sign."

They smoothed the bedspread. Then, with the chair

and floor lamp still out of place, they went out the door. Derrick sagged in relief as Henry tossed him the key.

"Thanks," Henry said. "But maybe next time you could throw in some complimentary champagne."

"Huh?"

Anna laughed and took his hand as they walked toward his car, squeezing it just before she let go to head for the passenger side. Neither of them spoke until they pulled onto the highway.

"Where do you think that came from?" Anna said.

"Both of us, I guess."

"Well, I did tell you to keep me busy." She reached over and squeezed his knee.

They stopped for dinner at a Chinese place on the way back, the only customers at the hole-in-the-wall joint on Route 50. The electricity of their moment in the motel room lingered throughout the meal, and they amped it further with spicy food and a bottle of wine. When they reached his house, Henry didn't even have to invite her inside.

"What do you think?" he said, switching on a light. "Tackle the letters, or wait till tomorrow?"

She answered by switching off the light and seeking him out in the sudden darkness. He pulled her closer. She spoke into his ear.

"Here's the better question. Couch or bed?"

34

Helen looked out the window onto the bleakness of East Germany. She had hopped off the Hamburg train in Spandau, where she changed clothes and adjusted her wig in a bathroom stall before boarding a train to Wolfsburg. From Spandau the train had exited West Berlin across the Wall without incident. The East German border authorities had barely glanced at her Canadian passport. They zipped open her bag but didn't touch its contents. No search or seizure. No escort from the train for questioning. For the moment her biggest problem was that the wig was making her scalp itch.

Her rail pass was now good for another thirty days, and by then, she'd be . . . where, exactly? And in what sort of condition? Still on the run? Locked in a cell? Facing an interrogator? Or, maybe, with no place else to go, she'd even be back in Wixville, shamed and disgraced, exiled once again to the boring brick rancher by the woods. Living with her mom and dad in a place she'd been trying to leave behind since the age of ten. If it came to that, she vowed to at least supply her mother with a better brand of vodka, something made by actual Russians. They'd drink together. It would be their shared secret.

She was already weary of checking for surveillance. But whenever she contemplated giving it a rest, the thought of Gilley prodded her. Elimination was his specialty, and he seemed to have plenty of people to carry out his plans.

Even so, she fell asleep for more than an hour, awakening with a start as the train neared the next border crossing into West Germany. Looking around, she saw that all was calm. God, but this was dreary countryside. The view was of chockablock houses and drab industrial buildings—gray Stalinist rush jobs from the 1950s, concrete monuments to state-sponsored anonymity that were already crumbling.

The train clattered along, skirting a village now, fluttery leaves from linden trees showering down. She spotted a line of women outside a bakery, all of them in dark coats, holding empty shopping baskets. Beetling down a potholed road was one of the clunky autos of the East—a squatty Trabant the color of putty.

Before she'd fallen asleep they'd stopped at some bleak industrial town, the name already forgotten, the depot little more than a concrete platform with exposed rebar, populated almost entirely by VoPos, or Volkspolizei, who stood ready to seize anyone who might try to jump on board to escape the "Workers' Paradise," as Herrington always delighted in calling East Germany. Helen's passage to Wolfsburg meant she wasn't supposed to leave the train during its transit through this forbidden land. Until they crossed back onto free soil she might as well be riding in a sealed car, like the one the Swiss had used to send Lenin back to Russia in 1917, transporting him as carefully as if he were a virus.

But who could Helen possibly endanger apart from herself? And, with her career and reputation already terminal cases, even that was a moot point. Only one potential victim sprang to mind—Kevin Gilley. She might still infect him, she supposed, as long as she collected enough incriminating evidence, and distributed it to enough of the right people before the Herringtons of the world shut her down. But how likely was that? Success probably depended on her contact in Paris, the woman she knew only as CDG.

It was then that Helen remembered something that CDG had said during their first phone conversation. *If you're ever in a jam, and the usual channel isn't an option, ring me at the same time as today. Twenty hours.*

A phone number in Paris, but for the moment it was beyond reach. In a panic, she tried to remember it. Gone for good, unless she was able to relax. She drew a deep breath, looked out the window at more falling leaves, and then shut her eyes as she tried to clear her head. She recalled the moment when she had first unfolded the typewritten message that had contained the phone number, and in a flash she saw it again, as clearly as if the sheet of paper was in her lap.

Exhaling, Helen again committed the number to memory, repeating it to herself three times to make sure. Her lifeline was still intact. She decided then that she would hop another train in Wolfsburg, on a route that, with one more switch, would take her to Paris.

Contemplating all the contingencies made her think of NASA, and all those space missions she'd followed so raptly as a young girl, hanging on every word from Walter Cronkite, whose grandfatherly tone had always reassured her in moments of peril. Don't worry, he'd say, NASA had backups for backups.

But what if, once she got to Paris, CDG recoiled in horror? Or cut her off? Or, worse, turned her in? Alas, Helen was not NASA. There was no backup for her backup. All hopes rested on CDG.

At the very least, she would finally see the City of Light. If her plans never got off the ground, then she would try to take in a few sights as a final consolation prize before turning herself in. The Louvre, a café, the Eiffel Tower. Then she would throw herself on the ramparts at the Agency's Paris station and be done with it. She ordered a coffee from a passing cart. Bitter and lukewarm. With renewed alertness she again grew cautious and watchful, her sense of well-being cursed by everything she'd ever learned in her training.

A curly-haired young man wearing a backpack and dressed like a hippie in a tie-dye shirt and jeans wandered by her compartment, glancing inside as he passed. It was the third time she'd noticed him in the past fifteen minutes. He looked either lost or stoned, but maybe that was an act. He might also be someone's scout—Gilley's, or Herrington's, or Edward Stone's. Helen memorized his features.

The woman seated across from her was also beginning to get on Helen's nerves. She had seemed almost preternaturally alert throughout the journey, eyes flicking in all directions. No book or newspaper to distract her. No aimless gazing out the window. Watchful and still, like a heron waiting to spear a fish.

A gray concrete monolith passed on their left, followed by a watchtower and then a long line of razor wire. The train began slowing, brakes squealing. Outside, police whistles sounded on the platform. She almost couldn't bear to look, but when she finally did she saw there was no commotion, no uproar. Just the usual collection of VoPos, loitering and smoking and looking officious. They had reached the crossing for West Germany. Wolfsburg would be next, and then, another nine hours beyond it, Paris. She took out her

Canadian passport, smoothed her wig, and prepared her smile for the authorities.

On the third stop after Wolfsburg, a trim young man in a light gray suit boarded the train and seated himself on the opposite side of her compartment. He was fresh-faced and smiling, as American as Johnny Appleseed.

"Hi!" he said cheerily. "Are you American?"

"Canadian," she said, after nearly answering in the affirmative. He'd almost tripped her up. Was that his job? Her radar began to beep.

"Where are you headed?" Why was he so curious?

"Here and there. I'll know when I'm there."

"Must be nice having that kind of freedom. I've been on a schedule for two weeks running. Between that and the food I'm about to have a coronary. Where do you live in Canada?"

"Montreal."

"How lucky. Your French must be great."

Shit. She'd meant to say Toronto, a place she'd actually been. Her French consisted of a few dozen words left over from high school, most of which had to do with food. He smiled again, as if coaxing her to do the same. Was he trying to get a read on her, or trying to pick her up?

"I'm Hal, by the way. Hal Douglas." He offered a handshake.

"Nice to meet you." Helen offered neither her hand nor her name. She pointedly turned to face the window, although she kept an eye on his reflection. Hal opened his mouth to say more, seemed to think better of it, and then waited a while longer for her to turn back around and give him a second chance.

Should she change compartments, or would that arouse further suspicion? He was probably a harmless Chamber of Commerce type from the Midwest, peddling widgets or office supplies, a lonely sales rep looking for an easy lay, or maybe just a sympathetic ear. So this was life on your own in the secret world, then, a heightened existence in which you always assumed the worst.

Hal picked up an attaché case from the floor and placed it on his lap. He popped the latches, raised the lid and reached inside for something. Helen's view was blocked by the lid, but she braced herself for action. If he pulled out a gun she would kick his shins and slap the barrel to the side. All the while she kept her face averted and watched the reflection.

He shut the case and she saw he was holding a copy of the *Financial Times,* which he shook open and began to read. Her brain sounded the All Clear while her heart beat time to the clacking of the train on the tracks. She wiped her damp palms on her slacks, and recalled something Baucom had told her on a fine summer night in a beer garden about the demands of staying safe in hostile territory.

It gets easier after a while. You get used to the whole idea that you need to notice everything, and I mean everything. But of course then you start to get comfortable, because you've convinced yourself that you're covering all the bases. And that's when you're the most vulnerable. That's when you're the most likely to make a mistake and get somebody killed.

Somebody like yourself, for example.

The man flipped a page of his newspaper, the sudden movement making her flinch. She checked her watch. Seven more hours until 8 p.m., and she was already a wreck. Helen sagged against the wall. But she kept her eyes open, and continued to watch the reflection.

35

At ten minutes before 20:00 hours, Helen sat on a stone wall near a phone booth in a suburb east of Paris, waiting to place her call. As a security measure she'd left the train a stop early. She'd then spent the next half hour strolling residential streets as she wound her way toward the city's outskirts. Her role was that of a happy-go-lucky Canadian tourist—from Toronto, not Montreal—keeping to herself and annoying the occasional passerby with questions in English. Now she would finally learn if she still had an ally in Paris.

A teenage girl darted into the phone booth five minutes before the hour, but the girl finished her call with two minutes to spare. Helen practically ran over to secure her spot. At precisely 20:00, she dropped in a few coins and dialed. CDG picked up on the first ring. No static this time.

"I had a feeling I'd hear from you tonight. I'm also guessing that your first name is Helen."

"I guess they've sounded the alarm."

"Full alert to all stations, I'm afraid. A matter of greatest urgency is how my COS put it. Apparently they're even worried you might be one of *them*. I'm guessing you're not or you wouldn't have called. So in that sense I suppose I should be relieved to be hearing from you."

"Is that your way of saying you shouldn't even be talking me?"

"It's a risk. I won't deny it."

Helen wondered if this would be their last contact. CDG didn't sound nearly as friendly, or as eager to help, as she had during their first call. Understandable, given the nature of their profession. And if the woman's wariness extended to letting someone from the Agency listen in on their call, then she was finished.

"I'm sorry. I shouldn't have expected you to even answer."

"I guess I had too many questions not to."

"That's only fair. Ask away."

"If you're not one of them, then what are you, exactly?"

"The same thing I've been all along. A girl in over her head. They canned me this morning for my curiosity about you know who. Sent me home to pack my bag for a flight to the States. I slipped out the fire escape while my handler was watching TV. And now here I am, a glorified clerk who decided to go it alone. My operational debut and swan song, rolled into one, with only one target in mind. Which is why I called. For help and advice. And, yes, I know I'm being indiscreet, but frankly right now you're all I've got left. Oh, and I'm in France, by the way."

She expected a reaction of shock, or even horror. Or, worse, a quick recalibration in which her would-be savior would cagily lure Helen into a trap. The good employee protecting her career. Instead, Helen heard laughter.

"I have to say, none of what I've ever done before could have prepared me for that answer. You ditched your handler out the fire escape?"

"He thought I was in the shower."

"Splendid!"

"Yes. But now I'm completely at your mercy. If you're planning on turning me in, at least let me know now so we can do this as gracefully as possible."

"It crossed my mind. But if you're still truly interested in taking down that certain someone, then I can hardly say no. That *is* still your main interest?"

"Yes. I just don't know if I'm up to it."

"Look, you've had the same training I did, and now that you're here it will be that much easier for me to help. Makes it far less likely this call will be screened, for starters. Although I still won't utter your last name, or his, because God knows what sort of filter this conversation might be passing through before the night is over, especially if French intelligence has decided to cooperate."

"That hadn't even occurred to me."

"Sometimes you luck into things, even in this business, and it sounds like so far you've been fairly lucky. But from here on out we'd better start banking on a little more skill, agreed?"

"Agreed."

"I'm going to need some time to figure out what we should do next. Do you think you'll be able to keep moving and call me back in two hours?"

"Yes. Same number?"

"God, no. Let me give you another one."

"For another phone box?"

"Of course. You don't think I'd have you calling the office, I hope?"

"No. Sorry."

"It's all right. In your shoes, I'd be thinking the same thing. It's a wonder you can trust anyone at this point."

"The bigger question is why you're trusting me."

"Who says I am? Maybe you're a mental case, the office malcontent."

"Oh, I'm definitely the latter."

"Same here. But I also know your motivation. Ever

since I saw what I saw, I've been wanting to hang his scalp on my saddle. So let's make the most of this while we can. Ready for the number?"

"Yes."

Helen wrote it down, even though she knew she should have committed it to memory.

"Oh, and I'm Claire. Claire Saylor. So when they flutter you later with the lie detector, I suppose that'll be the first thing that pops out. But if we're smart it won't come to that, because I'm going to arm you with the information you need and send you on your way for more. For a day or two, at least, we're going to beat him and all the rest of them at their own game. How does that sound?"

"Better than anything I've heard all day."

"Splendid. Talk to you in two."

Helen hung up and looked around. No one was watching. She strolled a few blocks, already feeling calmer. Then she caught another bus and crept closer to Paris. The sky on the horizon shined with the glow of the city.

She didn't fret as much about picking a phone box for the second call. Stay alert, but stay loose. She dropped in more coins and punched in the number.

"Hello there," Claire answered. "How about lunch tomorrow, and a little shopping?"

"Shopping?" For cover, of course, which Helen

should have realized right away. "Sounds great. Where would you like to meet?"

"Le Bon Marché. Rue de Sèvres, on the Left Bank. A grand old department store, and for your purposes what could be better?"

Helen knew exactly what she meant. During their counter-surveillance training on the streets of Baltimore and Washington, department stores had always been the toughest places to maintain contact with a target. Too many mirrors. Too many racks of clothing, nooks and crannies, exits and entrances. Then there were the dressing rooms and all of that easy-to-grab apparel for disguising yourself on the fly, if necessary.

"The store's name means 'the great deal.' The prices are anything but, although it's definitely worth the trip. The cosmetics counter alone is a floor show. You'll be wishing you were French within half an hour. After you've had a nice look around, go next door to the food hall, La Grande Épicerie. I'll be on the second floor in the main café. Is noon all right?"

"Perfect. How will I know you?"

"You won't. But I'll know you. Just look over at the tables and I'll wave."

"See you at noon."

"In the meantime, *bon chance*."

Oui, Helen thought. *Bon chance,* indeed.

36

By 11 p.m. Helen was seated in a café near the Gare de Lyon with a Michelin map spread on the table and a Fodor's guidebook in her lap. In her purse was a box of hair dye that she'd bought at a drugstore. She couldn't wait to ditch the wig.

A young man sidled up to flirt and Helen shooed him away by telling him she was Canadian, as if that was supposed to make her totally undesirable. She traced a forefinger down the streets on the map, marveling at the names she'd been hearing since she was a girl. A line from an old storybook popped into her head: *In an old house in Paris that was covered in vines, lived twelve little girls in two straight lines.* Perhaps she would bump into Madeline.

A waiter brusquely cleared away her cup and saucer and cleared his throat, eager to close, so Helen got down to business with her map. First she found the location of the department store where she would meet Claire. Then she scanned the neighborhoods just across the Seine from where she sat now for a likely place to hole up. She settled on the Latin Quarter, partly because she'd heard of it, partly because its bohemian reputation made her feel more like a writer or artist than a disgraced spy. She also liked the look of its streets on the map—crooked and squeezed together, offering the illusion of a maze where she'd be harder to find. Plus, the guidebook said it was a good place for finding rooms after hours. She noted the location for a small hotel that the guidebook included in its "Rock Bottom" section, saying that it offered "snug rooms for the young in legs and spirit (no elevator)." Then she folded up the map, paid the waiter—who responded with a disdainful flip of his towel, no Lehmann for sure—and was on her way.

She caught the Metro and promptly nodded off, missing her stop and having to double back after awakening with a start. At first she thought someone had stolen her suitcase, but it had only slid forward from the motion of the train. Her purse lay on the seat next to her, where it easily could have been snatched, and she thought of how idiotic it would have been to be foiled by a common thief.

The sullen innkeeper refused to speak a word of English even though she seemed to understand everything Helen said. Helen took a key heavy enough to weight her to the bottom of the ocean and climbed to the fourth floor. Gloomy. A window shade the color of stretched skin filtered the light from the streets, and the bed smelled like an ashtray.

She took a lukewarm shower, and then made herself spend the next hour dyeing her hair blond at the tiny sink. Then she covered her head with a plastic bathing cap and rolled into the valley in the middle of the sagging mattress, where she immediately sank into a dreamless sleep.

In the middle of the night she awakened suddenly and inexplicably, and sat up in bed. A couple of jolly young drunks were passing in the street below, chattering loudly. The room was stuffy. She considered opening the window, but was reluctant to raise the shade lest someone spot her silhouette and drop her with a single shot. Voices rumbled from the room next door—a man and a woman who seemed to have just returned. There was laughter, the woman's like a bell and the man's husky with mischief. The headboard of their bed banged the thin wall as one of them collapsed onto the mattress, and then a second time as the other one followed. For the next few minutes they talked, the sound of confidences being shared. Fortunately they were soon silent. Helen found herself missing their company and hoping they were merely asleep, and not dead. A silly idea, but there it was.

Maybe she should give up. Not by turning herself in, but by flying away. Travel back across the Atlantic. Become a Canadian. Live a tranquil life in the 'burbs of Toronto. Marry a bland businessman who drank Molson and followed the Maple Leafs.

Then she imagined Claire, alone at a table at La Grand Épicerie, checking her watch as she worried on Helen's behalf. Duty called, and Helen could not afford to be a no-show when Claire was risking so much for their cause. For Anneliese's cause, too. It was this thought that finally emboldened her to climb out of bed, raise the shade, and throw open the sash.

Cool air, the sound of distant music. The two drunks were still talking loudly but were nearly a block away. For a moment it almost felt like freedom. Then she saw the glow of a cigarette in a doorway across the street. Probably nothing, or they would have come roaring up the stairs by now. The figure was in shadow, but it had a man's size and posture. Why would anyone keeping an eye on her make himself so easy to spot? The cigarette glowed again. Helen lowered the shade and returned to bed just as the headboard in the next room again banged the wall, followed by a cry of pleasure and a succession of further thumps, which soon fell into a rhythm as frantic as that of a screen door banging in a gale.

So this was Paris by night. Noisy lovers and silent men in the shadows, biding their time.

Sometime later Helen fell back to sleep. By then the room next door was quiet and the fellow with the cigarette was gone from the doorway across the street.

A bright morning, a croissant and a coffee, and there she was on a Paris sidewalk, rejuvenated, a girl from Wixville strolling the Boulevard Saint-Michel. Even for someone more recently from Berlin it was impressive. On the corner just ahead, two North Africans, as thin as pipe cleaners, were selling plastic windup birds, releasing them into the breeze to attract the attention of tourists. The fluttery mechanical wing beats were as annoying as those of the pigeons. She smelled baking bread, the exhaust of a moped, the rainwater freshness of hosed-down cobbles. A feast for the senses.

Then there were the women. It wasn't what they wore, but how they wore it. She could have assembled exactly the same wardrobe and would have still stood out as the pretender. Maybe it was how they carried themselves, plus that bored look on their faces that said, *Of course I'm marvelous, but so what?*

Helen's dye job had been surprisingly successful, and she had dumped the wig in a trash can along Boulevard

Saint-Germain, observed only by a boy in shorts on a bicycle who'd laughed aloud.

A gust of cigarette smoke caught her unawares—Gitanes, like Baucom's, and she briefly wished he were here, more for advice than for comfort. Then she drew a deep breath as exhilaration swelled behind her breastbone. I can do this, she thought. Win or lose, I can do this for a few days more.

From overhead came a popping noise, and she glanced up to see a woman shaking a bedsheet from a high window. It startled her just enough to jolt her confidence, and she thought of all the people who must be looking for her by now. She nearly tripped on a crack in the sidewalk, and something like panic rose in her throat. Seeking shelter, she ducked into a small grocery to look out through the window, scanning the sidewalk crowds above rows of apples and oranges for possible surveillance. It took a moment for her to collect herself and head back out, and even then she paused a block later to remove her compact from her purse so she could check behind her while pretending to powder her nose.

It reminded her that, back at the Farm, when she'd finished at the top of her class in spotting surveillance, her male classmates had groused about this technique—*Hey, we can't stop to powder our noses!* But her skills had gone deeper than that. As their training officer had said, "She notices shit that you guys miss." Like socks and shoes, for example, or other small giveaways that male operatives tended to pay scant attention to when assembling their own wardrobes.

Beyond that, she'd developed a sort of sixth sense that had allowed her to spot anomalies in crowds and in movements. But that was during training, when she had relished the role of underdog, and many of her pursuers had also been trainees, lacking in finesse. Besides, she was out of practice. Would she again be able to function with the same easy sharpness?

She glanced at a reflection on a shopwindow and kept moving toward her rendezvous.

37

The department store, Le Bon Marché, was as grand as Claire had said, with colonnaded arcades and wrought iron railings, a hall of wonders three stories high. Crisscrossing escalators rose toward a magnificent skylight. Mirrors here and there offered an almost panoramic rear view. But with noon approaching Helen was so anxious that she scarcely took notice, and her palms were sweating by the time she climbed to the second floor of the vast food hall next door.

She paused behind a potted tree as the café loomed into view, and took stock of the clientele, hoping to pick out Claire from all the faces. Every table was full, and nearly all the customers were women. Only three sat alone, and each of them looked as effortlessly resplendent as the women Helen had been admiring out on the sidewalks. The air buzzed with conversation and the clatter of cutlery against china.

Helen was on the verge of breaking cover when her training and a shard of lingering doubt stopped her. She backed away and made a quick reconnaissance. Almost no men anywhere, except for a few beleaguered-looking older fellows toting bags in the wake of their wives—not that this was any guarantee of harmlessness. She tried to glance through the square windows of the kitchen's swinging doors, from which servers emerged every few seconds balancing trays with one hand. Behind them, in the flash openings, she saw chefs in white hats amid steam and smoke, and heard metallic scrapes and chops, the sizzle of a griddle. Satisfied that no one looked overly watchful or ready to spring into action, she stepped into view.

One of the three solitary women smiled across the room at her, a brunette with darker lipstick than Helen was used to seeing on Americans. Her hair was pulled up in a bun, and she wore a blue scarf around her neck, just so. Alert brown eyes. When she waved, Helen waved back and began weaving through the tables.

Claire stood in greeting. She was about the same height, and wore a yellow linen dress the color of sunlight. There were two shopping bags at her feet. You never would have guessed she was here for anything but pleasure. You never would have guessed she was anything but French.

They hugged like old friends. For cover, Helen

supposed, because she was resisting any sensation of relief. As they settled into their chairs, the situation still felt as if it might tilt in any direction.

"I thought it might be you," Claire said.

"You saw me earlier?"

"Checking the lay of the land? Yes. Smart."

Helen was a little crestfallen to have been spotted so easily when she had been so careful, and her discomfort went up another notch. She looked into Claire's eyes and cut straight to the point.

"You'd tell me wouldn't you?"

"Tell you?"

"If this was a setup. If they were about to come charging out from those swinging doors to take me in."

At first, Claire looked hurt. Then she smiled ruefully.

"I suppose I should be reassured by that question. I'll admit that it did unsettle me a little when you seemed to trust me so easily."

"I'm sorry. I've insulted you."

"No. You've asked the right question. And, to answer it, I never would've let you down so easily as this. They would have nabbed you the moment you walked into the store. And all of them would have been carrying one of these."

Claire reached into her handbag and slid a photostat across the table. It was a picture of Helen. They'd used the photo from her Agency ID, which they'd snapped on the morning of her arrival in Berlin following an overnight flight.

"It came in last night."

Helen slid it back and swallowed hard, staring at the table as she imagined the photo being distributed at CIA outposts all across Europe.

"And now it's my turn to be a little harsh. So please look me in the eye again, if you don't mind, because this game of precaution works both ways. I need to see the identity you're traveling under. You can pass it under the table."

Helen took the Canadian passport from her purse, slipped it to Claire, and then watched her flipping the pages in her lap, checking entry and exit stamps to make sure there was nothing alarming.

"It's quite good," Claire said.

"I suppose it is, if it's taken me this far."

"Who got it for you?"

"A friend. But he doesn't know about you."

"Must be quite a friend."

Helen blushed, but said nothing more. Claire handed back the passport and then took her hand across the table, as if preparing to swear a blood oath.

"Thank you. I know it's hard putting your fate into someone else's hands, so I'm going to reciprocate. We're in this soup together now, my friend, and will be until we've either emptied the bowl or one of us has knocked it to the floor, and broken it into a thousand pieces. All right?"

"All right."

Claire released her hand but not her gaze. Helen began to relax. Confidence was half the battle, and she sensed that she was at last in competent hands.

"The dye job is quite good, too," Claire said, her tone lightening. "Impressive."

"Speaking of being impressed, how do you manage it?"

"Manage what?"

"To look just like the rest of them." She gestured to encompass the room. "Who needs cover when you can pull that off?"

Claire smiled and dipped her head, an appealing show of modesty. She, too, was lowering her guard.

"In the end it was osmosis. I went through a full year of trying, all to no effect. Finally I just gave up. Then one morning I woke up and I just knew."

"Knew what?"

"What to wear, how to wear it. How to walk, how to speak, when to look people in the eye. The right expression of disdain. How to drink my coffee and sip my wine. When to flirt, when to ignore. At first I thought I must be imagining it. Then within a week three different Frenchwomen, in from the provinces, stopped me in the street to ask for directions."

"Amazing."

"You're from North Carolina?"

"Yes. Wixville."

"You don't have an accent."

"An act of will. It was that or never be taken seriously by anyone north of the Mason-Dixon line."

"Then maybe we really *are* sisters. I'm from north Georgia, a town with fewer people than are in this store right now, and here we are speaking like newscasters on the eleven o'clock anchor desk."

"When did you get rid of yours?"

"College. Georgia Tech. Part of it was my roommate, Marion from Massachusetts, as cool as a codfish. Spoke like a proper Brahmin, and there I was drawling and y'alling my way through rush week and first semester. Then one night we're watching some late-night talk show and there's Lester Maddox, our esteemed former governor who used to chase blacks out of his fried-chicken joint with an axe handle. He's sitting on a stage in Manhattan, making an ass of himself in front of the whole country, all the while sounding exactly like me and three-quarters of the freshman class. You're damn right I got rid of it."

Helen was about to reply when Claire leaned forward as if to impart a confidence. Still smiling, but with eyes now glittering with intensity, she lowered her voice and said, "Don't turn around, but there is a silent and resolute-looking fellow in a smart suit standing in the corner just over your left shoulder, over by the register.

Get out your compact and tell me if you recognize him."

Helen did as she was told.

"No. I've never seen him."

"I think he's with store management, so it's probably fine. Just wanted to make sure. Down to business, then. Here."

Claire reached into her handbag and handed over a copy of *Paris Match*. The photostat from the office had gone back into Claire's purse without Helen noticing.

"I brought that article I told you about. The one about overly aggressive men?"

A few extra pages had been neatly and expertly attached in the middle of the magazine.

"Thanks. Looking forward to reading that."

"Take extra good care of that. It's one of the last two copies, and I'm not sure I'd be able to lay my hands on the other one."

"Oh. I see." Helen placed it reverently into her handbag.

"I could always write a new one from memory, but it would never have quite the same weight. Not in a case this sensitive."

Helen checked her compact again. The man in the suit was gone.

"I think we're safe for now," Claire said. "We should have a drink to make ourselves feel better, don't you think?"

"Yes. A drink is exactly what's called for. When I

finally start to breathe again, I might even want lunch."

"I can order for both of us, unless you'd like me to translate the menu?"

"Please. Do the honors, as long as the drink comes first."

Claire picked up the wine list.

"Let's see. A little early for an aperitif, but I think the occasion calls for one."

She raised her right hand and a trim young waiter appeared almost instantly. Claire rattled off a stream of French. He nodded and departed. Within seconds he returned with two wineglasses and a beaded bottle, which he expertly corked and then placed into a silver ice bucket after filling their glasses.

"To our success," Claire said, raising her glass. "And to the continued survival of Elizabeth Waring Hart."

Helen clanked their glasses, a little too sharply. Then she smiled and sipped, expecting only wine but getting something stronger and more interesting, with a hint of orange peel.

"What is this?"

"Lillet. A Bordeaux that got itself mixed up with a dose of liqueur and a touch of quinine, chilled to a turn. It can be an acquired taste."

"I've acquired it. It's perfect."

She took another swallow and sank back in her chair before speaking again.

"I have to say, all that training is coming in handy,

and I don't just mean the surveillance games. In school I was always the clumsiest girl in gym class. But at the Farm I got to do things that had always been for men only—handling guns, rappelling off a helicopter skid with an M-16 strapped to my back, self-defense drills with karate chops and body throws."

"Same here. I remember how fresh it all felt. How new. All the boys had to do was revert to their natural state. They stopped shaving, did chin-up competitions, and generally acted like adolescents, thrilled to be blowing things up. And there I was, getting up every morning before the five a.m. run so I'd have time to wash and blow-dry my hair."

Helen laughed and took another sip.

"I held my own," Claire said, "that was what counted."

"Me as well. I've never forgotten."

"And as your reward, you get to have more of this."

She refilled Helen's glass. Here was yet another Agency employee bucking up her resolve with an exquisite drink. Baucom had never been willing to say much about what made him want to help, apart from sex and personal loyalty, but Helen sensed that Claire's motives might be had for the asking.

"Tell me something," Helen said. "Why are you doing this?"

"I thought we'd established that. To stop Gilley."

"That was earlier, before I'd left my sanity behind, before I was a runaway. Back when all we were doing was sending notes through the mail. Now? You're risking your career. Maybe more."

"My career? Let me tell you what that consists of these days. For the last two weeks they've had me keeping tabs on a high-ticket prostitute who might—repeat, *might*—be having an affair with a French cabinet minister. As if anyone in France would actually mind. No sign of the minister, of course. If it goes on for another week I'm going to invite her out for drinks just to break the monotony. Oh, *merci*!"

The waiter had appeared with their lunches. Helen's was a mushroom omelet with a salad. Routine enough, she supposed, but the aroma made her realize she was ravenous. She dug in.

"Does everything in Paris taste this good?"

"What, you're not homesick for currywurst?"

Helen smiled.

"Anyhow, that's my career, such as it is. I've asked for better assignments, but all of those go to the lads."

"Lads?"

"It's what a Brit friend of mine over at the local MI6 shop calls the boys in her outfit. Lads. They act about fifteen, and never show the slightest interest in what I'm doing. Unless, of course, I'm away on an unexplained absence for more than an hour at a time." She briskly checked her watch and made a quick scan of the room. "Otherwise, I'd be perfectly content to stay here drinking Lillet until six."

len picked up her handbag and stood to go.
out even a glance over her shoulder, she weaved
ugh the tables toward the back and headed down
hallway, where she opened the emergency door,
ckly shut it behind her, and ran down the echoing
irwell.

By the time she reached the ground floor it was all
e could do to hold down her lunch. Once again she
as on her own, with more than seven hours to kill.

"Do you need to leave?"

"I can talk a good enough game to explain away this afternoon, so don't worry on that score. Besides, I don't think you realize how deeply I feel about our cause." She nodded toward the magazine poking from Helen's purse. "You'll see, it's all in there."

"Bad?"

"It wasn't just rape. It was torture. Hours of it. Justine, one of our agents, was bleeding when I found her. The only reason I found out is that he overstayed his time at the safe house. I showed up to meet a contact, and there they were. Ten minutes later and I would've missed him. He was getting dressed and she was lying on the bed. When I asked what was going on he said it was a private matter, none of my business, and she wouldn't say a word. So I slipped her my phone number and two days later I guess she finally got up her nerve, so we met and she told me everything."

"What did you do?"

"The first thing I did was arrange for a new cover for Justine, to keep her safe."

Helen should have thought of that. It might have saved Anneliese. She put down her fork with a piece of omelet speared at the end, her appetite gone.

"Then I wrote it up and filed it as an addendum to my weekly report."

"To your chief of station?"

"Yes. Or, as I now think of him, my POS COS. Piece of shit."

"Ah. Like mine. What did he do?"

"Nothing."

"What did he say?"

"Unsubstantiated rumor. The ravings of a woman scorned. He said Justine had a history of that. He said it so many times that I started thinking there might be something to it. I hadn't been there until the end, after all. Maybe she'd embellished it. Then I heard about Marina. I hope you'll meet her, but I can't say anything more about that yet. Her cover's too deep, in a place far too dangerous for me to discuss it here. But she's going to tell you her story."

"When?"

"As soon as Audra and I make the arrangements."

"Audra knows what we're doing?"

"I had to tell her if we were going to get any help at all from higher up."

"I suppose so. It's just that . . ."

"I know. The fewer the better, now that you're on the run. But we *will* need help, because Gilley and his people outnumber us, and if he suspects you're still on his trail, this will be the first place he looks for you."

"Why?"

"Because he also knows about me, and Marina, and both those reports came out of Paris. So where else would you go if you were intent on assembling all the

pieces? That's why I spent a full surveillance techniques on my way which, don't look now but our man I think it might be a good idea if you omelet."

"Do you recognize him?"

"He's not from our talent pool, I know just an overly attentive floor manager. Be sorry, though. Do you see that hallway shoulder, the one by the kitchen doors?"

"Yes."

"There's a ladies' room toward the end. Ju is an emergency exit. As long as you open and door within three seconds, no alarm will sound follows you, I'll cut him off at the pass."

"And do what?"

"Charm the socks off him, of course." She smi "Let's meet again this evening. By then I should ha worked out some further arrangements. Eight o'clock.

"Where?"

"A safe house on the Rue Burq. Number five. Acros the river in Montmartre, near the Place des Abbess Metro station."

"One of ours?"

Claire shook her head.

"Some place Audra picked out for us."

"Eight o'clock, then. And thank you."

"Thank me later, when we've beaten them."

"Do you need to leave?"

"I can talk a good enough game to explain away this afternoon, so don't worry on that score. Besides, I don't think you realize how deeply I feel about our cause." She nodded toward the magazine poking from Helen's purse. "You'll see, it's all in there."

"Bad?"

"It wasn't just rape. It was torture. Hours of it. Justine, one of our agents, was bleeding when I found her. The only reason I found out is that he overstayed his time at the safe house. I showed up to meet a contact, and there they were. Ten minutes later and I would've missed him. He was getting dressed and she was lying on the bed. When I asked what was going on he said it was a private matter, none of my business, and she wouldn't say a word. So I slipped her my phone number and two days later I guess she finally got up her nerve, so we met and she told me everything."

"What did you do?"

"The first thing I did was arrange for a new cover for Justine, to keep her safe."

Helen should have thought of that. It might have saved Anneliese. She put down her fork with a piece of omelet speared at the end, her appetite gone.

"Then I wrote it up and filed it as an addendum to my weekly report."

"To your chief of station?"

"Yes. Or, as I now think of him, my POS COS. Piece of shit."

"Ah. Like mine. What did he do?"

"Nothing."

"What did he say?"

"Unsubstantiated rumor. The ravings of a woman scorned. He said Justine had a history of that. He said it so many times that I started thinking there might be something to it. I hadn't been there until the end, after all. Maybe she'd embellished it. Then I heard about Marina. I hope you'll meet her, but I can't say anything more about that yet. Her cover's too deep, in a place far too dangerous for me to discuss it here. But she's going to tell you her story."

"When?"

"As soon as Audra and I make the arrangements."

"Audra knows what we're doing?"

"I had to tell her if we were going to get any help at all from higher up."

"I suppose so. It's just that . . ."

"I know. The fewer the better, now that you're on the run. But we *will* need help, because Gilley and his people outnumber us, and if he suspects you're still on his trail, this will be the first place he looks for you."

"Why?"

"Because he also knows about me, and Marina, and both those reports came out of Paris. So where else would you go if you were intent on assembling all the pieces? That's why I spent a full hour using counter-surveillance techniques on my way here. Speaking of which, don't look now but our man in the suit is back. I think it might be a good idea if you didn't finish your omelet."

"Do you recognize him?"

"He's not from our talent pool, I know that. Probably just an overly attentive floor manager. Better safe than sorry, though. Do you see that hallway over my left shoulder, the one by the kitchen doors?"

"Yes."

"There's a ladies' room toward the end. Just past it is an emergency exit. As long as you open and shut the door within three seconds, no alarm will sound. If he follows you, I'll cut him off at the pass."

"And do what?"

"Charm the socks off him, of course." She smiled. "Let's meet again this evening. By then I should have worked out some further arrangements. Eight o'clock."

"Where?"

"A safe house on the Rue Burq. Number five. Across the river in Montmartre, near the Place des Abbesses Metro station."

"One of ours?"

Claire shook her head.

"Some place Audra picked out for us."

"Eight o'clock, then. And thank you."

"Thank me later, when we've beaten them."

Helen picked up her handbag and stood to go. Without even a glance over her shoulder, she weaved through the tables toward the back and headed down the hallway, where she opened the emergency door, quickly shut it behind her, and ran down the echoing stairwell.

By the time she reached the ground floor it was all she could do to hold down her lunch. Once again she was on her own, with more than seven hours to kill.

38

The safe house was on a steep, picturesque street in Montmartre— a third-floor apartment far swankier than any location Helen had ever come up with in Berlin. Pretty as a postcard, in fact, near a patisserie and a bookstore, and with a beautiful terrace that overlooked a narrow cobbled lane. Yet, from the moment Helen entered something didn't feel quite right, and it must have showed on her face.

"What's wrong?" said Claire, who'd arrived earlier. She sat with legs crossed, right arm stretched across the back of a couch with a cigarette going—the very image of style and self-assurance, posed as if for a photo by Cartier-Bresson. Helen still wore her outfit from that morning, which was beginning to droop as much as she was. She had arrived hoping for rest and refuge. Instead, her radar was sending out small, wary beeps.

"Hard to say," Helen said, continuing to inspect the room from the foyer.

Maybe it bothered her that the rent here must be through the roof, or that the furnishings looked downright lavish, a Langley bean counter's nightmare. She was also taken aback by the sight of a well-stocked liquor cart stationed next to the umbrella stand by the entrance, like part of a welcoming committee.

"That's certainly an innovation I never thought of, putting the fun right up front," she said. "Is this how they do it in all your safe houses?"

"Can't say I've ever seen that before, either. Like I said, Audra procured this place. This is my first time here."

"Have you checked to see if the equipment's on?"

"No, and now you've made me feel like a fool, because that's an excellent point."

Helen followed Claire down the hallway. Plush carpet runners and embossed wallpaper, king beds, everything spotless, luxurious, and beautifully maintained. Except for the equipment, which they found easily enough in a hall closet. Helen frowned again.

"Something wrong?" Claire asked.

"Just a little outdated."

"All I know about recorders are those sleek little body models they give you for clandestine work. Nagra SNs. Swiss, I think. Supposedly the East Germans like them even better than our people."

"Well, this one's Dutch. A Philips."

"They're no good?"

"Oh, it's probably fine. But I've never seen this brand

on our requisition list. Probably bought before I came on board. Still, a little strange they wouldn't have updated, given what they must be paying for this place. You said this house isn't on the usual list of locations?"

"Not one I've ever come across, and the locale is certainly a bit touristy for my taste—too many foreigners with cameras walking around—but keeping these places running isn't my department. I figured maybe it was reserved for a separate group of case officers."

"That would be one way of doing it, I suppose."

"You don't do it that way in Berlin?"

"I wasn't aware that any station did. But I've put in some of my own rules for our houses, so maybe whoever runs the show in Paris has done the same."

"Audra might know."

"No sense troubling her over it. Housekeeping trivia. Just shows what I've been reduced to. The only part of our business I really know."

"Pretty valuable info, I'd say, so don't sell yourself short. How 'bout a drink?"

"Perfect. But if I have any of the hard stuff I'm liable to curl up on the couch and fall asleep."

"I was thinking wine. Let's check the kitchen."

They headed for the back. The fridge was well stocked. Prepared foods from a specialty shop, filet steaks in butcher's paper. The wine was of the best vintages. Helen wondered who the tenant must be. A fairly prosperous male, judging from the clothes and other items she'd seen in the bedrooms. Her preference was always for tenants of more modest means, plain-living types who weren't likely to draw attention to themselves or their dwellings.

"Cheers," said Claire, after pouring each of them a glass. A white Bordeaux, exactly what she needed. The first swallow pooled in her stomach with a sensation of spreading coolness. Helen sighed and leaned back against the counter.

"Well, I've learned one thing already," she said.

"Yes?"

"I wasn't cut out for this. All along I've thought I deserved to be in the field, but I doubt I'd last a month, much less a year or more."

"You're blown and on the run, so of course you're overwhelmed. Most operational work is entirely different. With my assignments, the biggest challenge is boredom. I've never truly gone undercover like you. Or not since I was twelve."

"Twelve?"

Claire smiled.

"Our church needed a minister, and my dad was on the search committee. For the better part of a summer he piled us into the station wagon every Sunday to scout prospects all over Georgia. Augusta, Waycross, Tifton. We'd arrive just in time for the eleven o'clock service. Dull sermons followed by covered dish suppers on church lawns."

"Sounds awful."

"The good part was that Dad swore us to secrecy. If anyone asked why we were there, we were supposed to say we were just visiting from out of town. We even used fake names—the Martin family from Atlanta. Sanctioned to lie in your Sunday best, fibbing to all those nosy little church ladies while we ate their fried chicken and congealed salads. I enjoyed it way too much. I think it's half the reason I fell for the CIA. That, and maybe because the recruiter who came to campus looked like Robert Redford."

"They got me with the same setup."

Claire drained the last of her wine and set the glass in the sink.

"Shall we do business?"

They went into the living room. Claire took the couch, Helen an easy chair. She noticed then that Claire had brought a large tote bag, which appeared to be full.

"Marina, you said. She's my next contact?"

"Yes."

Just before Helen could speak again, a small but distinct click sounded from across the room. Claire must have heard it, too, because she frowned and looked in that direction.

"What was that?"

It happened again. It seemed to be coming from a cabinet just below the television. They went over for a look, opening the cabinet door to find another tape recorder.

"Testing, testing," Helen said, and the reels sprang into motion. After a few seconds they clicked to a stop.

"Voice-activated," Helen said. The machine confirmed her conclusion by again slowly spinning into motion. She reached down and shut it off.

"Not the usual location for that kind of thing, is it?" Claire asked.

"No. Or not under the guidelines that the Property and Personnel Branch sends out to all stations. The hardware's a bit clumsy, too. We never should have been able to hear it, and it's even older than the one upstairs. Another Philips."

"This place is starting to give me the heebie-jeebies. I'm not sure I feel comfortable telling you what you need to know here."

"What do you suggest?"

"There's a little café, not far from here. Quiet and usually uncrowded."

She gestured toward the door.

"First things first."

"The tape?"

"You did say Marina's name."

Helen removed the take-up reel, snapped the tape with her teeth, and unspooled the recorded portion. She carried the spaghetti pile to the bathroom and flushed it down the toilet. They watched as it swirled out of sight toward the sewers of Paris.

39

The waiter set down their demitasse cups of espresso. They were the only two customers in a small nook in the back. The big tote bag was underneath the table. A rear door was open onto a small garden where a caged parakeet cheeped.

"Marina was one of our agents," Claire said. She paused, glancing toward the open door as the parakeet went silent. "She moved back and forth between here and Marseille. Now she's working across the border."

"Germany?"

"Spain. Our records in Paris officially list her as inactive."

"Since when?"

"Since five months ago, when she filed a complaint against Gilley. Something similar to what we both witnessed, or so I was told. That's the problem. I never saw it, and now it no longer exists. Expunged."

"By your COS?"

"Yes. She then went into deep cover and disappeared, apparently with the help of her old case officer. It was only through Audra that I was able to track her down. She's in San Sebastián."

"Spain?"

"The Basque country, where she's keeping an eye on ETA, the separatist terror group, through an off-the-books arrangement with Madrid station. ETA would kill her in a heartbeat if they found out, which tells you all you need to know about how much she fears Kevin Gilley. Fortunately she's a natural for the posting. Paris-born, but to a Basque mother, a Harki father."

"Harki?"

"Algerian, but fought for the French in the war. When the rebels won, he immigrated here. Their families haven't exactly been accepted with open arms, which is one reason Marina is such a good agent. Grew up never knowing who she could trust. Audra sent word this afternoon that she's needed here, to meet with you."

"But if Audra could find her, couldn't Gilley?"

"Probably. But two of his people took out an ETA bomb maker a few years back, and ETA does tend to hold a grudge. Marina found a way to betray both Gilley operatives to the Spanish. You might say that she and Gilley are now blood enemies for life. Given the choice, he'd kill her before you. But he's certainly not foolish enough to go after her there. It's why she feels safe, relatively speaking."

"Why don't I go to her?"

"At this point, the fewer borders you cross, the better. We can't be sure that Canadian identity is still secure. Besides, ETA would be every bit as brutal with you, and once you were down there I'd have no way of helping you. The more isolated you become, the more likely you'll be found."

"Right. Either by our people, or by Gilley's."

"Aren't those one and the same?"

"I think now he may be recruiting people off the books completely," Helen said.

Claire raised her eyebrows. Helen explained what she'd learned about Delacroix and the way Gilley operated in Berlin.

Claire set down her cup with an agitated rattle in the saucer.

"That makes our job even tougher. And if Marina knows this, it would explain why she's playing hard to get."

"She's refusing to come?"

"Not refusing, but she has asked for logistical help, more than Audra is equipped to give her. More than I can give her, too, but I'm working on it."

"Why not just make another statement, or even a tape, and send it through a courier?"

"After all she's been through, she no longer trusts the

usual channels, not for this. In person or nothing, that's what she's saying."

"Even if it means risking a trip here?"

"Irrational fear and mistrust. An occupational disease, I'm afraid. What all this means is that you may have to sit tight for a day or two."

"I can think of worse places for waiting around." She smiled, but Claire was all business.

"Even if she comes, she'll only meet you on her terms, and through her arrangements. I won't be able to vouch for either. If Gilley has set up any trip wires to alert him to her return, then you'll be just as compromised. All I'll be able to do is make sure she knows how to find you. With Audra doing what she can from afar."

"Audra again. Our Oracle at Delphi."

"Yes. The word 'records' in her job title apparently covers just about everything we'd never have the clearance to see."

"Our records officer in Berlin seems to be in awe of her. Claims she knows a little bit about everything."

"That would explain how she got wind of Gilley's extracurriculars. I know it's how she saw my report, back before my COS incinerated it. But Marina's account never made it to Langley, in *any* way, shape, or form, which is why you have to collect her story firsthand. And this time it won't just be something on a piece of paper."

Claire reached into the tote bag and withdrew a small

but clunky cassette recorder and placed it on the table. A cheap Japanese model, like the kind you might buy in any electronics store.

"Voice-activated, but not as clumsy or as loud as that one in the safe house."

"But not one of those sweet little Swiss numbers, either."

"It's for the sake of cover. Get caught with a Nagra and they'll know your profession right away, even here. This way, if you're searched by any authorities, you're a bird-watcher who likes to record their songs. You're in Paris to take a little break from your jaunts into the countryside. Two birdsong cassettes are already in this bag with the rest of your things, along with a field guide for the birds of Europe."

"I didn't exactly bring outdoorsy-looking clothes."

"But I did."

She pulled a blue canvas overnight bag out of the big tote and unzipped the top. It was packed full.

"There are some traveling clothes in here as well. Also a few scarves, a light cardigan, an extra pair of sunglasses, even another wig—quick-change items to keep with you at all times in case you're trying to lose someone. I had to work fast, so I hope you don't mind the selection."

Helen checked one of the labels.

"How'd you know my size?"

"I guessed. I'm pretty good at that. In the bird book,

one of the pages is bent at the corner. The page number is the address for a small hotel on Passage de Flandre, where there's a room reserved under your cover name for a late arrival tonight, so I hope you didn't leave much back at your hotel."

"Only a toothbrush, a few clothes. You think I shouldn't go back?"

"It's best if you don't. And you definitely should avoid the Latin Quarter. If Gilley's hiring college boys, that's the perfect place for them to blend in. Your hotel tonight is up in the 19th arrondissement, where the streets are a little calmer, more plebeian, with fewer snap-happy tourists. Although if we're still not ready to pull this off tomorrow, then we may need to move you again, preferably a little farther northeast."

"Why northeast?"

"Because I'm guessing that's where Marina will end up. She grew up in Bondy, one of the banlieues."

"Banlieue?"

"Means suburb, but to any Parisian it says slum. With high-rise concrete *cités*, pockets of Algerians who've never quite fit in. Gang graffiti on the walls, mosques in trailers. You still see plenty of old-fart Maurice Chevaliers in berets, but it doesn't feel at all like Paris. It's Marina's old stomping ground, one of the places she can be assured of having a surer footing than Gilley. The good part of all of this is that Marina's story should be the last piece of the puzzle. Then you'll have enough ammunition to come in from the cold, and we can put you on the first train back to Berlin."

"And then?"

"If they have any brains, at the very least they'll be impressed by what you were able to accomplish right under their noses. Not to mention their immense relief that you didn't go over to the other side. And this way you'll have some leverage for cutting yourself a deal before they send you home. Or at least more leverage than you had before."

"Except then I wasn't a wanted fugitive."

"True. But can you think of any other way?"

"No. I can't."

They sat in silence, sipping their coffee.

"Speaking of sins," Helen said. "If I include your report, won't they know exactly where it came from?"

"I've covered my tracks pretty well. I made sure it got into the hands of at least half a dozen people before they quashed it, so they'll be under as much suspicion as me. Will they question me? Sure. I'm fine with that."

"What if they flutter you?"

Claire laughed.

"Let them try. In our training against Soviet interrogation techniques, I beat the polygraph three out of four."

"Nerves of steel!"

"Or the world's greatest liar. It'll certainly come in handy if I ever get married."

Helen laughed, a welcome release. She'd rarely met anyone whose company made her feel so invigorated, so vital. The circumstances certainly had something to do with it, but she had a feeling that they would have hit it off no matter what.

"It's too bad we can't pal around a bit more."

"Agree completely. But I'm afraid that, for both our sakes, you're going to be mostly on your own from here on out. I can help a little after-hours, but I can't afford any more prolonged absences without arousing suspicion. The COS apparently noticed my lengthy lunch today, and was asking around. All of this is my way of telling you that we may not see each other again, so we should agree on a daily contact time, by phone if necessary, and late enough in the day for me to relay any further news from Audra."

"Sixteen hundred hours?"

"That works. For tomorrow I'll call you at your hotel. If we need to change the arrangement we can do it on the fly."

"Okay. Any parting advice on how I should pass my time tomorrow? I doubt it would be a good idea to just stay in my room all day."

"You should get out and about and play your role, even if it means mixing back into the Instamatic crowd. Remember, you're a frugal Canadian with birdsongs on the brain, vacationing out of season to cut costs, and maybe a little overwhelmed by the City of Light. In fact, it would probably be a good idea to let a few shopkeepers take terrible advantage of you, so definitely do some shopping. Buy something gloriously tacky."

"All right. I will."

"And when the time comes to set something up, I'll know where to find you, so maybe you could check in at your room a few times along the way. Otherwise, be as carefree as possible, even though you'll always be one false step away from being found. Either by the Company or by Gilley."

Helen swallowed hard.

"How cheerful."

"Intentionally so. For every precaution you've taken up to now you'll need twice as many in the next day or two. All of it while keeping a dopey, touristy smile on your face."

Helen shook her head.

"I really don't know half of what you do. Or how you do it."

"Sure you do. You're just out of practice."

"I've never gotten *into* practice."

"You've managed to survive, and you're halfway home to what you hoped to accomplish. You're nimble and smart and you're not what they're accustomed to. So do us proud, all right?"

"All right." Claire squeezed her hand. "I will. Then, if they ever let me out of prison, I'll—"

"Seriously? Prison? Is that what you think they'll do?"

"Well, won't they?"

"After what you'll be giving them, it will be all they can do to buy your silence. Same thing the Brits do with all of their wayward sons. The last place they'll want you to end up in is a court of law, where you'll be free to say whatever you please—under oath, no less, while you tell the American public what its government servants have been up to. No, no. Make it back to Berlin and they'll have to deal with you on your terms. It's the in-between that's the tricky part."

"What's the worst they'd do? I mean, assuming it isn't Gilley."

"I think they'd kill you, dear girl. As quickly and cleanly as circumstances allow."

"Then I suppose I'd better get moving."

Claire nodded and looked around. A glance out the back door, and another over her shoulder toward the front entrance. A woman whose radar, as far as Helen could tell, was never switched off.

"It's probably better if we don't leave together," Claire said.

"Of course."

Helen stood, tried to muster a smile even as she began to feel weak in the knees.

"Goodbye, then. And thank you."

"I'll keep doing what I can. With regard to logistics, anyway. And while I'm not the least bit religious, I'll say this, anyway. Godspeed."

Helen walked briskly away, and did not look back.

40

Henry woke up at four in the morning. The moon was gone, and so was Anna. He sat up, listening. The night bugs were no longer singing, and the oppressive silence made the house feel deserted, a little spooky. Had she walked home? Henry stood and stepped across the room, nearly tripping on a pile of his clothes that Anna had tossed to the floor. All that passion seemed remote now, like something that had happened in another life. Stupid him. Words that he couldn't take back. He groped for his boxers, pulled on his trousers, buttoned his shirt. Pausing, he listened again, and thought he heard a rustle of paper, the dull knock of a glass being set down on a tabletop.

Moving into the hallway, he noticed that a light was on in the living room, and when he rounded the corner he saw Anna, fully dressed and seated on the couch in an amber glow of lamplight. He smelled coffee, and saw a steaming mug on the table in front of her. She was reading her mother's letters.

Henry, not wanting to startle her, cleared his throat, but she didn't look up as he approached. He walked past, taking care not to touch her, but she bristled away from him, anyway.

"You made coffee?"

"In the kitchen."

He returned with a mug, and took up a position at what he hoped was a suitable distance.

"Making progress?"

"Just getting started." She still hadn't looked up, and her voice was a monotone. "It's clear that all of the letters are from just two people."

He watched for a few seconds as she pulled folded pages from another envelope and flattened them on the table. Then she finally looked him in the eye.

"I've still got some questions. About what you told me last night."

It had happened during the languid aftermath, as they lay side by side in the moonlit bedroom. That's when Henry had experienced the ill-advised urge to come clean about his hidden role in this affair. Full disclosure, he decided. It was the only way forward with a clear conscience. Anna's eyes had a lot to do with his decision. Her gaze was so deep and longing that it worked on his mind like a truth serum. Guilty thoughts of his duplicity simmered to the surface, demanding to be skimmed. And the conditions for confession could not have been more amenable. A breeze stirred the curtains, wafting in honeysuckle. Anna reached forward to stroke his cheek.

"Beautiful, isn't it?" she'd whispered. "This whole night."

"It is. All of it."

"You don't think this was a mistake, I hope?"

"Not at all."

"It's just that, well, you've got this look in your eye, like you're kind of uncertain."

So she'd seen it, then, reading him perfectly, even if drawing the wrong conclusion.

"No regrets at all. Not about this."

"About what, then?" Her eyes again, for the final decisive push.

"There's something you should know about me. About my work."

"Oh, God. *You're* not CIA, are you?" She smiled, still not attuned to the import of what he was about to reveal. It gave him one last opening to exit. Instead, he plunged forward.

"No. But I didn't come to Poston just to hang out between jobs. It was part of a new job."

"For the U.S. Attorney?"

"It grew out of the same connections, but a different employer. Somebody in the national security apparatus, if I had to guess. Although that part has always been a little hazy."

"I see." Anna went very still, like she feared what was coming next.

"They put me here to keep an eye on your house. Or, more to the point, your mom."

"My mom?" Her voice barely a whisper. "You were spying on my *mom*?"

"Not spying. Observing. What they mostly wanted to know about was visitors, everyone who came and went."

"Oh, *observing,* big difference! So when she left the house, you followed her?"

"No. I never followed. I stayed here."

"Well that makes it much better. Fuck. And what did you do with all this . . . *information* you collected?"

"Phoned it in to a guy in Washington."

"Who?"

That was when Henry realized he couldn't tell the whole truth. Not without wrecking things. It might even put them in danger. He had done enough damage by revealing half. But, for now, half was all that was manageable.

"I don't know. I didn't even have a name." His first lie, although Henry doubted that Mitch was a real name, so it wasn't much of a lie. "All I had was a phone number."

"Then call it and ask."

"It's no longer working. They were as freaked by what happened as me, and they cut off all contact." Two more lies. Deeper and deeper. "I was about to skip town when you came knocking."

"Which is when you should have told me all this."

"Yes. I should have. And now I am."

"Goddamn it, Henry! For all we know, your boss was Merle's boss!"

"No!" He shook his head, relieved to be back on solid ground. "If they were behind this, do you really think they would've hired somebody to keep track of all the comings and goings? And then left me here, like some loose end?"

"Then why *did* you hang around?"

"I told you. Because of you. I'm working for you, now."

"Then use your goddamn skills and find out who it was!"

"I will. Or I'll try. But first don't you think we should deal with the letters?"

She watched him closely for a moment. Then she slapped him, hard, across the jaw. He barely flinched and never looked away. Her shoulders sagged and she began to sob, quietly but with her body shaking. He moved closer and held her. Somewhat miraculously, she let him, but only briefly. Then she pulled free, sighed loudly, and climbed out of bed.

"I need to sleep on this. I'm too tired to walk to the

B&B, so I'll crash on your couch. Lay another hand on me and I'll press charges."

"I really am on your side."

"So be on my side. But not on top of me, and not in bed with me. I'll decide in the morning what I want to do next. In the meantime, leave me the fuck alone."

And, now, here they were—a few hours later, again face-to-face, but still awkward and uncomfortable.

"How long did you do it?" she asked. "Spy on my mom, I mean."

"Six weeks and a day."

"Jesus! *Six weeks?* And hasn't it occurred to you, even once, that whatever your employers were looking for might somehow be related to what *we're* looking for?"

"Of course. Especially once we found out your mom was ex-CIA, and started digging up all this weird crap about Merle. It's one reason I knew I had to tell you. Although the sum total of everything I observed in those six weeks was so run-of-the-mill that I'd be amazed if any of it had the slightest bearing on what we're looking for now."

"You saw nothing out of the ordinary?"

"Nothing. And I never saw Merle, or even anyone who might have been Merle in disguise. I did see your brother walking around on his own a few times, heading off toward the fields. But he was never carrying a gun. Maybe he got it from the barn, or around back where I couldn't see him. He went off with your mom to the store a few times, or I'm assuming it was the store because they always came back with groceries. With your dad, too, once or twice, in the pickup. But nothing ever felt strange or suspicious, about him or anybody else. Like I said, it was the visitors my employer mostly wanted to know about."

"Why?"

"They never said. And I wouldn't have expected them to."

"Well, what visitors *did* you see?"

"Practically none. For your mom, anyway."

"None at all?"

"Unless you count Mrs. Furr, from around the corner. Or the mailman, and a couple of Jehovah's Witnesses. It was so uneventful I started wondering why they'd hired me at all. There were a few guys from Washam Poultry, but they were always for your father. He also got a visit from three buddies probably to play poker or something. Plus some older guy who picked him up one morning to go fishing."

"Everett Anson?"

"That's the guy."

"So you reported that, too?"

"It was part of the job. Anyone who came and went. You can see the log book if you want."

"No thanks." Then, after a pause. "Or, yes. I will take a look, if you've still got it."

He nodded and retrieved it from a dresser drawer. She flipped the pages, scanning the daily notations of names and tag numbers, the times of day, his brief notes in the margins. She shook her head when she put it down, and sagged a bit on the couch.

"An hour ago I'd made up my mind to fire you. Maybe even to turn you over to the cops, for God knows what. Peeping Tom? Massive fraud? Then I started thinking, well, maybe it's a plus if you're more of a pro than I thought. Not that I didn't suspect it. But if you can help me figure out what happened, great. Just don't expect any further unqualified trust. From here on out, we're strictly employer and employee, and even that's looking shaky."

"Got it."

She gestured toward the letters.

"Back to work, then. Provided you don't have to report in to your masters first."

"I told you, that's over," the words almost sticking in his throat. Last time he'd checked his phone he'd found three angry texts from Mitch, asking why he'd gone silent. He didn't dare turn on his phone now.

"Okay, then." She looked wrung out, but resigned to moving forward. She stood and crossed the room. "First, let's get some more light in this mausoleum of yours."

She pulled open the curtains to let in the day's first pale light. Henry couldn't help but stare, because there before his eyes was the incriminating view again—the Shoat house, on display like the darkened screen of a drive-in movie. He knew then that he never should have said a word. By trying to split the difference on the truth he had only deepened the deception.

She was right about one thing. Work was the only way forward.

41

"I've only read the first two letters, but I've checked the names and postmarks on all the others," Anna said, glancing at some notes. "There are twenty-nine in all. Thirteen from someone called IAD, sixteen from CDG. They refer to my Mom as TXL. Most of IAD's letters were postmarked in McLean. CDG's came from Paris until the last four, which are from York, Pennsylvania. And three of those arrived during the last four months, beginning in April."

"Including the one your mother never opened."

"Yes. And neither have I. Not yet. I think I'm almost afraid of what I'll find."

"That's a lot of recent activity."

"I thought so, too. IAD's last letter came in April, but there's been nothing since then."

"Wonder if something's happened to her?"

"Jesus, what a thought!"

"Well, it's something we have to consider. And hers

were the ones from McLean, down near Langley?"

"Yes, until 2006, when her postmark changed to Currituck, that town in North Carolina. She wrote the first of the letters, in August of 2002. Here. Read it and tell me what you think."

Henry unfolded the pages.

TXL,

I completely understand and fully share your concern, and suggest that in response we reactivate secure Sisterhood communications for as long as it takes to allay further worry. Toward that end, I am copying this message to CDG. As for your inquiry, I can report only that "Robert" is now officially inactive, although several of his assets remain in the field. His most recent assignments (unverified) were:

—Muhammad al Farooq, Amman, November 2000
—Dragan Jovovic, Novi Sad, July 1998

My only thought as to why he has chosen to reappear now is that he needs to be reassured of your continued compliance with past agreements as he prepares to enter a more public phase of employment.

I remain ever at your disposal,
IAD

Henry put the pages aside while Anna awaited his reaction.

"Looks like this *was* all about the scary guy you saw at the mall. And it's clear your mom initiated the correspondence."

"Robert, they call him. Although I guess the quote marks mean it's not his real name."

"Probably not, when they weren't even using their own names. Any idea why your mom would use TXL?"

"No. But something about the initials for all three of them looks familiar."

She was right, but Henry couldn't put his finger on why. Maybe another jolt of caffeine would do the trick. His hangover and all the turmoil had left him feeling the way he used to after a transatlantic flight. Then it hit him.

"Airports."

"What?"

"Their code names are airport symbols, like the ones on luggage tags. TXL for Tegel, in Berlin. I oughta know, having flown in and out of there a few times. CDG for Charles de Gaulle in Paris. IAD for Dulles, meaning Washington. Or maybe Langley."

"Because that's where they were based?"

"And still were, for the other two, based on the postmarks. It probably also means they all worked for the CIA. Why else use code names?"

"So then who's Robert?"

"Somebody who got your mom fired? He could be the whole reason for the severance agreement, based on what the letter says. What's the wording?" He read it aloud: "'He needs to be reassured of your continued compliance with past agreements.'"

"If he was a Berlin guy, how would the other two have known him?"

"He could've moved around, I guess. Maybe they all worked with him on something that went terribly wrong."

"Like Anneliese Kurz. Why else hang on to that old newspaper story?"

"The timing fits, but there's no mention of her in the letter. And what about those other names, the two for Robert's last assignments? We should Google them."

"Or maybe it's explained in the rest of the letters. Keep reading."

The second letter, which was the first one from CDG, had been mailed from Paris only two days after IAD's. It concurred with IAD's suggestion that they remain in regular contact. Henry read it quickly and set it aside.

"Hand me the next one."

"We should read them together."

She slid closer on the couch as Henry picked up a white envelope from IAD postmarked in August 2003, roughly a year after the first two letters. Their curiosity was overcoming their awkwardness.

The correspondence was fairly routine through the

next several letters. IAD and CDG offered brief but news-less updates to TXL in August of 2003, 2004, and 2005. Everyone seemed to be doing well. IAD mentioned in her 2004 letter that "Robert appears to still be on his best behavior, so far as I have been able to determine, or at least he is no longer making his presence felt." The following year, IAD noted that she would soon be retiring, which she said would leave CDG as "the only active member of our group."

The tone and timing of the letters shifted abruptly in May 2006, three months ahead of their usual annual updates, when CDG wrote, "I do believe I've spotted 'Robert' in a photo from 6A of this Tuesday's NYT. Not named, of course (When is he ever!?!), but lurking in the background as always, this time on Capitol Hill. This would seem to confirm IAD's earlier theory that he may be operating 'in a more public phase,' albeit in his usual shadowy way."

She'd enclosed a clipped newspaper photo. The focus of the picture was a witness testifying before the terrorism subcommittee of the House Committee on Foreign Affairs. Four faces were visible behind him, and CDG had circled in red ink the one on the far left.

"That's him!" Anna shouted. "That's the guy from the mall."

"You're sure?"

She nodded.

"It's that same half smile, smug and threatening. Yes, it's definitely him."

"Now, if we only knew his real name."

"But we do know one thing," she said, frowning now. "He's not Merle."

"People can grow beards, you know."

She shook her head.

"His age isn't right. This is from eight years ago, and even then he looks ten, fifteen years older than the way everyone describes Merle."

The next letter was from IAD the following month. She wrote that a few discreet inquiries had revealed that Robert "has assumed an advisory role among select GOP congressmen, including several with aspirations to higher office. Please keep in mind that although I no longer have the unlimited archival access I once enjoyed, my connection in that area remains strong, should either of you need access to Agency documentation on this subject or others."

"So she worked in records?" Anna said.

"Or was close to someone who did. All we know for sure is that she must have had a high security clearance."

"Now, if we only knew what my mom did. Or CDG, her buddy in Paris."

"They do seem like buddies, don't they? Even in this stuff."

"IAD strikes me as kind of buttoned down. CDG, a little more fast and loose."

In 2007 and every ensuing year through 2012 the letters were routine annual updates. There wasn't a single mention of Robert. Yet, even during this uneventful span CDG's correspondence crackled with more life and color. You sensed a personality behind the words, as opposed to IAD's gray tone of business-by-the-book.

Their letters from only a year ago, postmarked in August 2013, also had no news of Robert. But CDG's letter included a postscript that, judging from its personalized nature, she must have added only on her letter to Anna's mom:

PS—I'll be retiring in a few months, several years ahead of the customary age for going on the shelf. It's partly because I would like to enjoy my life and my travels while I'm still energetic enough to do so to the fullest. I suppose I'm also weary of bucking the same system that thwarted both of us in those earlier days, even though the gals new to our biz have been telling me for ages that opportunities for them have never been greater. Hell, by '89 they'd even opened an on-site day care center, right there at Langley. More power to them, but alas for us. One good thing about putting myself out to pasture is that I will now dare to send you a cornball holiday snapshot in the coming season. Maybe I'll even join Facebook! Although I gather that is still frowned upon by the powers-that-be. Regardless,

I will always fondly remember our adventures together, both past and more recent.
Yours, CDG.

"Recent adventures?" Anna asked. "Would you write it that way if you were only talking about letters?"

"I wouldn't, but I'm not CDG."

Anna moved on to the last few letters. The next one, from CDG only four months ago, was the first one postmarked in York, and Robert finally reappeared.

"Our friend Robert has at long last surfaced by name in the public sphere," CDG wrote, "or at least is now clearly visible just below the waterline, as you'll see in the current issue of *Newsweek*. 'Spooky,' indeed, although the story doesn't even come close to describing his real duties, not to mention any of the unsavory things we were witness to. With his star so obviously on the rise, I now ask of you both: Is it time for us to act?"

"We need to look up that story," Anna said.

Henry flipped open his laptop and quickly found *Newsweek*'s online archive, where he clicked on a tab for 2014. A gallery of all the year's covers popped up.

"What's the date on that postmark?"

"April 19th."

The cover story for the corresponding issue was headlined "Death on the Farm."

"Good God," Anna said. "Talk about irony. Although

I'm betting none of those farmers were murdered in their beds."

They clicked through the rest of the issue—a piece from Moscow about Russia's vulnerability on energy, a primer on how to cheat on your federal taxes, a story on the seductive dangers of menthol cigarettes. They lingered for a moment on a story about a mysterious State Department contractor who got involved with Freemasons in a scheme to topple Fidel Castro, if only because it sounded like something that an ex-CIA man might get mixed up in. But there was no likely suspect.

"There it is," Anna said, pointing to a story headlined "The Spooky Six."

"No matter who is elected president in 2016," the story began, "odds are that one of these half dozen men will have a lot to say about the winner's stands on matters of intelligence and national security."

The bulk of the piece was six thumbnail bios—of six paragraphs apiece—about each of the aforementioned "Spooky Six," whom the article described as "the most respected and sought after, yet also the most reclusive and camera shy, of campaign advisors from the security and intelligence arena." As if to verify the "camera shy" observation, none of the thumbnails came with a photo. All six supposedly had extensive backgrounds in intelligence. None was named Robert. Henry and Anna ruled out two whose backgrounds were in the National

Security Administration and the Defense Intelligence Agency. The other four had all worked for the CIA, but there wasn't enough further information to say which of them was Robert.

Henry wrote down the names in alphabetical order:

Alex Berryhill, Winslow Edinson, Kevin Gilley, John Solloway.

"So close, but so far."

"Google them. It's bound to give us something."

Precious little, as it turned out. Apart from the *Newsweek* piece, there was no other media coverage. The only other possible references were a few Facebook pages, some database listings offering addresses and phone numbers, a few property records and court citations—none of which included criminal charges— and a couple of business listings that had nothing to do with intelligence work or government employment. An image search produced a few photos, but none matched the anonymous face that CDG had circled in the 2006 clipping from *The New York Times*.

"Fuck."

They clicked around a while longer before admitting defeat. They felt certain they now had Robert's name, they just weren't sure which of the four it was.

"Back to the letters?" he asked.

"Only three to go."

IAD's last letter, also from four months ago, was her

response to the *Newsweek* piece. The most intriguing thing about it was that she also appeared to be responding to whatever TXL, or Anna's mom, must have said about the story.

"While I agree with TXL that the time is near for exposure, in my measured view we should first marshal our available resources and then await the next opportune moment of public acclaim, in order to inflict maximum damage."

"'Maximum damage,'" Anna said. "If you're this Robert fellow, and you get wind of that, not too hard imagining how he might react."

There was no follow-up correspondence to indicate what TXL and CDG thought of IAD's recommendation, but the next two of the three remaining letters—both from CDG in York—were as interesting in their own way as the correspondence about Robert.

The first one was postmarked in late June—only two months ago. The personal tone suggested it was a message CDG had sent only to Anna's mom. It was stapled to a *Washington Post* obituary for Clark Addison Baucom, a former intelligence agent who had passed away at the age of ninety.

"Very sad to read of the passing of your onetime beau from Berlin," the note said. "Yet, how interesting to find here the possible answer to one of your oldest questions about all those bodies of water, yes?"

"'Bodies of water'?" Henry said, but Anna had zeroed in on something else.

"Her onetime beau was *ninety?* Good lord, he was thirty years older than her."

"And when she left Berlin he would've been fifty-five, the old goat. But what's this big secret she's talking about?"

They read the obit, parts of which were as interesting as an adventure tale. In the final years of World War II, Baucom had been posted fresh out of Yale to Moscow by the State Department. It took him four days to reach the Soviet capital, a harrowing journey by plane, train, a bicycle, and, finally, by oxcart rattling through the ruined city. It was there that he began his work as a spy, an occupation that kept him busy throughout Europe until 1991, when he was mustered out of the CIA from a posting to Prague, two years after the collapse of the Iron Curtain.

They noticed that CDG had made a small checkmark next to a paragraph describing his work just after the war, which said:

In 1946, Baucom became chief of the political section of the U.S. embassy to Hungary. In Budapest he was assigned control over an intelligence network run by a small, secretive U.S. spy organization known as the Pond, which remained in operation until it was disbanded in 1955.

Baucom left the organization in 1948 to join the then-new CIA, and his earlier work for the Pond only came to light following the discovery of the organization's lost archives in a barn in Culpeper, Va. Those records, transferred to the National Archives in College Park, Md., were only recently declassified by the CIA.

"The Pond," Henry said.

"You've heard of it?"

"Vaguely. There were a few stories about it a couple months ago, right around the time of this obit. They didn't get a whole lot of attention, but maybe your mom saw them."

Anna shook her head.

"My mom never read any news except what was in the Easton paper. It was a willful disconnection, almost like she was scared of what she might find."

"Well, this letter sure did grab her interest. This was the week she got her research card at the National Archives."

"To go look up stuff about an old boyfriend?"

"Had to be for more than that, don't you think? Look at what CDG wrote. Bodies of water. The possible answer to one of your oldest questions. And . . ." Henry's voice trailed off.

"And what?"

"Jesus. This letter arrived the week before I got the phone call asking me to come do this job—to keep an eye on your mom, and whoever was visiting."

"You think it's connected?"

"I don't know. Maybe she found something, and somebody else noticed. The only way to know is to take a look ourselves."

"At the Archives? With Merle still out there?"

"Our leads on Merle are almost nonexistent. At least this is something."

"Okay, after we finish the letters."

The next one—the last one that Anna's mom had actually opened—had been postmarked only two weeks ago. It might even have been the last item of personal mail Anna's mother had ever read.

Dearest TXL,

This is to confirm that I have received your parcel, and also the copy of your recent documentary find. As to the latter, I would caution that the evidence is not conclusive. Nonetheless, I will of course guard all of this material with my life, just as you have done for so many years, in order to ensure that it will be available when the time comes. In the meantime, I will await further news of your inquiries.

Best,
CDG

"The parcel," Anna said. "Do you think she means the big envelope my mom kept at UPS?"

"Let's hope so, because that would mean it's in safe hands."

"But maybe you're right about the Archives. Sounds like she found something."

"And was looking for more."

Henry picked up the last envelope, still sealed. He handed it to Anna, who went very still and then turned it so Henry could read the front.

"Look at the date of the postmark," she said.

"Is that—?"

"Yes. This was mailed the day Willard killed them."

Anna took a deep breath to collect herself. The only sound was of paper tearing as she ran a fingernail along the top to slit the upper edge. Inside was a single folded page. Anna opened it and placed it on the table so they could read it together. There were only four handwritten lines.

Having reviewed your parcel and your latest correspondence, I have made a few discreet calls. Be aware that the worst is true and the strands have crossed. High alert and greatest caution. Keep your snow globe handy.

Anna put a hand to her heart.

"It's almost as if she knew what was about to happen."

"I think we better go take a look at those old papers."

42

It wasn't Henry's first trip to the National Archives, so he was prepared for the majesty of the vast reading room, which overlooked a forest through a curving wall of floor-to-ceiling windows. The holdings were a wonderland of undiscovered secrets and hidden treasures, there for the taking by anyone curious and dogged enough to dig them out. Anna was suitably impressed.

"Who *wouldn't* want to work here? Any idea where we should start?"

"Over there," Henry said, leading her toward a narrow, glass-walled room where a few researchers and archivists sat a tables, filling out requests for the next round of "pulls" from the many corridors of documents stored on the floors above and below. "There's bound to be a resident expert on this stuff. Or let's hope so. Otherwise we're in for a real slog."

Before leaving Poston they'd gone back into Anna's mother's office to take another, closer look at the ugly snow globe from Paris, if only because CDG's final message had seemed to assign it some sort of significance. They blew off the dust, turned it over, tapped the base for any signs of a hollowed-out space, and peered through the glass for any possible clues that might be gleaned from the kitschy model of the Eiffel Tower and all those plastic snowflakes, suspended in water. Nothing.

They'd then checked online about the Pond materials during the two-hour drive to College Park, and had been daunted by the sheer volume of materials that awaited them—eighty-three boxes, filed under Record Group 263, the holdings of the CIA. A staffer directed them to a reference guide for the Pond materials, but said they probably wouldn't make much headway without assistance.

"The guy you need is Larry Hilliard," she said, pointing across the room toward a big fellow with a slight potbelly, in khakis and a polo shirt. "Good luck, though. He's pretty busy."

Hilliard was seated at a long table, flipping through a thick leather-bound volume, totally absorbed. Henry cleared his throat, but Hilliard kept on turning the pages.

"Excuse me. You're Larry Hilliard?"

He sighed and looked up. Milk chocolate skin,

hair graying at the temples, gold wire-rim glasses. His eyes were a little on the sleepy side, yet they shone with curiosity and a touch of impatience. The overall impression was that of a docile bear who had just emerged from hibernation deeply hungry, only to be interrupted in his foraging.

"And you are?"

"Henry Mattick. We're interested in the Pond materials."

"You mean the Grombach archive."

"Grombach?"

"Colonel John 'Frenchy' Grombach. That's who started the Pond and ran it till its dying breath."

"In '55?"

"Well, at least you know that much."

"And not a whole lot more."

"I'm afraid you're going to have to navigate alone. For a few days, anyway. I'm working under a deadline, but I'll be happy to authorize your records requests. Just bring them over when you've filled them out, you and your assistant here."

"I'm not his assistant. He works for me."

"Whatever you say, Ms. . . . ?"

"Shoat. Anna Shoat."

He stared at her. For the first time since approaching him, they had his undivided attention, and when he next spoke his voice was almost reverential.

"Any relation to Helen Shoat?"

Anna reached into her jeans pocket for her mom's research card and handed it to him.

"I'm her daughter."

He shut the heavy volume and looked at her closely.

"Yes. I see the resemblance. Let's take this to my office."

Hilliard led them to a cubicle at the opposite end of the room. They sat facing him across a cluttered desk.

"I'd offer coffee, but you know the rules up here." He shook his head in amazement. "Your mother was an impressive woman. It's always a pleasure working with people who have that much enthusiasm. I gathered she also had some sort of personal connection to the material. Then when I heard about what happened . . ." His voice trailed off.

"It's all right," Anna said. "You can talk about it."

"I was just going to say how sorry I was. Shocked, too."

"We were all shocked."

Hilliard briefly bowed his head.

"What can I do for you, then? Are you looking to pick up where she left off?"

"Actually, we didn't even know she'd come here until a few days ago."

"What we could use first," Henry said, "is a little background on how this stuff even came to light. The story we saw said it was locked away in some barn?"

"Yes. It had moved around from one place to another for years, mostly because Grombach never wanted any outsiders getting their hands on it. After he died in '82, everybody pretty much forgot about it. Sort of like the Pond itself."

"I know I'd never heard of it," Henry said.

"That's the way Grombach wanted it. Frenchy was a strange bird. Born in New Orleans, his father was French. West Point, class of '23, although he got kicked out. A good boxer. Fenced, played football, polo. Commissioned into the Army as a second lieutenant, where, oddly enough, he ended up doing some work with the NYPD and FBI. Dabbled in coaching for the Olympics. Kind of a man for all seasons, and a big-time anticommie.

"So, then. The war began. And in '42 some general from Army Intelligence decided that he hated the brand-new OSS—the spy org that eventually morphed into the CIA—and wanted to set up his own intel network, even apart from Army G-2. He picked Grombach to run it. Not on his own, but hand in hand with a lot of big multinationals that kicked in money, office space, and commercial cover for agents and operatives. Companies like U.S. Rubber, American Express, Philips, Remington Rand, Chase Bank. The Pond was sort of a public-private hybrid, and Grombach liked that just fine."

"Were they any good?"

"Depends on who you ask. Grombach would tell

you they were the greatest, and once the war ended he wanted to keep the whole thing going. Of course, the OSS wanted to keep going, too, and a few years later it won the power struggle, and pivoted straight from fighting Hitler to fighting Stalin. But, if anything, Grombach's people had started fighting the Cold War earlier. He was raising hell about commie infiltrators even before Hitler was dead. And not long after the war he set up a private channel of communication with Senator Joe McCarthy and some of the other big red-baiters on Capitol Hill."

"What finally put him out of business?"

"The CIA. They signed up the Pond as a contractual contributor after the war. But Frenchy and the CIA never got along worth a damn, so in '55 Allen Dulles pulled the plug on them. Grombach didn't go down without a fight, and there was a lot of back-and-forth about trying to keep it going, maybe by taking it deeper underground, with more corporate support. That's just a fraction of the material here, but I mention it because it was one of the angles your mother was most interested in. That, plus Grombach's obsession for code words."

"Code words?" Henry said.

"He had a mania for it. Not just for agents and ops, but for cities, countries, public figures, departments of the government. You name it, Grombach had a code word for it, and he used them all in his correspondence, which can make for pretty crazy reading unless you know what the heck he's talking about. Which reminds me . . ."

He raised a finger in the air and swiveled his chair toward a filing cabinet. He opened the drawer, rummaged around, and pulled out a stapled sheaf of papers that he tossed on the desk. The title was in caps: GROMBACH CRIB SHEET. It was a glossary for the code names and buzzwords Grombach regularly employed.

"A historian who's researching a book came up with this, and kindly let me make a copy. Nineteen damn pages, double-spaced. Boy, did your mother's eyes ever light up when she saw it. In fact . . ."

Hilliard paused to look down at the floor. Then he cleared his throat.

"Yes?" Anna prompted.

"I was just going to say you could keep this particular copy, because it belonged to her. To your mother. I kept it here so she wouldn't have to check it in through security every damn visit. And, frankly, because for whatever reason she never seemed all that comfortable about taking any copies home with her. She never said why, and I never asked. So I ended up keeping quite a few items for her. Anyway . . ."

He handed it to Anna.

"As you'll see, she circled the words that interested her the most. She also made a little list of her favorites, right up there at the top of the first page."

"Yes." Anna began reading from it. "'The Bay, the Lake, the Zoo, Effies, Jack, the Hump, the Vee People."

"That's right. She almost laughed when she saw those. The Bay was the CIA, the Lake was the War Department, or Pentagon now. The Zoo was the State Department, the Effies were the FBI, and Jack was good old J. Edgar Hoover himself, another big-time buddy of Frenchy Grombach's, partly because they both hated the OSS and CIA. The Hump was Capitol Hill. The Vee people was a reference to Philips, the company I mentioned earlier, one of Grombach's corporate sponsors. It was Dutch, and I think its full name was Philips N.V."

"Why'd she zero in on those?" Henry asked.

"She never said, but I got the idea they were something that had been bugging her for years."

"One thing I can tell you," Anna said, "is that she used to work for the CIA. Way back in 1979."

Hilliard's mouth dropped open. Then he laughed aloud, while shaking his head in amazement.

"I'll be damned."

"You truly had no idea?"

"None whatsoever. My guess was that someone in her family might have been involved with Grombach. But the idea that she was in the same business? Granted, with a whole different outfit, but still . . ." He shook his head again. "She hid it well."

"If it's any consolation, I was more surprised than you were. Not a clue until the week after she died, when they called about a severance check for her two years of service."

"Still, you said 1979? That was decades after the Pond closed shop. Wonder what got her interested?"

"You said a second ago that you kept some other items of hers?"

His smile turned sheepish.

"We don't offer that service for all researchers. But, like I said, she was always reluctant to take anything with her. So whenever she made copies, she left them behind."

"Can you show us?"

"Be happy to. In fact, it's funny you'd be here today at all. I was just thinking about that stuff, wondering if I should throw it out. So it's all yours, if you want it. There isn't all that much, so if you'd like I can guide you through it. Probably wouldn't take more than an hour or two."

"That would be great," Anna said. "Thank you."

Hilliard checked his watch.

"It's getting on toward one o'clock. Are you two hungry?"

"Now that you mention it," Henry said. The only thing in his stomach was the cup of coffee from early that morning, and he was already running low on energy.

"We've got a pretty decent cafeteria. Why don't we grab some grub and take her pages out on the patio. That's where she liked to take her breaks, and it's as pleasant a spot as any."

43

"There were really only two main things she was interested in," Hilliard began.

He wiped his mouth with a napkin and shoved aside a plate with the last crumbs of his lunch. Then he dropped a file folder onto the table filled with maybe fifty pages of documents copied onto blue paper.

Anna was still picking at a salad, with seemingly little appetite. Henry had devoured a double cheeseburger and was working his way through a pile of fries.

A cardinal was singing cheery notes in the nearby woods, and their table was shaded by an umbrella. Nearly everyone else was eating indoors, so they had the patio to themselves.

Hilliard opened the folder.

"The first item was a group of individuals. A small one. This was her list."

He slid forward a folded sheet of white lined

notebook paper, the only item in the folder that wasn't a copied document. Anna's mother had printed out three names:

Clark Baucom (code name?)
Edward Stone (aka "Beetle")
Cryptonym "Lewis"

"That first fellow on the list, Clark Baucom, well, there was quite a bit on him, but that was hardly surprising. He's one of the few personalities in this outfit who went on to bigger, better things elsewhere."

"We saw his obit in the *Post*," Henry said.

"My mother had a copy of it. We think that's where she first found out about these archives."

"His Pond cryptonym, or code name, was 'Joy.' Based in Budapest. Joined up with the Pond just after the war ended and the Russians were taking over in Hungary. His big job in '47 was to smuggle out members of the Hungarian aristocracy before the tanks rolled in. Baucom didn't stay with Grombach very long, though. Joined the CIA in '48, and that was the best way possible to burn your bridges with Frenchy, who hated the Bay, as he called it."

"Who's this Stone guy, code name Beetle?"

"His name is on the cheat sheet, some operative they hired fairly late in the game, in the early fifties, a fellow with commercial cover based in Vienna. But we couldn't find more than a few mentions of him. Your mom seemed a little disappointed by that. The first was in one of Grombach's personnel memos, when he was discussing some new hires in '52."

Hilliard flipped through the relevant pages for them as he spoke.

"Then, as you'll see, there were a couple of Beetle's field reports—one from Essen, in West Germany, the other from Salzburg, in Austria—but neither was anything special. They're here, though, if you want to read them later."

He flipped through another few pages.

"Okay, then. This was the stuff that seemed to intrigue her the most—any and all correspondence having to do with Grombach's efforts to keep the Pond up and running past its shelf life. Officially it went out of business in '55. But there are rumblings here and there of him looking for a more secretive way forward. Trying to line up support from his buddies in the business world, or on Capitol Hill. Shadowy references to certain Army generals and diplomatic types who might help. Here's one example, a letter he sent to a bunch of folks in July of '54, right after the CIA had made it clear they wouldn't be renewing the Pond's contract. Take a look. The money paragraph is down toward the end."

We are informing our people that this is really a security blackout, and that is definitely the truth. We merely don't know how long it will have to last, but we do know that our association with the Bay must end. We hope that we may be able to reactivate under new and different auspices the first part of 1955. We hope to do so even if we must do it privately, entirely supported by private funds, and even if we have to go underground even further than we have so far.

"Wow," Henry said. "Is there a lot of that in here?"

"Dribs and drabs. But the bulk of it is in a strange little collection that Grombach called the 'Jewelry' file."

"Jewelry?"

"Partly because of all the code names he used in that correspondence—Tiffany, for the Department of the Army. Van Cleef and Arpels, with Van Cleef supposedly being some Hungarian. Nobody seems to have a clue as to who Arpels was. Then there are all these other names that no one has yet identified: Mr. S., Mr. N., the Shark. There's a fellow Grombach calls the Bishop, who may have been a retired admiral. Another name, Durrell, was apparently an Army general. 'Staying in the jewelry business' became Grombach's euphemism for staying in the intelligence game. But with some of this stuff, even if you know the code names it's all so cloaked and convoluted that half the time you can't really tell *what* he's saying. Your mom loved it, I suppose because it's so rich with the whiff of conspiracy, and of unresolved actions. Let me show you another typical paragraph, from June of '55."

He flipped to another of the blue pages and tapped his finger on the third paragraph.

The only thing I have to suggest as a brand-new idea, but I imagine our ecclesiastical friend would have to check with Mr. van Cleef, is to let Bishop carry the ball in a new and different approach on Durrell. My suggestion is to let Mr. Bishop approach Durrell and tell him he knows of the desires of Arpels and of the reasons for those desires, and of the efforts of Arpels to find out about the organization.

"Now, skip down to this paragraph." Hilliard poked a sentence farther down the page.

As I see it with the Jones boys still in command here, the only possible chance of a resurrection is away from here and with great quiet, which is exactly the answer provided Durrell can be convinced.

"Care to guess who Grombach meant by 'the Jones boys'?" Hilliard asked.

"The Dulles brothers?" Henry said.

"Bingo. Allen Dulles was running CIA, John Foster Dulles was secretary of state. Frenchy despised them both, and the feelings were mutual."

Hilliard heaved with gentle laughter.

"What became of all this?" Anna asked.

"Nothing, obviously. The Pond went out of business right on schedule. The CIA let one or two ongoing ops proceed to their natural conclusion, but even those were wrapped up within a year. Grombach himself went into the corporate security biz. That's when he must have stashed away all these papers."

"And what became of all this talk about staying in the jewelry business?"

"It just stopped. He was mentioning it on one day, saying nothing the next. Like it never even existed."

They pondered that for a few seconds before Anna spoke up.

"But isn't that exactly what you'd do—clam up and get real quiet—if you'd managed to succeed by taking everything even deeper underground?"

Hilliard smiled.

"Young lady, you think just like your mother."

He closed the folder and slid it forward for them to take. Then he leaned back in his chair.

"Tell me, if you don't mind me prying just a little. Any idea of why she found all this material so fascinating?"

Anna started to speak, and then stopped, so Henry picked up the thread.

"For one thing, Baucom was a former lover."

Anna blushed, making Henry wish he'd used a more delicate word.

"Ah. So *that* was the personal connection."

"One of them, anyway," Anna said.

"You think there were more?"

"Well, maybe these other two names, Lewis and Beetle, this Edward Stone guy."

"You may be right. Although I didn't note any warmth or affection when they were mentioned. I was also a little surprised by her interest in the 'jewelry' material. I mean, that was in '54, '55? She would've barely been born, I'm guessing."

"Born in '54," Anna said.

"Yet, it was almost like she believed the Pond was still a going concern. It was like she *knew* it. That was her whole approach."

"Did you ever ask what made her so sure?" Henry said.

Hilliard shook his head.

"Why not?"

"Because she told me she was going to take a break for a while to run down some other leads, and then she'd be coming back for more. I always figured I'd be able to ask her later."

Hilliard sighed deeply. A breeze ruffled the pages in the folder, and the cardinal again cried out cheerfully from the trees.

44

"You've been mighty quiet over there," Henry said. They were halfway back to Poston, and she had spent most of the time staring out the window.

"Trying to take it all in. Between your little bombshell last night and what we just learned, it's been quite the day."

"True."

"At the moment my biggest question is this: Who are we supposed to be more worried about? This guy Robert, an aging Washington power broker who seemed to be trying to clear the way for his last hurrah? Or some ghost of a presence from a possibly dead, possibly live spy organization that I'd never even heard of until a few hours ago?"

"Don't you figure that by now the Pond is gone for sure?"

"Mom didn't seem to think so. Maybe she saw

something in those papers that only she could understand."

"Maybe. And it's not as if private intelligence orgs have exactly gone out of vogue. The Pentagon was up to its elbows with one a few years ago in Afghanistan. But all those guys from '55 would be dead or out of the biz by now."

"Still . . . There's one line from that last letter of CDG's that has really stuck with me. I mean, apart from the whole sense of imminent danger."

"'The worst is true and the strands have crossed'?"

"Yes. You think she was talking about *these* two strands—Robert and the Pond?"

"No way to know unless we can find out what was in the parcel, or CDG herself. And without a name or a return address, the latter isn't likely. At least for now, Merle is still the key. Find him and we find his controller, or his case officer—whatever the hell you want to call him—whether it's Robert or some spy zombie who crawled out from the depths of the Pond."

"One thing I could do right now is look up those two names from that first letter in the pile, the one that talked about Robert's last two ops."

"Go to it."

She checked her notes and got out her phone.

"Okay. The first name was Muhammad al Farooq. Amman, in November of 2000."

"Good luck with all the alternate Arab spellings."

She clicked away for a few seconds and began cursing under her breath.

"You weren't kidding. An 'o' instead of a 'u' in Muhammad. A 'k' instead of a 'q' in Farooq. Hold on . . . Found something. In Amman, too, and the date matches."

"Source?"

"*The Jordan Times*?"

"Reputable. It's an English-language daily."

"If this is our Muhammad al Farooq, then he's pretty hot stuff in the Palestinian hierarchy. Has a few links to Hamas, but also to more moderate elements. Definitely not a friend of U.S. interests, or so it says in this one piece . . . Well, now."

"What?"

"He's dead."

"As of when?"

"November of 2000. The same month as Robert's op."

"Assassinated?"

"No. Freak accident. Took a fall while visiting some desert ruins."

"Sure he did. Just happened to fall off a cliff right around the time Robert was in town."

"I'm just quoting the story. It says there were multiple witnesses."

"Sure there were."

"Stop!"

"Try the second name."

"I'm already on it. Dragan Jovovic, Novi Sad, in July of 1998."

"Serbian?"

"And a little too proud of it, apparently. Implicated in Bosnian war crimes but never charged. Joined an ultranationalist political party that was on the rise back around '97. Anti-EU, anti-Western."

"Meaning anti-American."

"Well, it's from a British newspaper, but yes."

"Anything happen in July of '98?"

"Just found a story from that month. Three guesses."

"He died?"

"Of a sudden illness. Bacterial infection. Happy as a clam one day, dead as a doornail the next. Leaving a vacuum of leadership in his anti-Western political party, which proceeded to disintegrate not long after his death."

"Still think poor old Muhammad in Amman fell all by his lonesome?"

"What I'm thinking is that I'm no longer all that worried about some ghost creeping out from the slime of the Pond. My money's back on a connection with Robert."

It was past time for dinner when they got back, and they agreed that it would be best to go their separate ways for the rest of the evening. Henry dropped Anna off at the bed & breakfast. As he drove up Willow he couldn't help but glance at the darkened Shoat house, and the image stuck with him as he pulled into the gravel drive of his rental house.

He'd been looking forward to finding Scooter waiting on the doorstep, but there was no sign. Maybe the old mutt also wanted some distance. With neither man nor beast to look over his shoulder, Henry switched on his phone. There were two more texts from Mitch, and the tone was angrier than ever. The second one said, "Last warning: Turn on your damn phone!"

He considered calling back. Then, in a rush of residual guilt still fresh from that morning, he decided to wait at least one more day. Feeling uneasy about it, he climbed onto a kitchen chair to retrieve the exiled bottle of rye and a juice tumbler. He downed two shots in rapid succession, and then nodded off on the couch as darkness fell, only to be awakened seemingly seconds later by the jolt of something slapping hard onto the front porch.

It had sounded like a fat Sunday newspaper, except it was the wrong time of day, and instead of the squeaky wheels of the paperboy's bicycle he heard the roaring engine of a car, hightailing it onto the highway from the end of Willow.

Henry rose from the couch and looked out the screen door. Scooter lay waiting for him, which lifted his spirits until he saw that the dog was unnaturally still, and his head was matted and misshapen. He opened the door and stepped gingerly around the dog, his heart beating painfully hard as he stooped for a closer look.

Scooter was dead, with a smashed and bloodied skull. Had a car hit him? Henry doubted it. The blow looked more like something that had come from a tire iron, or a baseball bat. He listened for the noise of the departing car, but it had already moved beyond earshot.

"Fuck. You poor old mutt."

He went back indoors for a towel from the bathroom, which he wrapped around Scooter's body. Then he carried the dog around the side of the house across the dewy lawn in the dark. The body felt terribly bony and sad. He reached the back of the property, next to a small stand of pines, and laid the bundle on the ground. After retrieving a shovel from the shed where the lawnmower was stored, he dug a grave and buried Scooter. Then, while the crickets and katydids sawed away, he brushed some pine needles over the raw dirt. All the while, he wondered what he should do next. His stubbornness no longer seemed to be serving much of a purpose, except as a salve to his vanity, and he vowed that no one else was going to get hurt on behalf of his pride.

He washed his hands at the kitchen sink beneath the buzzing fluorescent light. Then he switched on his phone and dialed Mitch's number. The voice that answered was the same as always—flat, businesslike.

"I take it you got my last message."

"The one that was hand-delivered?"

"Yes. What do you have for me?" No gloating, no emotion at all. In a way, that made it worse. "I *said,* what do you have for me?"

"Hold on. I'll get my notes."

Henry told him about their discovery of the stashed letters, and their findings about Robert and Merle. He offered the four names from the *Newsweek* piece, half hoping that Mitch would cite one of them and say, "He's your man," so that he could at least salvage one positive thing from this call. Instead, Mitch listened in silence until Henry finished the story of Robert's appearance on the week Anna went off to college. Maybe out of pride, maybe out of caution, he withheld the information from the final letter, with its dire warning that the strands had crossed.

"Good stuff. Exactly what we hired you for. See? It's easy. Just do your job. Anything else?"

Henry numbly described their trip to the National Archives for research on the Pond. He was halfway through his summary of their findings when Mitch stopped him.

"That shit's ancient history. Is this really the best use of your time?"

"By all indications, Helen Shoat was up to her neck in this right around the time she died."

"It's a blind alley. Cease and desist."

"I'm guessing you know more than you're saying or you wouldn't be so sure."

"What I'm saying is, don't waste your time or mine."

"Maybe if you could offer a clearer rationale."

"For once in your life, Mattick, just do as you're fucking told."

"I plan to. But, per your instructions, I'm supposed to keep both clients happy, and the other one wants to pursue this. Hand in glove, right?"

A pregnant pause.

"Then you'd better find some way within the parameters of her assignment to steer her in another direction."

"The parameters of her assignment? Mitch, you've been in Washington too long."

"End this, Mattick. Right now. Unless, of course, you'd like all of my messages from this point forward to arrive hand-delivered. Understood?"

"Loud and clear."

They hung up.

Henry waited a few seconds, feeling like he'd learned something important when he'd least expected it. He then dialed another number with a Washington area code, and instead of an answer there was a beep, which Henry responded to by punching in an access code. A male voice answered after the first ring.

"Go ahead."

"Did you get all of that?"

"Affirmative. Stay on it, both tracks."

"Will do."

"And Henry."

"Yes?"

"Be careful."

"Too late for that, I'm afraid."

They disconnected. Henry again retrieved the bottle of rye. He needed another two shots before he could sleep.

45

Helen switched on the bedside light, unable to sleep. What she needed was a nightcap, anything to calm her nerves so she could wake up rested for what promised to be a long and eventful tomorrow. It wasn't yet midnight, so she threw back the sheets and got dressed.

Claire had booked her a spacious room on the third floor of a modest five-story hotel on a one-way street. French doors opened onto a narrow terrace with potted geraniums and a wrought iron railing, with a commanding view of the street below, although at the moment the wooden shutters were closed.

Helen had made a quick reconnaissance right after checking in. At one end of the hundred-yard block was the Canal de l'Ourcq, with a tree-lined roadway running alongside it and a pedestrian bridge that crossed to the other bank. At the other end was the Avenue de

Flandre, where busy sidewalks were populated mostly by Parisians, just as Claire had said.

She was about to head out when she remembered the copy of *Paris Match,* with Claire's report stapled inside. It sat on a console table, trying to look inconspicuous among a few tourist magazines, but Helen didn't feel comfortable leaving it there. Figuring it was easier to hide the report than the magazine, she loosened the staples and removed the pages. Then she took down a framed Chagall print that hung above the bed, pried out the back panel, slid the folded pages between the backing and the poster, and hung the frame back on the wall.

Downstairs, the empty street felt a little spooky, although it saved her time by not having to decide whether any bystanders were there to keep an eye on her. She chose her destination by sound, turning in the direction of the noisier Avenue de Flandre, and within a few blocks she found a brasserie on a corner next to an entrance to the Metro. A few hardy customers sat at sidewalk tables in the October chill, but Helen opted for the smoky coziness within. An older man had just stood to leave a table by the door, so she took his place.

The brasserie was nearly empty, which suited her fine. Two tables down, a pair of backpacking young Germans—and, yes, it figured that any tourists in this neighborhood were bound to be backpacking young Germans—bent low over a massive Michelin map.

They jabbed forefingers and made pencil marks, as if planning an assault on the Arc de Triomphe. Only her second night in Paris, and Helen was already viewing Germans as uncharitably as the locals. Or maybe she was just tired and on edge.

They, too, soon departed, just as Helen's whiskey arrived in a cut-glass tumbler, borne aloft on a tray by a bored waiter in a smudged apron. The Germans folded their map but left behind a newspaper, which made Helen realize she hadn't seen or read a shred of news in the past twenty-four hours. She had thought about buying an *International Herald Tribune* earlier that evening, but hadn't been sure if that's what a Canadian would do. Now she no longer cared.

She stepped over to the empty table and grabbed it before the waiter could clear it away. It was today's edition of the *Frankfurter Allgemeine Zeitung,* a little conservative for her tastes, but written in a language she could understand. She sipped her whiskey and settled in for a nice, restorative read.

As had been the case for weeks, the big news was out of Iran, where student protesters and the new leader, Ayatollah Khomeini, were freshly outraged because the deposed Shah had just landed in the United States. Yet another reason Berlin station wasn't getting much attention, although she supposed her little escapade must have turned a few heads in Langley by now.

She flipped the page. More foreign news. A bit of

domestic politics. Nothing about any CIA personnel going AWOL. Not that she'd expected it. The Agency did its best to keep these kinds of internal breaches quiet. She flipped another page. Some jerk in Bavaria had gotten himself arrested by making a Hitler salute on a subway car.

A story in the corner caught her eye: "Auto Accident Claims Life of SPD Policy Maker." The victim was Werner Gerntholz, forty-five, "a prominent thinker in Social Democratic circles, known for outspoken views on relations with the United States, especially with regard to nuclear policy."

The same fellow whose keys had been copied by Kathrin and Anneliese for Kevin Gilley and his young American helper, Kurt Delacroix. She recalled the details: a red key for a garage, and one that fit a BMW. The story said Gerntholz's BMW had run through a guardrail on a high mountain pass. He was alone, and had apparently fallen asleep. His body showed signs of carbon monoxide poisoning, leading authorities to suspect he'd passed out due to a faulty exhaust system.

Helen dropped the newspaper, took a deep breath, and then gulped half the remaining whiskey. She gazed out the window onto the sidewalks of Paris. Sleep was no longer an option. She quietly paid her bill and left.

In the morning, rather than being rattled, she was surprised to find that the news of Gerntholz's death had steeled her resolve. She hit the sidewalks with a swagger in her step, attuned to her surroundings. With the better part of a day to kill before her daily contact with Claire at 4 p.m., she decided to spend the next few hours plotting out escape and evasion routes in the blocks near her hotel, figuring that she might as well prepare for the worst.

She carried out her reconnaissance under the guise of shopping, all the while scouting for stores with rear exits, stairways, side doors, and other passages that she might employ to her advantage later. She also mulled the wide variety of quick changes she could make to her appearance with the help of the wig, scarf, sunglasses, and other items that Claire had assembled for her in the tote bag.

Confident that she was up to the task, she then amused herself by looking for the ugliest, tackiest item of tourist kitsch a bird-watching Canadian woman might want to take home. The pickings for such items were fairly slim on the Avenue de Flandre until she hit the jackpot at a small shop that offered hundreds of replicas of the Eiffel Tower of almost every imaginable size and style. There were gold ones, ceramic ones, plastic ones, and they could be had as key chains, paperweights, refrigerator magnets, clocks, and tree ornaments. Then there were the snow globes. Some with an entire miniature Paris inside. Red, blue, yellow, and gold, from small to large.

Finally she settled on one of the larger snow globes— nearly six inches in diameter, with a gilded Eiffel Tower inside. It had a massive and heavy plastic base on which "Paris" was chiseled in blocky blue letters—to her eye, the single most tasteless item in the store. She carried it gleefully to the register, where the proprietor searched in vain for a price tag and then, sensing her eagerness, quoted the outrageous figure of thirty francs, or around six bucks.

"Done!" she answered in English, although the moment she left the store she knew she would have to take it back to her room rather than lug it around for the rest of the day. What a dreadnought it was! Two pounds, at least. She smiled to herself and hoped she would have a chance to show it to Claire, and then she checked her watch. Just after 1 p.m. Less than three hours before she would find out whether Marina was ready for a rendezvous.

46

Claire sat in her windowless office, wondering how Helen was faring, hunted and probably scared. It was already after 2 p.m. Less than two hours before the daily check-in, which Claire would have to do by telephone unless things changed in a hurry. If she hadn't heard from Marina by then—which would be impossible unless she could sneak away long enough to check her Sisterhood mailbox—then she'd have to scout out a new hotel for tomorrow.

She rolled a clean sheet of paper into her typewriter and stared at it. Then she unrolled it and surveyed the sorry state of her career as symbolized by her current plot of Agency real estate. Hers was the smallest, bleakest office in a building that offered most of its residents splendid views of the gardens of the Champs-Élysées, the Place de la Concorde, and the splendid Hôtel de Crillon. The view from Claire's desk was of a blank wall with thumbtack holes left by the previous occupant, a fidgety man named Bewley who'd posted family photos alongside nudie snaps from one of the tawdrier floor shows in Pigalle. He'd rated out so poorly that he now worked for a private security firm in Oslo that specialized in crowd control for touring rock bands. Maybe that was her next destination if things went poorly for Helen. Claire tried to imagine booking limos for Aerosmith in Trondheim and had to suppress a yawn.

Then she thought again of Helen, living like an infiltrator on enemy soil, which in turn reminded her of a conversation at Langley two years ago, right before her posting. Peggy Mullen, a kindly old gal from counterintelligence, had sought her out in the CIA cafeteria to wish her well. Mullen, pushing sixty, had been based in London during the war for the OSS, enduring the Blitz along with all the heavyweights like Wisner and Angleton. She'd helped prep operatives for parachute drops into occupied France, and decades later she still talked about it with great animation as she discussed the pressures of knowing you couldn't afford to overlook a single detail.

"Get the slightest thing wrong—the button you sewed onto their shirts, or even the lint in their pockets—and they might never come back. You were always on a wartime footing."

That's how Claire felt now—a wartime footing,

worrying about every detail. It was the most urgent matter she'd handled in months, even though it was completely off the books. She absently picked up the sheet of paper once again, and was on the verge of rolling it back into her typewriter when there was a knock at her door.

"Yes?"

It was Maguire, her chief of station, oozing with forced charm as he entered with a hearty hello, which could only mean that he had some sort of disagreeable assignment. Get bogged down in scut work now and she might not even be able to reach a phone booth at four to call Helen. It would be unthinkable to phone from the office.

Maguire was past his prime, but had enjoyed some glory days during the latter years of de Gaulle's reign, when the French had pulled out of NATO and flirted with the Soviets. He was not unkind, and not a groper, but he was too old-school to see what Claire had to offer. Although she enjoyed calling him her POS COS, she sometimes felt sorry for him, especially when the younger males laughed behind his back.

He had been resistant to Claire's posting from the beginning. When informed that a woman would soon be assigned to operations at his station, Maguire had requested that the slot be filled by a "contract wife," meaning a female employee married to a CIA male. Instead, he got Claire, all by her lonesome, so his next move was to try to slot her in an office job. On her second night in Paris he'd taken her to a bar to explain why.

"I don't really believe in women ops officers," he'd said, smiling unctuously.

Claire, who wasn't above being a suck-up when the occasion called for it, maintained a game face and said, "You're certainly in position to know best, but why do you feel that way?"

"Because, well, you know, women have babies. Eventually. I know you're not married, not yet, but you might still get pregnant—this is Paris, after all, city of l'amour—and then of course you'd need all that time off even if you were right in the middle of something big. So you see?"

"Oh, absolutely. You're quite right." Having established the nature of the hurdle, Claire then proceeded to vault it in a single bound. "But that won't be a problem for me, you see, because I've been fixed." She said it with a winning smile, even as Maguire's jaw dropped.

"Fixed?"

"Yes. You know, like with a dog or cat?"

It was a lie, of course. An utter fiction. Not that Maguire would ever know.

"Oh."

His smile turned queasy, the discomfort of a man backed into a corner by his own words.

"Well, then. I suppose you're a reasonable enough candidate."

And that was that.

While getting acquainted with her new co-conspirator the previous day at lunch, Claire had discerned that if Helen lacked one vital office skill it was probably tact, or the willingness to suffer fools when necessary. Maguire would have loathed her, and she would have lost by fighting back. Yet the Agency needed women with attitudes like Helen's, just as much as it needed ones who knew how to play along.

"So, how is my favorite cabinet minister?" Maguire asked. "Has he yet frequented the love nest of our scarlet damsel?"

"He has not. But one thing I've noticed, only yesterday, is that I'm not the only one who has taken an interest."

Maguire frowned and sat down.

"Tell me more."

"A certain ambitious young reporter for *Le Figaro* has been lingering in a bar across the street from her place, two of the last three times I was there."

"Did he make you?"

"God, no. But I made him, and he wasn't just there for a drink. There was a camera in his bag and he was taking notes as he gazed out the window. He was none too subtle."

"What do you think?"

"I think we're not the only ones who've been peddled this story. Although why the French would even bat an eye at a sex scandal is still a mystery to me. But if they would, then I suppose our journalist will be willing to run with it much harder and longer than we'd ever want to."

"Meaning that any interest on our part—"

"Is probably a moot point, although I'm certainly willing to keep plugging away."

She expected him to respond as he usually did—by gloomily telling her, yes, plug away a while longer. Instead, he perked up and said, "Actually, this news couldn't have come at a better time. I have something else for you that's much more urgent."

"I'm all ears." She wanted to groan.

"Remember that full alert we got the other night, on the renegade clerk from Berlin station?"

Clerk. Poor Helen, although it was probably a blessing in disguise if everyone was underestimating her.

"You mean the brunette with the nice eyes?" She knew Maguire would respond better if she spoke in his language.

"They *were* nice eyes, weren't they? I'm told she also has quite a figure."

"Well, that's helpful to know."

"Anyhow, they still haven't found her, and I was wondering if, well . . ."

"If I could join the hunt?" More good news. And if

Maguire was assigning Claire, then he definitely saw Helen as a low priority. Gilley, unfortunately, probably saw things differently.

"Yes! I was thinking the search could use an injection of feminine intuition."

"I see. Great minds thinking alike, and all that."

"Exactly. Knew you'd see my point." He seemed relieved that she hadn't frowned and called him some sort of pig.

"Any reason to think she's in France?"

"None, really. But she hasn't turned up anywhere else, and, well, how many different places could she go?"

"A few dozen?"

"Well, yes, but . . ."

"But she's only a clerk with a limited imagination, and France is right next door, so . . ."

"Exactly."

"I think I might have some insights on her mentality, if you'd like me to get on it right away."

"Perfect, Claire. I knew you'd see what I was after. Her clearance was pretty low, so no one's all that worried about what she might spill. Still, it would be a real feather in our caps if we could run her down for Berlin."

A feather in Maguire's cap, he meant. But now Claire had carte blanche to make sure that everything would work better for Helen. Her eyes flicked around the room as Maguire prattled on. Her coat hung by the door. She thought her handbag was atop her bookshelf, but then she spotted it over to the side. She glanced at her watch. Even after accounting for the usual counter-surveillance techniques, if she left now she should have enough time to swing by the mailbox before going to Helen's hotel for their four o'clock contact. She stood from her desk.

"Where are you going?"

"To check with sources. If anyone like her is looking for help, they'd be the first to know."

Maguire stood, too, and smiled again.

"Of course! Good to see you jumping right into the fray. Happy hunting, Claire."

"Thank you, sir."

He gracefully stepped aside as she breezed out of the office.

47

Claire sensed she was being watched from the moment she stepped into the street. That man on a bench, reading *Le Monde*—hadn't she also seen him at lunch, when she'd dashed out for a sandwich? A TV repair van on the opposite curb eased into traffic in the same direction she was heading. Why would it have even been there? Both the embassy and the Hôtel de Crillon handled those kinds of jobs in-house. Maybe it was her excitement, maybe it was her sense of urgency, but her instincts told her that she had better shake not only the van but also the fellow on the bench, who had just stood and folded his newspaper.

She reversed course. Two blocks later she hailed a cab, ordered the driver to make a U-turn, and then a mile later hopped out and doubled back in the opposite direction of traffic on a one-way street. She didn't care if they knew she was trying to lose them, and that made the job easier. She went into the front entrance of a fruit vendor and exited out the back. She caught a bus, and another cab. Finally, a half hour later, she found herself alone and unobserved as she entered the main gate of the Cimetière de la Villette, in the 19th arrondissement. Her Sisterhood mailbox was beneath a stone planter by a stone crypt for the Famille Gérard.

She had chosen the location by the same rationale she had used to pick Helen's hotel, orienting herself to the northeast for its proximity to Bondy, where she expected Marina to turn up. Looking around, Claire saw that no one else seemed to be inside the stone walls of the small cemetery. The view from the surrounding houses was blocked by a canopy of trees, which were in all their autumn glory.

She strolled up a cobbled path beneath shedding maples to the Gérard vault, where she reached beneath the planter and yanked free an envelope. Normally she would have opened it in a more secure location, but she was in a hurry. She slit it open, unfolded a sheet of paper, and read a single line of typewritten characters: *18:00, the vista, Parc de Belleville, the bench.*

So there it was. A meeting was set, either with Marina or a cutout. She had more than an hour to relay the message to Helen, and now that she was free of surveillance, she could deliver it personally. Helen was supposed to take any four o'clock phone calls in her room, so that's where Claire would meet her.

She arrived at the hotel on Passage de Flandre with more than twenty minutes to spare. No one was manning the front desk, so she went straight upstairs. When there was no answer to her knock, she easily picked the lock with a small tool from a vinyl packet in her handbag. Then she plopped onto the end of the bed to wait.

My, but this place was dusty, and her nose wrinkled in response. Then she sneezed. A moment later, feeling a second one on the way, she reached into her purse for a packet of tissues she had bought that morning.

Instead of the softness of the tissues she felt a single tissue wrapped around something hard and heavy. She pulled out the packet for a closer look. It was the density of lead. Unwrapping it she found a small black box with a tiny red light on the end, flashing at one-second intervals.

It was a radio wave tracking beacon.

She cursed her stupidity, or maybe it was carelessness. Beacons like this were impractical for tracking individuals, because there was no way to strap them onto someone unawares. Unless, of course, you could slip one into their briefcase or handbag. Fearing the worst, she stepped to the window and peered between the slats in the shuttered door.

Nothing suspicious. She exhaled slowly, and was

about to turn away from the window when a TV repair van turned onto the street and pulled onto the opposite sidewalk.

"Fuck!"

She backed away from the window. Her first impulse was to smash the beacon, but then they'd know it had been discovered and would plan accordingly. Still, the damage was done. This was the only hotel on the street—the only hotel for blocks. They'd know for sure that Helen was staying here, and they'd snatch her the moment she showed up.

Who could have planted the beacon? It had to have been someone in Paris station, probably a confederate of Gilley's. Hansen, a recent arrival, had phoned her at around noon to come critique one of his reports. It had seemed a bit odd at the time, but nothing alarming, and she had left her office door open. Meaning at least two people had been involved. When you did work like Gilley's, you put out feelers everywhere, she supposed—people to do small favors with no questions asked.

Claire checked her watch. Eighteen minutes before four o'clock. Stay calm and think fast. She should have taken the Metro on the way over. Going underground would have killed the signal for sure. But it was too late now. Adjust and move forward.

"Think, goddammit!"

Claire opened Helen's overnight bag and took out

a baggy blouse that she'd bought for her the other day. She threw off her own jacket and pullover and hastily buttoned up the blouse. She took out a pair of bobby pins, pulled her hair up into a bun and pinned it into place, and then put on an orange scarf from her handbag, along with a pair of reading glasses. Then she unfolded the message from Audra with the details of the rendezvous and scribbled a handwritten addendum.

She moved the beacon to the console table, to ensure a clearer signal to the van. That's when she noticed the copy of *Paris Match* that she'd given to Helen the day before. If Helen was unable to return, she'd never retrieve it, so Claire stuffed it into her handbag. What else? Nothing she could think of, so she left the room, took a back staircase, and pushed through an emergency door into a rear alley. Fortunately, no alarm sounded.

She worked her way to a courtyard that opened onto Passage de Flandre near the canal. Helen would approach either from there or from the Avenue de Flandre. Fifty-fifty. An incorrect guess could be fatal, and Claire might already be too late. She decided that if she were Helen, she'd want to return by the least populated route, so she headed toward the canal.

She reached the street that ran along the canal. No sign of Helen. Across the road was a concrete stairway to a footbridge over the water. Claire climbed the steps to a landing halfway up, trying not to hurry now that she was out in the open. She took up a position at the railing with a commanding view.

It was now fourteen minutes before four. The van was still parked on the sidewalk, engine idling. The fellow whom she'd seen outside the embassy now stood on the near corner of Passage de Flandre, keeping a lookout along the canal just as Claire was doing. He gave no indication that he'd recognized Claire. Hoping to keep it that way, she pulled out her copy of *Paris Match* and pretended to read. Flipping open the pages she noticed right away that Helen had removed the report, probably to hide it in her room. Shit! Nothing was going right.

The lookout's attention was suddenly drawn to the other end of the street. He stepped around the corner and peered past the van toward a young woman who had just turned off of Avenue de Flandre, two hundred yards away—too far to see whether it was Helen. If Claire had guessed wrong, her friend was doomed.

She again checked her flanks. To the right was a man approaching on a bicycle. To the left, a couple of boys in shorts, playing tag. Behind her, a houseboat motored along with a *pop-pop-pop*, keeping time with her pulse. She glanced right again—and there she was!—making her way forward beneath the plane trees along the canal footpath, maybe forty yards away. Claire headed down the steps, restraining herself from breaking into a run.

She stared at the sidewalk in hopes that Helen wouldn't recognize her and call out her name.

The lookout's attention was still diverted in the opposite direction, so she quickened her pace while planning her move. Helen carried the bag on her left, so Claire eased to that side, reaching Helen about twenty-five yards short of the intersection. She pretended to trip on a tree root and threw herself forward, grabbing Helen's left shoulder while dropping Audra's message into the tote bag.

"Turn around!" she rasped. "They've staked out the hotel. Go!"

Helen faltered, but only for a second. Without a word she pivoted back down the canal, away from danger. Claire turned in the opposite direction. To a bystander it must have looked as if they'd bounced off each other, like atomic particles in a cloud chamber.

The lookout had taken notice and was now pursuing Helen, and ignoring Claire. His mistake. Claire reached into her handbag for the sharp tool she'd used to pick the lock and set off on a collision course. He didn't look up until she was almost on him, and by then it was too late. Claire jammed the splinter of steel into his left ear canal, feeling something pop as he shrieked and fell to the sidewalk. No one else had yet emerged from around the corner where the van was parked. The only other people nearby were the two boys, who looked up in surprise, and an older man carrying a grocery bag, twenty yards off.

"Help him!" Claire shouted in a burst of French. "He's hurt himself. I'll go for a doctor!"

The man put down his bag and stepped forward. The lookout held his head with both hands and writhed in agony as blood trickled from his left ear. Claire took off in the opposite direction from Helen. Having helped clear her friend's path to safety, it was time to disappear while she had the chance. Later she could discreetly work her way over to Helen's rendezvous point, in case help was needed there.

A few blocks later she checked her flanks. Gilley's people were gone. She hoped Helen had made it.

48

Helen's ears were ringing, a high-pitched whine like the wail of an inner alarm. Only as she emerged back onto Avenue de Flandre, one block up from her hotel's cross street, did the noise begin to subside. She still wasn't quite sure what had just happened. All she knew for certain was that she was back on the run, and that Claire had dropped a message into her bag.

It had to be Gilley's people, but how had they found her? Had she made a mistake? Lowered her guard? Whatever the case, thank God for Claire. She slowed her pace. Walking faster than everyone else was a sure way to draw attention. Deep breath. Think. Don't look over your shoulder. She glanced into a storefront window, but the reflection was a wavering riot of colors with a bus, children, their moms. A shriek of laughter to her right startled her, but was harmless.

Fortunately, she was in the very block where she had plotted her course of escape and evasion that morning, seemingly ages ago. She put her plan into motion, heading into a corner dress shop she'd already scouted. Two changing rooms were in the back, obscured from view by a long rack of clothes. She ducked into one and got to work, pulling off her jeans and slipping on a beige skirt from the tote bag. She took out a handbag. Then she put on the sunglasses, discarded the jeans, folded the tote bag, and tucked it under her arm as she exited the store from a side door and then walked down the cross street.

Rounding the next corner, and still walking at a normal pace, she made a beeline for another shop at the end of the block. This time she accomplished her quick-change on the move behind a rack of clothing, pulling up her hair under a green scarf that she tied beneath her chin. She pulled out the red cardigan from her purse and slipped it on as she exited by a rear door.

Two blocks later she reached the tree-lined Rue de Crimée, which also had plenty of shops and pedestrians. She walked against the flow of the one-way traffic until she spotted a bus rolling to a halt just ahead. She hopped aboard, using the transit pass she'd bought earlier. Only two other persons boarded with her, both of them women who had already been waiting at the stop. She sat in an aisle seat, away from the window, where she pulled off the scarf and sunglasses, lowered her head, and slipped on the auburn wig. Then she took off the red cardigan. She stayed aboard until the bus had crossed the canal that ran near her hotel. Only then did she feel secure enough to check the message in her bag.

Helen unfolded the tote bag and dug out the sheet of paper. The first line was typed: 18:00, the vista, Parc de Belleville, the bench.

Below, in handwriting that must have been Claire's: *Do not return to hotel! Call our first number at 4 tomorrow.*

So, then. Marina had been in touch, and a rendezvous was set for an hour from now. Helen got out her tourist map and found the park, a few miles to the south of where she was now, in the upper reaches of the 20th arrondissement. But there was no marking for anything called "the vista." She took out the Fodor's guidebook, looked up the park, and read about its "spectacular view from the end of Rue Piat."

Helen began moving toward the meeting point, via bus and Metro. She changed her appearance one more time as she gradually closed in on her destination. Finally, with seven minutes to spare, she reached the northeast side of the park, strolling down the narrow, one-way Rue Piat and then entering the park at the upper end of a sloping series of wooded hill and dale, with lush arbors and even a few waterways tucked into the creases of the park. Spreading out below was the grandeur of Paris, with the Eiffel Tower spiking the horizon to the southwest. It was only a few minutes after sunset, and everything was bathed in amber and russet, a beauty that calmed her as she stepped deeper into the park.

She looked for the nearest bench, but there wasn't one in view. A group of tourists had gathered earlier to photograph the sunset, but they were all standing. She headed down a walkway to her left. Ahead were espaliered grape vines, but no bench. To her right, a set of steps led downhill to a parallel path, maybe fifteen yards below, where she now saw a single bench.

She took a seat. No one was in sight except the tourists, who all had their cameras out. She was watching them when she sensed someone approaching on the path to her left, an older woman, shuffling heavily, in a worn gray overcoat. Carrying a shopping bag, she heaved herself onto the other end of the bench and sighed, as if in exhaustion. Her coat smelled like mothballs.

Helen looked straight ahead. She waited through a few tense moments of silence and, finally, the woman spoke under her breath in heavily accented English.

"Take the taxi that stops on the street behind us, Rue Piat. Ask the driver for number four. In a moment I will walk there, and you will follow."

Helen nodded.

The woman took a few more seconds to catch her breath and then stood, scattering a few pigeons that had assembled on the path. Helen fell in behind her, a few yards back. They ascended the sidewalk toward the tourists. Right on cue, a taxi glided to the curb as Helen reached the street. The rear door opened. As she climbed in she saw a man was hunched down on the other side of the backseat, staying out of sight. He nodded as if to reassure her.

"Number four," she told the driver, who pulled away from the curb.

There was a sudden commotion to their rear, and Helen looked out the back window to see that the older women had fallen to the ground on the narrow street. At first she was alarmed, but then realized what was happening. A second taxi had wheeled into view but was now blocked on the narrow street as several of the tourists rushed to the aid of the fallen woman.

The rear door of the other taxi opened. Was that Claire getting out? If so, then Helen had just lost her escort, her backup, her safety valve.

"Here," the man to her left said. He was sitting up straight now and he handed her a black piece of cloth. She took it, not knowing what she was supposed to do next. He mimed pulling it over his head. A hood, then, to keep her from seeing where they were going. When she hesitated, he sighed and snatched it back, and roughly pulled it down over her face. It smelled of sweat and cigarettes.

"Down!" he ordered.

"It is down," she said.

"No, *you*. You down!"

She lowered herself out of sight.

"Yes. Good," he said, although she could no longer see him. She no longer saw anything—not the city nor the streets, and certainly not Claire.

49

Claire hopped out of the cab as the driver fumed. She tossed a wad of francs onto the seat, which still didn't shut him up because that's how Parisian hacks were born to behave, so she leaned into his window and silenced him with an insult that covered half his ancestry, and then she stepped away to the curb.

She looked up the street, but Helen's taxi was out of sight. Hopeless.

"You must be Claire," a male voice said from behind. She turned abruptly.

Everyone else in the vicinity was still gathered around the fallen woman, except for this fellow, an American who had materialized at her shoulder. He was older but fit, even a little dashing, and wore an outdated wardrobe—trench coat and fedora, the standard spy uniform of the 1960s.

"Who are you?"

"I'm not with Robert, so you can set your mind at ease on that score. Where have they taken her?"

"Somewhere safer than where she was a few hours ago."

"Nice to know."

"Are you going to tell me your name?"

"Not here."

He looked around. The older woman in the street was showing signs of a miraculous recovery, and was loudly declining offers of help as she tried to disengage from the crowd.

"That one should get an Oscar," he said.

"Who are you working for?"

"As I said, not here. But we should compare notes. How 'bout a drink?"

His manner was oddly reassuring, even though she supposed that he, too, might represent some sort of threat. An Agency fixer, perhaps, summoned to round up all the miscreants and put a stop to this whole escapade. The end to her career, to their entire operation.

But that wasn't his vibe. In any event, there was little to be gained by running now that Helen was safely on her way, so Claire nodded and said, "Lead the way."

They found a café on the Rue des Envierges. Claire tried out some French on him as they walked through the door, just to show him he was out of his league, only to have him reply with an impeccable Parisian accent. As if to rub it in, he got out a pack of Gitanes, offered one, and then, without even consulting a menu, ordered something that made the waiter nod approvingly before disappearing into the cellar. A moment later she discovered that the man certainly knew his brandies.

"I'm guessing you're from Berlin station."

"Yes. But I'm not here in any official capacity, and I'm certainly not here to do either of you harm. If at all possible, I was hoping to lend a hand. Clark Baucom."

He extended a hand in greeting, but Claire was too surprised to take it.

"I've heard of you."

"Not from Helen, I hope?"

"No, no. From the station Old Boys, the ones who tell all the tales. I wasn't even sure you were still active."

Baucom smiled ruefully.

"Well, that's quite the tribute. My chief of station often feels the same way."

"My God, are you Helen's . . . ?" She let the words hang.

"Not anymore. On that front, at least, she's come to her senses. Well earned by me, alas."

Claire shook her head, less in wonder at Helen's choice of men as in admiration of how she had instinctively chosen the one fellow who could be invaluable at a moment like this.

"You supplied her with the passport, didn't you? The false identity?"

His sheepish smile told her all she needed to know.

"How in the hell did you find her?"

"By finding you."

"I thought only Gilley's people knew that connection." Her suspicion was aroused anew. Had she been lulled into a premature surrender?

"I knew because I cheated. I stole one of your messages from the mailbox she'd set up. She made it too damn easy for me, and so did you. Did you really think a code name like CDG would baffle a mossy old frequent flier like me?"

"Clumsy, I agree, but that wasn't my idea."

"And it didn't take much of a review of Paris station's lineup to settle on the likeliest suspect. Female, field person, roughly the same age and training class as Helen. That narrowed it to one. Then when I saw you checking your own bolt-hole in that cemetery, well . . ."

"I can't believe I didn't shake you before then."

"You lost that other crowd easily enough. How did they find the hotel?"

She told him about the tracking beacon. He frowned.

"Women and their goddamn handbags."

Claire laughed in spite of herself.

"So you saw the whole fiasco outside the hotel, then."

"Where I lost her again. I decided to put all my remaining money on the other horse still in the race."

"Are you sure no one knows her whereabouts at any official level?"

"As of this morning that was certainly the case, and I can't imagine it would have changed. They're slow-playing it, and secretly hoping she's gone off on some kind of drunken vacation. It also hasn't hurt that everyone in Langley is preoccupied with Tehran."

"That's good news."

"Yes. But it's also good news for Robert. Gives him a clear field for hunting. And from the look of things outside that hotel, I'd say he's well reinforced."

"So what do we do now?"

"Depends on where you think she's gone, and what that means."

Claire told him about Marina, and what Helen hoped to accomplish.

Baucom nodded, seemingly impressed, but then he leaned across the table and lowered his voice.

"You won't bring him down, you know, no matter how much ammunition you gather."

"That's smug of you. How can you be so sure?"

"His work. They'll be too determined to protect it. Or to protect everyone he's ever reported to."

"Then why are you here? Why are you helping us?"

"To save our girl, Helen. That's the one thing all your findings might be useful for, to keep those bastards from burning her at the stake."

"That's not enough. For me or for Helen."

"I understand, but right now our biggest priority should be to get her safely home."

"Agreed."

"Did you make any contingencies for contact later?"

Claire mentioned the designated phone call, due at four o'clock tomorrow afternoon.

"That's a lot of hours to be hanging fire."

"Yes. I should have set it for sooner, but I was in a hurry."

"Seeing as how you've both been flying by the seat of your pants, I'd say it's all gone pretty admirably up to now."

"The problem is that she may decide it's too long to wait. I'm worried that if things work out for her this evening she might try to make a run back to Berlin."

"Tonight?"

She nodded. He grimaced.

"That would be a mistake. Maybe a fatal one."

"I agree. He knows he's spooked her. He'll have all the stations covered."

"You have any other ideas?"

To her surprise, she realized that she did.

"Just one. But it might work. We've only just met, Helen and I, but if I've read her correctly . . ."

"Lead the way."

50

Helen hunched low in the taxi. The hood was making her nose itch as she tried to follow their progress by sound and by feel. For the first few minutes they bumped along cobbled lanes and swerved violently, the driver cursing under his breath. Then, sudden smoothness and a climbing sensation that ended on a level slab where they were moving at high speed with the noise of traffic all around them. The grinding of gears of large trucks— the blast of streaking motorcycles. She guessed that they must either be on the Périphérique, the city's ring road, or the A-3, the motorway that stretched out toward the banlieue of Bondy, Marina's home territory.

She tried to get comfortable, which wasn't easy when her minder kept shoving her lower whenever she straightened her spine. They continued on smooth roads for another fifteen minutes, slowing at times in congestion marked by car horns and with more cursing by the driver. Finally, they exited onto a smaller street with potholes. There was a mumbled consultation, and someone opened a window. She heard people on the sidewalk, a blast of bouncy Arabic music. Cool air poured into the car. They passed in and out of the glare of street lamps.

A few moments later, her minder yanked her into an upright position and pulled off the hood, snagging her hair enough to bring tears to her eyes, which she blinked back lest they see it as weakness. The car stopped in an alley. Massive concrete high-rises rose to the front and left.

"Go there," her minder said, pointing to a battered steel door dimly visible across a sidewalk to their left. "Up three stairs." She nodded, assuming that he meant she should climb three flights of stairs. "Then, number eight. Yes?"

"Yes."

"After, you will come back here. If not?" He shook his head and drew a finger across his neck. "Yes?"

"If you say so."

He didn't seem to like that answer, or maybe he didn't understand it, so he took her by the shoulders and again said, "Yes?"

"*Yes*. I understand."

He released her, and she climbed out. The steel door was unlocked but jammed shut, and she had to pull with all her strength to wrench it free. The stairwell was dark and stank of urine, although it brightened a bit as she climbed, and by the end of the second flight of stairs she could hear voices and smell cooking—peppers, caraway seed, and cumin, the spices of Algeria. But as she made the final climb the noises disappeared, and she emerged into an empty hallway that had either been gutted or was being prepped for renovation. She found number eight on a wooden door with a peephole, and knocked.

"Entrez," a woman called out.

Helen entered a large room with a scuffed linoleum floor and bare walls. A dim ceiling light offered the only illumination. Heavy curtains were pulled shut across the only window. There were two chairs. One, a blue wing armchair by the door, was empty. Facing it from about twenty feet away was a wooden folding chair, occupied by a younger, smaller woman with olive skin and drawn features, and black hair cut in a choppy bob. She wore a white, baggy peasant blouse, canvas painter's pants, and sandals. She was smoking. Next to her was a small table with a smudged glass of water. The woman's pose somehow communicated that she was not to be approached without permission. Helen spoke first.

"Marina?"

"You are Elizabeth Hart?"

"Yes."

"You will sit, please."

Helen pulled the Japanese cassette recorder out of her handbag and showed it to Marina.

"Bring it here. I will operate."

Helen crossed the room as carefully as if she were auditioning for the ballet. Marina took it without a word, switched it on, and placed it on the table.

"Where would you like to begin?" Helen asked after returning to the wing chair.

"With Robert," Marina said, her voice a monotone. "There will be no questions. I know what is needed, and I have no fault of memory."

She began her story in Marseille, where her case officer had come to her a year ago and said she would be participating in a special operation that would be directed by another operative, Robert, who she would soon meet. The first two meetings were businesslike. Marina, still being the careful employee, did not tell Helen what the operation's objective was.

The third time she met Robert, at a safe house of his choosing, he offered her a drink, backed her into a corner of the kitchen, and then overpowered her and raped her. The description was similar to what Helen and Claire had witnessed. The main difference was that Marina fought back more fiercely than the other two victims, although Robert eventually subdued her with several blows to the head.

Three days later she complained to her case officer in a written report, which the case officer forwarded to the chief of station in Paris. Three weeks after that she was shoved in front of a tram in Marseille near the Rue Grignan, saved only when her momentum in falling left her at an angle that caused the tram to bump her aside. She broke two ribs and badly bruised her hip, but the act had been so artfully carried out that eyewitnesses later recalled that she seemed to have tripped on her own.

With the help of her case officer, who was acting without authorization, she secretly obtained a new identity and an off-books posting to San Sebastián, although he agreed to help only on the condition that she no longer pursue her claim against Robert. Since arriving there she had twice had brushes with ETA operatives, yet she still believed it was safer to remain there than return to France. She had come here at great risk, she said.

"And now you are at great risk," she said. "So I must ask, why have you come for my story?"

"Turn that off first," Helen answered. Marina nodded and did so.

"There are others besides me who want to get out the word about Robert. Three of us. We're working together. That's all I can tell you."

"It is official, then? This action you are taking?"

Helen considered lying, then decided there was nothing to gain by doing so.

"No. I'm sorry. It's not official."

Marina nodded.

"I never thought it would be." She stubbed out her cigarette on the table and tossed aside the butt. She stood, walked the recorder over to Helen, and said, "When he finds you, you must tell him nothing of how you came here."

"He will not find me."

Marina smiled ruefully and shook her head.

"All right. But what you must know is that you cannot tell him anything about these arrangements."

"There's nothing to tell. They hooded me, I saw nothing. I don't even know where I am."

"But you know many small things, and he is skilled at adding small things into something larger. So you must say nothing for one day. One day, at least, to give me time to return."

"A day?"

"No matter what he or his people do to you."

Helen swallowed hard and gripped the recorder as if it were a lifeline back to safety.

"They're waiting for you downstairs," Marina said. "You will go now."

"*They?*" Had she already been betrayed? Was this a setup?

"The taxi that brings you here. They are waiting."

"Right. Of course." Helen was letting fear get the best of her. She exhaled slowly, wanting to show Marina that she was up to the task at hand. Marina lit another cigarette as Helen stood. They did not speak again.

Half an hour later Helen was back within the environs of Paris, dropped off in the middle of a traffic circle only a few blocks inside the Périphérique. Checking the road signs and then unfolding her map as cars whizzed by, she saw that she was on the eastern rim of the 20th arrondissement, at the intersection of Rue Belgrand and Boulevard Mortier. She ran the gauntlet of the circle and crossed to a quiet block of Rue Belgrand, where she ducked into a bar. It was a fairly prosperous neighborhood, with a clientele to match, and for the first time in several hours she was able to relax.

She ordered a whiskey and checked her watch. Nearly 9 p.m., meaning she would be at loose ends for nineteen hours until her next designated contact with Claire. It felt like far too long to wait. From here it would be easy to take cabs and buses back into the outer suburbs, where she might board a train toward Germany at a station less likely to be manned by Gilley's people. Or maybe instead she should find a room for the night, to give her a safe place to think.

A room. It made her remember Claire's report, one of the last copies, and maybe the only one that could be easily obtained. It was still hidden at the other hotel, a place that was now off-limits. She sipped her whiskey, and then cursed herself. It seemed foolish in the extreme to take all of these risks only to leave behind a third of the evidence that all of them had worked so hard to compile in the case against Gilley. Claire's message had been emphatically clear: Do not return to your hotel! But they needed all the ammunition they could get if they were going to stop Gilley. And if she could escape undetected across a rooftop in Berlin, then why couldn't she enter via a rooftop in Paris?

She paid her bill, found a store that was open, bought a few clothes, a small backpack, and a few other supplies, and then spent the next hour wandering before stopping in a cozy place for a light dinner, plus a glass of wine to bolster her resolve. Toward eleven she hopped a Metro to a discotheque that the guidebook had said "stayed open until the sun came up," where she kept herself awake with coffee and club soda while watching Parisian couples dance until 3 a.m. Two men asked her to dance, and she politely declined.

Just before leaving she changed clothes in the washroom, emerging in black jeans and a black pullover. She stuffed her remaining belongings, including the tape but not the recorder, into the backpack, which she secured snugly to her shoulders. She jammed a penlight into her pants pocket. Half an hour later, after vaulting onto the fire stairs in the back of a building near the end of the Passage de Flandre—unnoticed by anyone in the street below, as far as she could tell—she climbed five stories to the roof and began making her way down the block.

The going was more difficult than in Berlin. The roofs of two of the buildings were sloped, and the footing was tricky. She slid once all the way to the gutter, barely catching herself and making a terrible clatter. Worse, there were recessed windows along the edge, and she had to climb around them. She did so with her heart beating crazily, not daring to glance downward. She worried about all the noise she must be making in the rooms below, and at one point froze as she heard a window rattle open, followed by a quavering voice that called out, "Hallo? Hallo?"

She waited for the window to shut, and then practically crawled to the next rooftop.

Her hotel, fortunately, had a flat roof, and she easily found the ladder down to the fire stairs. If Gilley's people were posted below, then she needed to remain as quiet as possible. She reached the steel landing by the window at the end of the fifth-floor hallway. Locked. Shit. The fourth-floor window was locked as well.

She crept down toward the third floor, alarmed by the creaking of the stairway. Straining her eyes in the darkness, she tried to detect any sign of movement from the alley below. All was quiet. As she reached the landing she saw with immense relief that the window was ajar. She slid it open and hopped quickly inside, the cat burglar in black. Her room was up front, so she had to walk the length of the hallway, fearing all the while that someone would open the door and call out in alarm. No one did.

She got out her key and listened carefully. No noise in the stairwell. No slamming doors or clattering footsteps. She had made it.

She let herself in and switched on the flashlight, taking care to keep the beam from shining toward the window or any mirrors. She slid off the backpack and set it gently on the floor. Easing past the bathroom door toward her bed, she directed the light toward the wall where the poster was, only to see that the poster was gone. She then saw the report itself, folded neatly on the console table by the tourist magazines, which made no sense at all unless—

There was a sudden movement to her rear, a shadow darting out from the bathroom. She pivoted quickly as someone strong and fast knocked the flashlight from her hands. A second person grabbed her arms from behind and, quick as a flash, bound them in plastic while a hand clamped across her mouth just as she attempted to cry out. She tried to kick outward, but someone yanked her legs out from under her and bound her ankles with another band of plastic, and then he dropped her sideways to the floor, which nearly knocked the wind out of her. Someone slipped a gag into her mouth and tightened it, and her cry of pain emerged only as a mumble.

Someone picked her up, a strong and easy lift. Then, with a mighty heave, he tossed her onto the bed like a bundle of laundry. She bounced once and might have rolled off the side if the second man hadn't caught her and rolled her back toward the middle of the mattress.

The ceiling light went on, bright in her eyes.

Now she saw them. The man by the bed, stouter and shorter, spoke rapidly in French to a taller and more muscular fellow who stood at the foot. The taller man answered by shaking his head and speaking brusquely. A third fellow then emerged from over by the window, where he must have been standing all along. He and the stouter man nodded in reply and they both left the room, the door shutting with a click. Helen heard one set of footsteps receding down the hallway, meaning that the other one must have remained just outside.

The taller man looked down at her with an expression of triumph. He was about forty, she thought, as she tried to memorize his face. Slim but fit, with short dark hair gleaming with either sweat or pomade. He wore a black ribbed turtleneck, black running shoes, and a pair of black jeans. Then he spoke to her in English.

"Welcome, Miss Abell. What a pleasant surprise."

When he stooped down to reach for her, Helen kicked out at him with her bound legs, but he easily evaded the blow and laughed lightly, as if to say it hadn't been a very good joke.

"Can we calm down now, Helen?" Perfect English, with a slight British accent. "Oh, yes. I suppose you can't really answer with that gag in place." He reached behind himself, toward his belt, and produced a long and slender knife, which he displayed for a second or two as if to give her the best possible chance to gauge its possibilities.

"Here's what we'll do, then. I'm going to cut off that gag so we can talk. At the first sign you're about to scream or start shouting for help, I'll cut your tongue out as well. Then it won't matter how loud you scream, because I'll be out the door with that report and also your backpack, which I am guessing has an item of interest to us. And then, after all of your hard work, you won't even be able to tell the police what happened. Remain quiet, however, and you get to keep your tongue. At least for now. Do we have a deal?"

She nodded, which wasn't easy while lying on her side with her hands and ankles bound.

"Very good."

He leaned closer, and with alarming deftness he sliced free the gag. She coughed and tried to push herself back toward the headboard so she could at least raise up her torso.

"No, no," he said, again showing the blade. "None of that. All you need to do is speak. Remain still."

She obliged.

"Good. I want you to tell me all about this afternoon, then. Not a rundown on how you got away from us, but on who you met afterward, and where."

"I didn't meet anyone."

"Is that so?"

"Yes."

He lunged toward her, and with a flash of his hands he pinned her torso against the bed and landed with his knees on her chest. He placed the point of the knife against her neck, near her artery, and then pierced her skin, just deep enough to sting. She felt a warm trickle of blood dripping toward the duvet.

"This is my lie detector, you see." He shifted his weight, pressing his knees so hard into her diaphragm that she could barely breathe. "Like the needle on the machine when they flutter you. Except this one jumps a little deeper every time you lie or don't cooperate. Do you understand?"

"Yes," she whispered.

"Louder please. A whisper is insufficient."

"Yes."

"Yes, what?"

"Yes, I understand."

"If drawing blood is insufficient, then we'll begin collecting your digits. First your fingers and then your toes, one by one, and it will get a lot sloppier than either of us would like. So how about if we avoid all that and just get talking, all right?"

"Yes," she said weakly, and for a moment she thought she might pass out.

Then she remembered Marina, and how broken the young woman had looked. Now she knew why. She also recalled Marina's final admonition: Hold out for one day, to give her time to make her way back to safety.

Twenty-four hours? Helen doubted she would even last for one.

51

August 2014

Even with the helpful sedation of the rye whiskey, Henry awakened before dawn. The fleeting image of a dream hovered in the half-light—Willard Shoat, barefoot and bloodied, lumbering down the grassy shoulder of Highway 53.

Henry stood and pulled on his trousers as he recalled the forensic report's map of bloody footprints. He threw on a T-shirt, laced up his shoes. One more try, he decided. One last look.

Pulled along like a sleepwalker, Henry headed out the door. The only thing that slowed him down was the sight of Scooter's half-filled bowl. He thought of the lonely grave in the back, covered by pine needles, and he scanned the street for any strange cars. Reassured that nothing looked out of the ordinary, he headed down Willow and was soon making his way up the shoulder of Highway 53.

Bugs jumped in the grass. The dewy blades reached the tops of his ankles. It was probably only a matter of days before a state mowing crew would roll through, shredding every remaining scrap of evidence.

Henry watched for litter and debris as he marched forward. Not a single car was in sight, although somewhere in the distance he heard a tractor already at work, a farmer up with the chickens. Then it stopped, and all was quiet. Just as before, the red lights of a radio tower pulled him toward the sign at the edge of town. He stooped to check a wad of paper, but it was a discarded grocery list. He continued, slower now, his ears ringing from the silence. No more bugs and no traffic, as if the world had paused to let him concentrate. In quick succession he passed a crushed can of Bud, a receipt from a convenience store, a fast-food wrapper smeared with ketchup, a Styrofoam hot dog box, a shred of foil. The sign was only fifteen yards away, and he was about to lose hope when he spied something just ahead to his left, peeping from a tangle of clover six feet off the pavement—a small orange cylinder.

He bent down and picked up an empty plastic pill bottle, the lid gone.

WILLARD SHOAT was written on the top, with his address on Willow Street. Dr. Ridgely's name was off to one side. Just below, in a white rectangle with a red border, it said, ZOLEXA 100 MG TABLETS. TAKE 1 TABLET BY MOUTH EVERY MORNING AND 1 BEFORE BED.

He imagined Willard standing there in the dark, shaking the final tablet into his mouth, swallowing it without water and then tossing aside the cylinder. Had he done it while coming or going? Did it even matter? Henry shivered, and kept reading.

There had once been sixty tablets. The prescription had been issued about a month ago, in July, around the same time that Willard's "new doctor" had claimed his old files from Dr. Patel's office. The pills were from a Walgreens in Cambridge. There was a twelve-digit prescription number.

Henry pocketed the bottle and looked around. The road was still empty in both directions. He headed back toward the house at double time, and after fifty yards he broke into a run. Half an hour later, showered and eager to get going, he was knocking at the front door of Anna's B&B.

Gail Hollis, the innkeeper, was already up, bustling around the kitchen with bread in the oven and coffee brewing. The smells were welcoming and warm. She was familiar with Henry by now, so she waved him upstairs with barely a pause. He wondered fleetingly what she must have thought when Anna hadn't returned the night before last, and then he knocked at the door.

"Yes?" she called out sleepily.

"It's me." His voice was breathless. He tried to calm himself. "I found something important. I'll be downstairs."

She groaned, but he heard her feet hit the floor, so he headed downstairs.

"Can I get you something to eat?" Hollis asked. "I'm about to take out a pan of muffins."

"Thanks. That would be great."

"Help yourself to coffee. Just filled the carafe."

Henry poured a mugful and pulled a folding chair over to a table that was set for one, figuring it was Anna's usual spot. None of the other guests was up, hardly surprising since it wasn't yet 7 a.m. He was too excited to sit, so he paced as he sipped. Ten minutes later he heard steps on the stairs, and Anna rounded the corner. She stopped short when she saw him.

"Are you okay?"

"Yes. Sit down."

She pulled out a chair. He reached into his pocket for the pill bottle and set it on the table.

"Where did you get this?" Her voice a whisper.

"By the side of the road, out near the sign." He didn't need to say which sign.

"When were you out there?"

"Just now, less than an hour ago. I dunno, I woke up and just had a feeling. I was thinking of that map, the one the crime scene techs drew, and, well . . ." He didn't feel like explaining that it was the second time he'd made the walk.

"We should go to the Walgreens," she said.

"They open at eight. It's fifteen miles."

"Then I guess we've got time for breakfast." She managed a weak smile. He pocketed the pill bottle and turned toward the coffee.

"I'll get you a cup."

When he returned to the table she was frowning at her phone.

"News?"

"A voicemail. Must've come in last night, after I was already dead to the world."

She put it up to her ear to listen. He waited until she was finished.

"Who was it?"

"Cilla Miley, the one who Stu Wilgus called about."

"Because she'd seen your brother hunting with somebody, right?"

"Yeah. I'd tried her the other day and left my number."

Anna started punching in a number.

"You're calling now?"

"They're farmers, they'll be up. Besides, she sounded pretty upset."

Anna turned away for privacy, nodding her head a few times and saying little. When she turned back around her brow was creased with worry.

"She said she found something, out where she saw Willard with his friend."

"Found what?"

"She wouldn't say. She said I had to see it for myself,

but you could tell it shook her up. She said she barely slept a wink."

"Where's their farm?"

"Toward Cambridge. We could stop on the way."

The innkeeper brought out a basket of muffins and a platter of eggs and bacon, but they ate little and hardly spoke. Anna looked troubled, and Henry was still haunted by the vision of Willard, out there on the shoulder as he swallowed the last of his pills.

The Miley farmhouse was up a long gravel drive, with soybeans to the right and corn to the left. After a curve there was a small green lawn to the left that sloped down to a new-looking cottage along a tidal creek, with a picturesque view and its own dock.

"Is that theirs?"

"Used to be. They sold it a while back to help make ends meet. Two acres on the water, probably worth more than all fifty acres of their beans and corn."

"What kind of name is Cilla?"

"Short for Priscilla. There she is."

A thin woman with a gray bun crossed the broad front porch of a two-story frame house and came down to the lawn. She wore jeans and a flannel shirt. The house was white clapboard with green shutters, with big oaks to either side. Cilla, moving with urgency, was ready with a hug the moment Anna stepped out of the car. Anna introduced Henry as a friend, but Cilla barely nodded in acknowledgment.

"I'm sorry I didn't make it to the funeral, sweetheart. I was just so, well . . ."

"No need to explain. It was a circus."

"It's just a shame what you've had to go through. Your poor, poor mom and dad. Your poor brother. And now after what I've seen." She shook her like she was trying to make it disappear.

"Stu said you saw him hunting with a friend, out on the edge of your property?"

"Some friend." She shook her head again. "You'll see. It's out in those woods." She pointed toward the soybeans, over their shoulders, and then set out across the field. She didn't seem to notice she was treading on the beans as she went.

"Willard was the only one of 'em with a gun. That's why this shook me up so much, because it must have been him doing this."

When they came closer to the woods, Cilla stopped and pointed.

"See that path, running into the trees?"

"Yes."

"Take that. You'll find it. I'm not going back in there. Not ever." She had crossed her arms, like she was trying to stay warm, even though it was sunny and pleasant. "I'm going back in, so I'll say goodbye now." Then, to Henry, "You take care of her, now."

She turned to go, this time picking her way carefully across the rows of beans.

"Goodness," Anna said.

The path entered the trees between thickets of briar and poison ivy, so they proceeded in single file, stepping carefully. Beneath the canopy of oak, maple, and cedar was a tangle of underbrush, although the path had clearly gotten some recent use. A wren called out in alarm at their approach and flitted toward the clearing. They walked twenty yards, then thirty.

They broke free of the trees. Anna, leading the way, nearly fell back into Henry. She wobbled and then steadied herself, but would go no farther. Now he could see what had upset her. He eased alongside her, and they stared in silence.

Just ahead in the clearing, fifteen or twenty feet away, was a large sheet of plywood propped upright against an oak. Drawn across it in black ink, probably by a felt-tip marker, was a crude silhouette of two human torsos, at about the same level as a couple sitting up in bed. The plywood was shredded by bullet holes. Ten feet away from the target, the muddy ground was pounded flat by boot prints.

Anna sank to one knee and put her hands to her face. She cried out, either in anguish or rage, and he knelt beside her and put an arm around her shoulder.

"Target practice," she said, voice shaking. "We have to get this bastard. Whatever it takes."

"We will," he said. "We will."

The Walgreens was a brick building surrounded by asphalt, with a green metal awning over the front entrance and the name splashed across the top in red script. Over to the right was a drive-through window for the pharmacy. Henry looked at Anna.

"You okay?"

"Yeah. I've decided to just stay angry. That's the only way forward. What's our plan?"

"We'll ask if their records show what time of day the prescription was issued. Because it had to be Merle who picked it up. Once we nail down the time, we'll ask to see their security footage. All these pharmacies have cameras trained on the registers. It's one of the highest-risk spots for a robbery."

"You think they'll let us see it?"

"I've got a plan for that. It involves some deception, but . . ."

"Fine. You're good at that."

He winced. They sat in silence for another few seconds. Then Anna unlatched her door.

"Hold on," Henry said. "I was just thinking about the way someone like Merle would handle this."

"And?"

"Well, he's already sticking his neck out with a forged prescription and a fake ID, so the last thing he'd want to do is put his face in front of a checkout camera."

"You're thinking he'd use the drive-through?"

"Yep. Better for him, but maybe better for us, too. Maybe the outdoor camera wouldn't pick up his face, but it would definitely get his tags. Meaning all we have to do is look for a 2010 silver Camaro with a Virginia registration. Let's go."

A yawning pharmacist in a white smock frowned when Henry explained what he wanted.

"You'll have to see the manager."

The manager, no older than twenty-five, hustled over to the counter after they paged him. He was shaking his head before Henry could even finish.

"Okay," Henry said. "Then we'll get a warrant. But if you really want to make nice with the feds, you'll spare us the trouble and show us the footage. In exchange, I won't ask for a copy and I can promise you won't have to testify."

"Testify? Now wait a minute, what's this all about?"

"Department of Justice," Henry said, flashing the ID he still had from his stint in Baltimore. "But I'm not at liberty to say anything more about the nature of our investigation."

The manager frowned and put his hands on his hips.

"Then I guess you better get that warrant."

"Fine." Henry got out his notebook. "What's the best day of the week for you to give a deposition? Are Wednesdays okay?"

"Deposition?"

"In Washington. No more than a few hours of your time. Although we'll probably need to get your pharmacist under oath, too. To nail down the chain of evidence."

"Whoa, now. Didn't you say earlier you wouldn't need a copy?"

"Not if you let me see it now. But if we have to take this to a judge, well, like I said . . ."

"Hang on a sec."

With a defeated sigh, he set off toward the back, disappearing into an office by the pharmacy.

"Is that ID even valid?" Anna whispered.

"No. But he'd have to phone Baltimore to find out."

She smiled and shook her head. A moment later the manager poked his head out the door.

"Will there be any official record of this transaction?"

"None whatsoever."

"Then come on back. But first have Irene scan that prescription label, to get the time of day."

The pharmacist, who by now seemed somewhat excited about the idea of helping a federal investigation, happily obliged. The scanner beeped as she watched her computer screen.

"Nineteen hundred hours, forty minutes, and he used the drive-through."

"Thank you kindly, Irene."

The manager ushered them into the office, where eight video screens displayed images from around the store. He started typing on a keyboard.

"Number five up there is trained on the drive-through," he said. "You're lucky. We used to toss this stuff every month, but the DEA wanted us to beef up our capacity, so now everything's archived for a year."

"How long will it take to find it?"

"No time at all. We'll go to ten minutes before the prescription was filled and roll it from there."

The first image they saw was of a pickup truck pulling away from the drive-through. They fast-forwarded from there, and a few seconds later a car flickered into the frame.

"That's it," Anna said. It was a Camaro.

"Sweet ride," the manager said, just like Derrick at the motor court.

They stopped the image when they had the best possible view, and then zoomed it. Virginia tag. Three letters, four numbers. Henry wrote them down.

"Need to log this in," he said.

Henry stepped out of the office and walked up the empty aisle for cold remedies, to make sure he had privacy. He punched in a number that he used only sparingly, lest he wear out his welcome.

A familiar raspy voice answered.

"Bales."

"It's Mattick."

"Still on that job?"

"More or less. I need you to run a tag for me."

"Can't your employer do that?"

"It will be cleaner this way."

"Now, what could that mean?"

"Will you do it or not?"

"Give me the number."

Henry said it twice, and then listened to the clatter of keys on a laptop. Rodney Bales gave him a name, a DOB, and an address. He thanked him and was about to hang up before deciding that he might as well make one more request while he had the chance.

"Got a minute for some advice?"

"About?"

"My employer."

"Stop right there. I don't even know who that is, nor do I *want* to know."

"Weren't you the one who gave them my name?"

"I gave your name to a third party, who was probably just a cutout. All he told me was the sort of talent they wanted, and at the moment you fit the bill. But I will say this: Whatever you're doing is making some interesting ripples, some of which have even reached my little Island of Misfit Spooks. A distant acquaintance I haven't spoken to in ages contacted me during the past week to ask what I knew about you, and not in a way that was encouraging."

"Name?"

"I shouldn't even have told you that. Let's just say his interests are private."

"Meaning corporate?"

"Meaning not government. You want advice? Here you go. Whatever you're doing, wrap it up. Soon, and without contacting me again."

He hung up and turned around, and saw Anna eyeing him skeptically through the window of the office. He flashed her a smile that he hoped was convincing and gave her a thumbs-up. But he had to steel himself on his way up the aisle. Who were these people, and what were they after? Equally important, what did they *not* want him to find out?

He put on a game face and reentered the office.

"Thank you, sir," he said to the manager. "Exactly what we needed."

"And, um, you're sure I won't have to testify?"

"Absolutely. We'll keep your name out of this completely."

"And the Walgreens name? I mean, in case corporate asks?"

"Only to note your helpful cooperation in my report to the U.S. Attorney."

They shook hands and were on their way.

52

"Who did you call just now?" Anna asked. They were back in his car with the door shut.

"An old pal on the Hill. He ran the tags for me."

"That old job of yours is coming in pretty handy." An unmistakable note of suspicion.

"Do you want the name or not?"

"Of course I want the fucking name. It's just . . . All right. Go ahead."

"Kurt Delacroix, age fifty-four. With an address on Winding Brook Way in Stafford, Virginia."

"Spell it," she said, calling up a search engine on her phone.

He obliged her.

"I'm on it."

Henry eased into traffic as the first results popped up. She began scrolling.

"There are some property listings. There's a Facebook

account for an Australian surfer dude. There's a blog in French." She laughed. "Well, here's some comic relief. There's a YouTube, very schlocky, of a German rock band that calls itself the Kurt Delacroix Singers. Good God, the lead singer looks like that John Waters character, the one in drag."

She went quiet for a few seconds, checking further hits.

"Here we go. There's a quote from a Kurt Delacroix in a story from *The Hill*."

"They cover Congress."

"Where's your notebook?"

He handed it to her. She flipped through the pages and checked her phone.

"This has to be him. He testified before that same Foreign Affairs subcommittee hearing, the one where *The New York Times* took the photo with Robert in the background."

"In May of 2006?"

"Yes."

"So he's connected to *Robert*? The CIA guy who makes people disappear?"

"Unless they both just happened to be at the same hearing, which sounds like a stretch. The story refers to Delacroix as, quote, 'an expert on policy toward radical Islamist movements in unstable Arab states.'"

"What did he say?"

"I'll read it verbatim: 'Resorting to military

intervention in some of these situations would be like using a chain saw for an appendectomy. You'd end up killing the patient when all you needed was surgery to remove the enflamed tissue. So I would say that the most important byword is precision.' "

"As in targeted killings."

"You think that's what he's talking about?"

"Don't you? Especially if he works for Robert. Does the story give his employer? What's his job title?"

"Doesn't say. Just calls him 'an expert.' "

"Pull up the website for the Federal News Service. They transcribe every hearing on Capitol Hill."

They drove on in silence while she found the site and then searched for the May 2006 subcommittee hearing. There was a subscriber fee, which she avoided by signing up for a seven-day free trial.

"I'm in," she said, like a safecracker.

"Keep an eye out for those four names from the *Newsweek* story. They're in my notebook."

"Got 'em. Alex Berryhill, Winslow Edinson, Kevin Gilley, John Solloway. Good God. This transcript goes on and on. On my phone it'll take forever."

"We're almost to Poston. We'll pull it up on my laptop."

They practically ran into the house. They logged on to the site, found the sixty-four-page transcript, and searched for "Delacroix." And there he was, on page 19, stating his background and qualifications. He told the subcommittee he had worked for the CIA "in Berlin, Prague, Jerusalem, Beirut, a few other places." Then they found this exchange:

REPRESENTATIVE HARTNETT: *And what is your current employment, Mr. Delacroix?*

MR. DELACROIX: *I am a field advisor for a Washington consultant who I believe is already known to several members of this committee.*

REPRESENTATIVE HARTNETT: *I daresay you're correct, Mr. Delacroix, and while I know your boss prefers to stay out of the limelight, just for the record could you please state his name, and then we'll move on.*

MR. DELACROIX: *Yes, sir. Mr. Kevin Gilley.*

They looked at each other. Here, at last, was the elusive Robert, and their man Merle was his employee.

"Where's that picture of Robert?" Henry said.

Anna retrieved the letters from the bread drawer and found the clipped newspaper photo. CDG had circled Gilley's face on the far left end of the row behind the witness. Henry jabbed his finger at the fellow seated just to Gilley's right, who was stout, late forties, and even in 2006 had a salt-and-pepper beard.

"There's Kurt Delacroix. Merle. The chicken catcher and the forger. The UPS man who picked up your brother's prescription."

"And the son of a bitch who took him hunting. These fuckers set up the whole damn thing."

Her face was lit by anger and exhilaration, and both were contagious. Then a new thought sobered him up.

"The Sisterhood," he said. "What about CDG and IAD? If these guys knew about your mom, wouldn't they also know about the other two? Shouldn't we try to warn them? I mean, if he's really that good, and that ruthless?"

"The parcel," Anna said. "The one my mom sent away. What was it CDG said when she got it?"

"I'll guard it with my life."

"Do you think we're too late? They had to have heard about my mom by now, don't you think?"

"Unless Gilley and Delacroix got to them at the same time. But how are we supposed to find them? All we've got is postmarks."

Bewildered silence. Anna reached down to the stack of letters and began going through them slowly, one after another.

"Maybe there's a way," she said, plucking out the one postmarked from York the previous August, almost a year ago to the day.

"Here we go. Listen. '*I will now dare to send you a cornball holiday snapshot in the coming season.*' Mom kept last year's Christmas cards. I saw them in a box in her closet."

They walked quickly down the block to the Shoat

house. The smell of disinfectant was still strong in her parents' bedroom. Anna went straight for the closet, avoiding any glance at the headboard or the bloodstained wall, and reached above the thin line of dresses to a box on the overhead shelf. She carried it past Henry, saying, "Let's do this in the kitchen." He gently shut the bedroom door behind them.

They found the two Christmas cards easily enough in the stack of a few dozen. The one postmarked from Currituck, North Carolina, was in a plain white envelope, and the card was staid and sober, showing a snowy church with a wreath on the door. There was a signature, "Warmly, Audra," but there was no return address. The one from York, Pennsylvania, was in a red envelope, with a decidedly secular card featuring a crashed sled and an angry Santa. As CDG had promised, there was a photo enclosed—a spirited-looking woman in a Santa hat, standing with martini in hand in someone's kitchen, where a party seemed to be in progress. The signature, "Love, Claire." It, too, had no return address.

Anna's mouth flew open in surprise. Henry smiled.

"Do those names ring a bell, Miss Anneliese Audra Claire Shoat?"

"How the hell did I not figure that out earlier?"

Then she picked up the two letters and looked again, as if seeking tracings in invisible ink.

"Why did she never tell me?"

"Too dangerous?"

"That's the charitable explanation."

"But we're still stuck. Not even a last name to go on."

"Maybe not."

Anna dug deeper into the box. She pulled out a handwritten list of names and addresses, maybe three dozen in all. Some were crossed out, some had been revised. They were in two columns, one labeled *Friends,* the other *Family.*

"Of course," Anna said, finding the names almost instantly. "She listed them under family."

"The Sisterhood," Henry said.

Claire Saylor lived on Smallbrook Lane in York. Audra Vollmer's mailing address was a bit more vague, a post office box in Currituck, but at least now they had her full name.

They walked back to Henry's and went to work. Audra Vollmer remained maddeningly elusive. A search for her name turned up no phone number, no street address, and no property records. Claire Saylor, on the other hand, was an easy mark, which they grimly realized also made her an easier target for Gilley and Delacroix. Her phone number popped up almost immediately.

"Shall I do the honors?" Anna said.

"Put it on speaker. I just hope she's okay."

A man's voice answered after the third ring.

"Hello?" He sounded tentative, uncertain.

"May I please speak to Claire?"

"Who's calling?"

Anna paused ever so briefly before saying, "A friend."

"Just a moment."

They waited through a few seconds of muffled consultation. It sounded like someone had put a hand over the mouthpiece. Finally, a woman answered.

"Yes, hello?"

"Claire?"

"Who's calling?" Anna looked at Henry with a puzzled expression. This was a young voice, probably closer to their age.

"My name is Anna, Anna Shoat. My mother was Helen Shoat, or Helen Abell as you probably knew her. Is this Claire?"

"I'm afraid I don't know you. Can you say why you're calling?"

Henry shrugged and shook his head, having no idea how to proceed.

"I'm calling because we're worried that you might be in danger."

"We?"

"My friend Henry and me. Am I speaking to Claire?"

"Just a moment." Another muffled interval. What in the hell was happening?

"It would be better to talk face-to-face," the woman said. "How soon can you be here?"

Henry, who had already checked the mileage, mouthed the words, and Anna repeated them.

"About two hours, if traffic's okay."

"Where are you coming from?"

"Don't answer that," he whispered. "Hang up."

"We'll see you in two hours," Anna said.

She frowned, hesitated, and then hung up just as the woman was saying, "Hello? Hello?"

"Well, that was disturbing," Anna said. "There were clearly other people in the room, and that definitely wasn't Claire. She sounded very cagey."

"So did you. Maybe they're as wary as we are."

"Or maybe Claire was with her, and was just being careful."

"Maybe."

"Only one way to know for sure."

They locked up the house and headed for York.

53

Anna kept working the phone on their way to York, and the results kept getting stranger.

With no phone number or street address for Audra Vollmer, they decided to call the local police for help.

"The Currituck County Sheriff's Office looks like the best bet," Anna said, scrolling a website. "The sheriff is a woman. Looks like the no-nonsense type."

She called the headquarters in the town of Maple, and spoke to a Sergeant Crosley while Henry listened. Anna explained who she was and said she was trying to reach one of their older residents, Audra Vollmer, because she was concerned for her safety.

"Oh, we're well aware of Miss Vollmer. She's been down here a good while now. Keeps to herself and likes it that way."

"Right, and I don't want to disturb her. But, like I said, I'm worried about her, so if you knew some way to get in touch. Maybe a phone number?"

"I wouldn't worry about Audra. She's got quite the security apparatus out on her island."

"Her island?"

"Yes, ma'am, out in Currituck Sound. Don't even know if it has a name, so we just call it Audra's. Tell you what, though. The boat from our beach patrol unit over in Corolla usually runs by there a couple times a day, so if you'd like we could check on her next time through and pass along your name and number."

"That would be great." Anna gave him her particulars, as Sergeant Crosley put it. "Oh, and if you could please add that I'm the daughter of Helen Shoat."

"Will do, ma'am."

The connection ended.

"Security apparatus?" Anna said.

"Probably just cop speak for a nice alarm system."

"Nothing that Delacroix and Gilley couldn't get through in about ten seconds."

They drove on in silence, worried they'd be too late, and their mood didn't improve much when they saw Claire Saylor's house. It was a fine-looking, two-story stone home with black shutters and a slate roof, on a wooded lot with azaleas and boxwoods. There were neighbors to either side, but all the greenery made it feel secluded, which, under the circumstances, didn't seem like a good thing. The driveway was empty, the garage door was shut, and all the curtains were drawn.

"Looks dead," Henry said, as they eased into the driveway.

"Poor choice of words."

They strolled to the porch, listening for any sounds of life from within. Anna knocked.

"Who is it?" It sounded like the young woman Anna had spoken to earlier. Henry saw movement behind the peephole.

"Anna Shoat. I'm here with my friend."

"Just a second."

Muffled consultation, same as before, followed by a brief delay before the lock finally rattled. The door flew open, and they immediately found themselves staring down the barrels of two revolvers—one on the left, one on the right, held by two policemen.

"Hold it right there," the cop on the right barked. "Keep your hands where I can see them and walk slowly through the door." They stepped inside. The second cop holstered his gun and came forward to frisk them.

"What the hell?" Anna said, but Henry warned her off with a look.

"Just do as they say," he said.

"Smart man," the second cop said. "They're clean."

"Check their IDs."

He took Henry's wallet from his back pocket and got Anna's from her handbag.

"Checks out. Same names she gave over the phone."

Only then did the other cop lower his gun and call out over his shoulder.

"You two can come out now."

A swinging door flew open and a young man and woman appeared from the kitchen, wide-eyed and moving cautiously toward the living room. They sat on the couch while the cops stood guard.

"Take a seat," the man said, gesturing toward a couple of chairs that someone had brought in from the dining room. A fair amount of planning seemed to have gone into preparing for their arrival.

"Sorry about all that," the first cop said. "But after what happened this morning we're all a little skittish. And until we know more about what's going on . . ."

"What happened this morning?" Anna asked.

The young woman answered.

"They found her car. Over at the mall, York Galleria."

"Claire's?"

She nodded.

"The door was open." She paused and shut her eyes a second. "There was blood on the front seat. But no Claire."

Anna put her hands to her mouth and lowered her head. Too late. Probably for Audra as well. Every last member of the Sisterhood, gone.

"When do they think all this happened?" Henry asked. "I'm Henry Mattick, by the way, and this is Anna Shoat."

"Skip and Susan Turner," the man on the couch said. They all shook hands and settled back into their seats.

"Are you her daughter?" Anna asked.

"Oh, no. We're the neighbors, from next door. Friends, too. I don't think Claire has ever mentioned any kind of family. As for when this happened, yesterday I was out picking tomatoes from our vegetable garden, and Claire came over to chat. She invited us to dinner and then asked if Skip and I could help keep an eye on her place for the next few days. She said she was going to run over to Sears and be back around six for dinner.

"Well, I said yes, we'd love to. So, six o'clock rolls around and we knocked at the door, and nobody answered. We checked around back in her garden and she wasn't there, either, and the whole house was locked up. We waited a while and then opened our bottle of wine and sipped it out on our front porch, figuring she'd show up all in a whirl with a big take-out order or something."

"She's been known to do that for dinner parties," Skip added, smiling.

"Yes. But after an hour or so we figured it must have slipped her mind, or maybe she got tied up on something else. I did look out the window just before we went to bed and noticed there still wasn't a light on, and that worried me a little. But I figured she must have come home without us noticing, and went straight to bed.

"Anyway, first thing this morning I walked over here

and the place was still locked up, and when I checked the garage her car wasn't there, so that's when I called the police. And they told me they'd just found her car over in the parking lot at Sears, with the door ajar and the dome light on and, well, you heard the rest, about the blood and everything."

Her voice was breaking by the end. Skip put his arm around her, gave her a hug, and she shook her head.

"I let the police in to search," Skip said. "Claire gave us a spare key. We've tried her cell phone, but there's no signal, and they didn't find it in her car."

"What's she like?" Anna asked. "Claire, I mean."

"She's great. Like no one we've ever met." She turned toward Skip and he nodded.

"I mean, *look* at this place," he said. "The paintings. The rugs. The prints and artifacts from God knows where. She never dwells on it, but enough little dribs and drabs come out along the way for you to realize that she's been pretty much everywhere."

"I think she might even have lived in Paris for a while," Susan said, her eyes going wide.

"She did," Henry said. "For at least thirty-four years, as far as we've been able to tell."

The Turners' mouths dropped open in such perfect synchronization that it was like watching a couple of marionettes. Henry had to hold back a laugh.

"That long?" she said.

"Yeah. Then there's the whole CIA thing."

"CIA?" Their mouths remained agape.

"She worked for them in Paris."

It took a few seconds for the implications to sink in.

"You don't think that all this has anything to do with . . . ?"

"Possibly," Henry said.

"Like the Russians or something?" Skip said.

"Or maybe some kind of terrorists?" Susan said.

"No, no. We think it's, well . . ."

"A little more domestic," Anna said. "And personal. But it's nothing you or the other neighbors would have to worry about."

"How did you guys get involved?" Susan asked.

"My mom used to work with Claire, ages ago, over in Europe. But I didn't find out any of that until she and my father were . . . they were killed a few weeks ago. And that's why we came looking for Claire."

"Your parents were *killed*?" Susan asked, her voice almost a whisper.

"It's a long story," Anna said. "But it might be connected."

"Wow," Skip said. "But what about you guys? Are *you* in danger?"

Anna and Henry looked at each other.

"Get back to us in a week or so and we'll let you know."

They laughed uneasily as the two cops returned from the kitchen.

Skip then asked, "Do the police know about all this? The whole CIA thing?"

The first cop stopped in his tracks.

"CIA?"

"Another long story," Anna said. "Where would you like us to start?"

"How 'bout at the beginning."

He got out a notepad and settled onto an easy chair while the other cop stood behind him.

Anna told the story in broad brushstrokes, focusing more on the Sisterhood letters and what they'd discovered recently about Gilley and Delacroix than on her brother and her parents. The whole time, Skip and Susan Turner stared as if they were at the movies, raptly attentive. When Anna finished, the cop with the notebook whistled and said, "Maybe it's time to get the feds involved."

"Shit," his partner said. "Pardon my French. You're probably right. But that's not our decision to make."

"We better go report all this in. And how 'bout if I get some cell numbers for both of you. Will you be around a while longer?"

"Probably," Henry said. "But we're easy to reach."

The policemen said goodbye. It felt like the end of a dinner party, when the guests begin drifting home. But now Susan, having had time to digest everything, was more curious than ever.

"Why York?" she said.

"Excuse me?" Anna replied.

"I mean, I'd already wondered that a few times about Claire, but now even more so. Why would a woman who'd spent thirty-four years working in Paris for the CIA, and who's been just about everywhere, why would she end up here, of all places?"

"Did she have family here?"

"Not that she's ever said."

"Was she ever married?"

"If she was, she hides it well. I mean, it's a nice neighborhood and everything, but we wouldn't be here, either, if it wasn't for Skip's job."

"No idea," Henry said.

Anna shrugged.

Another mystery, another anomaly.

"I guess we should all go," Susan said. "Leave this place in peace."

Henry looked at Anna, and they both thought the same thing at once.

"Actually," she said, "do you mind if we have a look around first?"

Susan and Skip exchanged a glance as if suddenly suspicious. Then Anna explained about the most recent letter in the correspondence between the three women, the one in which Claire acknowledged receipt of "the parcel" from Anna's mom, and pledged to guard it with her life. Not only did Susan and Skip consent, they eagerly joined in. It wasn't every day in the suburbs of York that you got to search the home of an ex-spy.

They proceeded quickly but respectfully, taking care to not make a mess. It was indeed an elegant house. The closet in the master bedroom was its own revelation. A vast and stylish wardrobe for any and all occasions, from dresses to gowns to shoes of every variety, everything in its place. This was no farmhouse wife, like Helen Shoat. This was someone who had remained in close touch with the wider world.

"Tell me something," Henry asked Anna. "Does this look to you like the closet of a woman who shops at Sears?"

"More to the point. Does this look like the closet of a woman who would admit to her next-door neighbor that she shops at Sears?"

They smiled and moved on.

But they found no strange records, no letters, no inexplicable correspondence. No papers at all, in fact, except the commonplace homeowner detritus of bills and warranties and receipts.

The only oddity was a brand-new reel-to-reel tape recorder, still in the box it had come in, although the packing materials had been removed, indicating it may have been used at least once. They found it just inside the stairwell leading from the kitchen to the basement, perched on the landing as if she'd recently set it aside for storage.

"Oh, that thing," Susan said, laughing. "She came over a few weeks ago asking if we had one she could borrow. We didn't, of course. I don't think *anybody* has one of those anymore. So she went online, and the nearest place you could buy one right away was at some specialty audio store down in Baltimore, fifty miles away. So off she went. She never did say why she needed it."

But Henry and Anna had stopped listening to Susan. They were too preoccupied by the idea that Claire had suddenly needed a reel-to-reel tape recorder.

"The parcel, don't you think?" Anna said. "It must be a tape."

"And the timing's perfect."

"Let's keep looking."

They checked inside the box for the recorder. But there was no tape mounted on the spindles. Nor did they find any tapes—or any nine-by-thirteen padded envelope—down in the basement, or up in the attic, or anywhere else. Like Helen Shoat, Claire Saylor must have kept her correspondence with the Sisterhood in a safer and more sacred space.

They were about to give up when Henry said to Susan Turner, "You mentioned that you had a spare key. Did she have one for your house?"

"That's right."

"Do you know where she keeps it?"

"Sure. She showed us."

They followed Susan into the kitchen. She rummaged through a wicker basket where keys and other odds and ends were piled together, and quickly located a key with a red ribbon attached.

"Right here."

Henry pulled the basket across the counter and poked around. Seconds later he plucked out a small, numbered key that looked exactly like the one for Helen Shoat's UPS letter box.

"Look familiar?" he said.

Anna smiled.

"Henry and I have an errand to run. But we may need to get back in a little later to use that new tape recorder. Would it be all right if we borrowed your key to the house?"

Skip looked hesitant, but a smile from Susan did the trick.

"Just drop it off in our mailbox when you're done. But only if you promise to tell us later what you found."

"Deal."

They looked up the nearest UPS Store, which was only a few miles away. The mailbox was the same size as Helen's. The key fit. The only item inside was a nine-by-thirteen padded envelope that had been shipped from Stevensville, Maryland, about two weeks earlier.

The parcel. Claire had either stashed her Sisterhood letters somewhere else or had taken them with her, in which case they might be gone for good.

Inside the envelope were two documents, one of them folded and rubber-banded to an old cassette tape, plus two smaller padded envelopes, both labeled "Alt-Moabit Safe House," and both marked with the same date from October 1979. "Afternoon" was written on one, and "Night" on the other.

"My mother's handwriting," Anna said. She opened them. Each held a reel of audiotape. They ran to the car.

"What are the documents?" Henry said, as they made their way back to Claire's house.

"The one that was clipped to the cassette looks like a transcript from an interview, probably from the cassette. It's dated about ten days after those others, from October of '79. Good God!"

"What?"

"The transcript says the interview was recorded in Paris. And my mother did the interview. With somebody named Marina. No last name."

"A cryptonym, maybe? The right people would probably know exactly who she was. What were they talking about?"

"Robert, it looks like. Kevin Gilley. From something that had happened earlier that year."

"An assassination?"

"No." Anna's voice trailed off. She had turned to the

second page and was scanning the words as fast as she could. "Looks like it's about something that happened to Marina personally."

"Something Gilley did?"

"Yes, she . . . This is terrible."

"What?"

"He raped her. In a safe house in Marseille. She says it here. Oh, God, and it's very graphic. He fucking *raped* her! One of his own agents, and in a CIA safe house."

"That would explain why he'd go looking for your mom. Killing people with Agency sanction? They'll cover for you on that until your dying breath. But raping your own agents as a personal sidelight?" Henry shook his head. "This stuff must be the ammunition they were talking about—Claire, Audra, and your mom. They were just waiting for the right moment to use it."

Anna's eyes got wide, and she turned to look out the back window of the car.

"Anything interesting back there?" Henry asked.

"No. But I'm not sure I'd know the difference. We need to find someplace safe for all this stuff."

"We need to find someplace safe for *us,* don't you think? And what should we do about the Turners, not to mention the cops? If all of them start yakking, then everybody will know exactly what we're up to."

"And we'll be as dead as my mom and dad."

They drove on in silence a few seconds longer.

"You know," Anna said, "when we were sitting around

Claire's house with the Turners, all of this felt like a big treasure hunt, or a manhunt, my chance to even the score. I'll bet my mom and Claire felt that way, too. They probably took a lot more precautions than us, and look at what it got them. Audra, too, for all we know."

For a few seconds, neither of them spoke.

"What's the other document?" Henry asked.

She shuffled through the papers, trying to refocus.

"It's a field report from Claire, from March of '79. She seems to have walked in on a rape. Gilley and some agent at another safe house, this one in Paris."

"So he was a serial offender."

"And from the looks of it, no one ever did a thing about it."

They were in a somber mood as they pulled up in front of Claire's. Henry drove around the corner to park out of sight like the cops had done. They doubled back on foot, and crossed through the Turners' backyard.

"Don't open any blinds or curtains," he said. "We'll play the tape in the basement."

They set up the recorder on top of the washing machine. It was a little spooky down there, with deep shadows and a few cobwebs, plus a damp, earthy smell. The only light was the glow of an overhead 60-watt bulb with a chain pull.

They decided to proceed chronologically. Anna took the reel marked "afternoon" and set it on the spindle. She threaded the tape through the channels and onto the uptake reel, which, in her nervousness, led to some fumbling and swearing. Finally, everything was ready to roll.

Anna drew a deep breath.

"Here we go."

She pressed the button for play.

54

Paris, 1979

The man in black pressed his knees to Helen's sternum, and he again showed the blade of the knife.

"Let's have a better answer this time. Tell me where you went this afternoon, after you ran from us."

"To the Parc de Belleville."

He lowered the blade to her cheek, placing the point near the base of her nose.

"That is a large place, Helen. Many acres. You're going to have to do better than that."

"A bench." He pressed the point harder.

"Speak up! I told you, whispering is insufficient!"

"I said a *bench,* near the vista point at the upper end along the Rue de . . ." She couldn't remember the name of the street. What was the name of the goddamn street!

"The Rue Piat?"

"Yes." She exhaled with relief, and immediately felt

worthless for doing so. At this rate, she wouldn't last ten minutes.

"Much better, Helen. And the name of this contact?"

"It was a cutout. I don't know her name. An old woman."

"Describe her."

"Old. I don't know. Heavy. I made it a point not to look at her directly, and I didn't care once she told me what she came there to say."

"Describe her!" He pressed his knees again, and moved the blade within inches of her eyes. "Tell me what you observed or you will observe *nothing*, ever again."

"Gray hair, wrinkles. I told you, she was old and heavy. Her coat smelled like mothballs."

"Good. Like mothballs."

He shifted slightly to relieve the pressure on her chest and leaned away again. He then frowned and glanced to his left, as if something had just distracted him.

That's when the wooden shutters of the French doors crashed open in a hail of splinters. He looked over in alarm as someone vaulted toward the bed from the terrace. He tried to react, but his awkward posture rendered him momentarily helpless as the intruder knocked him off of Helen and onto the floor.

It was Claire.

"He has a knife!" Helen shouted.

He scrambled to his feet, but by then Claire was

nearly on top of him, and in quick succession she rammed a knee to his groin, kicked a shin, and grabbed his right arm. In an instant she had knocked the knife out of his hand and had put him on the floor.

But he was not so easily defeated.

He quickly sprang onto the balls of his feet and deftly struck Claire with a kick that knocked her off balance. A second kick put her on the floor, while Helen watched helplessly from the bed. The tide turned in a series of thuds and grunts, and he pounced forward, climbing atop Claire to achieve the same position he had earlier taken on Helen, with his knees pressed to her chest.

They were too close to the bed for Helen to see Claire any longer, and for a few seconds the man also disappeared from sight as he bent lower in their struggle. Helen heard only grunts and gasps and then, incongruously, a crinkly rustle of plastic, followed by a resounding, thudding crack, like that of bludgeon against bone, or sledgehammer to skull. The man's torso reeled slowly backward, like a falling timber. Helen saw his eyes roll back in his head, and then he collapsed.

Claire grunted as she extricated herself from the tangle of his limbs and struggled to her feet, victorious. In her right hand she held the hideous snow globe, its base now chipped at the edge.

"The perfect souvenir," she said.

She bound the man's wrists behind his back with a pair of plastic handcuffs that she seemed to produce from nowhere. Then she bound his ankles. She walked toward the door, returned with his knife, and cut the bindings from Helen's hands and ankles.

"There's at least one more," Helen warned. "He might even be on his way upstairs if he saw you go through the window."

"Not to worry. Someone else has already taken care of him, and also the one in the van. While you were out seeing Marina I was able to recruit an ally."

"Who?"

"You'll find out soon enough. Take a deep breath. You're safe now."

Helen tried to stand, then faltered as she realized she was shaking.

"Sweet Jesus," Helen said, "am I ever glad to see you!"

Claire gave her a bear hug, and tears sprang to her eyes, which Helen blinked back. Claire touched a congealing trail of blood on Helen's neck, and inspected her closely for further damage.

"We're putting you on a seven o'clock train back to Berlin."

"But if more of Gilley's people are—?"

"They won't be a problem now, not after he hears from those two friends of this fellow. I'm also making a phone call. We'll keep moving for a few hours while the dust settles."

There was a groan from the floor.

"Good," Claire said. "I was hoping he'd come around."

Helen sat up to watch. When the man tried to raise himself, Claire placed her right foot on his chest and pinned him like a butterfly. She crouched low enough to speak into his ear.

"Your friends out front are gone. They're taking a message to Robert, and you're going to do the same thing. Are you listening?"

He nodded slowly.

"Good. Because you need to remember all of this. Tell Robert that he is never to fuck with us again. None of us, not if he ever hopes to walk free anywhere again on this planet. Operationally or otherwise. Do you have that?"

"Yes," he rasped, barely audible

"Louder!" She pressed her heel deeper into his chest.

"*Yes*."

"Yes, what?"

"I'll tell him. Tell him not to fuck with you."

"Any of us. And there are three of us, and he damn well knows it. Plus Marina, which makes four."

"Three of you, plus Marina. Okay."

She removed her foot.

"C'mon," she said to Helen. "Grab that report off the table. We'll wash that cut and get you packed. I'll gag him and put out the 'Do Not Disturb.' We'll leave him for the maid."

Helen laughed, a release from deep inside that lasted for only an instant.

"Okay," Claire said, nodding to signal she was ready. "Let's finish this."

55

At the Gare de l'Est, Helen bought a ticket to Berlin via Mannheim. They had thirty minutes until departure They ordered a pair of double whiskies at the station café while everyone else sipped coffee. The waiter didn't bat an eye.

Helen felt stretched as tightly as a rubber band on the verge of snapping, but the first swallow of whiskey helped. The second, more so.

"What will happen to Marina?" she asked. "I didn't have time to tell them much, thank God. But I would have. I was about to. That damn knife."

"Stop. Don't do this to yourself."

"Where were you all that time? How did you even know?"

"I didn't. It was a hunch."

She told Helen about her earlier trip to the room, when she'd discovered the tracking beacon.

"I grabbed the copy of *Paris Match* on my way to warn you off. Later I saw that you'd removed the report, and figured you must have hidden it in the room. When I remembered how you gave them the slip in Berlin, I thought you might try the same thing in reverse here."

"Good God. We even think alike."

"Here's to that." They clanked their glasses.

"I dressed up like an old charwoman, broke into a vacant room next door, and sat tight. Once the fun started, I waited for the van to be taken care of out front. Then I climbed over to your terrace and body-slammed the shutters. Here's to shabby French construction."

They tapped glasses again. An educated guess, a single act of daring. Without either of them, she'd be dead.

"As for Marina, she's getting a fresh set of documents and a passage to somewhere safe. My understanding is that she was pretty much fried."

"That's how she seemed to me. A refugee with a price on her head." She paused, sipped. "What about you? Won't this end badly for you, once everyone finds out what happened?"

Claire smiled.

"That call I made an hour ago? It was to my COS, to let him know I'd bagged the wayward clerk from Berlin. He's bursting with pride. If anything he'll probably advance me a pay grade, and now that word is out that you're back in Agency hands, Gilley has no choice but to back off. All the same, it's probably best if you show up at Berlin station unannounced."

"The goon with the knife, do you think he'll really deliver the message to Robert?"

"Damn right he will."

"But did we really need to send it? I mean, I guess I'm thinking that as long as I make it back to Berlin with the goods, Robert will soon be out of business. Right?"

"Oh, Helen." Claire frowned with concern.

"What?"

"I hope we're not expecting too much from all this."

"Why shouldn't we? We've built a foolproof case against him."

"Yes, it's great work, all of it. Something the three of us can always be proud of. But these reports, these tapes and eyewitness accounts, well . . ."

"Well what?"

"I've done some thinking about the realities here— with a man like Gilley involved, and what he does for a living."

"What do you mean? Who have you been talking to?"

"Look. Of course we'll try to bring him down. Maybe we'll succeed. But our only chance to do that is if you can first work a deal for yourself, and these materials will help you. They're your ticket back to freedom, so use them that way."

"Well, sure. But once they've seen everything . . ."

"You don't get it, do you? Our evidence is the very reason they'll be willing to give you a pass, by making you agree to hand everything over and keep your mouth shut. My guess is that they'll get lawyers involved, for him as well as for you. You'll want that. The first thing you should ask for, in fact, is a lawyer. You'll probably have to sign something fairly disagreeable. But don't give it up for nothing. Make them pay, one way or another."

"I don't want them to pay, I want *him* to pay." Claire's expression told her exactly what the chances were for that. "Oh, Claire, I fucked this up for all of us, didn't I? For Marina, too, and for Anneliese. If I hadn't just taken off like that . . ."

"No. You didn't. We put together what we wanted to put together, and now more people than ever will know. One way or another, word of this will creep into more corners than it ever would have otherwise. Okay, so maybe it won't take him down. Given what he does for the Agency, maybe *nothing* could take him down. But they'll watch him closer. They'll tighten his leash."

"How can you know that?"

"I can't. But it makes operational sense. He'd be jeopardizing everything if he doesn't clean up his act. They'll know that now, and so will he."

Helen tried to take solace from that, but there was little to be had. So instead she finished her whiskey.

"By the way," Claire said. "So you'll breathe a little

easier on the train, you should know that one of our people will be on board the whole way. In fact, he's here now."

Claire nodded toward a spot over Helen's right shoulder. Helen turned and saw Clark Baucom a few tables over. He raised a coffee cup in tribute, and then smiled like a boy who'd been caught copying someone else's exam.

"How did he . . . ? And you . . . ?"

"I'm sure he'll be happy to tell you. I gather that the two of you know each other rather well." Helen blushed. "It's quite all right. Your secret is safe with me. All of your secrets are."

"He's no secret to anyone in Berlin. But I'm going to take you up on the last part of that promise."

"Good. It's the least we can do for each other. Trust and share, the three of us. Stop doing that and we're no longer the Sisterhood."

Helen smiled, and then the PA system called out a boarding announcement for her train. They stood, and hugged one last time. Baucom was already making his way toward the platform, while keeping Helen in his field of vision.

"I won't follow any farther," Claire said. "Your very able escort will take over from here."

A final smile, and Helen turned to go.

Nine hours later she was in Berlin.

56

Helen Abell waltzed straight past security with a flash of her ID. Apparently no one had bothered to tell the Marine guard that she was persona non grata. She then used a key that Baucom had given her to enter Berlin station, and was well into the depths of its offices and corridors by the time anyone happened to look up from their typewriters and desks to see her standing there, alone and defiant, holding a file folder like a weapon.

Eileen Walters, who had just rounded the corner from the hallway back to records, stopped in her tracks. Helen heard an actual gasp from the typing pool, followed in rapid succession by a "Holy shit!" from points unknown.

"Well?" she announced loudly, playing the moment for all it was worth. "Is someone going to tell Herrington I'm here, or should I just go on back and deliver his heart attack personally?"

This line at least provoked smothered laughter from some unknown quarter. In the meantime, someone else must have already managed to sneak away toward the back, because Herrington then appeared, looking shocked and out of breath.

Helen turned to confront him from twenty feet away, clutching the folder. She gave him an opening to speak first, and when he didn't seize it she filled the breach by holding aloft her office key and saying, "You'll probably be wanting this."

She then raised the folder.

"Before you take it, you'll want to look at a few things I was able to dig up out in the field concerning Kevin Gilley, aka Robert, while I was away. And, yes, I was working. So I expect to be paid."

Herrington, ashen, spoke in a low but steady voice with a pleading undertone, as if he were trying to will everyone else to get back to work and stop listening to this embarrassing exchange.

"Let's discuss this in private, Miss Abell, if you don't mind."

"Not without a lawyer present. And a tape recorder."

"Fine. But let's at least refrain from further discussions of sensitive material in such an open forum."

That was the moment at which everyone who was listening realized that Helen Abell had—at least for now—won. Like so many bullies before him, Ladd Herrington was not very fearsome once you got in the first blow. Seizing her advantage, Helen nodded and replied, "I'm all for discretion, sir. Your office or mine? Either is fine, as soon as my lawyer has arrived."

Later, of course, well after the flush of this initial victory, it would be those same lawyers who would work the most assiduously to disarm her, by turning the entire process into an exercise in slow-motion capitulation, geared toward nothing other than her own defense. In other words, events proceeded almost exactly as Claire Saylor had predicted.

So it was that, roughly twenty hours later, Helen found herself in a conference room on the neutral ground of the U.S. consular office, where she was reading the fine print of a final document while, to her left, her cheapo American lawyer who'd been recommended by a friend did the same. The room was quiet, the mood somber but relatively civil. Her energy was nearly spent.

Then a door opened, and Helen might not have even looked up if Herrington hadn't nervously cleared his throat. With a glance she saw it was Kevin Gilley, dapper and official-looking in a dark suit and a red power tie, as if delivered fresh from the campaign trail by his own motorcade. He nodded at Herrington, who smiled tightly and swallowed in a way that made his Adam's apple bob.

Gilley did not come to the table but instead took a chair by the door. He folded his arms and looked straight at Helen. She put down the document and stared back. His eyes were the same blue-green she had noticed that night at the safe house. But then they had at least looked like something belonging to a living being, burning and intense, fired by scorn and sexual energy. Now they seemed to be coated by a dull sheen, like cough lozenges.

His stare was unwavering, and almost clinical in its assessment, as if he was still gauging what sort of threat she might pose. Helen felt a cold spot creeping up her backbone. She had to make an effort not to shiver.

"All of the revised language looks in order to me," her lawyer said. He obviously had no idea who had just entered the room. "Is something wrong?"

"Nothing that a well-placed gunshot wouldn't fix," she muttered beneath her breath.

"Excuse me?" He sounded a little alarmed.

"Nothing. Nothing at all."

She glanced for a final time at the document—a severance agreement—then she scribbled her signature and the date they had all agreed upon. A date that will live in infamy, she thought. She slid the papers across the desk toward Herrington before the lawyer could justify charging her for another billable hour.

"Well, then," Herrington said, neatening the stack with a little pop against the desktop, and then adjusting his tie. Still not a word from anyone to acknowledge Gilley's presence, which infuriated Helen so much that she decided to address the issue herself.

"Do I have your personal assurance, sir, that this document will protect me from the likes of him? Do I have the Agency's full assurance on that matter?"

"Protection?" Herrington said, as if the very idea was ludicrous.

"Yes, protection. If you need any background, just check the recent status of Anneliese Kurz, aka Agent Frieda. Or read my report, if you haven't already shredded it."

Gilley kept his arms folded, but the corner of his mouth curled ever so slightly, like he was holding back a smile. Her impulse was to climb across the table to slap him as hard as she could. Instead she clasped her hands together below the tabletop and squeezed hard, as if crushing the bones of his face.

"Well, then," Herrington repeated. "This concludes our business. I believe we have achieved the best possible outcome for all concerned."

He got up, and so did his deputy and then his secretary, and they walked single file from the room. Helen turned to her lawyer.

"You're dismissed."

If he had said anything about a bill at that moment she wasn't sure what she would've done, but it wouldn't have been dignified or polite. He coughed, picked up his briefcase, and left, nodding obliviously to Gilley on his way out. Gilley smiled and nodded back. She stood and stared at him, knowing she would have to walk past him to leave.

She stepped around the table toward the door, and then stopped.

"Well?" she said.

"Well what, my dear?" He spoke the latter words the same way Baucom did, which infuriated her more. "I presume there will be no further trouble from these matters to interfere with my duties?"

"As long as there is no further trouble toward me from you."

"Oh, and thank you for the lovely message via Joseph in Paris, from you and that other tart. You flatter yourselves to think you'd be of any further interest to me."

Later, Helen would think of at least half a dozen retorts, all of them witty and crisp and poised. But at that moment she only wanted to be out of his presence, then and forevermore. And she was already clinging to an unmistakable note of surrender she'd detected in his final comment. By trying to dismiss Claire and her as inconsequential, he had in his own twisted way announced his compliance with the truce.

So, instead of replying she walked out through the open door. Then, as she heard him rising to follow, she shut the door behind her. She did not hear it reopen before she rounded the corner and moved out of sight.

*

A few hours later she was seated in the main concourse at Tegel, waiting for her flight to be called. Nonstop to JFK, economy class. Still more than two hours before boarding. There had been no need for a security escort this time, although she'd heard that Herrington had discreetly inquired about the possibility. Cooler heads had apparently prevailed.

"Let her wander all she wants," the logic had been. "She's free as a bird now, but at least we've clipped her wings."

With the better part of an afternoon to kill, Helen had briefly considered a quick farewell tour, with stopovers at her favorite café, maybe a bar or two, and a walk on her favorite wooded path around Schlachtensee, where she'd always found solace. Then she decided to hell with it. Better to spend her final hours in the sterility of an air terminal, a clean and quick severance. She hailed a taxi and opened a newspaper as soon as it pulled away from the curb, lest she be tempted to look out the window along the way.

And now here she was, with her clipped wings and her future in ruins. Where would she go now? What would she do? She was literally hanging her head beneath the gloom of such thoughts when Clark Baucom's voice snapped her to attention.

"You look like you could use a dose of Lehmann's finest, my dear."

She looked up to see him standing ten feet away, with a tweed jacket slung over one shoulder. In his right hand was a brown paper bag from which he then produced a bottle of the genuine article, the brandy to salve a thousand wounds. It was the first time she had seen him since the train ride to Berlin, nine hours that had passed without a single word. Nine hours in which she had withheld hundreds of questions, mostly out of pride.

Now Helen smiled grudgingly. Part of her still wanted to hate this man for stealing the tapes, but he had atoned brilliantly in Paris.

"Does Lehmann loan that out for special occasions?"

"Come on." He nodded over his shoulder. "One of the ghastlier airlines runs a nice little departure lounge right around the corner for frequent sufferers like me. They won't mind if we provide our own tipple."

She stood with her shoulder bag. It felt like as appropriate a farewell as any.

"Lead the way."

"Your friend Claire used those same words not so long ago. She's a sharp one."

"Yes, she is."

She eyed him askance as they crossed the terminal to the darkened lounge. What could he possibly want, at this point, except either a thank-you or an absolution?

Or maybe he was simply being human, in search of some warmth, a final affectionate note to say that all had been worthwhile.

They sat in a corner. The cocktail waitress, who of course knew Baucom on sight, brought two empty glasses, no questions asked. He had been good at this sort of thing for far too long, she supposed, and it made her smile. First time all day she'd done it so freely.

"I won't ask what that was for," Baucom said as he poured her a measure. "Drink up."

She swallowed. As good as she remembered. She was almost sorry there wouldn't be a bed to climb into afterward.

"Thanks for coming," she said.

"Had to. Special delivery mission. News, first of all. Herrington's out as chief of station."

Helen's mouth flew open in surprise.

"I'll definitely drink to that," she said, brightening as Baucom tapped his glass against hers. "Where's he landing?"

"Langley. No job title yet, but the word is that he'll have three supervisors to keep him busy, and a male secretary."

Helen laughed. It felt like the first time in ages. Baucom reached again into the paper bag, and with another act of conjuring pulled out a large padded mailing envelope.

"Brought this for you as well."

She accepted it warily, as if it might be filled with incriminating items.

"Go ahead. Take a look."

She pressed the edges to splay open one end, and inhaled sharply as she looked inside. The tapes, both of them.

"Where have they been, all this time?"

"Enjoying a limited run to an exclusive clientele. Interesting listening for one and all."

"Who?"

He shook his head, as she knew he would.

"At least tell me what the reviews were like."

"Pretty much as you'd expect with regard to Robert. He'll be watched a little closer, but you already knew that. As for anything further?" He shrugged, frowning. "As I said before, the nature of his work puts him almost beyond reach. For now, anyway. But later, when we're all older and grayer? Maybe that's one reason I thought you might want it back."

"And the other tape? With all the water music, for lack of a better description. Why give that one back?"

He frowned again.

"So far, at least, my efforts on that front have come to naught. Apparently certain people have decided that these revelations were either not all that surprising or that they're so inconsequential as to not really matter."

"And what do you think?"

"I think that, for the moment, someone is gaming the system better than I can. They've either got a more powerful rabbi than me or better information. Maybe both."

"You know what it's all about, don't you?"

"Let's just say I think you should hang on to it, but keep it secure. For your own good as much as for the Company's. A bite from anything that potent will always be potentially fatal."

"Then why should I keep it at all?"

"Insurance, against some future rainy day? And you've been in the game long enough to know that by rainy day what I really mean is a fucking deluge, a flood with waters deep enough to drown you. So let this keep you dry, then, Helen Abell."

He placed a hand on her shoulder. She wanted to bristle, to duck away, but it felt good—calming and secure—so instead she reached across the table to caress his cheek, lightly and only for a moment. Then she demurely returned her hand to her lap.

"I'll miss you," she said.

"I do get back to Washington now and then."

"I'm aware of that."

He studied her eyes for a few seconds as if waiting for more, and then smiled ruefully when it became clear that no more would be coming.

"Message received."

Then he corked the bottle, placed it back into the bag, and stood. He moved to her side, a lumbering jet taxiing for departure.

"You're not to leave this lounge until you've finished that glass," he said, "if only for Lehmann's sake." She smiled and kept her seat. "You'll have a fine life, my dear."

"I plan to. A quiet life, too."

"Highly advisable."

He squeezed her shoulder and was on his way. She watched until the door closed behind him.

57

The reels of tape began to turn in the silent basement. The first sound they heard was the voice of Anna's mother, reciting poetry.

> *How can I keep my soul in me, so that*
> *it doesn't touch your soul? How can I raise*
> *it high enough, past you, to other things?*

"Oh, my God," Anna whispered. "It's *her*."

Her mother paused, as if to accommodate her daughter's interruption. There was the sound of footsteps, and then Helen Abell continued.

> *I would like to shelter it, among remote*
> *lost objects, in some dark and silent place*
> *that doesn't resonate when your depths resound.*

Then, more footsteps, as if she were crossing a fairly large room. The volume seemed to fade and grow, as if she were walking past a series of microphones. It lent a sense of movement to the mind's eye. Henry watched Anna, whose face was rapt, as the poem and the footsteps continued, with a pause between each stanza:

> Yet everything that touches us, me and you,
> takes us together like a violin's bow,
> which draws one voice out of two separate strings.

"It's beautiful," Anna said. "But why? What is she doing?"
"A sound check before the main event?"
"Maybe."

> Upon what instrument are we two spanned?
> And what musician holds us in his hand?
> Oh sweetest song.

Then the voice went silent but the footsteps continued, picking up pace before fading, as if Anna's mom had moved beyond sight, or perhaps further into the past, again unreachable. No, she was going up a stairway.

Anna wiped her eyes with her fingertips. No sooner had she collected herself than there was a rattling sound from the speaker, and then the sound of an opening door followed by footsteps. They were heavier than those of Anna's mom, but they, too, crossed the room. A cabinet door opened, the click of a latch followed by the clank of bottles and glasses, a drink being poured. Then someone pulled up a chair and took a seat. No words were spoken.

Where was Helen Abell all this time? In another room? On another floor? Was she listening, or was she unawares?

A few minutes later there was a second arrival, and a conversation began. Two men. One was older and wheezing, the other one younger and healthier. Their first few words were barely audible. Then the older man spoke up, and his words emerged clearly in a trancelike monotone, as if he were repeating an oath of allegiance:

"*To swim the pond you must forsake the bay. You may touch the lake, but you must never submerge, and you must always return to the pond.*"

"*And the zoo?*"

"*Dry. To all of us, anyway. The pond is also dry, to the zookeeper.*" A pause, a wheezing intake of breath. "*All of their people believe it to be long since drained, and its waters shall forever be invisible. Except of course to those of us with special eyewear. And that's what we're offering, if you're interested.*"

"*Eyewear?*"

"*So to speak. A new way of seeing. And access,*"

opportunity. More than you've ever dreamed of."

And so on, just as Anna's mother had heard it through headphones thirty-five years ago while standing in her stocking feet in the upstairs of that safe house in Berlin.

"The Pond," Anna said. "It still existed."

By the time the conversation was finished and the tape was done, the ramifications of what her mother had recorded that day were quite clear: She had stumbled upon evidence of the continued existence of the Pond, twenty-four years after it had supposedly ceased to exist. What's more, this meeting seemed to have been some sort of recruitment of a CIA operative, enticing him to leave behind "the Bay" for the freedom of "the Pond." At best, a bit of duplicity and disloyalty, at worst an act of treason, depending on what the Pond had been up to by then.

Helen Abell probably hadn't realized any of that until as recently as a few weeks ago, when she had visited the Archives, and, based on what Hilliard had told them, had finally deciphered the significance of all she'd overheard. Or, as Claire had written in one of her final letters, the one with the Clark Baucom obituary, Could this be the answer "to one of your oldest questions"?

"That's certainly some political dynamite," Henry said after the tape ran out.

"Do you think it still exists?"

"Thirty-five years later? I guess anything's possible.

Doesn't sound like Gilley was involved, though. Not one mention of Robert."

"Let's put on the second tape. Maybe Robert stars in the sequel."

He did. Or, at least, that was the name the young female on the tape used for her case officer in the first words of their conversation. Her name was Frieda, and even though their meeting sounded harmless enough early on, Henry and Anna were on edge from the beginning after having read the reports of Robert's actions in the safe houses of Paris and Marseille.

Soon enough, there were sounds of a struggle. At first, based on Gilley's exclamations, they wondered if maybe Frieda had gained the upper hand. It was then clear that he was in control, and they heard the sound of clothes being torn, and of buttons bouncing on the floor.

"Hold still! Stupid whore!"

Anna put a hand to her mouth. It sounded like a large piece of furniture was being shoved. Then it began to creak and judder. By that point, Frieda had been reduced to the occasional whimper and gasp.

"Nein!"

"God," Anna said. "This is horrible."

Then, like a shock, like a rescue, like a deliverance, there again was the voice of Anna's mother:

"Stop it!"

Footsteps hammered down the stairs.

"*It's you! The goddamn station busybody!*"

"*I was . . . I was sleeping upstairs . . . What the hell are you doing to her? You're . . . you're . . .*"

"*It's not what you think. Frieda likes it rough. Enjoys it more when there's a tussle. Isn't that right, Frieda?*"

There was an incoherent answer by the other woman, so Gilley prodded again.

"*Speak up, my dear.*"

"*Ja. Yes. It is as he says.*"

"*So you see?*"

"*I know what I saw. And I know what I heard.*"

"*Then do as you must, of course. Go ahead and try it. But if anyone's out of bounds here, I'd say it was you, interrupting a private meeting between a case officer and his agent. Sleeping, you said? Like hell you were. Nosing around where you shouldn't be, more likely. Way out of your depth. Probably grounds for dismissal, or at the very least, reassignment.*"

Not long afterward, they heard Gilley depart. Helen and Frieda conferred in subdued tones. Evident through it all was Frieda's deep fear of being exposed, and of what Gilley might do if Helen pursued the matter further, although Helen made one last attempt at getting Frieda's assistance in further intervention:

"*Tell me your name, at least. Your real name.*"

"No!"

"Your coat. Here . . . Please, use my taxi. I'll give the fare to the driver."

"No!"

Then, footsteps, followed by the rattle and creak of a door opening, the hiss of a downpour from outside, and a final entreaty by Frieda.

"You will look out for me, yes? Not to report this, but to see that he does not reveal me to the others. You can do this, yes?"

"Yes. Of course."

"Safe house."

Frieda spoke those final words in a tone of utter disdain. The only sounds during the next several minutes were of tidying up, five or ten minutes in all. Then, a pop and a hiss, signaling that Helen Abell had turned off the recorder. Henry fast-forwarded the tape, listening for the chipmunk squeaks that would indicate further conversation. But the rest of the tape was blank, and the verdict against Kevin Gilley as prosecuted by the Sisterhood was now clear—three rapes at three safe houses.

"My mom wouldn't have let that go," Anna said, "not even to save her own skin. And she sure as hell wouldn't have let it go for a goddamn severance check. Unless . . ."

"Unless what?"

"She *did* pursue it. And then Frieda turned out to be right—about what Gilley would do to her in return.

Don't you see? Frieda was Anneliese Kurz. Look at the dates. The newspaper story was from only a few days later."

Henry nodded. He removed the reel from the spindle and put it back in the envelope. The house and neighborhood were quiet—so quiet that they both jumped when Anna's phone rang in her purse.

"Hello?"

The caller was a woman. Henry could easily hear both sides of the conversation.

"Is this Anna? Anna Shoat?"

"Yes."

"Thank goodness! I'm so relieved you're safe. You *are* safe, aren't you?"

"Yes. Who is this?"

"Audra Vollmer, one of your mother's oldest friends. I was told you were trying to reach me."

"Yes! Of course! And I'm glad *you're* safe. We're at Claire Saylor's house, in fact, and . . ." Her voice trailed off.

"Please tell me that nothing has happened to Claire."

"I'm afraid she's disappeared, and, well, it doesn't look good."

Anna told her about the abandoned car, the empty handbag, the blood on the seat.

"Oh, my . . ." Her voice faltered. There were a few seconds of silence. "First your poor mother and father, and now Claire."

"What about you? Are you sure everything is all right. Should we call anyone for you?"

"I'm taking extra precautions, I can assure you. Living in a remote location has its drawbacks, but also its advantages. Having said that, it is imperative that we meet. The sooner the better."

"I agree."

"I know it's asking a lot, but would you be willing to come here? I'm rather old and immobile these days, you see, and . . ."

"Of course. I'd be happy to."

"Wonderful. And, well, I'm not quite sure how to put this, but I believe that Claire may have recently taken custody of a valuable item of your mother's. For safekeeping."

"She did. We found it, and it's—"

"Please! Not over the phone!"

"Of course. Sorry."

"Not to worry. I'm relieved that it remains in safe hands. Would it be too much to ask for you to bring it with you?"

"Not at all."

"Wonderful. But do take care. With it, and with yourself. Let's discuss your journey, then. I'm going to suggest some rather elaborate precautions for you to begin employing immediately. Then I'll make arrangements to secure the way for you. Do you have something to write with?"

Henry handed over his notebook and pencil.

"Yes. Go ahead."

Audra Vollmer gave them their marching orders.

58

In two days her daughter would be drifting away to another world, probably forever, by heading off to college. Helen knew firsthand how dramatically that experience could change a young life. How was she spending these precious final hours with Anna? By shopping for clothes at the mall. Dreary and all-too-predictable, she supposed. Much like the rest of her life.

Look at her now. A farm wife in her late forties, going soft in the middle and gray on top. Who would have expected it? Certainly not Clark Baucom, who'd be pushing eighty by now yet was probably still imbibing ambrosial brandies that cost half as much as her weekly grocery bill. Maybe he was even still seducing women half his age.

"What do you think of these?" Anna emerged from the dressing room in something horrible.

"No. Out of the question."

"I knew you'd say that."

"Then why'd you ask?"

Anna turned and went back inside. Two more items to try before they moved on to the next stop in retail hell. Speaking of things that cost half as much as the groceries, the toll of this little excursion was already making her wonder which of her five credit cards she'd be able to use without exceeding the limit. She also needed to call Tarrant, to remind him to check the hinky ventilation fan in the second chicken house. A malfunction on a scorcher like today and they'd have thirty thousand reeking corpses and another black mark on their balance sheet with Washam. It was like working for a loan shark.

Anna emerged again.

"Much better."

A tasteful design, a decent fit, and best of all it was 30 percent off. But Anna's attention was elsewhere. Something had caught her eye from across the shop floor, so Helen turned to look as well. And that's when she saw him. Dark suit, arms folded, and those unforgettable eyes. Kevin Gilley, older but no less menacing, stood only fifty feet away, and he was staring at them.

Helen involuntarily put a hand to her mouth in horror. He raised his hand as if to wave, and then dropped it to his side. He did not approach them, but he did not look away.

"Why's that man staring at us?" Anna asked from over her shoulder. "Do you know him?"

"I used to," she said, her voice robotic. "I want you to remember his face, Anna, okay? Take a good, long look."

"Why?"

"Just do it, all right?"

"Okay. I think he's leaving. Don't you want to say hi?"

"No."

"Who was he?"

"Someone I used to work with, a long time ago. I wouldn't worry about him."

"I wasn't worried."

"Good."

Helen was about to say more when the shopgirl who'd been waiting on them came forward. In her hands were two other items that they'd already set aside for purchase.

"Will you be adding that blouse?" she asked.

"Oh. Yes." She was flustered, caught between two worlds like in one of those science fiction films, where half of your psyche gets left behind by a botched teleport. "Put them on my Hecht's card. No, wait. Here, use the MasterCard."

Anna went back to the dressing room to change. The

salesgirl waited until she was out of earshot, and then whispered to Helen, "That man gave me something for you."

Helen did a double take as the girl held out a folded slip of paper.

"What do you mean?" she said, recoiling.

"This note. He told me to give it to you, but first he made me promise not to read it." She was smiling conspiratorially, seemingly tickled to be playing courier for a pair of aging lovebirds who probably weren't even married to each other.

"Give me that," Helen hissed, angrily snatching it away. The girl, crestfallen, retreated to the safety of the register and began ringing up their purchases with a pouting lower lip.

For a moment all Helen could do was stare at the folded paper while all the old horrors returned. The photo of Anneliese, the knife against her throat, the eyes that were blue-green lozenges, cool and lifeless. She unfolded the paper and began to read.

How pleasant to see you again, Helen. Just a note to let you know that, although I haven't forgotten, I still fully expect you to continue to forget even if my name begins appearing in the news from time to time, as it may soon do. Your agreement is still binding, and I will hold you to it even if our old employer won't.

P.S.—Your daughter is quite the young beauty. She will

*go far. Provided, of course, that her mother's curiosity
isn't unduly reckless.—Yours always, Robert*

"Mom, are we buying this one or not?"

It was Anna, tugging at her shoulder. Helen stuffed
the note in her purse. She was trying not to shake. She
took a deep breath before speaking.

"Yes, we're buying that, so take it on over."

"Are you okay?"

"I'm fine. But that man you just saw, the one I used
to know?"

"Yes."

"If you ever see him again, I want you to tell me, all
right?"

"Okay."

"Anywhere. At home, at school, with Willard—
anywhere—and I want you to let me know right away."

Anna looked away, a little unsettled, but Helen
wanted her full attention.

"I'm serious. Do you understand?"

"*Okay.* But who was he?"

"It's not important." Then, sensing the ridiculousness
of her answer after everything she'd just said, Helen
sought to come up with a way of identifying him without
uttering his name, lest Anna blurt it out someday and
put herself in danger.

"I'm sorry. It *is* important, but you don't need to
know his name. Just his face. He once knew a friend

of mine, a woman I worked with. They're the reason you're named Anneliese. Okay?"

"Okay."

Helen turned toward the sales counter to complete their purchase. All the while, as the register beeped and clicked to record the rising total, she was already composing the first lines of a letter she would write that evening, an emergency message to two of her oldest colleagues. A plan of action took shape in her head. They would write, they would stay in touch. They would reactivate their network, and they would again protect one another—and Anna as well.

She had failed Anneliese Kurz. She would not fail her daughter.

59

Audra Vollmer's directions to Anna and Henry were a model of care and planning. They were reassuring. They were also a little disconcerting, at least to Henry.

"She's been retired for more than eight years," he said. "She must be calling in some very old chits. This is damn serious."

They were seated in Henry's car with the windows rolled up, parked on the lowest level of an underground garage three miles from Claire's house. A silver 2012 Honda Civic with Delaware tags was due to arrive any minute. They were supposed to switch vehicles with the driver. Henry's car would supposedly be waiting at his house in Poston when they got back.

They would be driving south on a route that Audra had detailed in an email to Anna—330 miles without a single tollbooth, to minimize the chances of video surveillance. They were to use cash only, and avoid public rest stops, and they were not to approach the boat dock for the crossing to Audra's island until an hour after sunset, which in Currituck would be at 7:48 p.m.

"Obviously, she's still well connected," Anna said.

"If I wasn't so grateful, I might be a little creeped out."

"She's made me feel safer. And I'll admit that when we were sitting in that basement, I was starting to wonder if we shouldn't just crawl into a bunker for a while."

"Well, from the sound of it, her island is a kind of a bunker. Your mom had some pretty interesting friends. Do you think all this stuff will bring down Gilley and Delacroix?"

"Audra seems to think so. What I'm wondering is whether it can help Willard."

"It can't hurt. Keep him off Zolexa and he's a different person."

"It's already helped me, just by knowing what happened. You've done your job well. Thank you."

Henry nodded and looked away. He hoped she still felt as grateful once she found out the rest.

The Honda arrived from around the corner with a squeal of tires. It parked behind them, blocking their exit, which was momentarily worrisome until the driver stepped out and dangled a set of keys. He looked government-issue—white guy, mid-twenties, trim build, brush cut, wearing khakis and a dark polo—and he didn't say a word as they exchanged keys. Henry and Anna drove the Honda up and out onto the darkened streets of York toward Interstate 83.

An hour later they stopped at a diner for omelets, hash browns, and beer. In the middle of the meal, Anna looked up and exclaimed, "Oh, no! Who's going to feed Scooter while you're away?"

Henry looked down at his eggs.

"You know how Scooter is. Lives by his own calendar. He's probably not due back for at least another night."

"Maybe you should call a neighbor?"

"Tomorrow. He'll be fine."

He pushed away his plate and called for the check, while thinking of that dimple of freshly turned earth beneath the pine needles.

An hour and a half later they reached the night's designated stopover, the humbly named Value Place Hotel on U.S. 29 near Manassas, Virginia, where they registered, per Audra's instructions, as Mr. and Mrs. John Pulver. She'd advised them it would be safer to stay in one room, and Henry sensed Anna's relief when they opened the door and saw two double beds. They had no luggage apart from Henry's shoulder bag—with all their papers and tapes—but they'd stopped along the way to buy fresh underwear, socks, and toiletries.

"Well, now," Henry said, dumping the plastic bag full of items on a table by the door. "Ugly bedspreads, the hallway smells like an ashtray, and the mattress feels like a slab of granite. But there's flat-screen TV and free Wi-Fi."

"She said not to use that."

"Yes, ma'am. Is ESPN permissible?"

"Only with the volume down. I'm ready to crash."

"You know the real reason she picked this spot, don't you? Convenience for our babysitters."

"You really think so?"

"We're, what, half an hour from Langley? It's straight down I-66 from here."

"I'm glad she has someone looking out for us."

"Yeah, very warm and fuzzy. Remind me to shut the curtains."

"Okay, Mr. Pulver. I'm showering, putting on my Walmart undies, and going to bed."

Henry was almost asleep by the time Anna emerged from the bathroom, toweling off her hair. She switched off the light and he heard her sigh as she slid between the sheets.

"What a day," she said. "Do you really think we can pull this off?"

Henry wasn't sure what he thought, other than mildly troubled by how easy it suddenly seemed. A clear path south, along which they would apparently be watched by unseen protectors. Upon reaching their destination, they would hand over their findings to a veteran spy, to let her do battle by proxy against the forces of darkness.

"Hope so. By this time tomorrow I guess we'll know for sure."

"I've been thinking again about that last letter from Claire."

"Me, too. 'The worst is true and the strands have crossed.'"

"Meaning Kevin Gilley and the Pond, don't you think?"

"But crossed in what way? Had he gone to work for them, or did he find out about it and do something extreme?"

"The *Newsweek* piece," she said.

"That thumbnail on Gilley? It hardly said a word."

"But wasn't there some reference to his preference for private intelligence firms?"

"Probably because he was working for one. But we could look it up."

"Audra said not to use the Wi-Fi."

"Oh, for God's sake."

"We'll check it tomorrow, on the way down. Oh, and don't forget to call about Scooter!"

"Right."

That ended the conversation. It was nearly midnight. They switched off the lights.

Two hours later, Henry was still wide awake.

He climbed quietly out of bed, pulled back the edge of the curtains, and peeped through the opening. All quiet. Their room was on the second floor, and there were certainly enough cars and vans in the parking lot to shelter an unlimited supply of surveillance personnel. He paced the room, stopping at the mini-refrigerator for a look. A whiskey, a gin, a couple of beers. He could polish off those in no time and then sleep like the dead. But he needed to be sharp in the morning, so he shut the door. The condenser began to buzz.

Something was making him uneasy, and it wouldn't go away. He listened to Anna's breathing, steady and secure. He took his phone and his overnight bag into the bathroom, where he flipped on the light and then put down the lid of the toilet for a seat.

Using the Wi-Fi whether Audra liked it or not, he found the *Newsweek* story from four months ago. The six paragraphs still told him very little, although the reference Anna had remembered was intriguing in light of what they knew now: "Gilley believes the intelligence community's burgeoning ties to the private sector could be exploited to even greater purpose."

He reached into the bag for the pile of blue papers, their copies from the National Archives. They'd been so busy that they hadn't had time to go back through them since Hilliard's quick summary.

He reviewed the "Jewelry" correspondence—Grombach's frantic attempts to keep the Pond up and running past its sell-by date. Obviously something in these pages had clicked for Anna's mom, but even upon closer reading Henry couldn't find it. Nor was the

Grombach crib sheet much help. Most of it still read like gobbledygook. Hilliard had characterized Grombach's people as far-right ideologues, in line with Senator Joseph McCarthy. If they'd stayed in business, presumably they would've always had a receptive ear in certain corners, and he supposed that the right mix of corporate clients could have kept them going right up to today.

He flipped through the remaining pages—Baucom's field reports, the stray mentions of "Beetle." He yawned, and his back began to ache from his uncomfortable perch. At the bottom of the pile were a few pages Hilliard had never discussed, because they had nothing to do with Anna's mom's main areas of interest. When Henry read them he wondered why Helen Shoat had bothered to make copies. They were memos from Grombach about seemingly trivial shoptalk. One, dated from the Pond's supposed final month in 1955, was a list of tradecraft tips to all field operatives—how to best choose a dead drop, advice on their newest ciphers, how to deal securely with hotel switchboards, how to choose cryptonyms in a hurry.

It was the final item that caught Henry's eye, and when he read the words a second time he felt a prickling sensation at the nape of his neck.

One sure way to avoid wastage of time is to adopt this system from Tempest, an assiduously efficient young archivist we've recently hired to put our field reports in the best possible order before the close of our import-export business. She suggests that on such occasions one may simply take a name from the three-letter airport codes that have come into common usage during the past few years.

Just as the Sisterhood had done.

He checked the crib sheet for the cryptonym, Tempest. Nothing, although Henry doubted it was a real name, because Grombach even used a code name for his personal secretary, Virginia Schomaker, known as "Honeyshu." Grombach's code names were rife with puns. "Church," for example, stood for the Pond's liaison with the CIA, Lyman Kirkpatrick, whose real-life nickname, Kirk, was the Scottish word for a church. "Bishop" was the code name for a retired admiral named Knight, a bit of chess wordplay. What could have been the origin of Tempest?

Using the Wi-Fi again, he searched for the origins of Audra's last name, Vollmer: "Germanic. Composed of the elements volk, or folk (people) and meri, mari (famous)."

Famous people? Not really a tempest, or anything to do with one.

He looked up Audra: "Anglo-Saxon. Variant of Audrey, used since 19th century."

A second source disagreed, saying: "Lithuanian. Means 'storm.'"

Storm. Tempest.

"An assiduously efficient young archivist," Grombach had written. And a brand-new hire. They had already surmised that Audra had something to do with record-keeping at the CIA. Maybe it was nothing, and maybe it was something.

Did the dates work? If Tempest had been hired at the age of twenty-one in 1955, then she would be around eighty now, or about twenty years older than the other two women in the Sisterhood. Plausible. It would also mean she hadn't retired until the age of seventy-one or seventy-two. Not unheard of, but a little unusual.

If Audra *was* Tempest, what did that mean? For one thing, she might want possession of the first tape, the one featuring evidence of the Pond's later existence, even more than the one implicating Gilley as a serial rapist. That thought sharpened Henry's vague sense of unease. He considered waking Anna, but figured she would either be pissed off or laugh him out of the room. But Helen Shoat had seen the reference and copied the page.

He thought of something else as well. Helen could have mailed off the tapes to either or both of the other women—accomplishing the latter by making copies—but instead she had chosen Claire. And Claire, judging from the reply, had written back only to Helen.

Henry's brain was abuzz with doubt. Dwell on this long enough and he might link Audra to the JFK assassination. He was making a big assumption based on a single vague reference in one stray memo. And maybe also because of the odd way Audra had sealed herself off on a secluded island. Plus, Claire's final letter, with its alarming tone. The lateness of the hour was surely another factor.

Sleep on it, he thought. But first, just in case, he would make a phone call.

A sleepy voice answered, but didn't sound surprised. They spoke in lowered tones for the next ten minutes, and by the time Henry hung up he felt better. He got up stiffly from the toilet seat and switched off the light. Then he groped his way back toward the bed. Anna was still snoozing. It was up to Henry to be the designated worrier, the resident skeptic.

The next morning, he made his case at the breakfast table, while they sipped coffee in the booth of a diner on U.S. 29 in Northern Virginia.

Anna scoffed.

"Go ahead," Henry said. "Say I'm crazy. But your mom copied it, and she sent the tapes to Claire, not Audra. And now Audra is desperate to have them."

"Desperate? Yes, she wants them, but that's because of Gilley. And if she was covering for the Pond why would she go to all this trouble to keep us safe? Safe from Gilley, I might add."

"I didn't say it was foolproof."

"It's not even plausible. And based on what, because

the name Audra *might* be the Lithuanian word for storm? I've seen more convincing theories about the Royal Family running the international drug trade through the Trilateral Commission."

"Then why did your mom copy it?"

"For some other reason? Or maybe because she was amused to find that they weren't the first people to use airport codes? Nor will they be the last, I'm betting. Besides, while I do think Audra is older, I really didn't get the sense she's eighty."

"Didn't get the sense? Very scientific."

"True, it's not as scientific as basing your whole theory on the name Tempest, the Lithuanian storm sister. Oh, and by the way, did I hear you talking to someone in the bathroom late last night, or did I dream that?"

He blushed, and hoped she didn't notice.

"I'd texted a neighbor about Scooter. He must have been up at the time, because he called me right back."

"Well, at least you took care of that. Let's order."

Henry buried his face in the menu. Even he had to admit his theory wasn't nearly as convincing by the light of day. He'd nonetheless felt like he'd owed it to Anna to make the case.

But his worries did not go away.

60

The breeze from across the sound was soft with humidity, tangy with brine. In the water below, two crabs fought for supremacy, swinging claws like switchblades in the murk of the pilings. Henry watched by the glow of the light at the end of the dock. Without it they would have been standing in darkness. The new moon was a mere sliver, and the only other illumination came from a distant thunderhead, popping like a flashbulb out over the Atlantic.

Anna gazed off toward the sea. She was quiet now that they had reached the point of departure for their final destination. Somewhere out in the blackness was Audra's island, and from across the chop they now heard the rising whine of an outboard engine, right on schedule.

"Do you think that's the boat?"

"Don't know why anyone else would be out there at this hour."

"God, these mosquitoes!" Anna brushed at her arms.

"Maybe that's what we're hearing. The mother of all mosquitoes."

Then they saw the running lights as the boat appeared from around a stand of saw grass. The man at the helm wore black jeans and a black T-shirt. Given the momentous feel of the occasion, Henry half expected to see his face smudged with antiglare blacking, like a commando on a night raid. His hair was slicked back, his muscles chiseled. More bodyguard than waterman by all appearances. The boat was no-frills, about fifteen feet with a small cuddy cabin and an open rear deck. The boatman looped a line around a piling but didn't bother to tie up.

"Hop aboard," he said. "There at the stern."

Anna went first, Henry followed. They joined him at the wheel, partly out of curiosity, since he was their first human contact with Audra's insular little world.

"How long is the ride?" Henry asked.

The man shrugged, turning the wheel as he set his course.

"Maybe ten minutes. Light chop tonight. Nothing to really slow us down."

"Do you work directly for Ms. Vollmer?" Anna asked.

He teeth showed in the darkness.

"Not to be rude, but I'm not paid to answer questions."

The teeth flashed again and he looked straight ahead. Henry headed back to the stern and sat along the port side, letting the wind scour off the last of the bugs. Anna joined him.

"Well, that was pleasant," she said in a lowered voice.

"I guess Audra's people operate by the 'need to know' doctrine."

"Old habits die hard."

They settled in for the ride. Henry thought he noticed something glide beneath the hull, like a ray or a large fish, but it could have been a trick of shadows from the running lights. He hadn't realized until now how cut off they were going to feel. By daylight it probably would have been quite pleasant, with views in all directions and other boats within sight. Maybe Audra had insisted they arrive after sunset to make an impression. If so, she'd succeeded.

"Doesn't this strike you as odd?" he asked. "A powerful woman like her, holing up like this? It's usually men who do that. Howard Hughes, Salinger. Charles Foster Kane."

"Emily Dickinson, Greta Garbo. And Kane was a movie character. Next you'll accuse her of being a dotty old cat lady."

They huddled closer on the seat as the boat rounded a point. Just ahead was a lighted dock. Beyond it, a row of trees and then a white clapboard house on stilts. It was of modest size, well lit and well maintained.

"Not as gloomy-looking as I feared," Anna said.

"Still . . ."

"What?"

"This whole business of having us arrive after dark. Look, I know you think I'm being melodramatic, but promise me one thing. If she shows as much interest in the first tape as she does in the one about Gilley, do me a favor and pretend we never listened to it."

"Why? Because that'll mean she must be Tempest?"

"Just humor me, will you? The less she knows about what *we* know, at least on the topic of the Pond, the better."

The boatman deftly secured the bowline to the dock. They scrambled ashore just as a brindled cat darted in front of them and disappeared into the night.

"Don't say a word!" Anna hissed.

A welcoming committee of mosquitoes arrived. The house was eighty yards ahead, across a trim lawn via a slatted boardwalk with footlights. Beyond were several outbuildings. One was as big as a barn, with concrete walls and a pitched roof of corrugated metal.

"This is quite the compound."

"She has to have *somewhere* to keep all the cat food," Anna said, but Henry was too nervous to laugh.

They climbed the steps to a screened porch. Henry was a little surprised Audra wasn't there to greet them.

"Maybe she's an invalid," Anna said, as if reading his thoughts.

At the door, he gestured for Anna to do the honors. She took a deep breath and knocked.

Brisk footsteps. The rattle of a knob. The door opened onto another hired hand in black, except this one wore a sport jacket with a bulge, undoubtedly from a handgun. Henry wondered if Anna noticed.

"Anna and Henry?" the man inquired.

"That's us," she said. "And you are?"

"Come with me."

He led them through a modestly furnished living room with a telescope on a tripod, aimed through a bay window toward the sound. They turned up a short hallway where he knocked at a heavy oaken door. A woman's voice answered from within.

"Show them in, Lloyd."

Lloyd opened the door and stood aside.

61

Audra Vollmer was no invalid. She stood on the opposite end of the room in front of a large mahogany desk, smiling broadly. Her posture was upright, her brown eyes clear and alert. She wore a navy business suit, as if she might have just returned from a day at the office, and her gray hair was pulled back tightly in a bun. She was considerably older than either Claire or Anna's mom.

She opened her arms and called them forward.

"It is such a relief and a joy to see you!"

Anna, approaching with Henry in her wake, held out her arms as well, but instead of a hug there was an awkward clasping of hands. Still, Audra's smile seemed genuine, and it was a second or two before she let go.

"You are the image of your mother. Did she ever tell you about us?"

"No. Nothing. I hardly know anything about that

part of her life, except from what I've read in your letters."

The smile seemed on the verge of collapsing, and she drew away a hand to dab at her eyes.

"Yes. And now it's only me, I'm afraid." She walked behind her desk. Henry saw a handheld radio on the corner, presumably for summoning any of her people at a moment's notice. She gestured for them to be seated on a couch to their left, and then rolled her office chair around to the same side of the desk to face them.

"And this is Henry Mattick, the one who's been helping me."

"Yes," Audra replied. "I know all about Henry and his help."

Odd phrasing, he thought. A little ominous. He wondered if she would ask him to leave. But she didn't object when he took a seat next to Anna.

"Well, then," she said. "Let's see what we can do about righting these wrongs that have taken away my two dearest colleagues. And also your father, dear girl."

"Where should we begin?" Anna sounded breathless, and who could blame her? Finally she was in touch with her mother's past, not just through a letter or a tape recording, but in the flesh.

"I thought I would leave that up to you. I'm assuming that you have lots of questions, and while in some cases I won't be allowed to answer them, I'm happy to tell you what I'm able." Another odd statement, Henry thought.

Would Audra really withhold information from Helen's daughter simply because it was still officially classified? But Anna seemed unfazed.

"What was my mom's job in Berlin? Her duties?"

"She was a keeper of safe houses. Four of them. It was a desk job, when what she really wanted was to be in the field. I'd had the same ambitions once, so I understood her frustration."

"How did she end up making the tapes?"

"On both occasions she just happened to be testing the equipment when the others arrived, unannounced. Or so she explained it to Claire and me. Quite extraordinary, really."

"The woman, Frieda, who was raped. Was she Anneliese Kurz?"

"You've done your homework. Yes, it was Anneliese, whose murder is still officially unsolved. Have you seen the name of the only eyewitness on the original police report?"

"No."

"Kurt Delacroix." Anna's mouth fell open. "Yes. His association with Kevin Gilley goes back quite a ways."

"They manipulated my brother, with drugs and God knows what kind of lies. We have proof of it now."

"I suspected as much the moment I heard what had happened. It's how Gilley has always operated—by careful use of the orchestrated accident, or the unwitting surrogate. He fancies himself an artist in that way."

"An artist?"

"Yes. An old hand in Athens once overheard him compare his work to that of a pointillist painter. Thousands of dots upon a canvas of his own choosing, each carefully rendered to form an illusion of suicide, or some other act of misfortune. Anything less elaborate would have wounded his vanity. That's probably what has saved your lives up to now. The case of Anneliese Kurz taught him that. Act hastily and someone will be tracking your scent right away, just as your mother tracked his. You're so much like her, you know. In your tenacity above all. Good work."

"But do you think it will actually do any good?"

"That will depend in large part on the materials you've brought me."

Anna turned to Henry, who zipped open his bag and withdrew the padded envelope. He handed it to Audra, who accepted it without looking him in the eye.

First she pulled out the two reports detailing Gilley's rapes in Paris and Marseille. She then removed the smaller envelopes and read the dated labels from the Alt-Moabit safe house in Berlin. She smiled, looking immensely pleased, and turned back toward Anna.

"Am I to gather you've listened to these tapes? To both of them?"

There was a hint of steel in her words, and for the first time Henry detected a flicker of uncertainty in Anna's eyes. She paused, so Henry rushed into the breach.

"We wanted to, but we didn't have the right equipment."

"Yes," Anna played along. "We were hoping you'd have a way for us to hear them."

Audra held her gaze.

"You're having doubts about me, aren't you." A statement, not a question. "Because of him, I'm guessing." She nodded toward Henry.

"Not doubts, really." Anna smiled nervously. "That's Henry's department."

"Henry's actions have gone well beyond the realm of doubt, dear girl. The word for him would be duplicity. But you weren't trained to notice these things the way your mother and I were, so you can be forgiven for taking a serpent to your breast."

"Serpent? If you're talking about the work he did before my parents were killed, he's already come clean about that."

"Has he, now? And did he also tell you about Mitch, the fellow in Washington who he continues to report to, day after day?"

Anna turned toward Henry, confusion giving way to dismay.

"Is that true?"

"It's not what you think."

"Predictable that he'd say that," Audra said. "Just as predictably, I'm guessing that he has already tried to poison you against me. For his own purposes, of course."

"She's only telling you half the story," Henry said.

"Half of *what* story?" Anna's voice rose. "Who are you still working for, and why?"

"We should go," Henry said. "She's lying for her own damn reasons, and we should leave while we can."

He stood, already glancing toward the door where he'd last seen the goon Lloyd lurking. Audra picked up the handheld radio and pressed a button.

"Lloyd? It's time."

"So you're not denying it, then?" Anna said to Henry.

"How do you think she knows all this?" Audra's words and actions had made several things clear to him, and none of them boded well for their survival. "And who do you think this guy Mitch really works for? He works for Audra. That's how she knows I've been calling him."

"So she's right, then. You've been lying."

"To protect you, which is what I'm trying to do now. We need to *leave*!"

He grabbed her arm. She shook him off. Lloyd appeared in the doorway, holding the gun in his right hand.

"The boats are coming," he shouted. "What should we do, ma'am?"

"Patience, Lloyd. Let it play out as planned."

Lloyd nodded and disappeared.

"What boats?" Anna said. "What's happening?"

Henry heard them now, engines buzzing across the water, moving closer to the island. The fruits of his nocturnal labors were paying off.

"Your friend Henry would tell you that it's a rescue party. The one he arranged for last night over the phone at the motel. I warned you to not use the Wi-Fi, but of course he ignored that. Not that we wouldn't have picked up the signal from our van. So you see, Henry? We were prepared. Come with me, then, both of you. We'll deal with Henry first. Then you and I, Anna, shall have a long chat."

"Then she'll kill you, too," Henry said. "She certainly can't afford to let you leave. Not now."

Anna, whose confusion gave way to a look of horror, shook her head.

"There's no need to *kill* him! Not on my account."

"It will be entirely on my account, I assure you." She pressed the button on the radio. "I need you back in here now, Lloyd."

Henry edged toward the door, wondering when the goon would return. He was about to make a run for it when someone else appeared in the doorway—a woman, trim build, late middle age, hair cut short, with black tights dripping water onto the floor. She held a gun that looked a lot like Lloyd's, and pointed it at Audra.

"Hello, Audra. Put down the radio and step away from your desk."

Audra's reply was almost a croak.

"*Claire?* But . . ."

"Do it now, please. I don't want to shoot you, but you know I will. *Now!*"

Audra dropped the radio with a clatter and robotically stepped forward.

"Never fuck with a field operative, Audra. That's something you pencil pushers always forget. Your gorilla is handcuffed and out cold, by the way. Worst-trained muscle I've ever seen." She turned toward Anna. "Hello. I'm Claire Saylor. Your mother asked me to look after you, so as soon as we're finished here you can come with me."

"What about him?" Anna nodded toward Henry.

"Oh, he's one of the white hats, although he probably didn't know for certain until a moment ago. 'Need to know' is a brutal rule to live by. Am I right, Mr. Mattick?"

"Yes," he said, thinking fast. "The abduction in York. That whole thing with your car."

"Staged."

"What about all those boats she was just talking about?"

"Most of hers never left the marina. And the one that did is now at the bottom of the sound. Oh, and you both should know that Kurt Delacroix is in custody, down at the end of the dock, with that cat of hers rubbing against his ankles, just to piss him off."

Anna looked warily at Henry, as if still uncertain of his loyalty. He nodded, to reassure her that everything was finally okay. This time he even believed it, if only because of the gleam of triumph in Claire Saylor's eyes.

Claire crossed the room to Audra, who had sagged to her knees.

"Anna, could you please help me tie up this scheming bitch?"

The words snapped Anna out of her fog, and she sprang into action. Outside, the boat engines had gone silent, and a voice on a bullhorn blared, "FBI! Drop your weapons!"

Claire and Anna got to work.

62

The three of them met in Washington a week later, at a French restaurant near K Street. A sentimental choice, Claire said, as the waiter seated them at a table for four.

"We'll pretend that the fourth seat is for Helen."

Anna glanced at the empty chair as if it might suddenly produce an apparition. Then she cleared her throat and looked down at her menu.

"Does this have anything to do with Mom's awful snow globe?"

Claire looked up with a start.

"She still had that?"

"It's on a shelf in her office."

Claire smiled brilliantly, a thousand watts of joy.

"Hideous, isn't it?"

"What's the story behind it?" Henry asked. "You even mentioned it in your last letter."

"No idea." Claire looked back at the menu but was still smiling. The waiter took their orders, and then Claire laid down the ground rules.

"Everything I'm about to tell you will stay between us. I'm only doing this as a favor to her." She nodded toward the empty chair. "Are we all agreed?"

"Well, I know Henry can keep a secret when an authority figure asks him," Anna said. "So, sure, I'll go along with that."

"I'm in," Henry said. "Anna, how's your brother doing?"

The question seemed to disarm her, piercing the shell of resistance she'd brought to the table.

"He's pretty much his old self, now that the Zolexa is out of his system. Telling him Merle was gone was like removing a spell. He's still not sure what happened, but from everything he's said it's clear that Merle convinced him he'd be able to change himself to be just like everybody else—smart, in other words—as long as he did as he was told, by destroying everyone's 'bad souls.' Then everybody would emerge brand-new, him included. But first he had to aim true, right at their heads, or it wouldn't work. So you were right all along about the sign. He was counting himself out, too. It was part of the reset that was going to make everyone better."

"And are you okay?"

"I've been better. This whole thing—in one way, all

it really did was postpone the collapse. It kept my mind working so hard that I never had time to grieve, or even say goodbye. The moment I got home from North Carolina I started to cry. I didn't leave my apartment for almost a week."

Henry took her hand, and she didn't pull it back. Anna cleared her throat.

Through it all, Claire remained silent, her face placid. It seemed clear she was awaiting their cue to resume, so Anna turned toward her and spoke.

"I think you're the one we really want to hear from. Tell us about Gilley and Audra. Was she really with the Pond? Were they working together all those years?"

"Heavens no to the latter. Although yes to your first question, so let's back up a few years." Claire checked for eavesdroppers, still the careful custodian of secrets.

"I think you both have a pretty good idea of what got this whole thing started—those tapes. Two sticks of dynamite, even if it took them ages to detonate. The second one, with Gilley? That's easy to read. A rape followed by a murder, with Delacroix to help him."

"But the tape about the Pond," Henry said. "Did no one figure that out until a few months ago?"

"I'm pretty sure a few higher-ups got wind of it right away, thanks to Helen's friend, Clark Baucom, but they never aggressively acted on it. The Pond had survived, yes, mostly with the help of a few obliging corporations, but it hadn't amounted to much. Small budgets and large egos, mistaking their insignificance for autonomy. They had a few patrons in the Pentagon, the occasional congressman, but I gather that certain elements in the Agency viewed it all along as a sort of glorified corporate security firm, whose people were sometimes useful. They were the whisper in an ear, the tap on a shoulder, and if you were a client they could always tell you what you wanted to hear. Remember the source Curveball and all that hokum that led us into Iraq?"

"That was from the Pond?" Henry said.

"One way or another, apparently."

"So, not always so harmless," Anna said. "Plus, what about that guy on the tape, talking about 'elimination, plain and simple.'"

"They were always pretty nasty to anyone who they thought might betray them. Which is of course what eventually made Audra such a danger to your mother."

"Audra was still part of it, even now?"

"She was their archivist from '55 onward. They were content to let Grombach's older papers rot in a barn as part of their cover, but her real coup was in securing an archival job with the CIA, in the late fifties, where she became the Pond's conduit for any CIA materials they might want to see."

"Did the Agency know *that*?"

"Not until a few weeks ago. And it was almost certainly Audra who got Helen fired back in '79. When your mom first started asking for records about 'Lewis,' the code name on the first tape, Audra tried to divert her by giving her more material on Gilley. That's when she first put Helen in touch with me, because she knew I had my own axe to grind about Gilley.

"So there we were, the three of us, seemingly united in our sub rosa effort to take down Gilley. Then Helen filed a request asking for the whereabouts of Edward Stone, the wheezing man, and Audra realized her diversion wasn't working. So, she told the Berlin chief of station that Helen was seeking information above her clearance. The next day, he lowered the boom."

"He fired her?" Anna said.

"First thing in the morning. But instead of going quietly, Helen went on the run. She was sure Gilley was the one who had brought her down, and was determined to return the favor. That's where I came in, helping her once she made it to Paris. And on the Gilley front, Audra was still willing to pitch in as well. Partly out of guilt, I suppose."

"What happened then?" Anna asked.

"Lots of things. Most of which I'm still not allowed to tell you. All you really need to know is that your mother was splendid under pressure, and was able to gather up the necessary goods without betraying either my role or Audra's. And for her troubles she got a severance package, and that murdering rapist Gilley got to keep his job, mostly because murder was his whole reason for employment. A deeply unsatisfying result, but that's how it can work in this business. And that's how it would have ended, too, if Gilley hadn't gotten cold feet about the arrangement when he moved into the public arena. I think he'd always suspected your mom still had copies of the evidence against him."

"Is that why he showed up that day at the mall?" Anna said. "To let her know she was in danger if she ever blabbed?"

Claire eyed her carefully.

"Something like that. And then, well, you saw the letters. When we found out Gilley might become a force in the White House, or maybe even director of intelligence, it was too much to stomach. So we laid our plans, and it all might have gone smoothly if I hadn't sent Helen that damned obituary for Clark Baucom. Because then she went poking around at the Archives, and finally discovered what the first tape was all about."

"And saw the reference to Audra," Henry said. "Is that when the strands crossed?"

"Yes, because by then Gilley was in touch with Audra. He had found out about her little secret through the back channels he'd always inhabited, so instead of threatening her he offered a deal. Help keep your gabby girlfriends quiet, and once I'm in power I'll usher your pals at the Pond out into the beautiful light of day, where they can finally flourish."

"That fits with what *Newsweek* said, about him being a fan of private intelligence gathering."

"Meaning that, for Audra, he was no longer the enemy. He was someone to be courted. That's when everything got dangerous for Helen, because Audra had a source at the Archives keeping her apprised of everyone who was viewing the materials."

"Not Hilliard, I hope?" Anna said.

"No. Some flunky who was happy for the extra pay. And when Audra realized what your mother had seen, she told Gilley we were planning to out him."

"Which was as good as killing her."

"Yes. Although, based on Audra's debriefing, she was as appalled as everyone by what happened. She thought Gilley would steal back the materials, or bully your mom into giving them up. But theft and bullying were never his preferred methods."

The table was quiet for a few seconds.

"Anyway, that's where Henry came in, right after Audra crossed over."

"Me?" he said.

"Helen mailed me the tapes for safekeeping after she figured out Audra's role. I took a sounding in the community and didn't like the rumblings, so I contacted a few sources. One of them got in touch with you, Henry. They'd heard Audra was looking for someone to keep an eye on Helen, so they dangled your name in front of them, the handyman from Justice who was looking for a new job. And, by doing so . . ."

"Used me to keep tabs on Audra's people, like Mitch."

"Correct."

"Everyone must have been overjoyed when I hired him, too," Anna said.

"It was a bit more involved than that. Stu Wilgus, that fellow who referred you to Henry?"

"*He* was part of this?"

"Oh, I doubt he even knew who he was helping, or why. But when Audra got wind that you'd made an inquiry about hiring a PI, she arranged for an old lawyer friend of Wilgus's to ask him to pass along Henry's name."

Anna shook her head in disbelief.

"So, if Audra was the Pond archivist," Henry asked, "where did she keep all the records?"

"Almost everything now is digital, but all the papers since '55 are in that barn of hers. Climate-controlled, state-of-the-art. I'm told the Agency is having a fine time going through it all."

"Wow," Henry said.

"Yes. No more Pond, even under its reduced circumstances. Not that you'll ever hear any of this in the news. The burial will be private."

"What about Gilley?"

"He's finished. Facing felony charges and a new investigation, Delacroix as well. I've been assured by the U.S. Attorney himself that this time neither of them will wriggle free. Although, if the Agency has its way, it will all be handled in private."

"No fucking way!" Henry said.

"I was hoping you'd say that. And if you're still willing to stick your necks out—figuratively, this time—then the U.S. Attorney would very much like to hear from you both. He, too, wants to make it public. Call this afternoon and he may even depose you this week."

She handed them business cards with the necessary phone numbers.

"Is that the real reason you asked us here?" Anna said, sounding a little disappointed.

"One of them."

"Whatever it takes," Henry said.

"My feelings as well. Now, then. As much as I've enjoyed seeing you, Henry, this is where I politely ask you to leave, so that Anna and I can discuss some further things about her mother."

"Oh. Sure. But first I'd like a private word with Anna, if you don't mind."

"As long as Anna's okay with it."

Anna looked back and forth between them, as if probing for signs of collusion. Then she nodded.

"I'll be in the bar," Claire said, standing. Henry rose as well, and clasped her hand in gratitude.

"Thank you, Claire. For everything."

"Thank *you*, Henry. You did good work."

"Yeah, well." He looked down at the floor, probably because he preferred not to remind Anna just then of how good some of that work had been. Claire departed, and he sat back down. When he looked up, Anna was eyeing him closely.

"Good to see you again," he said.

"I'd like to say otherwise, but I'll admit that I can't. So how have *you* been?"

"Rethinking some of my career choices. And my solitude."

"Sounds healthy enough."

"Anna, I haven't always been the greatest at figuring out what I want in life. But on the few occasions I have, I've been pretty determined to make it work. And that's how I feel about you. I'd like to make it work. So, if you've decided that you don't want anything more to do with me, tell me now. Otherwise, I'm going to keep trying to stay in touch."

"I may need a day or two to answer that. But if you can wait, I think you might like the result."

"I'm good with that."

"Provided you'll never duck another question."

"I'm good with that, too."

He smiled resolutely, like a man preparing to begin

a siege. Then he stood, nodded to Claire at the bar, and headed for the door.

Claire settled back into her seat as Anna watched him leave.

"You could do worse, you know," Claire said.

"He did lie to me."

"For all the right reasons. Mostly. And he did tell you more than he should have."

"Still."

"Yes. Still. This job will do that to you. Yet another reason I never stayed married."

"You were married?"

"Not your business."

"Is that why you live in York? Your neighbors were certainly wondering."

"Also not your business. Let's talk about your mother."

"All right, then. What was she like? At my age, I mean, and even younger?"

"She was bold, brave, witty, and resourceful. One of the most wonderful people I ever knew. And they never should have let her go."

"Wow."

"Here's another wow. We had more than one adventure together."

"What do you mean?"

"Tell me, did your mother ever run off on any sudden trips on her own, little family visits that maybe lasted a week or so but she never talked about all that much?"

Anna thought about it for a second, and her eyes widened.

"I remember her going off to Georgia a few times, to visit a couple of invalid aunts."

"These aunts, did you ever meet them? Or come across their photos in any family albums?"

"Unbelievable. Where was she really?"

"Maybe someday, when all the dust settles, I'll write you a long letter to tell you all about it."

"I think I'd rather hear it from you in person, when the time comes."

"I'm pleased you feel that way. Any other questions?"

"How well did she know Audra?"

"Not well. They didn't even meet until years later. In fact, Helen said you were with her at the time. On Capitol Hill, I think."

"Of course! The photo! We found it in her stuff, me and mom with an older woman on the Mall. I remember she took us to lunch. Some place with wood paneling and fussy waiters."

"The Old Ebbitt Grill. Her favorite haunt whenever she was in the city. And, as I said, I'm convinced Audra never wanted harm to come to your mother."

"She seemed ready enough to kill Henry and me."

"Yes, well, by then she'd crossed the line, and all by making a terrible miscalculation about Gilley. She'll take that to her grave."

"Good."

"I agree. She's earned her guilt. We all do in this business, one way or another. So there's the silver lining for your poor mother. She got out while her conscience was still clear."

"Except for Anneliese."

"Not her fault, but I'm sure you're right. It's why she reactivated our network, because she was determined it wasn't going to happen twice. You were the Anneliese she could still protect."

"But—"

"I know. You weren't aware of that. Which is why I brought you something, a note she sent me. One from Kevin Gilley on that day at the mall."

"He passed her a note?"

"While you were trying on clothes or something."

Claire took a folded paper out of her handbag and handed it to Anna, who slowly read the words with their pointed threat, their ghastly warning.

"So you see?" Claire said. "That's the one thing capable of saving us all. Not our compromises, or the things we withhold, and certainly not our betrayals. But the idea that what we're really doing is fighting for the people we love. You, in the case of your mother. That's really what I wanted to tell you today. For her sake."

Claire stood. She briefly placed a hand on Anna's shoulder, and then walked away.

Afterword

Yes, there really was an obscure U.S. intelligence agency once known as the Pond, and pretty much everything fictional archivist Larry Hilliard tells Anna and Henry in chapter 42 about its origins and its history is right on the mark. John "Frenchy" Grombach started the whole thing in 1942 at the request of a general in U.S. Army Intelligence, and it might still exist if Grombach hadn't lost out in a power struggle with the fledgling but much larger Central Intelligence Agency.

As Hilliard also points out, Grombach nonetheless managed to keep the Pond running until the CIA shut it down in 1955, and he was scrambling until the last moment to find a way to surreptitiously keep it alive, partly because he believed the CIA was too blind to Soviet infiltration in places like West Germany.

It's also true that Grombach's long-lost archives were discovered in a barn in Virginia in 2001, although they weren't declassified by the CIA until 2010. They're now available for public inspection at the National Archives in College Park, Maryland, where all eighty-three boxes are filed under Record Group 263.

Grombach's depicted mania for cryptonyms and coded language is no exaggeration. He employed as many as five names for himself: Mr. Dale, Jean, Dr. Ellis, Valentine, and Professor. As for that handy-dandy "Grombach Crib Sheet," which Larry Hilliard attributes to "a historian," well, it also exists, and the historian is Mark Stout, program director of the MA in Global Security Studies at Johns Hopkins University, and a former intelligence analyst with the State Department and the CIA. Stout, probably the leading authority on the Pond, generously gave me a copy of his invaluable crib sheet, or I never would have been able to make sense of the archives as I was researching this book. I also thank him for answering my questions about Grombach and the Pond.

As for the intriguing and somewhat whacky "Jewelry" file mentioned in chapter 43, in which Grombach writes in deeply coded language about his fevered attempts to keep the Pond going past its shelf life, that, too, is authentic, and I quote directly from one of Grombach's oddball messages.

So, then. Did Grombach manage to resurrect the Pond in some privatized form after 1955? Highly doubtful, but not out of the question. And many news stories in recent years have documented the rise of privatized intelligence efforts and their use by the Pentagon in places such as Afghanistan and the Middle East.

I am also indebted to several people and sources for helping me depict what it was like to be a female employee of the CIA in 1979. The first of these is Francine Mathews, an author of many fine novels who spent four years as an intelligence analyst for the CIA. I'm grateful that she took the time to share her thoughts and observations in a lengthy email, part of which made its way almost verbatim into Helen and Claire's conversation about their days of training at the Farm.

Declassified CIA archives offered multiple insights into the working lives of women at the Agency, and the evolution of their roles and responsibilities over the past few decades. One of the most helpful was the transcript of a panel discussion from about a decade ago by four women—Carla, Susan, Patricia, and Meredith (their last names were redacted)—who joined the Agency between 1965 and 1979. Their candid and illuminating stories and opinions helped shape several scenes and chapters.

Finishing this novel would not have been possible, nor nearly as pleasant, without the editing expertise of Sonny Mehta and Edward Kastenmeier at Knopf, and the valuable counsel of my agent, Ann Rittenberg. I am also grateful for the efforts of all of the other wonderful people at Knopf who make writing and publishing such an enjoyable and rewarding venture.

A letter from the publisher

We hope you enjoyed this book. We are an independent publisher dedicated to discovering brilliant books, new authors and great storytelling. If you want to hear more, why not join our community of book-lovers at:

www.headofzeus.com

We'll keep you up-to-date with our latest books, author blogs, tempting offers, chances to win signed editions, events across the UK and much more.

If you have any questions, feedback or just want to say hi, drop us a line on hello@headofzeus.com
or find us on social media:

@HoZ_Books

HeadofZeus

HEAD *of* **ZEUS**